THE LAST AUTUMN

By Daniel Scavone

For information, or to order additional copies, contact:

Beacon Publishing Group
P.O. Box 41573 Charleston, S.C., 29423.

800.817.8480 / beaconpublishinggroup.com

Publisher's catalog available upon request.

ISBN-13: 978-1-949472-98-1

ISBN-10: 1-949472-98-1

Publishing in 2018. New York, NY 10001.

First Edition. Printed in the USA.

To Cecelia Gleeson

Thanks for it all

"The only source of knowledge is experience."

—Albert Einstein

"A lot of people say you're not smart if you never went to college, but common sense rules everything. That's what I learned from selling crack."

—Snoop Dogg

I

Thomas Wolfe was right; you can't go home again. Not really. For the most part, Alex enjoyed the visits home. But for some inexplicable reason, from the first time he returned home during his freshman year, he felt part family member and part stranger. Summer vacations were no exceptions. Once all the special meals he missed so much had been eagerly eaten, recent neighborhood gossip absorbed, and hometown friends reacquainted, tension and restlessness would creep into his soul. By the time mid-August rolled around, and the days began to be noticeably shorter, everyone in the family felt quietly happy that Alex's stay was winding down.

As Alex would drive the New Jersey Turnpike, sometimes he would release his grip on the steering wheel to both bang to the rhythm of the music on the radio and to urge his Jetta ever forward. On occasion, his right hand would move toward the ashtray, reaching to take a hit off the half joint he had discovered in the glove box earlier.

Alex rode the turnpike to exit nine, New Brunswick. He took Route 1 south, passing corporate offices of many Fortune Five Hundred companies. The images of the buildings moved rapidly across his sunglasses. A lot of Princeton boys and girls working around here, Alex thought as he took one last hit off the joint and carefully threw the remnants out a crack in the window. No need to be worrying about roaches laying around. Not that he was a pothead. He usually only smoked on the weekends, or to relax after a very long night of studying. But at the beginning of every semester, this generalization broke down. For the first few weeks, Alex and his friends would go a little dope crazy. Amanda would be none too happy about it. She participated on rare occasion, but she never took it too far. "You don't have to do it to the point of stupidity," she would inform Alex when he would go overboard at one of their many small group parties.

"I'm fine," Alex would say while taking another hit, trying to avoid eye contact with his friends as that would unquestionably spark a laughing fit that would serve as proof positive of his girlfriend's point.

Senior year seemed especially promising. Although he had not seen Amanda since the visit to her parents' summer home this past July, they seemed to be getting along as well as ever. As evidenced by Alex's mother's complaints about data usage on his phone, they seemed to be on the same buzz. Additionally, he had come off his best academic year yet, made even more satisfying because he had done the least amount of schoolwork since coming to Princeton. This year he would have Mondays off and no classes scheduled before eleven o'clock the rest of the week. This, he had reasoned, would leave him plenty of time for crew practices, completing his required senior thesis, and pursuing matters of a less intellectual inclination. Finally, his living arrangements were ideal. As the roommate of his eating club's president, he was going to live right in the club and share one of the finest suites on campus. Come on man, get me off this highway.

Alex made a right turn off Route 1 in Princeton onto Washington Road. Immediately, one would feel change as the landscape shifted from a busy six-lane highway lined with strip malls and offices, to a two-lane road lined with majestic elm trees. In the distance, looking south, the first glimpse of the University, Cleveland Tower, became partially visible up high on a golf course hill. Then the road dipped, hiding the tower, and bringing the driver's attention to the upcoming stone bridge that traverses Lake Carnegie. Andrew Carnegie, an old alum, built the lake, and it was a beauty. Clearly visible to the left of the upsloping bridge stood the University boathouse. It sits alone like a large Tudor home, overseer of the cherished lake. Thanks, Andy.

Alex smiled as he thought about seeing Boder again. The first time Alex walked into his dorm room freshman year, he found Boder, lying on his bed, reading the arts and leisure section of the *New York Times*. On the floor, next to him was a large glass, half full of scotch and surrounded by a few finished Dunhill cigarettes. Boder was about to cast another newly finished butt onto the floor when he spotted Alex coming into the room. Boder had quickly thrown the paper to the side and attempted to rise as steadily as one could after lying down for some time, while consuming a couple of glasses of Chivas. He had greeted Alex enthusiastically, saying, "Hey, are you the new roomie? Or some psycho about to take advantage of my less than sober condition?" Boder held out his right arm perfectly straight and continued, "James Boderman. My friends call me Boder. My dad calls me a money sucking pain in the ass. And babes, well they just call. You must be Alexander Theodore Williams from far away Redding, Connecticut. Very nice to meet you, I hope." Slightly taken aback, Alex found Boder's searching right hand for a rather lengthy handshake. Boder bounced back onto his bed and continued talking without missing a beat, "I was actually hoping for a roomie with a slightly rounder ass, but I think you will do." Alex looked at Boder, slightly dismayed. Boder smiled and retracted, "Hey, only kidding, homophobe. Why don't you sit down and let's mingle? One word of advice though, don't mind anything I say and we'll get along fine. I'm fucking nuttier than a fruitcake." Alex was immediately inclined to lend full credence to the fruitcake assertion, and, through the following years of living together, Boder would do his best to live up to his boast.

After the lake, the University becomes the heir apparent. Collegiate Gothic architecture abounds with a sprinkling of period Modernism. Alex made a right onto Prospect Street, home of the most important aspect of life at Princeton: the eating clubs. Career paths, lifelong friendships, business ties, peer status, marriage possibilities, and general well-being, were often determined by which eating club a student selected. These clubs were not your run of the mill fraternity houses. Rather, they were impeccably kept, large, multi-story, brick or stone mansions, built in the Southern plantation style. Most came complete with gardeners, cooks, servers, and maids. Rumor had it that the clubs abolished the official ass-wiper position just a few decades ago.

In the more prestigious of the clubs, the current members did the selecting. Early in the spring semester there was "bicker week", when club members interviewed hopeful sophomores. If the club wanted a given prospect, he or she would be sent a bid to join. If they didn't think a prospect was good enough to eat with, or that they were possibly lacking legacy status, he or she was out of luck

In the beginning of junior year, Boder and Alex had "bickered" together, deciding that they would attempt to join the same club. This was not going to be easy, as they weren't exactly peas in a pod. Alex was reserved, very bright, an athlete, well-mannered, but he was neither from big money nor a legacy. Although Boder was from a very wealthy family and both his Senator father and grandfather Princeton alumni, he had more than enough drawbacks on the negative side. Extremely intelligent but you would never know it, Boder was slightly but affably obnoxious, a couch connoisseur given to jogging only when the pizza shop was about to close, and he did not appear to give a shit about anything.

After researching possibilities and probabilities, Alex and Boder decided on the O'Neill Club. It was probably second tier both in prestige and difficulty for gaining membership. The first tier belonged decidedly to Clover, Lionhead, and Cabin, all of which reluctantly admitted women to their ranks relatively recently under a barrage of lawsuits. Alex probably had the best chance of the two to "bicker" into one of the upper tier clubs. Boder, on the other hand, was definitely doomed. Given his escapades during the first two years, he had made too many enemies. Once, at Cabin, as the party was winding down, he raided their refrigerator in one of his legendary munchies binges. It probably wouldn't have been so bad if he had not tried to stuff a canned ham up his shirt for later use. Clover banned him after one of their parties when he threw his cigarette out a second story window, accidentally igniting the doghouse of the eating club's mascot, a bulldog named Beans. Unfortunately, the dog was inside sleeping. Before Beans realized it just couldn't be that hot outside, it was too late. Being a gentleman, Boder went back to Clover a few days later with a top-of-the-line bulldog puppy. This almost eased the tensions until one of the Clover members saw the nametag on the pup's collar – "Refried". They were not amused.

Boder was also an absolute no-no at Lionhead, and Alex was on the same list by association. In November of their sophomore year, Alex, Boder and another friend, Lawrence Hurley, nicknamed "Sheik", went to a party at Lionhead following the Princeton-Dartmouth football game. Attendance was by invitation only, but Sheik had scored an invite from a former high school buddy from Missouri who was a club member. Alex and Boder had forgotten all about the party until it was too late to scramble for an extra invitation, but not to worry. Sheik, who they say has talked his way into more women's pants than Kimberly-Clark products, managed to get them all inside without a hitch.

To say that Lionhead was packed that evening would be an understatement. The furniture had been moved out of virtually all the first-floor rooms to make space for the band, the beer tables, and the crowd, but they still could have used an extra living room. When Alex and his friends walked in, the band was taking a break. The temperature inside Lionhead was well over eighty degrees, causing all the partygoers to share sweat as the one common characteristic. Once he had a beer in his hand, though, Alex didn't mind the heat. With girls bumping against him as they tried to pass, Alex reasoned that there were worse places to be in the world.

Alex spotted two extremely good-looking girls talking to one guy over by the makeshift stage. He didn't know any of these individuals, but Boder once had a minor run in with the guy, David Shepherd. A year earlier, in Firestone Library during midterm exams, Boder made one of his rare visits. While sitting in a wooden chair with his feet crossed on a large oak table in one of the main study areas, Boder had inadvertently looked up from his Economics 101 text to spot Shepherd stealing a notebook from the table of a female who had left for a short break. Boder pretended that he didn't see Shepherd's move, but then followed him to the copy machine room, and then to the third-floor men's room. Shepherd exited the men's room without the notebook. Boder found it stuffed in the garbage can. Boder took the notebook and went back to the table where the girl, now in a complete frenzy, had returned. Shepherd, sitting a few feet away, turned as white as a ghost. "Sorry," Boder said, "I was studying here a few hours earlier and I thought this was my notebook. On the way out, I realized that I had made a mistake."

The girl quickly grabbed the notebook from Boder's outstretched hands. "I'm having enough trouble in this course," she hissed, "I don't need an asshole fucking me up any more. Now would you mind getting out of here so I can calm down and get back to work?" Red-faced, Boder quickly apologized again while making eye contact with Shepherd. Shepherd carefully kissed the middle finger of his right hand and blew it toward Boder. Boder then left the library, but not before carefully logging Shepherd into his memory for another day and another time.

At Lionhead, Boder elbowed Alex in the abdomen to direct his attention toward the stage area where the girls, a sandy blonde and a redhead, were still engaged in conversation with Shepherd. Shepherd was a year ahead of Alex and Boder and a full-fledged member of Lionhead. Boder, in his intoxicated state, mumbled something to Alex about this being the time and the place, but Alex was not sure what Boder was talking about. A few minutes later, Shepherd left the two girls to get them a couple of beers. "I'm going for it man," Boder informed Alex.

"Forget it Boder; they're talking to someone."

"Who, Einstein's ghost?" Boder asked mockingly. "I don't see anyone else over there."

"Boder, don't give me that shit; you saw him. It looks like he went to get drinks or something." Alex warned, though he knew that at this point there was no reasoning with Boder.

Boder responded, imitating the voice inflections of an old Jewish man, "He needs two girls?"

With the inevitable stare in the face, and Boder looking for just the slightest bit of encouragement, Alex surrendered, "You're right." Alex straightened Boder's shirt collar and brushed the shoulders of his sweater, "Go for it, kid. And if you get rid of that tall geek, I'll be right behind you."

"Don't you worry about that," Boder responded with an odd grin that made Alex just a bit uneasy. Boder left Alex and approached the girls. Pretty from across the room, they were even prettier up close. The sandy blonde had shoulder length hair, bright baby blues, a slightly upturned nose, and teeth so white and perfect that they couldn't be totally natural. Her clothes screamed New York Upper East Side. The redhead was slightly taller, and with shorter hair, but was just as pretty in her own way. She wore perfectly fitted blue jeans tucked into dark brown cowboy boots, and a simple white blouse. She had dark brown eyes that seemed capable of reading your entire life story on impact. Her cheekbones were high and very pronounced, and her body had that slightly muscular tone of a dedicated athlete. On the walk over, Boder had already decided to go for the blonde based on the simple deduction that she had bigger breasts. One thing about Boder: his reasoning always ran deep. His courage aided by legal and illegal substances, Boder inserted himself between the two girls, as they were talking to each other in hushed tones, and queried "Is it hot in here or what?" There was no reply. Unruffled, Boder continued, "My name is Jim. You beautiful ladies can call me Boder. All my fans do." Still nothing. "Do-a-you-a girls-speak-a da English?" he baited. The redhead sneered in Boder's direction. The blonde looked down at her shoes and desperately tried to hide a smile. Progress, Boder thought. Whatever it takes.

"We're waiting for someone," the redhead snipped.

"Can I wait with you?" Boder asked hopefully.

"Do what you want; just don't bother me."

Boder decided that the redhead was too high of a hill to climb. He turned his attention to the blonde; "I guess I won't be sleeping with her tonight, hey?" The blonde couldn't take it anymore. Covering her mouth, she began to laugh. Boder, ever diligent, and sensing the imminent return of Shepherd, continued, "Well it's about time we got a human response here." Boder looked up toward the ceiling with arms widespread, "Thank you, God!" Even the redhead could not resist a slight grin.

The band returned to the stage and opened the set with "Last Nite" by The Strokes, one of Alex's favorites. Alex was where Boder had left him a few moments earlier, tapping his left foot and watching Boder in action. Sheik was in another corner entertaining two different girls and trying his best to end the evening sans his friends. One of the girls was quite overweight and seemed to hang on Sheik's every word. Alex felt like going over to her, pulling her aside, and telling her, in the most discreet and polite way possible, that he was sure Sheik thought she was a major cock block, and that the only reason he was even giving her the time of day was to get into the substantially slenderer pants of her girlfriend. But hey, who the hell was he? Both of his buddies were carrying on conversations with women while he stood there kissing his plastic beer cup and dancing by himself. Even the overweight girl had the guts to get in the game. What was his excuse?

Over by the band, Boder did a slight twist routine and asked the blonde if she wanted to dance. The blonde, like girls sometimes do when in pairs, looked at the redhead as if she had asked the question. The redhead shrugged in response, and Boder sensed that even she was warming up to him. "I don't think so. You're drunk," the blonde said.

"I know, but I can really move my feet," he urged, and he did a little moonwalk to convince her. It was something he had learned from the landscaper at his parents' house. The blonde laughed again.

"If I dance with you once, will you leave me alone?" she bargained.

"Absolutely not!" Boder replied. Before the blonde could respond, Boder grabbed her lightly by her left wrist and pulled her a few feet onto the crowded dance floor. The blonde was as good of a dancer as Boder, and they smoothly dispersed other dancers on the crowded floor like hot lava burning through a rock bed. Boder looked over at the redhead and noticed that she was talking to Shepherd, who had now returned. Although Shepherd was trying to act disinterested, you could see he was keeping a watchful eye on the dancefloor activities. Boder lowered his mouth to the blonde's ear and whispered, "Do you know that guy talking to your friend?"

"His name is David. I just met him."

"Do you like him?"

"I might," toyed the blonde, as she did a slow three hundred and sixty-degree turn in a crouched position while moving slowly away from Boder. After the spin, she smiled at Boder, and he danced toward her.

"Too bad," Boder replied.

"Why? He seems very nice to me."

"He is an unadulterated asshole."

The blonde stopped her dancing and lost her smile. "A what?" she demanded.

"An asshole. Unadulterated."

"Do you really think that is necessary?" the blonde questioned, trying to control her temper. She wasn't sure if her anger was because of Boder talking about a new acquaintance, or because she was disappointed that this recent stranger, who she really thought she might like, was like a lot of men she had met at Princeton. It seemed they were always trying to elevate themselves by putting other guys down, like a giant dick contest. "And anyway, how do you know what he's like? Are you an asshole expert or something?"

Boder didn't feel like getting into the library story just then. It was too loud, too crowded, he was too drunk, and he felt he was losing her. "Yes, especially when it comes to unadulterated ones!"

The blonde had enough. She raised herself onto her toes to make sure Boder could hear her, and shouted, "Well you must certainly be very self-aware then!"

Boder knew he had gone too far. He was angry that he was going to lose her over Shepherd, and Shepherd wouldn't even have had anything to do with it. Boder tried a quick retreat, "Hey, I'm sorry. No more asshole dissection, I promise."

With that, the blonde shook her head, turned, and headed back toward her friend. Shepherd, watching the situation closely, moved onto the dance floor and lightly grabbed the blonde by her shoulders. Boder had followed the blonde and was standing right behind her, as the band began "Stay with Me" by Sam Smith. Shepherd leaned over and asked, "What's the matter, Kim? Is this jerk bothering you?"

"No not really, but I think Amanda and I should leave now."

"You don't have to. Why screw up your evening because of this moron? Just say the word, and he's out of here."

Boder knew he might have screwed up his chance with the Blonde. If he did, he wanted to screw it up all by himself. The last person he wanted for assistance was Shepherd. "Hey Shepherd, don't you have some spilt beer or something to clean up?" Boder baited.

Shepherd put his face only inches from Boder's. The excitement made Boder's heart race faster, pushing the booze and drugs through his body. He was rocking back and forth like a bowling pin, appearing undecided on whether to fall or stand. Shepherd's words interrupted Boder's internal tension; "The only thing I'm going to clean up, if you don't get the fuck out of here, is you, dickhead!"

Boder was dying to lunge at Shepherd's throat. But even in his inebriated state, he knew better than to hit a guy on his own turf. Especially when he was so fucked up that it would take his utmost concentration just to throw a punch anywhere near the intended target. Although he hated to do it, he would ignore Shepherd and chalk the Blonde up as a loss. There were plenty of other babes in the woods, and besides, he simply had too much fun for the day to ruin it now. "Fuck you Shepherd!" Boder jeered, "You're just not worth the time." Boder turned to the Blonde to apologize a final time, not expecting a response, but maybe to let her know he was not as big a jerk as she thought. It was the last thing Boder remembered from that evening.

Alex couldn't believe what he saw. A few moments earlier, out of the corner of his eye, he had seen Shepherd and Boder engaged in intense conversation. Alex knew that Boder was not a fighter, but, given Boder's intoxicated state, Alex thought it best to keep at least one eye on the situation. Alex saw Boder turn to his right to say something to the Blonde, leaving the left side of his face exposed to Shepherd and his glare. Suddenly, Alex saw Shepherd's right hand come up with a half-filled, Lionhead embossed, glass mug of beer. Shepherd continued to swing it around until it connected with Boder's left ear, sending Boder down on the dance floor amid a mosaic of beer, foam, blood, and broken glass.

Alex always felt that one of his biggest faults was taking too much time to make a decision. Take him out to buy a single shirt and it could be an all-day event, and he frequently sent the waiter away "for another two minutes," while he frantically decided what he was going to order. But in this moment, as he saw Boder's neck take an unnaturally quick jerk around and his figure disappear down into a sea of bodies, he honed in on Shepherd like a famished mother lion on an unsuspecting wildebeest. Alex had to get through at least twenty people in about twenty feet, but it seemed as though he was Moses and they were the Red Sea. About four feet before contact, Shepherd turned his attention to the oncoming predator. Like the wildebeest before the lion first clamps onto his hindquarter, Shepherd made a desperate attempt to escape the onslaught, but it was too late. Alex leaped, his crown landing squarely in Shepherd's chest. Together they went flying, returning to earth only when Shepherd's ass landed on top of the bass drum, smashing it, and bringing the cymbals down on them both. Alex only vaguely remembered throwing a few punches after that. Then, he woke up, very sore, in the redhead's bed.

II

Alex pulled down the long narrow driveway to the right of his eating club. Each club had a student niche - intellectuals, wealthy, jocks, partiers, etcetera. O'Neill had the reputation as the artsy club. Well, as artsy as you get at Princeton. Wall Street is full of tigers. Authors, musicians, poets and painters? Not quite as prolific.

O'Neill wasn't originally one of the clubs that had a bicker policy. Problem was, they always had more spots than candidates. By the mid-seventies, the coffers were dry, and the house was in disarray. Compared to the well maintained, estate-like quality of the other houses, O'Neill was in big trouble. The roof leaked; the brick exterior had cracks; the boiler was temperamental; the inside walls were screaming for new paint; and most contrary to its peers, their bushes weren't neatly trimmed.

Out in Ohio lived Morton Francis Hershfeld, Princeton class of 1954. "Morty", as he liked to be called, was a poet. Poets, as we all know, were not in great demand during the last half of the 20th century, so he never had a pot to piss in. He was married once, in 1968, to a Jewish intellectual from NYU named Joan Brenner. Joan was a very talented painter, but she had multiple sclerosis, which had thankfully been in remission for quite some time. Nonetheless, children were out of the question. Mentally, they were great equals, and you could almost see the neurons crossing between them. But by 1972, she was tired of his drinking binges, the bill collectors, and the constant moving from one bad apartment to one even worse. Joan moved back to New York, divorced Morty, and eventually married a Mercedes car dealer. Shortly thereafter, a Joan Brenner painting became a must have among the Upper East Side elite.

Joan only painted flowers, specifically, violets. She painted all types of violets; red violets, blue violets, and even yellow violets; young violets, old violets, and dead violets. Even diseased and bug-infested violets were not beyond her brush. She painted violets in a vase, violets in the earth, and violets on the sidewalk. The only thing she never painted were violets with people. A wealthy patron once offered Joan $100,000 to paint a portrait of her four-year-old granddaughter holding a bouquet of violets. She refused. Joan told the patron that humans and violets had been at odds for quite some time, and now was not the time for compromise. Besides, the simple fact was, Joan was getting about the same compensation for a single violet painted on a white background. Who needed her violets to be upstaged by some brat in a dress?

After separating, Morty and Joan never spoke to each other again, but, intermittingly, Joan would write to him, send him a few hundred dollars, and maybe detail her latest work for him. If Morty happened to be living in the same place for more than a few months, he would actually get the letter. And, if Morty happened to be in one of his brief periods of sobriety, he would sometimes respond.

By 1986, Joan's multiple sclerosis had left her mostly bedridden. She continued to paint but completed only one picture that year. It would be her only multicolored violet painting. She painted it while in her bed, positioning the canvas about five inches from her face. She would signal her assistant by blinking, directing her as to what colors to use and how much paint to put on the brush. She would then have the paintbrush placed in her mouth and work her craft. The violet she created appeared tilted through a pane of freshly broken glass, but the flower was in perfect condition. It was bright pink, white, purple, and yellow, and on each heart shaped leaf there rested clear dewdrops. There was one slightly larger drop that had just departed the blossom and was heading toward the glass-shrouded ground. Another half-dozen drops, which had already hit the ground, were painted blood red.

Knowing she was near death, Joan prepared her last will and testament. It was a very simple will for someone worth about eight million dollars. She bequeathed two million dollars to the New York Botanical Society for a special violet garden and their continued research on the flower. She would have left more to them, but she was convinced that most of it would get siphoned off by some New York politician who wouldn't know a violet from ragweed. Initially, Joan was reluctant to leave anything to Morty, as she knew he wouldn't care what she did with it. Besides the drinking and drugs, she felt he didn't understand about the violets. In the end, childless and her current husband well-to-do financially, Joan decided what the hell and left the rest to Morty. Joan died in early spring, 1987, just a few weeks before the violets would bloom in central park. That year, they were not as spectacular as they had been in previous years.

After Joan divorced Morty, his life went from bad to worse. At least when Joan had been around, she would clean and sober him up. After Joan left, forget it. Morty would wear the same piss stained paints for weeks at a time. By the late seventies, he had discovered crack, and his health, and sanity, began to deteriorate rapidly. He was arrested more than once for trespassing or drug charges. He was still composing poetry, but he kept it mostly in his head, rarely taking the time to put his works on paper. Instead, he would eagerly volunteer samples of his works to anyone who would listen.

Basically, Morty lived on handouts from a few individuals who, despite the sometimes-crude delivery, appreciated his literary talents. The hipsters in the flats area of downtown Cleveland were big fans of his recitals. In exchange for a few dollars, he would go on for hours before an enraptured and usually extremely buzzed audience. The problem was that Morty would get so stoned himself, that he would usually recite passages from William S. Burroughs' *Naked Lunch,* while the hippies nodded their heads in approval and amazement. *Stupid fucks*, Morty would think to himself.

In 1988, on a cold February morning, at a halfway house on East 55th Street in Cleveland, two well-dressed men from New York appeared at the door, looking for Morty. After almost a year, they had finally discovered his whereabouts through local police records. With neither a hint of disdain, nor of congratulatory salute, the men handed Morty a certified check for six million dollars, wrapped in a handwritten note. The two men nodded, forced themselves to smile, walked down a long corridor away from Morty's room, and toward the door where a limo to the airport awaited. Morty opened the note and looked at the check. He slowly closed his eyes, opened them, and looked once more. He tried to remember what drugs he must have snorted that morning. It read:

> Dear Morty,
>> Please take care of the violets for me.
>> Have and will love you always,
>> - Joan
>> P.S.
>> After cashing the check, please
>> use some of it for a haircut and a shave.
>> I'm sure you look like hell.

It was the first time Morty cried in as long as he could remember. When the tears finally stopped, Morty stuffed the note into the inside pocket of his beat up, corduroy jacket, and went to the nearest bank to open his first bank account.

There's no need to educate the reader about the possible ramifications of a known drug addict having a pile of newfound money. Old adages such as "fox in a hen house" don't begin to accurately portray this phenomenon. Morty went on a crack-pot-coke-meth binge, hitherto unheard of in the annals of Cleveland drug-addict history, and he even stopped reciting his poetry.

One sunny morning, in early August of that same year, Morty awoke from an exceptional weeklong, drug-induced carnival, to find that he had been sleeping smack in the middle of a large, vacant lot, where row houses, long gone, once stood. In the lot was a sea of rotted wood, old tires, rusted appliances, and broken glass. Very slowly, Morty lifted his groggy head in a feeble attempt to gain his bearings. Bits of dirt and shards of glass clung to the bloody and bearded cheek he had unwisely elected to lay on when he crashed there nearly fourteen hours earlier. His left shoe was missing, and his shirt and pants were dirty and torn. Morty guessed it must have been early morning. The scent in the air was a little too fresh to be otherwise. Over the course of a summer day on the eastside of Cleveland, the stench builds up like a heated pile of dog shit. Looking from left to right, like a lost tortoise, Morty saw nothing but refuse. In the far distance, he saw blurry figures making their way to their predetermined destinations. Then, when he had almost completed his scan, he saw it: the only sign of life on the whole lot, except for himself of course, and even that was questionable. About fifteen feet to his right, between a long empty Colt 45 can and a discarded empty box of condoms, stood a six-inch tall, recently sprouted, deep purple, violet flower.

Morty was not a religious man or particularly superstitious, nor a believer in paranormal phenomena. Nevertheless, Morty knew that once, maybe twice, in everyone's life, something happens that is so unexplainable, strange, coincidental, or just plain weird, that it's best for one's psyche and well-being to simply accept and go with the message. Morty had about five million, four hundred thousand dollars left. He had a hell of a last few months, but he knew this was a sign that he couldn't keep the rest of the money. But what to do with it?

Back in the spring of 1952, Morty was a much more

typical Princeton sophomore of his day. It would be hard to guess this, though, considering his activities after graduation. There was, however, a major difference that set him apart from most of his peers at the time: he was Jewish. Jews, and other minorities, had made inroads into Princeton over the past few decades, but in 1952 he was a Jew at WASP central. There was no way, for that that matter, that a Jew was going to bicker his way into any eating club. That is to say, any eating club but O'Neill. As Richard Wiggins, the recruiter for O'Neill at the time, told Morty, "Hey Hershfeld, we really don't care if you're Jewish. Christ, we don't even care if you sleep with Yaks. We need the money."

Morty took Joan's advice and got a nice shave and a haircut. He went to JC Penny's and purchased a grey suit. Shit, he thought, forty years later and their clothes still suck. He hired his only friend, Setrag Mooradian, an immigrant from India and now a taxi cab driver, and paid him a thousand dollars, plus expenses, to drive him from Cleveland to Princeton. Setrag had saved Morty's ass many times over the years during his drug binges, so he was glad to get paid for a change. Morty arrived at the front door of O'Neill at 10:14 a.m. on September 26, 1988. It was raining, so Setrag lent him his umbrella and waited in the taxi. Morty rang the doorbell and, after realizing it was broken, knocked loudly.

There had been many parties at the eating clubs the evening before. Prospect Street was peaceful except for the sound of discarded plastic cups blowing along the sidewalk. Charlie Cronin, the only one awake inside O'Neill, answered the door. He had just gotten up to take a leak. Cronin eyed Morty with a mixture of annoyance and contempt as he offered, "Sorry old man, we don't want any magazine subscriptions today. Maybe you should try the Quadrangle Club."

"No son, that's not why I'm here. Is the President in? I think it best I talk to him."

"Look pops, I really don't think you are going to get any further with him. It would be best if you just turn around and . . ."

"Look you little shit," Morty smiled and patiently continued, "I am an alumnus of both this University and this club. I am about to impose on O'Neill the greatest gift it has ever seen or ever will see. Now get the President, if you please." Cronin looked at Morty and then beyond him to Setrag sitting in the idling taxi. Setrag looked back at him and smiled, making visible his missing front tooth. Without another word, Cronin motioned for Morty to come inside and follow him upstairs. Cronin gave a knock on the door of Danny McPhearson, O'Neill's President, and, without waiting for an answer, he entered.

"Mac, this gentleman says he's an alum with . . . whoops!" Cronin paused when he realized there were two heads in the bed.

Groggy and looking up at the ceiling, McPhearson replied, "Cronin, why don't you and our guest just come on in, and we will have the meeting under the blanket via flashlight." McPhearson's bedside partner, a townie he had met the night before at a local bar, put her head under the pillow.

"Sorry Dan, I didn't realize you had company."

"That's why you're a history major and not a detective, Cron."

Totally naked, McPhearson stood up, reached an

outstretched hand toward Morty, and continued, "Danny McPhearson sir, my apologies. If I knew you were coming, I would have at least put my underwear on." Morty instantly liked him.

"Well Mr. McPhearson, I really don't have much time. I have my driver waiting downstairs, so I will get right to the point. I've had the good fortune to have come into some money, a lot of money. Certainly, much more than someone like me deserves. Besides, it's not really mine in a true sense. I'm just the caretaker, and not a very good one at that. If I continue my caretaking ways, I'll probably be dead within the year." McPhearson and Cronin had no idea where this was going. Morty looked at the bed and hoped that the faceless girl had not suffocated herself. He continued, "Anyway, this woman, a dear friend and more of mine, from the days when I had at least part of my brain left, would have wanted me to put the money where it would do the most good. No, let me rephrase that. To put the money where it could make a positive change. I've decided to give it to O'Neill."

"Sir, we're greatly appreciative," gushed McPhearson, while wondering if he was going to have to pay the taxi driver to take this nut away. "Would it be rude of me to inquire how much we're talking about here?" McPhearson asked.

"Five and change."

"Dollars?"

"Million." McPhearson and Cronin just stared at each other, their mouths open wide enough to take in a few softballs. An orgasmic groan came from underneath the pillow. Morty reminisced, "I learned a lot when I went to school here. I wasn't even very strange back then, but I was a Jew at Princeton University at a time when most of what went on here was off limits to my kind. This crap hole of a club took me in anyway. And you know what? Not once in the years of eating every meal here, spending all my social time here, and even getting laid here, did anyone ever consider me different than anyone else. Now, just walking through here, I get the feeling that this place has not changed much. In fact, judging from the needed paint job, I would say it has not changed at all, and that is good. Do you know why? Because if there was ever a place in this whole goddamn universe that is a microcosm of this country's social establishment, it's Princeton." Just then, Joe Cluffy broke into the room to ask if anyone wanted to play golf. McPhearson and Cronin politely brushed him away, and Cluffy slid out of the room. Morty continued, "I am getting a little long-winded here. I promised myself I wouldn't do that. Besides, another five minutes and Setrag will kick my ass. That goddamn Indian has got some temper. Anyway, gentlemen and, uh, ladies, the point I'm trying to make is this: Change is always good, and don't let anyone tell you differently. In every unit of life, there must be a force of change. I don't care if it's a family, a town, a country, the entire universe, or a fucking swim club for one-legged Eskimos. Change makes everyone in the unit grow, and I think O'Neill could be a force of change in this unit we call Princeton University. It could be the little thorn in the side, the little offbeat pain in the ass that occasionally comes up with an idea that everyone can use, even if they steal it. So, I'm going to give you people some cash, plenty of it. First, fix up this house. Just because you're different, that doesn't mean you must play on an uneven field. My God, I'm not even sure I could stay here, and I've slept in places where even the rats couldn't take it. Then, take the rest of the money and rattle some brains and bones around here. There is just too much creative potential here for most of you people to head to Wall Street to sell fucking bonds.

The room became deadly quiet and still for what seemed like an hour, but for what was really about twenty seconds. McPhearson and Cronin were experiencing one of those very odd and rare moments, when you know that what is going on before you will forever be remembered in the minutest detail. Morty reached into his jacket pocket and handed McPhearson a crumpled check. Morty then turned without uttering another word, went outside, and got into the waiting taxi. Morty's work was done. He would never write another poem in his life.

After a brief stop back in Cleveland, Morty and Setrag drove around the country for the remaining nine months of Morty's life. Finally drug free, Morty could usually be found in some roadside bar, creating some sort of special havoc.

III

Alex entered O'Neill through the back door. Classes wouldn't be starting for another week, and meals wouldn't be served at the club until then, so the kitchen was dark and sterile. Alex thought of Antonio, the cook, who exemplified the expression "nothing like a home cooked meal." Most members made a point of staying out of the club in the late afternoons, because the smells emanating from the kitchen would make them delirious.

A large metal door swung from the kitchen into the dining area. The dining area was swathed with solid oak floors and walls. The white ceiling hosted large oak beams two feet apart. There were thirteen mahogany tables, each lined with twelve matching chairs. Two large, colonial style chandeliers provided most of the evening light, accompanied by some matching sconces along the walls. Three, ten-foot windows lined the east wall, overlooking Prospect Street. A large, stone fireplace was in the middle of the North wall with windows flanking each side. Above the fireplace was an oil painting of Morton Francis Hershfeld. The portrait was painted from an old wedding day photograph. A book of his own poems was placed in his left hand, and a single, pink violet had been painted on his jacket pocket. The inscription below the painting, written on a small gold plaque, said: "The Violet Lives. Thanks, Morty." Alex made a right, moving toward the opening on the other side of the dining room, leading into the foyer and, from there, to the rest of the club. Immediately to his right cascaded a long, wide flight of stairs. Then, past the stairs, but still in the foyer, was a hallway that led to the living room, the billiard room, two studies, a bathroom, a guest room—which Antonio usually used after late dinner parties, a storage room, and Alex's favorite, the smoking room. The smoking room was painted a light baby blue, offset by an occasional white Corinthian column running from ceiling to floor. The room contained ten high, dark, black leather Chippendale chairs and two matching couches. Two mahogany coffee tables were littered, daily, with the latest reading materials.

Resting on one of the five end tables was a Spanish cedar humidor, which was usually filled with Cuban cigars. The cigars were courtesy of Javier Gonzalez's father, a small cigar distributor in Miami. Javier, a senior, was admitted to Princeton because of his soccer prowess. He wanted to be an architect, but he knew that desire alone would not get this Cuban into Princeton. Javier played soccer for his first two years, helping the University win two Ivy titles. In the beginning of junior year, Javier chose to concentrate solely on his schoolwork. Alex, grappling with the pros and cons of continuing on the crew team, asked Javier how he could just walk away from it like that.

"Because twenty years from now," Javier replied, "I don't want to be in some barrio of Miami, kicking soda cans at a brick wall, with a bottle of wine in my hand, while telling my buddies how I used to help some gringo kids up north win soccer games."

In the southwest corner of the smoking room was a large entertainment center containing a sixty-inch television, Apple TV and various video games. Nearby was a stereo system, whose music could be played throughout most rooms of the club.

The northwest corner contained a small, fully stocked bar, complete with refrigerator, small sink, and ice machine. In the remaining corner hung a well-used Taverner Genuine Bristle Dartboard. Alex's father had been a tremendous dart player, earning a good portion of his law school tuition by playing late night matches in the bars of upper Manhattan. Alex wasn't quite as good, but when teamed up with Mathew Zimmerman, a math whiz kid from San Francisco, no one on campus could beat them. The funny thing about Zimmerman, or "Zimmy" as he was usually called, was that he looked perpetually stoned, even when he wasn't. He wore basic, black framed eyeglasses, a quarter-inch thick. He had wiry, black hair and sideburns styled circa 1973. Zimmy, peering through those telescope glasses while throwing bulls-eyes, was quite a sight. On more than one occasion, minor scuffles had broken out because new challengers thought Alex and Zimmy were trying to hustle them.

The remainder of the room was decorated with an assortment of plants, a fireplace matching that of the dining room, and a wide glass double door, between the entertainment center and bar, which opened to an old stone patio. Alex took a good, long look around the now empty room. He smiled, knowing that he would spend many late hours in this very spot over the next ten months. Satisfied, Alex whirled around and backtracked to the stairs in the foyer, which took a U-turn to the third floor. He bounded up the old wooden stairs to the second floor, eager to see who had already returned to the house. Of the one hundred fifty members in the club, only about thirty lived there. Most of the bedrooms were still empty, mattresses sheetless and cold. Alex looked forward to them filling up very soon.

Alex heard loud music coming from the last bedroom on the left. Judging from the music, the Black Keys, Alex knew Tony Crummins must have arrived. Tony was about six-foot-three and weighed about 290 pounds. Most people called him "Big T" or just "BT". Alex liked BT a lot. He didn't drink, smoke, do drugs, or otherwise abuse his body, except for occasional hoagies he devoured every week from Hoagie Haven on Nassau Street. He could also play a mean guitar. If you could exemplify the definition of personable, you would point to BT, as Alex wasn't sure he had ever seen BT sad or irritable. As an infant, BT was adopted by a wealthy couple in Cincinnati. They had treated him well, yet BT once confessed to Alex, during a late evening conversation in the smoking room, that he wondered about his biological parents all the time. BT didn't wonder so much about why he was given up for adoption. Rather, he would find himself preoccupied with his birth parents' well-being: "Alex, someday I know I am going to need to search for them. I mean, blood runs deep man, real deep." At times like these, BT was like a big teddy bear, and Alex just wanted to hug him.

The speakers were blasting "Howlin' For You" as Alex turned into BT's room. BT had just stepped out of the shower and stood there soaking wet, his stomach overflowing a red and white stripped towel. The circus immediately came to Alex's mind. Upon spotting Alex, BT went into his Kravitz imitation. He slowly approached Alex, playing his air guitar, lip synching to the music, and placing one foot in front of the other like a woman in high heels trying to keep her feet dry from the puddles on city streets. About six inches from each other, BT put his face into Alex's, did some patented Kravitz crotch movements, and then shook his hair wildly, sending a shower of water all over Alex.

"Alexander!" he exclaimed. "What the fuck is happening brother? Get over here man!" With that, BT lifted Alex off the ground, eradicating any dry spots that remained on the front of either of them.

"BT, put me the hell down, man. You're getting me soaked." With that, BT plopped Alex onto his unmade bed, they slapped five, and began to bullshit about what they had been up to over the summer. They made plans to go out for pizza that evening, and Alex headed to his own room. Down the hall, up the stairs to the third floor, and all the way to his suite, the music continued to resound from BT's room.

Alex reached the top of the stairs on the third, and final, floor. Of the four doors, one led to a room that contained a few video game consoles, a card table, a pool table, a small stereo, a television, an old refrigerator and a few beat-up chairs, couches, and tables that were left over from the days prior to the late nineties' renovations. Wall hangings were limited to a poster of Walter White from *Breaking Bad,* and a 1932 O'Neill Club picture, taken when slick hair, no smiles, and heavy wool sweaters were very much in style.

The only other decoration in the entire room was stationed in a corner. It was a seven-foot tall, brightly painted, plastic statute of Marilyn Monroe, standing on the famous air vent pose from the movie, *The Seven Year Itch*. It had been in the club since June 1, 1955. That evening, four club members had gone to New York City to catch the movie premiere. They loved it so much, they decided to "permanently borrow" the statue display that was out by the ticket booth. For years, it had been dubbed the "X Room", where you were likely to experience just a little bit X-tra. Get togethers in this room were usually smaller, stranger, and a little less predictable than those taking place in the Smoking Room. There probably wasn't a member in the club who wasn't, at some point, involved in an activity in that room that would have resulted in serious student disciplinary action, if not actual jail time, if known to University authorities.

The other three doors led to various size bedrooms. The only single bedroom at O'Neill was also on this floor, and it was occupied by Patrick Roziewski, known by all simply as "Sheik". Sheik hadn't picked particularly well in the room lottery drawing, certainly not well enough to score the only single in the entire club. However, the male members of the club widely believed that keeping Sheik happy, and in a proper operating mode, would bode well for everyone else.

Alex had met Sheik during the first week of freshman crew. Sheik lasted about a week, until his late-night activities made him miss one morning practice too many. That morning, when he came to crew practice late, the coach deliberately halted practice to demonstrate the wrath that awaited anyone else who thought he was above the rules. With the coach about four inches from his face, reading him the riot act on maturity and responsibility to the team, Sheik's facial expression appeared as though he were sitting on his couch and watching the weather channel as the forecast called for 72 degrees and clear skies. When the coach was done berating him, Sheik was asked if had anything to say in apology to the team. Sheik simply took off his Kansas City baseball cap, turned to team members, who were patiently enduring this particularly chilly September morning and already sitting in their boats on the water, and said, "Gentlemen, may all your rowing be merry." With that, he put his baseball cap back on, nodded, and smiled to the coach without the slightest hint of disrespect, and headed up the hill away from the boathouse toward his dormitory, while whistling in the air. Even in that early stage of their college careers, Sheik's reputation was quickly being established. The coaches intended impact never really ensued, as the team watched Sheik disappear up the hill, knowing he would probably soon be in the arms of some new honeypot who would console him after his difficult day. Meanwhile, the team would be out in the cold, dank air, trying hard to keep their personal oars from receding into their bodies.

Besides Alex and Boder's bedroom, the remaining living quarter on the third floor was a suite of three bedrooms sharing a small living room and bathroom. Of the thirty members who lived in the club, fourteen were woman. This suite contained six of them. Of the remaining eight, most played on the women's ice hockey team. They enjoyed the more male dominated second floor: community bathroom and showers, hockey games in the hallway—if you put a hole in a wall your team lost a point unless, of course, it was the result of a good clean body check—yelling, screaming, pants optional, water fights, and general mayhem. The six women on the third floor were much more pseudo-intellectual types: Stephanie Gross, artist; Susanne Reilly, East Asian Studies; Rena Satz, Anthropology; Rebecca Harrison, writer and editor of the Nassau Literary Review; Elaine Freedman, Chemistry and head of the Lesbian, Gay and Bisexual Alliance; Sophia Yau, classical piano, real classical piano. The Princeton Admissions Office asks prospective students with special talents to submit materials demonstrating their level of expertise. As high school senior, Sophia sent the Dean of Admissions two tickets to her upcoming recital at Carnegie Hall.

As Alex's senior year wore on, he would come to realize that for some inexplicable reason, this was the first group of female roommates he had known who never argued with one another. Furthermore, combined, they would have the highest GPA of any other six students you could put together at the school. In a way, they were almost a club within a club. They were friendly, but only to a point, and never invited other club members into their suite, not boyfriends or, in Elaine's case, girlfriends.

Alex had not seen Boder since early July when he went to visit him at his parents' house in Washington. Boder's parents lived in a nineteenth-century townhouse in Georgetown. Additionally, they had a good-sized ranch out in Loudan County, Virginia. "My Nanny used to tell me that I was an only child because my parents stopped at perfection. Now, I think it was because my parents felt that even one child was a nuisance to their lifestyle," Boder once reflected. At the time of Boder's birth, his father, Frederick Boderman, was a freshman congressman from Virginia. Prior to that,

Fred had made a ton of money as co-founder of a very successful private equity fund. For the past eleven years, he had been a U.S. Senator, and for the last five, the most senior from his state. Alex believed Boder was a little tough on his parents. True, Boder's father was rarely at home. But when he was home, he was certainly very congenial. Once, he took the family, and Alex, to Bourbon Steak at the Four Seasons. He let the boys drink wine and was telling stories so funny that Alex thought he was going to bust a gut. Alex noticed that Boder hardly even grinned. Boder's mother seemed to be a model college mom, always sending Boder fancy care packages of food and clothing. At the Washington house, Boder's mother seemed to be absent a lot also, but the cook and the maid treated Boder as if he was their own child. In a way, he was. The housekeeper, Shirley Lewis, was Boder's nanny since he was a baby. She had come from Arkansas when she was just seventeen and was hired by Mrs. Boderman to care for Boder. When Boder was about nine or ten and no longer needed a nanny, Shirley implored Mrs. Boderman for another position. She was not terribly fond of the Boderman's, but had fallen in love with little Boder. Fortunately, Mr. Boderman was in the midst of his first senatorial campaign, and Mrs. Boderman was throwing a lot of dinner parties. Mrs. Boderman kept Shirley to do the cleaning and asked her if she could recommend a reliable cook. It just so happened that Shirley had recently befriended a slightly older black woman, who did some volunteer work at their Baptist Church kitchen cooking meals for the poor. Mary Robinson was living just a hair above the homeless line herself, but Shirley noticed that Mary always kept an extremely neat appearance and cooked like a champion.

Shirley approached Mary about the job. Mary, who had been unable to find full-time work for almost three years, jumped at the opportunity. Before bringing Mary to interview with Mrs. Boderman, Shirley asked, "Now Mary, I know you do some wonderful things with that slop we deal with down at the church, but can you make real gourmet meals for people who eat such stuff on a daily basis?"

"Darlin', you get me a couple of cat's asses and, after I'm done cookin' em, those people will think they are eating filet mignon!" Shirley laughed, and Mary laughed, and they have been laughing ever since.

The affection between Boder, Mary, and Shirley, was evident. At breakfast, they would tease each other and laugh until it hurt. Guests were not above being the subject of their humor. On Alex's first visit to Boder's home, Mary deliberately burned some corn in lard, placed some home fries, toast and a touch of parsley on a plate and, gave Alex the first plate of "Mary's Special Louisiana Grits."

Looking on from his seat, Boder played along, "How about it, Mary? I've been thinking about those tasty grits for months. Where's my plate?"

"Now Jimmy," Mary retorted, "you just hold your horses. Don't they teach you anything about manners at that Princeton place? I don't know about there, but around here it's company first." Alex would taste tiny bits of the lard-overdosed burnt grits and take large sips of his juice, too polite to ask what was so special about what tasted rather disgusting. It was not until Mary, Shirley, and Boder were literally on the floor in a desperate attempt to calm down and catch their breath that Alex realized he had been duped. Once Alex finally caught on, he alternated between gagging and laughing, all the while shouting, "Son of a gun! I should have known better!" Alex's decorum slipped rapidly as the fat dribbled down his throat, "Sons of bitches!" This sent the guilty trio's giddiness into the stratosphere.

On Alex's most recent visit, other than the usual bantering with Mary and Shirley, Boder seemed quieter and more tense than usual. Alex saw Boder's mother only occasionally, and the Senator not at all. At night, Boder and Alex were hitting the Georgetown Bars and Clubs, staying out until early morning, drinking, talking, laughing, and overall doing a pitiful job of attempting to pick up girls. Unconcerned, they usually ended up taking an Uber ride to Dupont Circle for some fried chicken and doughnuts at GDBs, before returning home and crashing until early afternoon. Alex made a commitment to himself that, when they got back to Princeton, he would ask Boder what was going on between him and his folks, as he was beginning to feel a bit uncomfortable with Boder's moods.

Alex already knew Boder was back at school. For the past few days, they'd had numerous text conversations. "Hey, Zander, when are you going to get your ass down here old boy? The Prez needs some help with official business."

"Like?" replied Alex.

"Like who am I going to smoke all this great gonja with? It came direct from Colombia via our lovely nation's capital?"

"I'm sure you'll be smoking just fine without me. Anyway, I'll be down in three days, I'm just wrapping up a few chores for my mom."

"But dude, the rest of us early arrivals miss you. The chicks won't even look at us until you get that big thang of yours down here."

"Boder, you are one fucked up dude."

"Yes, I am."

These types of conversations occurred about five times a day. Alex decided that trying to get things done at home was useless with Boder bothering him. Even Alex's mother told him to get back to school before she drove to Princeton herself and rung Boder's neck. That was one thing about Boder that bugged Alex: When Boder wanted something, no matter how minor, he wanted it right then, and he wouldn't stop until he got it. They almost came to fisticuffs one time during freshman year over it. Boder had gotten the munchies very early one rainy morning and woke Alex to go grab something to eat. He urged, "Zander, wake up man, put your shoes on."

"What? What's going on?" Alex asked, both dazed and confused.

"I'm starving, and I'm buying. Come on; let's hit the Princetonian Diner. I've just got to have a jumbo corn beef sandwich and a knish."

"What time is it?"

Boder looked at his wristwatch. "Four-thirty," he pronounced, sounding just like the information man at a train station.

"Are you out of your fucking mind?" Alex was now sitting straight up in bed, and, courtesy of Boder's omnipresent reading lamp, the orange letters PRINCETON were clearly visible on the chest of his grey T-shirt.

"Why? Couldn't you go for a monster 'wich?" Boder asked.

"You want to know why?" Alex's voice was rising as he

volleyed the question back, unsuccessfully trying to remain calm so he could go back to sleep. "First of all, no, I don't feel like a monster 'wich. Second, I am very, very tired. Third, it's raining like hell outside or is that sound coming from inside your screwball head? And oh yeah, silly me, I have crew practice in two hours and a fucking calculus mid-term tomorrow morning at eleven! How is that for why?"

"But dude, I'm buying, driving and..."

"I don't give a shit, Boder. I'm telling you, you're really starting to piss me off."

"OK, Zander. Christ, I thought I was doing you a favor. We'd have a little fun. A little chow. But forget it, relax man, go back to sleep." Alex didn't say anything, he just shook his head, puffed up his pillow, and slammed his head down hard. It was quiet in the room for about sixty seconds when, in that soft but somehow condescending voice of the train station information man, Boder said, "But maybe you'll feel a little hungry in ten minutes...."

Alex put his key in the lock of the old, but freshly painted, door. Alex and Boder had a mini-suite, consisting of a living room, two small bedrooms, and a bathroom. Being the "Presidential Suite", it certainly was the most nicely furnished. The other members didn't mind because, knowing Boder and Alex, everyone was welcome to hang out. Walking into the living room, it was immediately apparent that Boder had settled in. His stereo system was already set up and King Gizzard and the Lizard Wizard was vibrating through the speakers. To Alex's right, above the couch, was a framed 2014 Mardi Gras poster Boder had purchased in New Orleans early last spring. Alex didn't make that trip, opting instead to ski in Vermont. But, hearing the stories from Boder and the rest of the crew, he wished he had left his skis back home. Boder had also hung a large, unframed poster of his favorite group, Hozier, above the stereo system. Alex went to the small portable refrigerator in the corner and, as expected, found it already stocked with beer. Yuengling only. Alex smiled. America's oldest brewery, of course.

Alex walked down the short, narrow hallway, past the bathroom, to Boder's bedroom door. It was closed. Alex doubted that Boder was hanging out in there at 3:00 pm on a hot, but beautiful afternoon. As expected, he was nowhere to be found, but his belongings were strewn all over the room. Alex was neat, almost obsessive-compulsively neat, but Boder was just the opposite—one of the few downsides of growing up with people who did it all for him. Over the past three years, Alex helped change Boder's sloppy habits substantially, but, every September, he usually required a refresher course. By the looks of the room, Alex knew this year would be no exception.

Alex went into his own room and sat down on the stripped bed. He wanted to get himself all together before calling Amanda, as he had promised that he would as soon as he arrived. Amanda wasn't arriving until the Saturday before classes started, so Alex wouldn't have much time alone with her until school actually began. She would be flying in with her dad, who was staying until Monday morning to help her get settled. Alex felt a little annoyed by this. Besides the eating clubs, all the dorms were already open to anyone with an excuse to return early. Last year, Alex had noticed most couples would arrive, like he did, to enjoy a week of fun and nothingness. By November, many of the couples were no longer together, but Alex knew none of them would trade that first week back at school.

Alex would certainly enjoy the week, but he really wanted Amanda to share in the fun before school started. She took school very seriously, and Alex thought she worried about it too much. Once that first class began, until May, Amanda would be filled with nervous energy. She could go on for hours about her classes, her assignments, what she should take next semester, the eighty-nine she received on a test when she was positive she had aced it, and other school related topics. This usually bored Alex to tears, but he would listen politely and try to help when he could. The thing was, Amanda was so sincere. Alex received good grades partly because of his brain and partly because his competitiveness demanded them, but Amanda strived for good grades because she believed it was the right thing to do.

Alex and Amanda had gotten together twice over the summer, and, in the absence of school, she was much more relaxed. Amanda flew to Connecticut early in the summer and they spent a few days in Newport. They ate oysters at The Mooring, imagined being Vanderbilt's while touring The Breakers, and took long naps on Second Beach. Alex thought they laughed much more at the shore than when they were at school. About a month later, Amanda sent Alex a plane ticket, courtesy of her old man's frequent flyer miles. Although Amanda lived in Evanston, a suburb of Chicago, they spent a week at her family's summerhouse on the shore of Lake Michigan, just outside of Sheboygan, Wisconsin. Every day they would take the family's twenty-four-foot cruiser on the lake to water ski, fish, or just hang out. Once, with a devilish look in her eye, Amanda took off her bathing suit top and, with just her bottoms, sunglasses, and Chicago Cubs cap on backwards, commandeered the boat, driving it a few miles off shore. Not a word was spoken the entire way out, as they shared a lukewarm bottle of beer. Alex couldn't imagine any other place he would rather have been. Finally, Amanda cut the engine and Alex dropped anchor in the calm water. Amanda led Alex back to the captain's chair where, removing everything but her Cubs hat, she sat atop him. As Alex dialed Amanda's number, he wondered if he would ever experience that tremendous feeling of closeness and security with her again.

"Hello?" she answered the phone.

"Hi," Alex greeted excitedly.

"Hi Alex! Where are you?"

"I'm back."

"Great! How is it?"

"It's very hot. I just got into my room. Boder's about, but I haven't seen him yet. I saw BT. How are you doing? Any possibility of coming back a little early?"

"Come on Alex, we've been through this. I've got so much to do, and you know how my dad likes to get involved in my life. Anyway, I'm doing OK, but I really miss you."

"I really miss you too. I was just thinking about our boat ride."

"I think about it all the time too."

"I was thinking about painting the walls of my bedroom like a lake."

"Not a bad idea! Hey, can I call you back later tonight? My mom is waiting for me outside in the car. We're doing the back to school shopping thing." Alex paused. Her family was like a fifties television show. Amanda's dad worked and her mother was a full-time homemaker, even though Amanda was the only child of four who still, technically, lived at home. The family members were always impeccably dressed, and, whenever Alex visited Amanda, he couldn't believe how nice they were to him, how welcome they made him feel. Initially, he thought they couldn't possibly be all genuine, but, after a few days, he realized they were. He would get mad at himself sometimes for being envious.

"Is Victoria's Secret on the list?"

"Yeah right, more like white cotton panties from Target."

"I love you."

"I love you too. I'll call you tonight. I know you're going to party, but please be careful."

"Me? Careful?" Alex asked mockingly.

"Yes, you! I would rather take care of a nursery school class than you and Boder when you guys get going. Anyway, I've got to run. My mom's beeping the horn."

"Bye."

"Bye."

BT knocked on the door and asked Alex if he needed help unpacking his car. Alex wasn't about to deny the offer, especially from a fellow neat freak like BT, so they spent the next two hours bringing everything up to the room and putting it all away. Neither one could resist the urge to put Boder's piles in order as well.

After taking a shower, Alex decided to take a walk around campus, and to act on a hunch as to Boder's whereabouts. He was right; Boder was at a fountain just around the corner from the eating club; Boder loved that fountain. Just off Prospect Street, where most of the eating clubs were, the fountain stood next to Robertson Hall, home to the Woodrow Wilson School of Public and International Affairs. The building was one of those nineteen sixties, modern looking buildings, modeled after the architectural displays of the last New York World's Fair. The Woodrow Wilson School was a sort of think tank for some of the brightest undergraduates and graduate students who were interested in foreign affairs. It was also the professorial retiring grounds for many former U.S. Presidential cabinet members and advisors.

James Fitzgerald, designer of The Fountain of Freedom, as the brass sculpture was formally known, created the rather large, artificial geyser, to compliment the Woodrow Wilson School building. He placed the sculpture in the middle of a pool of water which was surrounded by a plaza of white stone, shielding it from the rest of the University with long rows of cherry blossoms. The pool of water was the shape of a rectangle with long sides bulging outward in the middle. As for the Fountain of Freedom, it was actually three separate brass sculptures close together. They consisted of very rough and jagged strips of the metal, rising over twenty feet towards the open sky. Throughout the sculpture flowed the fountain itself, spurting water through all the nooks and crannies, before descending into the large pool of water below. At its deepest, the water around the fountain was about two feet, which, on hot days, was besieged with students, locals, and a dog or two. As usual, in most social settings, Boder was easily spotted. He was lying in a floating chaise lounge with an iced tea in the plastic drink holder. He was wearing shades, a thin gold chain around his neck, and a Vineyard Vines bathing suit, with blue whales spouting all over it, which he had just purchased at the University

Bookstore. He was also reading John Grisham's latest novel. With his keen sixth sense of impending excitement, Boder looked up from his book and peered over the top of his sunglasses at the individual walking toward him. "Zander!" he exclaimed.

"Well, if it isn't the Bodster!" Alex replied as he stopped at the edge of the fountain. Lifting his hands from his pockets, he slowly opened them wide like a priest at a Catholic mass, "Here we are for the final run!"

"And what a run it will be, my friend," Boder replied, hopping off the chaise lounge and onto the edge of the fountain. They gave each other a high five, and Boder attempted to give Alex a wet hug.

"Get the hell away from me, man, I just took a shower."

"Aw, I wouldn't want to mess you up for the ladies. Have I got an evening planned for you."

"What's up?"

"Surprise, surprise. Unless of course you're going to ditch me because your old lady is back in town."

"Count me in. Amanda won't be back until Sunday."

"That's rough," Boder said, putting on his most serious look as he placed a damp hand on Alex's shoulder and consoled, "Listen, I'll try my best to make the next few days a little less difficult for you."

"Fuck you," Alex retorted, shaking his head as Boder laughed. Alex wanted to change the subject. His emotions ran so wide when it came to Amanda, he really didn't enjoy joking about her. "So, what are you reading? Is that the new Grisham book?" he changed the subject.

"Yeah, it's the only one I have left to read. My mom's really pushing this law school thing, so she bought me all twenty-nine of his goddamn works, and all of Scott Turrow's. To tell you the truth, I feel like I'm trapped in literary hell; all these books by lawyers about lawyers. Zander, you can't wait any longer. You've got to quit school and become a writer right now."

"It's a sad, sad thing. But hey, your mom's not around anymore," Alex quipped.

"This is true," Boder said, as he placed the book in a standing position on the edge of the fountain, "Just another one of the many fine benefits of college." Boder kicked the book about ten feet into the sky before it descended into the waiting water. Alex shook Boder's hand, and they walked back toward O'Neill.

IV

Alex, Boder, and a few other early birds, spent most of the next few days in a state of laziness, drunkenness, stonedness, stupidness, or some combination thereof. They were loving every minute of it. It was like having all the benefits of college without any of the responsibilities.

Alex and Amanda spoke on the phone once or twice a day, supplemented by numerous texts. The Thursday before school started, though, they had a bit of a tiff on the phone. After texting Alex on and off without any response for several hours, Amanda called Alex at about four-thirty in the afternoon. A crew of about seven revelers were in the Smoking Room, half-stewed, watching *Game of Thrones*. Amanda was more than a little annoyed when she heard herself announced to the group as "daddy's little student." Goddamn Alex, she thought, couldn't he keep anything just between them? She was further annoyed when Alex answered the telephone with a laugh in his voice. To boot, he was obviously inebriated.

"What's up?" Alex asked, unsuccessfully trying to stifle

his own laughter. He was even more unsuccessful in his attempt to wave the others into silence.

"Well obviously I'm a hit," Amanda said, concentrating deeply on maintaining her composure.

"What?" Alex said only half seriously. One thing Amanda was not, was stupid. But he was feeling his oats right now. It wasn't only the alcohol and pot making him feel this way either. The previous night, Ellie Gifford cornered him at a party at Cabin Club. Ellie had been after Alex since they met in Literature 131. Although he had dated Ellie a couple of times before meeting Amanda, she was too forward, even for him. He always felt just a little bit uneasy around her. She could get loud and overly opinionated in public, leaving Alex wishing more than once that he could have slid away. On the other hand, she was fun and, although she was always considered one of the best-looking girls on campus, now, in senior year, she was, well, a knockout. It was no accident. She ran three miles every morning, lifted weights every afternoon and yoga in the evening. Ellie also limited her meals to one a day, which she sometimes did or did not regurgitate. She had her teeth bleached, her nose shortened, and her eyes fitted with iris enhancing contacts.

The night before, Alex and Ellie had kissed and groped a bit on the back porch of O'Neill, before Alex's senses kicked in, and he told her that maybe it wasn't such a good idea. Even Ellie's pledge of silence couldn't convince him to continue. The next morning, Alex wondered if he stopped because of Amanda or because he didn't think Ellie could keep a secret. All Alex knew was that it had been kind of fun. Even the teasing by some of his friends who caught some of the action was, in a strange sort of way, exciting.

The simple fact was, but for Amanda, Alex would have slept with Ellie. Alex couldn't help feeling a little bit of resentment toward Amanda. It was very stupid thinking, Alex knew. Amanda wasn't there. Amanda hadn't said or done anything. If the situation had been reversed, Alex was sure Amanda would have done the same thing, although probably with a lot less remorse.

Alex could sense Amanda's annoyance growing as she said, "Alex, I really don't care if your friends want to humiliate me, but it does bother me that you do."

With an audience half watching the show and half eavesdropping on his conversation, Alex wanted to diffuse the situation. He implored, "Amanda, don't take it so seriously. Get a sense of humor will you." Some diffusion. There was silence at the other end. Alex eased the tone of his voice and continued, "Maybe we should talk about this another time."

"I think not," Amanda retorted, and hung up. Alex stood with the receiver in his hand, wondering if he should pretend to have a conversation leading to mutual harmony. No. Alex hung up the receiver and just shook his head. Boder was the first to jump in, "I know someone who's not getting laid next week!"

"That's what you think!" Alex shot back, laughing. The room began to laugh with him, but their laughter was more genuine than his. Alex sat back down and attempted to watch the movie, but his mind was racing with thoughts of his relationship with Amanda.

****

The ceiling slowly came into focus, then the curtains on the window next to the bed, and, finally, the redheaded girl sitting against the wall, with her chin on her knees. All Alex knew was that every bone in his body ached and this wasn't his room. He started to recall the fight he got into at Lionhead, after Boder was hit with a beer mug. He remembered knocking a guy into the drum set, but judging from the pain he felt, that must not have been the end of it. The redhead, sitting on the opposite bed, seemed familiar. Oh yeah, she was with the blonde, Alex remembered. This was getting weird. "What am I doing here?" Alex asked. That hurt. Alex felt his left cheekbone. Very sore. He ran his tongue across his teeth. They all seemed to be there. "What time is it?" he continued, "My friend who was talking to your friend…is he ok?"

"Keep your pants on," the redhead advised. She rose from the bed, went over to a small cooler on a desk, and put some ice cubes into a paper towel, making a neat package. She walked over to Alex and placed it on his cheek. Alex had a feeling this had replayed a few times already, while he had been passed out. It felt good. Alex closed his eyes. Then the redhead whispered, "OK, which question you want answered first?"

Even thinking hurt. "To be honest, I forgot what I asked you. So, why don't you decide? If possible, spare me any gory details."

"Well for starters, you and your friends nearly started a riot."

Alex removed the redhead's hand from his face, "What are you talking about?"

"After Shepherd hit your friend with the glass, you and

another one of your buddies . . ."

"You mean Sheik?"

"The really good-looking one?"

"Go on."

The redhead placed the ice back onto place and continued, "Like a good little hero, you jumped in to save your drunken friend. At first, you were on quite a roll. You knocked Shepherd into the drum set."

"I do remember that," Alex smiled.

"Thus, began your fatal mistake."

"And what was that?" Alex asked. He was interested in the story and the storyteller.

"It was on his home turf."

"So?"

"So?" The redhead asked, slightly incredulous. Then her voice took on a more matter-of-fact tone as she explained, "So, he had more friends than you, and they beat the shit out of you."

"Sheik?"

"Ditto."

"And Boder?"

"I think the beer mug to the head was enough. An ambulance came and took him to the hospital. Cindy, my friend with the big tits you guys were drooling over when you first came into the club, felt guilty and went with him to the hospital. They put four stitches in his left ear and sent him home to sleep it off. He'll be fine."

"We weren't drooling."

"Yeah, right."

"Just panting a little." The redhead pressed the ice firmly into Alex's cheekbone. "Ouch!"

"Oh, I'm so sorry," the redhead responded, mockingly.

"Yeah, right. So, you think it was wrong to jump in?"

"I didn't say that. I said it was a mistake. I didn't say it was wrong. If it was wrong, I wouldn't have saved you."

Alex put his right hand over his eyes and said softly, "I'm really afraid to ask this question, but did you just say you saved me?"

"Yes."

"What do you mean?" Alex asked with greater concern in his voice.

"Don't sweat it macho man, there isn't a man alive who has not been saved by a woman from his own mess."

"So how did I get out of that mess?"

"I think you mean we."

She is starting to get on my nerves, Alex thought. Nevertheless, he knew he owed her, and she was intriguing. "How did WE get out of this mess?" Alex corrected, with a forced smile.

"Just as the guys began pounding on you, I noticed that you were practically passed out. I screamed that you were a diabetic going into shock. Scared the hell out of them. I didn't know where you lived, so a guy friend of mine helped me carry you here. My roommate is visiting her boyfriend up at Yale, so here you are, snug as a bug in a rug."

Alex glanced over at a corner where he saw his jeans, shirt, and shoes. The redhead's eyes followed Alex's. As politely as he could muster, Alex began to question, "We didn't . . .?" Alex pointed to his clothes in the corner.

The redhead laughed. "First, from what I've seen of you so far, you haven't exactly wooed me. Second, from the looks of you after the fight, I don't think my dog back home would have wanted you, and he humps everything in sight. Finally, even if, for some kinky reason, I was attracted to a beaten up, drunken slob, I really don't think you were up for the performance. If your ego needs to know that bad, and judging by the ridiculousness of the question, it must be some ego, I took your clothes off so the blood on your clothes wouldn't get on my roommate's bed. OK, Stud?"

Slightly stunned, Alex stared at her in silence. Then he remarked, "Much more of your encouragement, and I'll be up and running a marathon this afternoon."

"Sorry, but you seem to have this habit of setting yourself up."

"What prompted you to become Madam Curie?" Alex asked, vainly attempting to change the subject.

"I guess I have this strange desire not to see people get beat up. And if they do . . . well . . . I don't like to see them lying helpless in their own bodily fluids." The redhead replaced the melting ice with fresh cubes and dabbed his face while encouraging, "But not to worry, these wounds look worse than they are. You'll be good as new in a week or so."

"Who are you?"

"Amanda. Amanda Fallon. Chicago."

"Have I met you before? You seem vaguely familiar, but I just can't place it."

"No, we've never met. I've seen you in the boats. Sometimes I come out and watch the practices. I go to most of the meets," she explained. Alex remembered a girl sitting in the same spot, all alone, on a hill, about one hundred yards from the boathouse, during some of the practices. That hill was quite a distance from the river. Now, up close, he recalled seeing her face at meets and acknowledged, "You've even come to some of our away meets. I can remember seeing you at Cambridge and Providence."

"Very good. Give that boy an 'A' for memory."

"Why do you watch?"

"Is it a crime? I like the sport. I kind of grew up with it."

"How come you don't row for the women's team?"

"I play tennis."

Fallon. Fallon. Fallon. It buzzed through Alex's head like an annoying bee. Finally, it stung. He blurted out, "Hey, you're not related to Ronnie Fallon, are you?"

"He's my dad."

"Holy shit!" Alex sat up, immediately apologetic, "Excuse me. Ronnie Fallon? The coach mentions him every day!" Ronnie Fallon, a.k.a. "The Cruiser," Princeton class of '81, was by far the best rower Princeton has ever seen. He went on to win three gold medals in the 1984 Los Angeles Olympics and, not satisfied, four more in Seoul circa, 1988. He was a fellow crewmember and roommate of Alex's current coach, Bob Diriglia. About a decade ago, they added a new boat tank to the boathouse for practice in inclement weather. It was named the Fallon Tank.

"Not that he would have ever used it," Coach Diriglia was fond of saying. Alex voice and body went into an imitation of his coach: "He would be out on that river every day, without even a sweatshirt. Toughest son-of-a-bitch I've ever met. And when it was hot, we could row for miles and he wouldn't even break a sweat. He made us find strength we never knew we had. We would win more for The Cruiser than for anything or anybody else. We knew if we lost a meet, it would never be his fault. That understanding put more pressure on the rest of us. Man, I would be out there rowing until it felt like my heart was about to burst, and the veins in my head were about to explode through my skin. Then I'd look at Fallon, moving in rhythmic motion like a finely tuned machine, his whole body going back and forth, back and forth, not missing a beat, not one sign of struggle. And it would just psyche me up more than I ever guessed I could be."

"Well, I would love to stay here and reminisce with you, but I've got to get to the library and do the reading for my Anthropology lecture tomorrow," Amanda said matter-of-factly. She added, "Do you mind if I take a few snapshots of you? The class would find them very interesting . . . evolution, that sort of thing."

"Are you always this funny? Anyway, thanks for the saving, the healing, and the hospitality. I owe you one," Alex said as he attempted to get off the bed. Once standing, he realized the inside of his head felt like there was a horse race going on inside. "Whoa," Alex whispered and slowly sat again.

"Maybe you'd better take another nap before you try that again," Amanda suggested.

Alex lay down on the bed. "You don't mind my staying here?"

Amanda smiled, answering, "No, as long as you don't pick a fight with my desk while I'm gone." With that, Amanda gave Alex a quick wave and left the room. Despite all that had happened the previous night, Alex's was consumed by thoughts of this girl. It's funny how, sometimes, you just know, during that first meeting, that the relationship is going to become something more significant, even if you can't pinpoint precisely why. Alex thought that reaction must be greatly magnified in those relationships like Lennon and McCartney, Jobs and Wozniak, Lenin and Trotsky, or Jordan and Pippin. Alex didn't think his new association with Amanda was going to change the world, but he did have a very strong feeling that it was about to change him. Soon, however, Alex's mind darkened as a deep sleep covered it.

When Alex awoke, Amanda was not around. He slowly lifted himself out of the bed and went over to the mirror. The swelling in his cheek had gone down considerably, but it still hurt like hell. He could see the beginnings of a black eye developing, and his stomach and back were a little sore. Nothing permanent, but he was not going to win any beauty contests for a while. Goddamn Boder, Alex groused. He had to stop getting caught up in Boder's antics. Alex looked at Amanda's side of the room. Adorning the wall above her desk were pictures of her family, the German Shepherd that humps everything, and one, probably very unhappy, cat. On Amanda's desk, Alex found her iPod. He turned it on and began scrolling through her music lists. Alex believed that you could learn a lot about someone from their taste in music. Katy Perry, Adele, Mumford and Sons, Taylor Swift, and the St. Vincent's soundtrack were the staple choices for most girls Alex knew. Amanda's was a bit of a surprise from what Alex expected. She had a lot of classical music, especially Mozart. Alex was no expert, but it looked to him as though Amanda had all of Mozart's symphonies and piano concertos, among many other pieces. Even Mozart's operas were well represented: Die Zauberflote, Don Giovanni, Le Nozze di Figaro, and Cosi Fan Tutte. Alex smiled in approval. One of Alex's favorite classes had been

Introduction to Music. Behind Economics 101 and Computer Science 126, it was the most popular course at Princeton. Alex was intimidated by Mozart, though. Not by Mozart's music, he found that just amazing. Rather, he was intimidated by Mozart's genius. Writing sonatas by seven, symphonies by eight, oratorios by ten, and operas by the old age of twelve. Dead at age thirty-five. A once-in-a-generation, pure genius.

All this thinking was making Alex tired again. His urges told him to snoop around some more, but his body told him it would have to wait, so he returned to the bed. Good timing, he thought, as the door opened and Amanda walked in, carrying a book on the writings of Descartes. She smiled at Alex. "Good morning," Alex said. "I thought you were preparing for an anthropology course?"

"The problem is that you should have said good afternoon. I did the anthro this morning. This afternoon, I was doing a philosophy paper."

Alex had no idea he had slept so long. "You're kidding," he doubted.

"Nope. Anyway, how do you feel?" Amanda came over and sat on the side of the bed. She squinted her eyes and looked intently at Alex's face. She noted, "Well, the swelling went down, but you're getting one hell of a shiner."

"Well, I was starting to feel a little better until I realized how late it is. I was supposed to get together with some other people from my Irish Drama class this morning to prepare a skit we're doing from Shaw's *Man and Superman*. This is the second Sunday in a row I screwed up."

"You've got to stop your weekend celebrations."

"Yes, I was thinking the same thing. Anyway, what time

is it? I'm starving."

"It's almost four."

"Would you like to join me at P.J.'s for a burger?" Alex asked. It was more than just not wanting to eat alone.

"I already had lunch. You wouldn't feel funny if I just came and had an ice tea or something, would you?"

"Feel funny? Look at my face. I am funny!"

On the way to P.J.'s, they stopped at the kiosk in the middle of town to pick up a *New York Times*. While they walked, Alex unfolded the newspaper to reveal the entire contents of page one. On the front page were articles about Gaza, Syria, Iraq, Afghanistan, Ukraine and Nigeria. "Jesus," Alex sighed, "I'm glad it's peace time." They walked the rest of the way to the restaurant in silence.

At P.J.'s, they had the usual small talk about school, friends, music, and their respective families. Amanda filled Alex in on The Cruiser's present-day habits. He was still up at dawn, did seventy-five pushups and jogged three miles every day. He owned a biomedical company that went public about eight years ago and made him very wealthy. Although The Cruiser talked about rowing since Amanda was an infant, he refused to row. The Cruiser hadn't been in a boat since he let go of the oar after his last race in the 1988 Olympics. "He told me," Amanda explained, "that when he crossed that finished line, he knew he'd pushed his body to that level for the final time; the peak had been reached. He knew that if he didn't voluntarily stop racing, his body would soon make him, and he believed that would be too humiliating. He couldn't stand the idea of going into a boat knowing that he would never be as good as he had been. I guess that's the Achilles heel of the perfectionist."

Alex didn't tell Amanda much about his dad, other than the fact that he was gone. He wanted to tell her all about him, and someday he would. He hated the inevitable sympathy. If he heard, "Oh, I'm so sorry," one more time, he thought he would vomit.

The conversation shifted to twentieth century plays, a topic on which, Alex happily realized, they were both knowledgeable. Amanda liked American playwrights the best because it was easier to imagine herself performing in them. "I like to read plays out loud," she offered. Alex's affinities leaned more to the British and Irish playwrights, especially Beckett, Pinter and Stoppard. Alex noted, however, that he was particularly fond of Edward Albee's *Zoo Story* and Eugene O'Neill's *Long Day's Journey into Night*.

"Did you know that O'Neill went to Princeton for a while?" Amanda asked.

"No kidding? Another Princeton literary dropout, a la Fitzgerald?"

"Bingo," Amanda agreed, adding, "He got kicked out in his freshman year for his pranks. He went to work in New York after that, and then became a seaman on ships overseas. He got tuberculosis and wound up in a sanatorium for a bit. I think he returned to school to study drama after he recovered."

"Here?"

"No, Harvard. I guess he didn't want to completely leave the sanatorium," she quipped.

"Did he graduate?"

"I'm not sure, but I wouldn't bet on it."

The waitress came with the check. Alex asked her for

more coffee. "Fitzgerald was the same way," Alex said, "he never graduated either. In fact, he was asked to leave twice during his junior year, due to poor grades, and in his senior year he gave it up altogether and joined the army."

Amanda shook her head. She used a straw to slowly stir the ice of her otherwise empty glass. She reflected, "It's amazing how the real great ones seem to know their own destiny. Look at Gates and Zuckerberg. I think, if I ever quit school, I would constantly worry about where my next meal was going to come from."

"I know what you mean," Alex agreed, "sometimes I feel guilty about it myself. My goal is to be a writer. Here I am in college, taking courses as a means towards this goal, yet sometimes I feel like I could experience life so much more outside of these walls. It is so antiseptic. I wouldn't mind taking some time and hitchhiking across the country. On the other hand, if I stay here, I know I'll get a degree that will help me pay the bills. I guess I might be a bit of a chicken."

"Alexander," Amanda began, Alex liked the way his name sounded when she said it, "so that's what you think this college thing is all about, just paying bills? I mean, as Joel said in *Risky Business*, 'maybe I should have gone to the University of Illinois.' "

"Yes, but with a degree from Princeton, you're able to pay bigger bills." They paid the check, and the two walked back to Amanda's room. This time, Amanda joined Alex in bed. Alex was recovering nicely.

*****

"Do you want a hit? Hey Alex, this is earth. Come in,

Captain Alex. It was Sheik offering Alex a smoke off a recently lit, turquoise colored bong. Alex's eyes came into focus on Sheik. He shook his head in an attempt to return to reality. The credits from *Game of Thrones* filled the television screen. Alex knew his eyes were open and watching the show, but his neurons had failed to send information back to his brain.

"Yes, I'll do one" Alex accepted, placing his mouth on the top of the bong and his finger over the hole on the side. He took a deep breath. The water on the bottom gurgled, and smoke filled the tube. His finger let go of the hole and the smoke disappeared into his mouth. Alex passed the bong onto the next participant, leaned back on the couch, and slowly exhaled the smoke. Maybe I'd better hold off on this Ellie thing, He thought.

V

Despite the tension prior to her arrival, things between Amanda and Alex softened as they came together after the long absence. The pair had some of their best times that September. O'Neill and the other clubs were in full swing, with back to school parties, renewed or new romances, start of the year jitters, and just plain hanging out.

Boder was drinking, smoking, and doing drugs, more often than Alex had seen before. Keeping his promise from the last Washington visit, Alex asked Boder if everything was fine on the home front. Boder assured him that his recent antics were a product of his usual dementedness, and nothing had changed. Alex decided not to pursue it any further, but, nevertheless, he sensed something was off, no matter what Boder said to the contrary.

Alex's partying subsided a little when he made the decision to row again. A thirty-minute telephone conversation with The Cruiser helped seal that decision. The Cruiser called Alex directly after Amanda told him that Alex was questioning joining crew in his final year. When Alex discovered The Cruiser on the other end of the phone, he expected to get a long liturgy on the benefits of rowing. Instead, The Cruiser began, "You know Alex, anyone who has any connection to the sport wouldn't blame you one iota if you didn't row again this year." He continued, "You want to know something? I would say that ninety percent of the time I rowed, I hated it. Absolutely hated it. You practice in rain and cold. You row until you feel sick, while the coach yells at you through a megaphone from his little motorboat, while sipping hot coffee from a thermos. Sometimes your scull tips over, sending you into muddy, smelly, cold water, and your hands get callouses the size of small grapefruits. But you want to know why I did it? I was very good at it, that's why. I wasn't the smartest kid in the class and certainly not the best looking. God gave me ears as big as my hands for Christ sakes. I couldn't shoot a basket to save my life, and I wasn't much on the social scene, but I could row a boat. And, with practice and dedication, I rowed a boat faster than anyone in college at the time. I'm sure your coach probably told you that I was a cool cucumber on the boat. But do you want to know something? On the morning of races, I would literally be lying in the fetal position on the floor of the bathroom in my room, my nerves twisted like a bowl of spaghetti. But, by race time, I would always manage to pull myself together. I had to, for, there, I was the king. I've seen you row, son., and you're good. Not as good as I was, but you are good. But that's not even the point here. Coach Diriglia has sent me some tapes of your team's races last year. You're in a good boat. Man for man, your boat is better than mine was, maybe the best Princeton's ever seen. With the possible exception of Carr and Johnson, no one's a star, but there is no weak link. Not only should you win the Eastern Sprints, but you guys have a serious shot at the Nationals, and maybe even a good showing at the Henley Royal Regatta. And son, if you haven't rowed on the River Thames in England, then you haven't rowed. The point is, Alex, you have the opportunity to be part of a happening. And you'll find that, in life, it's not often that you'll find yourself in this type of situation. For some people, it never occurs. To be part of something that is the best is a very rare lifetime experience. It doesn't have to be a sports thing either. It could be a big business deal, making a scientific discovery, or winning the damn national horseshoe competition. People respect the best, no matter what it is. If the opportunity presents itself, you should grab for the golden ring. I can tell you that no one who ever won the Super Bowl ever said the work wasn't worth it. There aren't many areas in which I'm an expert, but I do know rowing. I can tell you that, for you, at this time in your life, the golden ring is floating on Lake Carnegie."

The real collegiate rowing season began in March. Competitions usually involved two schools at a time. But, in the fall, there were a few regattas during which groups of schools, and clubs, raced to tune up for the upcoming spring events. The Ivy League schools agreed to leave the water the Saturday before Thanksgiving and not return until a mutually agreed upon date during the spring thaw. But this didn't stop then from practicing. They'd simply move inside the boathouse, where training in a rowing tank, on an ergometer, or in the weight room, replaced the challenges of the lake.

Princeton Crew practiced every fall weekday from six-thirty in the morning until nine, and from seven in the morning until noon on the weekends. As spring season approached, practices were sometimes held twice a day. The September practices were especially difficult on Alex. Most of the other heavyweights had spent the summer rowing for a club team, sculling, or at least lifting weights and practicing on the ergometer— a rowing machine, consisting of an oar handle attached by a metal lever to a flywheel. A timer in front of the seated rower displayed the revolutions of the flywheel, while another timer paced the rower, and a tachometer told him how powerful his stroke was. Besides an occasional jog around his neighborhood, Alex spent his summer totally out of the exercise loop. Come September, Alex found himself in a battle for a spot in the first shell. The numbers coming off the ergometer didn't even place him in the top ten. His performances in the weight room, and on timed runs, were also subpar. His rowing form in the shell, however, was surprisingly good, although he tired easily. At the end of each practice, Alex could usually be found lying on a bench in the boathouse, unable to get himself to the shower. He was so exhausted that he was falling asleep by eight or nine o'clock without even eating dinner. Boder told him to pack it in. Amanda told him to be careful.

By the last week of September, Alex was in much better physical shape. He improved dramatically in most of his practice exercises. Nevertheless, he had not yet earned a place in the first shell. Alex found himself in competition with Patrick McGill, a freshman from Groton, who was previously ranked the best high school rower in the nation. Alex was angry with himself. Had he exercised just an hour or two a day over the summer, he wouldn't be in this predicament. At practice, Coach Diriglia announced seven out of eight members who would be in the first shell. A 2000-meter scull race between Alex and McGill would determine who would fill the eighth and final spot.

Alex had mixed feelings about the coach's decision for a row off. He thought the coach should have given him the benefit of the doubt, as he had rowed three years for Diriglia and he improved dramatically every year. Except for Bob Carr and Neil Johnson, two rowers with Olympic potential, Alex would probably be the best rower on the squad if he were in shape. The last few weeks saw dramatic improvements in his physical conditioning, and it was just a matter of time before he was up to full speed. To make him compete against a freshman was humiliating. He considered that maybe he should just tell the coach to take an oar and stick it. No, he reasoned, it was clear the coach had his motives. The simple fact was, at least a dozen guys on the squad had done everything better than Alex had this fall. And McGill? Well he totally kicked Alex's ass. That kid might be a little rough around the edges, but he was clearly a star in the making. Princeton had sent The Cruiser to Groton to help recruit McGill, and the fact that he even selected Princeton over traditionally superior college crew squads, was something of a shock to the entire college boating community. Deep down, Alex knew the coach was right. To come back to campus totally out of shape was insulting to the team. The coach couldn't just ignore it. He was probably giving Alex a break by even letting him have this shot at the first scull.

Some shot. Alex did very little single sculling. He hated it. Just balancing oneself in a single scull was no easy feat.

The scull was sensitive to the most minimal of moves. A good sneeze and you would find yourself capsized. Although a scull was about twenty-six feet in length, its weight—complete with the rigger, slide, and stretcher—was only about thirty pounds. The rigger was a set of metal tubes affixed to the middle, top edges of the boat (e.g. the gunwale), through which the oars were placed. The slide was the rower's seat, attached to a track by wheels that moved back and forth with the rower's stroke. The stretcher was a footrest that held the rower's feet in place' so he could pull the slide forward at the end of each stroke. Except for the planking, the ribs and the keelson—that long piece of wood running lengthwise down the middle of the floor from bow to stern—most modern sculls contained little wood. Composite construction accounted for their light weight, toughness, and speed. There was no rudder on a scull, only a skeg, a small fin that is found on most surfboards. Steering was achieved totally with the two oars in each rower's hands.

The normal collegiate race distance was two-thousand-meters in the same direction. The McGill-Williams race would have a turn back at the one-thousand-meter mark. The coach gave one of the crew members an orange rubber buoy and had him paddle out to the one thousand-meter mark to drop it smack in the middle of the lake. At the turn, one rower would go clockwise and the other counter clockwise, returning in the initial lane of the other.

Alex left the boathouse and headed up the wooden dock toward the water. Other team members had already placed the two sculls in the lake. The oars were placed in the oarlocks, attached to the riggers. There was a definitive sense of excitement in the air, as there was something about a contest involving not only skill, but also the dignity of a person, that stirred the blood. Alex's stomach churned. If he had known about this race, he certainly would have skipped breakfast. McGill was already in his scull as Alex approached the end of the dock. Cocky bastard, Alex thought. As a senior, Alex felt he should have had a choice of scull. Not that it would really matter, he realized, but it was the principle of the thing. Alex wasn't going to hold that against him, though. Faulting McGill for that would be nothing but jealousy. Besides, Alex could be as competitive as anyone. Sure, McGill was in better shape and, to date, McGill certainly had been rowing better, but Alex would be damned if he'd let anyone knock him out of the first boat without a fight. He had spent too many hours on this lake wet, cold and tired, to be knocked out so easily. If he were to go down, he would go down kicking and screaming.

Alex carefully entered his scull, listening to a few good luck calls from fellow seniors, some less than sincere. Alex didn't have problems with anyone on the team, but he didn't particularly fit in either, they were a very cliquish group. Due to the nature of the sport, most of them were elite prep school graduates. This was the group Alex had the most trouble acclimating to when he arrived at Princeton. He felt many of them carried a holier-than-thou attitude, so Alex generally skipped crew social functions. If he lost this race, he knew there wouldn't be many tears shed in the boathouse.

Alex gripped the oar handles as a teammate pushed his scull from the dock. He would begin the race in the lane farthest from the dock. As Alex floated toward his starting position, he switched both oar handles to his left hand, and adjusted the stretcher bolts to properly fit his feet. Slowly,

Alex went back and forth on his seat to test the slide. Satisfied, he rowed to the starting line. McGill was already in position to start; his body was tilted thirty degrees forward, his oar blades were flat a foot above the water, his eyes were looking straight ahead, and his back was facing the course. Alex assumed the same position. The mumbling and chatter on the dock waned, then grew silent. After half a minute, the silence in the air was broken by Coach Diriglia, "Rowers, are you ready?" All was quiet. Alex stared intensely at his feet in the stretchers, his knees near his chin, his arms stretched out, and each hand clutching an oar. Diriglia continued the traditional rowing race starting call, "Ready all? Row!"

Alex quickly turned his oars perpendicular to the water as he buried them within. He pulled his wrists hard toward his chest and pushed his seat forward with his feet. His body leaned back in the direction of the bow and he caught a quick glimpse of the blue sky. Without hesitation, Alex's feet began to pull his body back toward the stern of the boat. Simultaneously, he lifted the oars a few inches out of the water, pulling them in the opposite direction of his moving body, and accelerating his movement back up the slide. Within seconds, he cycled back to the exact position he was in at the start of the race. He would be rowing at a rate of about thirty-six strokes per minute for the first minute. Then, once he got up to speed, he would decrease to about thirty-two strokes. Not wanting to lose his breath to the excitement of the moment, he made sure he inhaled and exhaled on every stroke.

Of all the differences between rowing a single scull and an eight, two were of significance. In a single scull, rowers used two oars, juxtaposed to the one oar used, known as a sweep, in the eights. More importantly, eights had a coxswain, which was the reason for the golden rule demanding that rowers never, ever, look outside the boat. In a single scull, however, the rower had to frequently look over his shoulder to assure that he wasn't headed toward the riverbank, or to check on his competition.

Other than the sounds of his oars splashing into the water, his slide moving back and forth, and his breathing, there was silence around Alex's boat. This was a sign he was rowing well. A bobbing scull or a splashing scull was a slow scull. About two minutes into the race Alex looked over his shoulder. At an angle ninety-degrees to his chest, Alex was shocked to find McGill nowhere in sight. He continued to turn his head toward the bow, finally catching sight of McGill about thirteen meters in front of him, a full scull length and a half. Alex's heart dropped. McGill was really moving. For a split second, he wondered how he would break the news to Amanda, his mother, and friends, about his demotion. But, just as quickly, he removed that thought from his mind and replaced it with bringing his stroke back up to thirty-six strokes per minute. With his thumbs gripped tightly over both ends, his remaining fingers grasping the handles like a condor on a tree branch, again and again Alex dipped the oars into the lake, sending ripples to the banks that would hit long after his departure. His heart pounded in his chest, no longer from nervousness but for more and more oxygen needed to feed muscles that were pushed to their breaking point. Alex looked over his shoulder again, spotting the rapidly approaching buoy. Since Alex's last look, McGill had not gained any more ground, but neither had he. One hundred and eighty degree turns, known as "turning the stake" in rowing circles, were not used in normal collegiate racing, and therefore not practiced. Alex wasn't sure how he would navigate the turn, but it was imperative that he make up some ground. Alex chose to let McGill make his move, and then decide on a different course of action in a gamble to catch up. McGill began to slow the pace of the oar's action on his starboard side. At the same time, McGill began to give more strokes to his port side, causing his scull to ever so slowly begin to turn around the buoy. It was apparent to Alex that McGill would not bring the scull to a standstill before turning. Instead, McGill attempted to make the turn with enough speed to provide momentum for the second half. Alex knew that such an election would cause McGill to make a wide turn, so he decided he would attempt to go inside. McGill was about halfway into the turn, about six meters past and parallel to the buoy, when Alex approached the turn. Alex lifted the oars from the water and, moving his arms away from his body, brought the oars perpendicular to the sides of the scull. Alex then turned the blades to a fully squared position and dug them firmly into the water. The muscles in Alex's neck and arms strained; his face reddened. Within seconds, the scull slowed to almost a dead stop. Without hesitation, Alex pulled at the water with the oar on his port side and pushed at the water with the oar on the starboard side. The scull turned ninety degrees in a matter of a few seconds. Meanwhile, McGill had completed his turn about five meters behind Alex's scull and was beginning to advance. "That's a bullshit turn!" McGill screamed.

Alex desperately wanted to respond, but he didn't want to waste any energy. Five quick, even strokes and he was in

McGill's original lane. Again, Alex dug the oars squarely into the water to bring it almost completely to a stop. It was much easier this time, since the scull wasn't going fast, and Alex immediately began turning the boat in the direction of the boathouse for the second stretch. Push. Pull. Push. Pull. Alex wanted to know where McGill was at this moment, but he couldn't look just yet. He had to build up some momentum first. Quickly, he pulled back on the oars, sliding his body forward while tilting his head upward towards the sky. Alex pushed his hands away from his abdomen and extended his arms straight, which caused his seat to slide back toward the bow. Alex repeated his stroke about eight times before looking over his shoulder to check his direction and his competition. Looking to his port side, about ten meters directly across, was McGill. They were dead even. Their eyes made contact. Alex forced a smile. McGill's face remained expressionless. The turn strategy worked, but it had by no means won him the race. Alex brought his stroke rate back up to thirty-six per minute and had no intention of slowing down. Pain was checking in, and exhaustion was knocking, but Alex was not answering. With four hundred meters to go, Alex glanced over his shoulder. McGill's boat appeared to be about two meters ahead. Shit, this kid is good. Alex didn't think he could go one millisecond faster. He attempted to bring his stroke rate up to forty, something he had never done in a single scull, but, then again, he had never been in a race to the death. Alex's lungs ached for more oxygen.

If there were any pain greater than the self-inflicted pain of a rower toward the end of a race, it would be difficult to imagine. The lungs screamed, the stomach cramped, and the arms felt as though they had been pummeled by a group of wild horses. Every muscle in the rower's body screamed at the brain to stop the torture. Alex looked over his shoulder, only two hundred meters to go, but McGill was still about the same length ahead. Again, their eyes met. This time, McGill smiled. Alex stopped keeping count of his stroke rate, instead, he stroked full out, faster than ever before. Alex no longer kept a breathing cadence. His veins were popping out at the temples of his reddened face. He was rowing like a wild beast. At one hundred meters to go, Alex glanced over toward the other lane and saw that he had gained almost a meter. Screaming with the finish of each stroke, like a wolf that has just been hit with an arrow, Alex wasn't even sure he was going in the right direction. There was no time to check. He had to push forward. There was a lot of yelling on the dock, but neither rower heard a thing. Alex was anticipating the dock coming into view on the port side when he heard it. The sound was unmistakable. It was McGill letting out that rare human sound that occurs during a moment of both shock and pain. He sounded as though he had fallen off a cliff. McGill had crabbed. A crab occurred when a rower's oar entered the water at an angle, instead of perpendicular. The oar sliced downward and out of control, floating in the water like a crab catcher's net. It was McGill's oar, on his starboard side, that crabbed, causing the handle to rip away from his hand. The force of the other oar, still in the water, caused the front of the boat to turn sharply to the starboard side. Off balance, McGill slipped off his slide. The combination of these various centrifugal forces caused the shell to capsize. McGill, his feet still in the stretchers, found himself upside down in the cool, dark, murky water.

Alex didn't look to the scene of the accident. After seeing the dock appear out of the corner of his eye, he slowed the boat, lifted the oars into the shell, and lay back in a semiconscious state. He couldn't tell if the clouds were moving rapidly in the wind, or if his head was spinning them onward. McGill, panicked, exhausted and out of breadth under the shell, released his left foot from the stretchers by jerking it hard out of the Velcro straps; however, McGill's right leg, which was unresponsive to his demands, would not release from the stretcher. He felt in the darkness with his hands for the elusive strap without success. Soon, as though he was being sucked into a wind tunnel by a giant fan, McGill felt himself fade away. A few crewmembers dove in, rushing to the capsized shell. Ripping the Velcro strap from McGill's right foot, they dragged him to the dock. McGill lay on the dock completely still, water dripping off his hair, racing shirt and shorts settling down into the cracks between wooden slats. Nervously, Coach Diriglia began mouth-to-mouth resuscitation. Within thirty seconds, McGill's chest began to heave, and his mouth spewed lake water. Someone called an ambulance. Although McGill soon appeared fine— or as fine a one could appear after rowing a mile as fast as possible and then nearly drowning—it seemed prudent to take him to the hospital for observation. As he was placed on the hospital stretcher, McGill called the coach over and asked, "Coach, did I pass the dock before capsizing?"

"Son, being a freshman in the second varsity boat isn't bad. Now you go and get some rest." McGill put his right arm over his eyes and began to sob. The first aid volunteers rolled the stretcher down the dock and into the ambulance. McGill's right arm never left his face, and Coach Diriglia watched and shook his head. Either this incident was going to help make that kid the best rower Princeton had ever seen, or he wouldn't be able to beat a tadpole. Only time would tell.

The slow grinding of the bow of the scull against the small stones of the riverbank brought Alex to his senses. He sat up, shaking his head awake after having given in so completely to the exhaustion. These sculls were fragile, and he was aware that the stones could do some considerable damage. On the other hand, Alex had won, and a broad smile came over his face. He closed his eyes to completely embrace the joy of the moment. Soon, Alex's attention was drawn to the dock, about one hundred yards away on the same shoreline. He saw the ambulance lights and McGill being carried away on a stretcher.

Alex slowly rowed back to the boathouse dock. Upon hearing some applause as he approached the dock, Alex deduced that McGill was not seriously injured. Crew members circled around Alex, eager to give him their opinions and analysis of the race. Coach Diriglia broke into the circle first, though, and silence ensued, as Diriglia stood face to face with Alex. Diriglia smiled and held out his right hand to Alex. He happily took it, as Diriglia shook firmly back and forth and praised, "Congratulations son, I knew you had it in you to row like that. I wished we clocked it, because your last hundred meters was one of the fastest single sculls I've ever seen. We get you into the right shape, and you can help us break some records out here."

Alex looked at the coach without a hint of emotion. As a coach, Diriglia was very well respected. He had brought forth rowing abilities in Alex that Alex never dreamed possible. When Diriglia put a boat on the water, it may not have always won, but the eight rowers in it would row to the top of their ability. But this time, Alex thought Diriglia went too far. "Would I have won if McGill didn't crab?" Alex asked.

"What the hell difference does that make?" replied the incredulous coach.

"Because if I wouldn't have won the race if McGill didn't crab, then I don't want the spot on the first boat," Alex responded. He paused slightly and continued, his volume rising a notch, "You put us in those sculls to see who would row the fastest. I want to know if I rowed the fastest."

The coaches' voice rose to meet Alex's, and then some, "I put you in the sculls to see who would win. Period. If it were for pure overall speed, I would have picked McGill without the goddamn race, but this sport is more than just speed." Coach Diriglia pointed to his head, expounding, "It's what's up here that counts. I could get any athletic lughead in a boat to row. I need guys who know how to win. And, as I suspected, though not without some doubts lately, you know how to win." The coach paused, stared at Alex, spit into the lake, and continued, "Now as for winning the race without McGill crabbing, frankly, I really don't know, and I really don't give a damn. I just need winners who win within the rules. In keeping with the deal I made earlier, I'm offering you a spot on the first boat. If you don't want it, let me know now, because I have a lot on my mind. I got a boy in the hospital, and I have a varsity boat to fill. In short, I'm not going to get into some psychological debate with some pansy ass on my dock."

Alex wanted to answer back, but his mind went blank. He

had never met a good coach whose wrath couldn't reduce a human to wreckage in short order. When confronted with an individual questioning his authority, any coach worth his salt could turn a Medusa-like challenger into a worm. Although it didn't sit totally right with Alex, nothing the coach said was wrong. Alex did win, and it was not luck. Winner got first boat. Simple as that. "What position am I?" Alex asked.

The coach smiled, as winner of another one-sided debate, and commended, "Congratulations, this year you've been promoted to seventh man, part of the stroke pair." Alex shook his head positively, pleased with the news. In an eight-man shell, the two seats closest to the coxswain, known as the stroke pair, were the seventh and eighth man. These rowers were the most precise on the boat. When the coxswain called for a change in the stroke rate, it was the stroke pair who had to lead the change smoothly and precisely. Those seats were numbered eight and seven respectively, and they would be occupied by Jim Daley and Alex. The next four rowers, given the seat numbers three through six, were the real power of the boat, the strong endurance guys. These rowers were given the cadence, and they got you there. Those seats belonged to Steve Hartshorn, Russell Simon, Stewart Haley and Keith Jackson— the only black rower on the team in the whitest of sports. The final pair on the scull were the bow pair. These two positions belonged to Bob Carr, seat two, and Neil Johnson, seat one. This pair required the overall best rowing skills and instinct. The bow pair kept the boat in balance and on course without ever turning an eye outside the boat. Alex and the coach shook hands again. Then, with his gruff poker face, the coach returned his attention to the rest of the crew, clapping and yelling for all boats and equipment to be cleaned and returned to the boathouse.

*****

Alex took a long hot shower, dressed, and went back to his room. It was about eleven o'clock, and Boder was still sleeping. Alex texted Amanda, and arranged to meet her for lunch before his next class. He didn't tell her about the strange events of the morning, though, because Alex needed a little more time to think about it himself. Alex lay down on his bed to relax for a few minutes. Dozing, he soon began to see images of McGill, trapped beneath the shell and unable to release his feet from the stretcher. Only it wasn't McGill this time, it was Alex himself. He couldn't breathe. Dark, black, water filled his throat. He jerked his legs until he felt his calves separating from his knees. A large, blue, illuminated fish passed slowly in front of Alex's face. The fish paused for a second, taking a long look at Alex before continuing. Alex looked up, and the light from the water's surface was getting dimmer and dimmer. He awoke, his body jolted up to a ninety-degree angle and covered in a light sheet of sweat, his mouth as dry as a radiator in an old New York City flat. It was three o'clock in the afternoon.

VI

Alex walked out of McCosh Hall and onto the Quadrangle facing the University Chapel. It was the first week of October. The air whispered, and some leaves on a nearby elm showed their first hint of a yellowish hue. Alex had just come from a meeting with his senior thesis faculty supervisor. It did not go well. All seniors were required to write a thesis, a project accounting for many of the year's credits. Alex's advisor, who also happened to be head of the English Department, was furious because it was obvious that Alex hadn't yet given any serious reflection to the project. Alex realized that this wasn't going to be a cakewalk.

Princeton students have a smaller project to do in their junior year, known as the "Junior Project" or "JP". The theory is that JP is good preparation for the larger senior year project. For Alex's JP, he wrote a sixty-page paper on John Milton's *Paradise Lost*. The title of the proposed paper: "Man's Conscience in Milton's Paradise Lost: Christianity or Humanity?" After reading Milton's entire work, a feat that took Alex nearly a month, he felt he should entitle the paper: "What the Fuck Right Do I Have to Critique a Work of This Magnitude?" Alex read at least a dozen books on Milton's works and at least thirty other writings specifically on *Paradise Lost*. In the end, Alex received an "A" on his JP, but he was not particularly satisfied. Not that he had plagiarized, but he felt his paper really didn't have a single new idea.

Because of Alex's dissatisfaction with his JP, he formulated two objectives for the senior thesis. Since he had already focused on work in the classical genre, he felt it was time to move into something more contemporary. Second, since the Milton paper made him feel as though he had put other scholars' ideas into his own words, he wanted to do something that was solely his own creative project. No one's ideas but me and my monkey, he thought, A novel perhaps? No, Alex wasn't about to step into that trap. There were always one or two students every year that tried that. Alex had gone to the library to read a few of the most recent attempts. They were a nice attempt at best, horrible at worst. Alex wasn't going to walk away totally risk free, though, so he decided he would attempt to write a play. A simple, one act play, if there was such an animal. He would include a limited number of actors, one or two stage settings and, hopefully, intense dialogue. Although he had all summer to do it, he had waited until a few days ago to sit down in front of his computer and come up with a few ideas. Alex didn't think the ideas were as weak as his advisor believed. He knew they needed some filler, but they were certainly workable.

Proposal 1:

Young couple meets and quickly falls very much in love. The man, a construction engineer, has an accident on the job and is paralyzed from the waist down. Play opens with man in the hospital and his girlfriend coming to see him. Both parties are very upset and swear their undying love to each other regardless of the outcome. They promise to marry as soon as he gets out of the hospital. The man would be in the hospital for a year recovering and undergoing rehabilitation. The play would focus on a series of meetings between the couple during that one-year period. After a few months, however, the inevitable would happen, the pair would begin to drift apart. The play would focus on his fear of losing her, and on her guilt as she slowly returns to a normal life without him. The play culminates with an intense emotional meeting between the two, where the woman finally tells the man that she is seeing someone else and she thinks it might be best if she stopped coming around. When she leaves, the man's soliloquy would leave the audience wondering if he will commit suicide. Author undecided at this point whether to introduce some symbol of hope e.g., a new hospital acquaintance, a priest, a letter from a long-lost friend asking for his know-how on a major building project. Or should man OD on painkillers?

Proposal 2:

Wife sends husband to the supermarket to pick up two cans of Progresso Plump Whole Tomatoes for her spaghetti sauce. The couple is retired, early seventies. The husband is a very dignified gentleman, who worked as an engineer for IBM for forty-six years. Dresses very well. Upper middle class. Lives in an old brownstone in Queens. He doesn't drive anymore, so he takes the subway two stops to the supermarket. The subway is crowded with high schoolers going on a field trip to the Botanical Gardens. The students are quite rowdy; yelling, dancing on the seats, and pushing each other. No teachers or supervisors appear to be around. There are a few other passengers on the subway car, but none seem to notice the commotion. The old man clutches a straphanger, ignoring the ever-increasing intensity of the students' behavior. Suddenly, he notices that one young student, a Puerto Rican girl, is being mocked and harassed by a classmate, a black boy. Not looking, the nervously laughing girl smashes into the old man and falls to the floor. The old man almost falls as well, but his grip on the straphanger narrowly prevents it. The black boy jumps in front of the old man and tells him he should watch where he is going. Thinking it is a misunderstanding, the old man starts to explain what happened. The young, black student will have none of it. The student starts calling the old man all sorts of names, accuses the old man of attempting to sexually gratify himself by rubbing against the girl. An argument ensues. The old man looks for support from other passengers. There is none. Other students join in. The old man cannot understand a word that is being said. The train pulls into a station. The boy pushes the old man to the floor. The old man's new Stetson hat falls off. Shaken and lying face down, he looks up and sees the Puerto Rican girl smiling at him. Then she kicks his hat out onto the platform, and all the students run laughing to a different car. The old man is finally helped to his feet and off the train by one of the remaining passengers. The old man is very upset, but he refuses to let it get the best of him. When he arrives at the supermarket, his hands are still shaking, and he has forgotten what his wife sent him to the store for. He tries to call his wife from his cell phone, but he is trembling too much, and he can't hit the right numbers. Wandering down the aisles, he comes across the canned Tomatoes and remembers why he is there. There are a dozen varieties of each type; stewed tomatoes, crushed tomatoes, tomato sauce, tomato paste, pizza sauce, etc. After about ten minutes he finds the whole, plump tomato section. Another five minutes and he finds the right size, but he can't locate the Progresso brand that his wife requested. He knows they must sell it, because his wife comes home with it all the time. He asks a woman, about fifty, who is also buying some canned tomato products, if she sees Progresso Plump Whole Tomatoes. She says she doesn't work there (or maybe she doesn't reply at all) and walks away. Soon the assistant manager shows up, about thirty, but still sporting some pimples. He tells the old man he must stop harassing customers or he will be asked to leave. The old man, an individual who has only become very angry a handful of times in his life, explodes. He demands to see the manager. The assistant manager says he will go get him. The old man thinks aloud to himself about how times have changed. He mumbles, "Is it a general lack of respect for all people? Or maybe there has always been a lack of respect for old people, people who no longer produce for society." His thought process is broken by the assistant manager's return. Instead of returning with the manager, the Assistant Manager has brought security to escort the old man out of the store. In vain, the old man briefly struggles with the much stronger guard. Suddenly, he has trouble breathing. The guard lets go of his hold on the old man, and he falls back into the shelves before slumping to the floor. He is dead, a dozen cans of plump, whole tomatoes, Progresso brand, lie on the floor around him.

That morning, when Alex printed out the proposals on his computer printer, it became obvious that one of his O'Neill playmates had hacked in. An additional, third proposal had been added:

Proposal 3:
ACT I. Dorky, geeky, Princeton English major with a little pecker (hereinafter referred to as "English Major" or "Alex") decides to write play for senior thesis project. Wants to write about the New York scene, so English Major goes into the city to get the proper feeling. After about two hours walking around, the only feeling of New York that English Major felt was the warm one of some homeless

person peeing on his leg outside the Port Authority Bus Terminal. Decides to take a subway ride, gets coat caught in closing door, almost hangs himself. Stares intently at people on subway, trying to connect with the city's underground. A bum tells English Major to stop staring, that it is not polite. Bum gets up, farts in English Major's face and spits on him. There is a ruckus going on in the car next to English Major's. He gets up off his seat to investigate. By the time he gets inside the other car, all he sees is an old man on the ground, with a young Puerto Rican girl standing over him. Probably trying to look up her dress, English Major concludes. Disgusted, decides it's time to get off. Sees new Stetson hat on the ground. Someone must have left it there. Tries it on. Perfect fit. Old man on floor looks at him incredulously. English Major figures old man must be a faguar. Enough of the Big Apple. After long day of research, English Major decides he needs to do something relaxing. A jog? No. Sauna? No. Rub down? Close. Blow-Job? Bingo. English Major goes back to his college. Seeks out his wench. Coincidentally, she is not only a fellow student, but also the daughter of his senior thesis advisor, Professor Dingle. English Major finds Dingle's daughter at her family's house, fortunately alone. She quickly goes to the task at hand. Actually, that should be "in hand." Professor Dingle, arriving home early from his lecture on Clothing Styles in the Literature of 1911, walks into his study only to find his daughter playing mouth music on English Major's organ. Believing in the principle that the best defense is a good offense, English Major criticizes the Professor for not knocking before entering the room. Enraged, the Professor lunges toward the pair. English Major's outstretched hands try to fend off the attack. The girl, completely frozen in fear, and not one to speak with her mouth full, can only mumble for peace. End of ACT I.

ACT II. Very short. Shot of English Major walking down a path with paperback books in hand. He is wearing a local community college sweatshirt.

Alex spent some time contemplating who in the house could have done it. He optimistically narrowed the choices down to thirteen suspects.

To lift his spirits after leaving McCosh, Alex headed back to his room to listen to some music. Going on Spotify, Alex decided to beef on his knowledge of the Brandenburg Concertos.

Alex went into Boder's room to see if he could find any pot. There were only two times when Alex would smoke marijuana alone: when he watched a movie or when he listened to music. Finding a joint in Boder's room was like finding rats in a garbage dump. Going back into the living room, Alex lit the joint with a match from a book of matches advertising tractor trailer driver's training. He took three hits and put it out. He had promised himself he would be completely weaned off by the beginning of official crew season in the spring. He didn't want to ever feel that excruciating pain in his lungs, like he felt in his race with

McGill, again.

Alex connected his earbuds to his iPhone. He was careful to select the concertos in numerical order—he would never have played four, five, or six first; he was a little anal about those sorts of things. He found a bag of barbecue chips on a bookshelf, pulled a Coke from the refrigerator, and laid down on the couch with a pen and notebook, hoping to get a little more definition around his thesis. Concerto No. 1 began, and the harpsichord seemed to sooth the tattered nerve endings of his brain. Alex put the notebook and the chips on the floor beside the couch. He closed his eyes. About twenty minutes later, by the time the orchestra got to the allegro assai of Concerto No. 2, Alex's mind had left the room. It floated with the flutes, high above the clouds. Notes for his senior thesis paper were left on the ground. As the concertos moved forward, different instruments brought Alex higher and higher: the violins, the natural horns, the harpsichord . . . even the oboe. The breeze from a cracked window caressed his face. What would Bach think, or do, Alex wondered, if he walked into the room and saw this half-stoned kid listening to his music; on this five-inch machine, for two hours; while lying on a couch, without any real instrument in sight? Alex smiled and took the final sip of his soda. Geniuses of that caliber don't fear change. They welcome it. Bach would probably put his ear to the earbuds and suggest that the treble be raised just a bit.

VII

No, it was not homecoming. But it was the Harvard game. Ninety-nine-point-nine percent of the American sports world could care less, but to that faction of American power, Harvard and Princeton alumni, it meant quite a bit. With deference to Michigan vs. Ohio State, it was the final score between Harvard and Princeton that reverberated in corporate boardrooms across America.

It wasn't just the alumni. The Harvard - Princeton social rivalry seeped into the psyche of the students on campus as well. Whether it was a football game or a debate team contest, when Harvard came to town, substantially more students went to the event than would otherwise go. Even Alex found himself drawn in. When it came to crew, the team seemed to dig in just a little deeper when the opposing rowers wore crimson tank tops with a large white H on the front. Unfortunately for Alex, for the past thirty years, Harvard had been an international powerhouse in crew, while Princeton wallowed in mediocrity. Alex and his teammates vowed that this year would be different.

The evening before the big football game, Alex, Amanda, Boder, Tina— a girl from Delaware he met last summer as a

Congressional aid, Sheik, Sheik's honey of the week, BT, Zimmy, Javier, and a few other stragglers, went to the Annunciation Bar & Grill for dinner. The food was horrible, but the beer was cheap. More importantly, fake I.D.'s worked well there. Two tables away was a group of about ten Harvard students, who were down from Cambridge for the weekend. As imbibing a few beers was apt to cause, a little taunting began. Boder raised the stakes by slipping a waitress twenty bucks to deliver a cheeseburger to the visitors with the words "Harvard Sucks" inscribed on the slice of American cheese. In an impressive return, one of the Harvard gentlemen quickly and discreetly hung a moon in the direction of Alex's table, revealing a bright, orange P, with the top half of the letter perfectly stationed on the cheeks of his ass, surrounding the anus. The rest of the Harvard table clapped and roared with laughter. BT stood up, and, lifting one of the beer pitchers off the table, began to recite the recently revised, sexually neutered, and now politically correct, school song:

> Let music rule the fleeting hour,
> The mantle round us draw;
> And thrill each heart with all its power,
> In praise of Old Nassau.
>
> And when the walls in dust are laid,
> With reverence and awe;
> Another throng shall breathe our song,
> In praise of Old Nassau.
>
> Till then with joy our songs we'll bring;

And while a breath we draw,
We'll all unite to shout and sing:
Long life to Old Nassau!

First BT's table, and then most of the other patrons in the restaurant, joined in. At the close of the song, the restaurant burst into applause. Unflustered, a member of the Harvard contingent stood up to contribute his verse:

Walking around the Canon Green,
I met a black and orange whore;
And with one swallow,
Among the halls so hallow,
She rang the bell on top of Old Nassau!

Jeers, crumpled paper towels, and French fries were hurled in his direction. The largest member of the Harvard contingent walked over to Alex's table, placed both hands on the table in the inverse position, leaned his face forward, and issued the edict: "I'll take on any one of you orange, fag-assed wimps in a drinking contest."

"I resent being called orange," Boder casually replied. The Harvard challenger smiled slowly and satirically at Boder, then imitated Boder's last statement, moving his head rapidly up and down and making Boder sound like...well, an idiot. The sneer returned as he continued his invitation, "Just pick, any one of you sad sacks to try and beat me. The losing table gives the winning table their shirts." Sheik exhibited a rare sign of concern and wriggled in his seat, probably because he always wore the most expensive clothes. The

Harvard gentleman left the Princeton table with one final comment, "I'll leave you ladies a little time think it over." Alex looked at Boder. Boder looked at Alex. It was clear something had to be done. Alex watched Boder's eyes turn toward Amanda, who was seated next to Alex. If Amanda's fingers squeezed her beer glass any harder, it would surely shatter. Her fingers were as white as chalk. She was biting her bottom lip, and her eyes were downcast. Alex had only seen Amanda like this on only rare occasions, usually when she was pissed at him.

"I want to take him," Amanda said tersely. Alex smiled at the rest of the table, convinced he hadn't heard Amanda correctly.

"Babe, could you please repeat what you just said?" Alex asked. Everyone else had been thinking the same thing.

Amanda didn't move, or change her expression. She repeated, "I think you heard me the first time, Alex. I want to take him."

"Don't be ridiculous! You don't even drink that much. I've seen you smashed on two glasses of wine. I can tell this guy is good. He's very athletic looking. I think he can pound 'em. Besides, you're—"

"A girl? Is that what you are about to say?"

"I didn't say it. You did," Alex quickly replied.

Boder jumped in, attempting to diffuse the situation, "People, people, people. Let us calm down. You two should have your daily argument another time, preferably when I'm not around. Now listen, these jerk offs have challenged us on our own turf, in front of a rather large audience, I might ad. We must accept, and we must win. Now Alex, I'm your best friend, but Amanda's kind offer should be seriously considered. First, you'll have to excuse Zimmy, Javier, and myself from competition. If the truth can be told, we're already flying on the gummy bears Zim brought back from Colorado; therefore, the desired, victorious outcome would be highly unlikely for any of us. BT doesn't drink, and you, Alex, have crew practice at seven-thirty tomorrow morning. None of the other ladies have been so generous as to make such a kind offer; therefore, Alex, I believe Amanda's suggestion is our best alternative."

Alex stared at Boder in disbelief. Boder stared back with the serious, yet satisfied look of someone who knew they held the winning hand. Alex looked at Amanda. He knew she was waiting for him to continue his protest, but Alex wasn't looking for a battle here. He really had nothing to gain. If she wanted to make a fool of herself, fine, so be it. "Boder, my apologies. I really hadn't thought it all the way through. You are one hundred percent correct. Amanda is not only an option, but she is a good option at that." Boder stared back at Alex with the uncertain look of someone beginning to feel as if he was playing in a rigged poker game.

Alex went to the Harvard table to accept the challenge. All parties concerned, and a substantial contingent of onlookers, moved to an adjacent bar room. Amanda, all five foot six, one hundred and twenty pounds of her, met the Harvard contestant at the middle of the bar. He was six three, two hundred and eighteen pounds. "Hey, didn't I see you two in a boxing match in Las Vegas?" someone yelled. The crowd applauded.

"What are they drinking?" someone asked.

"Let the lady decide," said the Harvard contestant.

"Jack Daniels, straight up. And a beer chaser if you like,"

Amanda said stoically. Everyone cheered. Alex put his hands on his face and shook his head.

The first two shots of bourbon were placed on the long oak bar. Next to each shot stood an open bottle of Heineken. Boder whispered something in Amanda's ear; she nodded in agreement, and then had the bartender replace her Heineken with a Yuengling. Alex noticed that someone had turned the music off. After assurances to both sides that he had recently migrated from Canada and had not attended either University, one of the bartenders; a stout, redheaded, red-faced, mustached man in his mid-thirties, not surprisingly nicknamed Red Eddie; was selected as referee. He laid out the rules, "When I give the signal, you must immediately and completely, down the shot in front of you. You may drink your beer whenever you like, to assist the shot process. I will repeat the call to drink every three minutes and thirty seconds. If you do not finish the shot within thirty seconds of the call, if you vomit, or if you decide to withdraw from the competition, your opponent will be declared the winner. There shall be no bathroom breaks. Now shake hands, and may the best man, uh, person win."

Alex couldn't stand it. He had to try one more time. He walked up to Amanda and whispered, "We can still get out of here."

Amanda looked him right in the eye and demanded, "Alex, step back and leave me alone."

Alex raised his arms in the air. "Fine, kill yourself," he retorted. He turned his back on the action as he heard the bartender yell, "Contestants, prepare to begin." The bartender looked down at his watch and then shouted even louder, "One . . . two . . . three . . . Go!" Both contestants easily swallowed their first shot and the second, and the third. In fact, after the fifth shot, the Harvard man chugged his entire beer, and proceeded to do an impromptu Indian rain dance around Amanda's barstool. The crimson members in the audience went wild. Amanda stared straight ahead. Her brown beer bottle remained full and covered in perspiration, which began to trickle down the side and onto the cocktail napkin that was imprinted with parts of Einstein's mathematical equations.

"One . . . Two . . . Three, Go!"

"One . . . Two . . . Three, Go!"

"One . . . Two . . . Three, Go!"

The Harvard contestant was taking long, slow swigs of his beer after each shot. Amanda's beer stood lukewarm, dripped in sweat and untouched.

"One . . . Two . . . Three, Go!"

"One . . . Two . . . Three, Go!"

"One . . . Two . . . Three, Go!

But for the clatter of shot glasses returning empty to the bar counter, and the familiar mantra-like chant of Red Eddie, the bar became possessed by an eerie silence, like that of the crowd watching a saloon high stake poker game in an old western movie. The eleven shots had taken a visible toll on both contestants. The Harvard contestant's usually active mouth had ceased to function, and he became very agitated at supporters who would tap him on the back following each successful shot. Amanda's eyes had become glazed, and she had to hold her head in her hands following each round just to keep her face from slamming into the bar. Alex was becoming concerned. He whispered to Boder that he was going to pull Amanda out. Boder replied, "Alex, you probably should, but I'll tell you this: if you pull her out now, she will never speak to you again."

"Well, she'll never speak to me again if she's dead, either!" he argued, but Alex knew Boder was right. Do or die, this was Amanda's show.

"One . . . Two . . . Three . . . Go!"

"One . . . Two . . . Three . . . Go!"

On the thirteenth shot, Amanda barely swallowed the last drops of the harsh, tea colored liquid, before the thirty-second limitation expired. Amanda felt herself beginning to regurgitate, and she swallowed hard, pushing the gooey, and ungodly substance back into her stomach. She couldn't go on. Her head was in a constant spin, accelerating by the moment. Amanda slowly turned on her stool and searched the crowd for Alex. She couldn't distinguish the features on anyone's face. Alex saw the look on Amanda's face and knew she was in deep trouble. He quickly approached Amanda, grabbed the shirtsleeves of her upper arms with both hands, and redundantly asked, "Amanda, what's the matter? Babe, are you OK?"

Amanda's head swayed back and forth. Finally, barely audible, she managed to speak, "Alex . . . I can't . . . I . . . can't go . . . on . . . .. I'm a . . . bout to . . . pass out . . .."

Alex looked over Amanda's shoulder at the Harvard contestant. He appeared to have just been on the losing end of a heavyweight fight. His white knuckles clawed at the ridge of the bar for support. His head bobbed back and forth like a buoy on the Chesapeake Bay. But his supporters began to cheer, as it appeared Amanda's surrender was imminent. Even Alex couldn't believe what he was about to say. He grabbed Amanda by her wrists, "Amanda, listen to me. He's almost down. I can feel it. You were right. You can take him!" Slowly shaking her head in the negative, Amanda attempted to rise from her stool. Stepping onto the floor, the spinning increased, reminding her of the roundabout ride at the park by her house, which she hated, even as a little girl. Her brother would spin her around, faster and faster, refusing to stop, even when she would scream, beg, or cry for him to do so. Alex held Amanda up, brushed away some hair that was sticking to her sweaty forehead and cheeks, and gently placed her back on the stool. Alex knew the bartender was about ready to make the call for the next round. The bartender poured the fourteenth shot. In a desperate attempt to regain some cognitive thought, the Harvard contestant opened his eyes as wide as he could, and then blinked several times in rapid succession. Alex spoke softly, but firmly, "Amanda, listen to me. I know he can't last much longer. Do one more for me, honey . . . just one more. Then, I promise, I'll take you home."

The bartender, sensing the end, made this call more stern and ominous, "One . . . two . . . three . . . Go!" The Harvard contestant, not feeling any need to hurry, stared at his glass as if it contained nitroglycerin. After thirteen shots, it might as well have. Amanda looked into Alex's eyes. His face seemed to approach her nose and then fade back. Then she saw his smile. Even with the nerve numbing effect of the whiskey, his smile felt good. Slowly, Amanda turned toward to the bar, her back facing Alex and the rest of the silent, but anxious, crowd. There was about fifteen seconds left. Amanda picked up her shot glass and looked directly into the eyes of her challenger, whose shaky hand was attempting to bring this final shot to his lips. He caught Amanda out of the corner of his eye and slowly turned to look at her.

"Well, what are we waiting for Big H?" Amanda slurred, "Let's do it." Amanda carefully lifted the glass to her lower lip and let the biting liquid pour down her throat. The Harvard contestant did likewise. Amanda's stomach felt as though it might explode, leaving its contents on the barroom floor, and, hopefully, providing relief. She grabbed hold of the bar to maintain her balance, and stared at the little plastic Clydesdale horses running in a circle around a light over the bar. Suddenly, Amanda heard a loud, crashing sound to her left. Some commotion and a huge cheer followed. The Harvard contestant's stool emptied as he fell to the floor, face down, half of the fourteenth shot still held upright in his now still hand. Alex immediately went to Amanda and hugged her. She collapsed into Alex's chest. Amanda didn't want him to ever let go. Then, her thoughts darkened and faded away.

Alex borrowed Sheik's car, a Mercedes 325i, to take Amanda back to his room. It was in a parking garage close to the restaurant. Once in the car, Amanda's head fell into Alex's lap. Alex looked down at Amanda's face; her hair was matted in sweat and smelled awful. Slowly she looked up at Alex, then turned her face back toward his lap, and vomited. To Alex's surprise, he didn't mind at all. He was glad she was getting the poison out of her system. There she was, semiconscious, sweaty, and sprawled across the front seat, vomit on her face and clothes, but Alex was never more attracted to her than he was at that moment. He began to laugh, first at the whole scene in the restaurant, and then at how pissed Sheik was going to be. Finally, he laughed at a group of individuals he'd spotted walking shirtless down

Nassau Street, with one poor, unconscious slob being carried along by his underarms, a large rip clearly visible in the back of his pants.

*****

Amanda skipped the game on Saturday, electing instead to keep her face buried in her pillow. Fortunately for her, the following week was fall recess. Early Saturday evening, Alex drove her to Newark Airport. Amanda didn't say much. She wore her sunglasses the entire car ride, even though it was raining. "Man . . . I feel like a bug on the bottom of Shaquille O'Neill's sneaker."

"I guess that means we're not going to do goodbye shots at the airport bar?" Alex joked.

"Please . . . one more remark like that and I'll puke on you again."

Alex wouldn't be going home for most of the break. Crew practice. The last push before the cold weather set in. Boder was hanging out until tomorrow, and then going home to Washington for a day, before flying to a Bermuda condo that was owned by some lobbyist his father knew. A few days earlier, Boder had invited Alex. "Dude," he tempted, "it's all expenses paid. How can you turn this one down? The babes! The Beach! The babes! The booze! The babes! The gonja! Did I mention the babes?"

"Sorry," Alex replied, "the boat calls."

"Oh yeah? What's it saying? Come freeze your ass off in some dingy, with a bunch of sweaty homos, instead of lying in the sand right by the big blue, with your head lying on a nice pair of big, warm titties?" Boder was on a roll now. He placed his right hand on Alex's shoulder, and in his best serious tone cautioned, "Xander," he was the only person who called Alex that, "you have to fold on this crew thing. It's cramping your style. This is it, bro. The last year of college. Before you know it, we'll be getting up every morning to spend the entire day listening to some old dude tell us what to do." Boder pulled a joint from the shirt pocket underneath his argyle sweater, lit it, exhaled, and prompted, "It's just not going to get any better than this." Then Boder inhaled deeply and passed the joint to Alex.

Alex looked at the joint with mixed emotions. He knew he got high too much with Boder around. On the other hand, it was always a lot of fun. If Alex smoked, he felt guilty. If he didn't smoke, he felt bad for missing out. He should have been Jewish. Alex waived off the joint. "Sorry Bode, duty calls," he explained, "Besides, I've got some work to do on my thesis, and my mom has been bugging me to come home this year. Do you realize, I live an hour from here and I have yet to go home?" Alex had spoken to his mother and had vowed to make it home at least for dinner over recess. "Speaking of home," Alex went on, "I've noticed you're not going to be spending much time there next week. In fact, I've noticed that you hardly ever call home lately. Last year, I felt like I lived with your mother. And the Senator? Jesus, I can't even remember what he looks or sounds like."

Boder's demeanor changed to something slightly more somber. He took a long hit, released the smoke above his head, and tried to move back to his half serious nature, teasing, "What, I have a nanny here now? I thought half the reason I chose this place was to live away from home?"

Boder attempted to pass the joint back to Alex. Alex

shook it off again. Boder shrugged his shoulders and continued to smoke solo, but Alex wasn't ready to let him off the hook. Boder usually did very little homework. Now he was doing none. Boder was always a good-natured wise-ass. Now he was becoming cynical and a little nasty. Boder was even bringing townies from the local bars back to the suite to party with various illegal substances. Not that Princeton was full of hooligans, but it was still making Alex a little uneasy. Boder used to talk about his parents constantly. He worshiped his mother. Although he complained about his father's long absences from home and lack of communication, it never stopped him from bragging incessantly about his father's contacts and lifestyle. Lately, Boder didn't speak a word about his parents, unless Alex asked about them. Even then, it was like pulling teeth. Sorry Boder, it's time to zero in, Alex thought, as he looked Boder right in the eyes. He noticed they were distant and gently began, "You know, bro, I think you're having a problem with your folks."

"Didn't we have this conversation a while ago?"

"Yes, we did," Alex replied, "I think you were snaking me then. Do you want to snake me now, too?"

Boder took another hit off the joint, placed it in a nearby ashtray, and looked down at his shoes. There was a brief silence as the white smoke slowly dissipated. "Tell me you never had any problems with your folks. You think I'm the only twenty-year-old in America not presently on the best of speaking terms with his parents?"

"I didn't say that," Alex responded, "and I don't really care about the rest of the twenty-year-olds in America. I care about you, Bode. Who really knows you better than me? I mean really? We eat together, sleep in the same place, get fucked up together, and study togeth—uh, never mind that one. Hell, remember those two chicks we met from Swarthmore as sophomores? We had sex in the same room together, for God's sake! But you're changing on me, bud. Maybe we're just getting older or something, I don't know, but I know you Bode, and you're moving in a direction that's concerning me. I guess all I want to say is, I'm here for you, man. If you need anything, please come to me."

Boder looked at Alex, smiled, and said, "Are we going to kiss now?" Alex smiled and shook his head in the negative. He wasn't sure if he had gotten through. Boder continued, "No, seriously though, I appreciate it. Yes, I am having a little thing with the folks, but it's nothing that won't blow over. I'm not the bleeding-heart type, and I do have difficulty relating my problems. Everyone just thinks of me as happy-go-lucky Boder, the rich senator's son. You know that's not always true. Anyway, I appreciate your concern. I do love you like a brother, and I want you to know that. If my problem gets any worse, I'll fill you in, OK?

"OK."

"But for now, can we let it be?"

"Sure, I think we cleared up a few things."

Boder nodded in agreement. Once again, a brief silence gripped the room. Finally, Boder spoke, "Now let's get the hell out of here and have a few beers before we start feeling each other up!"

The pair walked out of O'Neill shoulder to shoulder, unsure exactly what they had planned for the evening, but fully confident it would be another good night.

VIII

Alex spent most of fall recess in the water at Carnegie Lake. With colder weather creeping in, it was important that the team do as much practicing as possible. The coach had double sessions scheduled Monday through Friday, with a trip to Boston on Saturday for the Head of the Charles Regatta. Workouts included running, weightlifting, the ergometer, and strategy sessions outside the water, as well as sprint races and extra-long races in the water. Alex was in much better shape than he was in September, and he didn't even mind the practices. The team was coming together well, and the spring season was looking more and more promising. The Cruiser just might have been right about the gold on the lake.

At about four o'clock, Friday afternoon, the day before Halloween, Alex headed down to the boathouse for the trip to Boston. The next day was the Head of the Charles Regatta, an annual event featuring the largest assembly of sculls and shells in the United States. This event hosted all the best schools, and all the worst; major and minor rowing clubs, crews from around the world, and various collections of guys in boats. The event had become so large and chaotic in recent years, nearly eight hundred boats, which for a pure, boat against boat rowing race, there were certainly better events.

But for rowers—real, oars in the veins, tradition rowers, of any skill level—this was an event not to be missed. As Anne Sexton once wrote:

> I am rowing, I am rowing
> Though the oarlocks stick and are rusty
> and the sea blinks and rolls
> like a worried eyeball,
> but I am rowing, I am rowing,
> though the wind pushes me back.

Alex loved this event. During his walk to the boathouse, he realized that this would likely be his last trip to the Charles, at least as a serious participant. That was one of the bittersweet things about senior year at college: so many lasts. Alex handed his equipment bag to the bus driver and went to help the team's rigger load the shell trailer. Freddy Lewis, the team's rigger, in charge of maintaining the boat and the boathouse, always orchestrated the event as though he were sending his kids away to college. Nicknamed "Chief," Freddy was a short, quiet, black man in his mid-sixties, who was on the job even before The Cruiser rowed. First the oars, made of plastic foam, carbon fiber and fiberglass, and painted in the school colors, orange and black, were gently loaded onto the bottom of the open trailer. Then eight sculls were carefully loaded, one at a time. They were inverted to protect them from bad weather and loaded two across and four high; care was taken to tightly hook and strap them in. Tools, a few extra seats, some oarlocks, and an assortment of spare parts, were also loaded as insurance against unforeseen events. The crew teams, both the men and the women, some student fans, and a few alumni, boarded two buses for the five and one-half hour trip to Boston. Heading up Interstate 95 to Interstate 91, one couldn't help but spend some time staring at the leaves of the trees, bursting in the vibrant colors of their final encore. As the bus rolled north, it grew slightly colder, the trees had fewer leaves, and darkness settled in quicker than it had yesterday. Winter was just a frosted breath away.

At about ten-thirty, the bus pulled into the parking lot of the Cambridge Marriot Hotel. Alex was rooming with Jim Daley, a junior from Oklahoma. Daley was a meticulous individual. Although he considered himself rather organized, Daley was the only guy Alex knew who hung his blue jeans on clip hangers in the closet. Daley was never late for, nor missed, a single practice. He never had a bad word to say about the coach, no matter how hard practices became, although Daley never said anything good about him either. The fact was that Daley never said much at all; he just nodded a lot. Daley was not as athletic as the other members of the team, but he certainly was focused. If the coach wanted thirty-six strokes per minute, Daley would divide that up into exactly 0.6 strokes per second. Alex didn't know Daley very well. The reason they were assigned to be roommates was that they were the stroke pair of the first skull, and Diriglia liked to put the pairs together. Last year, as a sophomore, Daley wasn't in the first skull, but he was part of the stroke in the second. Daley didn't seem to be a bad guy, but Alex wondered if he would ever really be able to dig deeper into Daley's persona. One thing was for sure, Diriglia wanted lights out by eleven, and Alex knew that at precisely that moment, Daley would be in his pajamas, in bed, with the lights out. Alex, on the other hand, always had difficulty sleeping the night before a meet.

As The Cruiser had recently revealed during their telephone conversation, it was likely that Alex would also spend some time in the early morning hours throwing up. God, he hated that! It was just that the anticipation of the competition, the extreme pain, and the excitement that always appeared, just blew his insides up. Everyone handles the pressure in his or her own way. Alex knew that Carr always jogged just before bed the night before, just so he would be tired enough to sleep. Johnson, Carr's crew roommate, read the Bible aloud to keep calm. Alex tried these, and a half-dozen other techniques teammates used, with no success. Once he even called The Cruiser for advice. "Don't sweat it," The Cruiser told him, "If you weren't worked up, then I'd be worried. As for myself, hell, after a while I used to just make myself puke to get it over with." Alex knew he could never do that. He had a strong aversion to self-inflicted pain. Alex had seen the movie *127 Hours* about a Mountain climber in Utah who, to escape, cut his right arm off after falling and getting it stuck between boulders. Alex knew that, if that had been him, he probably would have ended up as lizard meat.

Alex wondered what Daley did to ease the tension. "Hey Daley," he questioned, "are you nervous about tomorrow?" Daley shook his head no and got into bed. It was ten fifty-nine. Still dressed, Alex shut out the lights and sat on his bed. Within minutes, Alex could hear two knocks resounding on each hallway door. The knocks were getting closer. It was Peter Henderson, a recent graduate, and now one of Diriglia's assistants. Two loud knocks on Daley and Alex's door. "Lights out, gentlemen. We row in the morning!" Alex rolled his eyes. "They are out, and no shit Sherlock," he whispered. Alex needed some air. Daley didn't seem like a snitch, not that Alex believed it should matter. It wasn't like he was going to sneak out and roam the streets all night, or meet some woman in the hotel lounge and go to her room for an evening of wild, impetuous, and gratuitous pleasure. Well, OK, maybe the second example was pushing Alex's maturity and responsibility levels too far, but the fact-of-the-matter was, he needed to take a walk to calm down. He put the light on to see Daley's predicted nonverbal answers to his impending questions. Daley's eyes popped open. "Hey Daley, I need to take a little walk around the hotel to unwind. You want to come?" he invited. Daley nodded in the negative. "You want anything?" Again, negative. "It's OK, right? I mean it does not bother you that I leave for a few minutes, does it?" Daley shook his head no. "I'll be right back. And don't worry, you won't even hear me come in." With that, Alex put on his jean jacket. Quickly and quietly, he left the room.

Alex walked down the long corridor away from the elevators and toward a back exit. He took the off-white, concrete steps down three floors to the parking lot. Upon opening the door, he was hit with a burst of frigid air. Alex could see his breath, buttoned his jacket, and walked toward the sidewalk in front of the hotel. Nearing midnight, it seemed quite bright outside. Alex looked up. The sky was crystal clear, as it gets only when it's very cold, and the moon was full. Alex crossed a quiet, four-lane highway to a 7- Eleven. He purchased a Lemon-Lime Gatorade and returned outside. He wanted to talk to Amanda. He missed her. Besides, talking to her always helped him take his mind off the race. Amanda was still back home in Chicago, and she told him that morning that she was going with friends to some country bar that evening. It was an hour earlier in Chicago, and Alex wondered if she would be home yet. Alex texted her but received no reply. He then called on his cell, but, after four rings, her message came on, "Hi, it's Amanda. Out for the evening folks. Leave a message, and I'll get back to you. For you hometown folks, I am heading back to New Jersey on Sunday night. And if this is Alex, I called you earlier tonight but didn't get a reply. I know you must be busy with the team, getting ready for the race. Good-luck tomorrow. I love you, babe! Bye!"

Alex did not leave a message. He was jealous that she was out having fun without him. Stupid, but undeniably true. He looked up from his phone, stopped short and felt a tingle in the back of his neck. A disheveled, dirty, grey bearded man, somewhere between fifty and sixty, appeared no more than six inches from Alex's face. He asked, "Do you have five dollars, son? I really need five dollars. They just kicked me out of the damn store. I need five dollars to get back in, to get some food. I just need five dirty, measly dollars." The man's breath reeked like the inside of a milk carton after a day in the hot sun. His teeth partially brown, black, and rotted.

"I'm sorry," Alex said, "I don't have my wallet with me. I don't have any money."

The man edged a little closer to Alex's face. Politely, but with a hint of sarcasm, he replied, "Well how'd you get that Gatorade there, boy? Is your ass a soda machine?" With that, the bum let out a haunting, throaty laugh.

Just what I needed, Alex thought, a homeless bum who thinks he is a goddamn comedian. Nevertheless, Alex did feel sorry for the guy. Alex never did buy the argument that homeless people were homeless because they didn't want to work. Not many jobs tougher than living in a cardboard box, in the winter, in Boston. "I already had that money in my coat pocket," Alex retorted, "but I may have a few singles in my wallet." Alex reached into his pants pockets.

"Well make sure it totals five dollars. Don't want any fifty cents or something like that. If I wanted fifty cents, I would have asked you for fifty cents," the man pushed.

A bum with big balls, Alex thought. Alex put the wallet very close to his face and peeked inside. The man put his face just inches from. Alex's hands, his long greying, dirty hair partially blocked Alex's view. "Hey, do you mind. I'm trying to find five dollars for you. I can't see my hand."

"Well excuuuuussssee me!" The man said sarcastically, raising his hands to either side of his head. "I didn't plan on this taking all day," he continued, "God forbid it totaled more than five dollars, eh, boy? Well I'll save you some time there, son, so we can both get some sleep tonight. You got yourself twenty in there. Now why don't you just hand it all over to compensate me for the wait?" Alex couldn't believe this guy.

"Are you always this forward in your begging?" Alex retorted, "Maybe I shouldn't give you anything. What do you think of that?"

The man's face turned serious. When he spoke, his tone was somber. He could have been a mid-level executive at a big corporation, giving a presentation to some superiors. "I apologize," he said, "I didn't take you for the prissy type. I thought you were just some kid who didn't think a few bucks was a big deal." For a few moments, there was silence, then just as quickly, the man's facial expression and voice returned to semi-crazed as he went on, "But I think you will give me twenty dollars, though! And . . . do you know why?"

Alex wasn't sure he should answer, but felt compelled. "Why?"

"Because you feel sorry for me and, even more importantly, you're scared shit of me."

"Listen old man," Alex bravely retorted, "I'm a lot stronger than you. So first, let's delete the scared to shit line."

"That is certainly a strong and impressive consideration, my son. But it still is no match for a knife." Alex wished he was back in his room. The image of Jim Daley sleeping soundly filled Alex's head. Not a worry in the world. Alex could just see it, Daley finding him tomorrow morning lying on the sidewalk in a pool of blood. Daley sadly shaking his head, but not for too long because he doesn't want to be late for the Regatta.

"Here, take it," Alex heard himself say as he deposited a twenty into the man's hand. "Now leave me the hell alone."

"Thank you, kind sir," said the man. His voice once again returned to that of the corporate executive. Smiling, he said, "It was a pleasure speaking with you."

Alex stood still and watched as the man walked past the entrance to the 7- Eleven, out of the parking lot, and into a small, unkempt, red-brick building with a flickering, yellow, neon sign that spelled out "Joey's Tavern," and a handwritten cardboard sign in the window that read "Big Drinks and Even Bigger Women." Angry, Alex sat atop a dispenser of the local newspaper. Alex looked up at the stars and then across the highway. "Anyone else want to take advantage of a stupid shit from Princeton?" he yelled.

*****

Early the next morning, Alex awoke with his insides in a knot. Every goddamn time, churning like a high-speed blender. Just once, he would like to wake up on a race day feeling normal. Alex's mind raced to the beggar of the night before, but he quickly tried to put it out of his mind. He just couldn't get into that right now. That whole episode needed considerable time to properly digest. Alex heard the shower running. He needed to pee. He quietly opened the bathroom door and was about to ask Daley how he felt, when the answer became all too apparent. Looking through the fogged glass of the sliding shower doors, Alex could see Daley soaping his penis a little too intensely to be considered appropriate washing. If he rubbed it any harder and faster, it would probably come flying off at the root and go splattering against the faucets. Alex quickly left the bathroom. He smiled, shook his head, and mumbled, "So, Mr. Perfect pulls predominately on his protruding protuberance. To each his own."

*****

By the time Alex got on the bus, everyone else was already there. "Hey Sleeping Beauty," Diriglia yelled, "Glad you could make it!"

Alex wanted to reply, "Well if Daley jerked off quicker, I would have been here fifteen minutes ago!" But he thought it best to leave that little tidbit to himself. He wouldn't even tell Boder that little gem. Telling Boder something confidential was like putting a Billboard on the Golden Gate Bridge. Alex vowed not to do it, no matter how much he knew Boder would enjoy the story.

It was a very brisk morning, and a heavy fog was just beginning to lift, as the bus headed for the Boston University Boathouse, the starting point of the race. As the bus rode within a few blocks of the boathouse, traffic came to a virtual standstill. There would be about two hundred thousand spectators at this event. Rowing for the common man. Instead of the usual two-thousand-meter race, this competition was about two and one-half miles. No two boats would start at the same time. Every fifteen seconds, for almost ten hours, a single scull or shell would leave the starting line, one by one, until everyone had their moment in the sun. The rowers were put into classes; prep schools, colleges, women, single skulls, veterans, or goof-offs; and released from the line in sequences to reduce collisions. Since the colleges rowers were some of the best, they usually went off near noon, when the crowds were at their peak. It was nine-thirty. Coach Diriglia had everyone get off the bus for a long walk to the Boston University Boathouse, to loosen up. Along the race route, there were ten different boathouses from which to launch. The better your class, the more likely your boathouse would be near the start. Only the actual crew and their boat were permitted near the river's edge by any boathouse, so, once a team was launched, they were on their own until the finish.

Along the walk, Alex watched other teams arriving in buses and cars, with small trucks towing carriers of sculls and shells, sleek, shiny and ready to go. Some shells had names tattooed on their bows: past coaches, great former racers, and generous alumni. There were flags and shirt colors of so many different schools, clubs, and countries. Then, there were the spectators who ranged from raggedy students to foreign dignitaries. People carried lounge chairs, blankets, and box seats. They wore wool pullovers and fur coats. They packed cookies and caviar, coffee and cognac. Alex's heart pounded. He breathed deeply. He noticed the water, the trees, the air, the boathouses, the shells, and the colors. If there was a more beautiful sport in existence, at that moment, Alex didn't know it.

The team hung out at the BU Boathouse, waiting for their shells to slide through the traffic. Finally, after forty-five minutes, the carrier arrived. The men and the women, the lightweights and the heavyweights, selected their shells and equipment and carefully carried and prepared them near the river's edge. Alex's race was scheduled to go off in about an hour. He grabbed McGill, now one of his closest acquaintances on the team, and went for a jog to loosen up. Alex and McGill jogged away from the river and onto some side streets in hopes of avoiding the crowds. It was useless. All the restaurants and cafes were buzzing, and McGill elbowed Alex every time he spotted a nice-looking woman. By the time they returned to the river, Alex's ribs were sore.

Alex was a little angry at himself for getting so worked up about a race that was really nothing more than a fancy scrimmage. Yet Alex also knew that the other teams would be watching his squad closely to see if the rumors of their potential were true. Alex, and most of his teammates, did not want the other teams leaving the Head of the Charles just thinking that his team had possibilities. They wanted the opposition to have no doubt about who the team to beat would be this spring. Alex wondered, though, if he and his teammates were putting too much pressure on themselves. Fuck it, he thought. They wanted to kick some ass. Alex watched as Chief made some last-minute adjustments to the oarlocks of the shell. Everyone knew that Chief was probably responsible for more Princeton Crew wins than anyone who ever set foot inside a shell. A framed inscription, entitled *The Five Points to Assure Winning*, hung in the locker room of the Princeton boathouse. It read:

> One: Row as a team.
> Two: Row as a team.
> Three: Row as a team.
> Four: Row as a team
> Five: Never, <u>ever</u>, interrupt
> Chief when he is working
> on your shell.

Diriglia called the heavyweight team over for a quick meeting. "Gentlemen," he said, "on one hand, we know this is only a scrimmage. On the other, this is our last chance before winter to go up against the best, see what we've got, and see what we need to work on. I'd like to send a little message to the rest of our fellow competitors today. We go off at four minutes after twelve. You must be at the starting line at precisely that time. Watch the team in front of you. The good news is: the team off the starting line in front of you is Harvard." The team cheered. Harvard had been the Ivy League champ for the past three years, and they were supposed to be very good again this year. Alex recalled the incident with the Harvard challenger and Amanda at the Annunciation Bar & Grill. He hoped this went just as well. Diriglia continued, addressing the coxswain, Joe Vales, directly, "Now Vales, keep your eyes on those guys. They'll probably do the fastest time in our class, besides us. If you gain ground on them, you'll know you're in good shape. And for God's sake, keep your eyes on other shells out there. There are a lot of crazy jackasses in this event and there will be shells all over the goddamn place. Remember, this is a very long race, so pace yourselves. Now everyone in here for a prayer."

The team gathered around and put their hands on top of one another. Neil Johnson, the team Co-Captain, led the prayer: "Dear God, thank you for giving us the ability to be here today. Bring us home safely and swiftly. Watch over Princeton. Amen." After a moment of silence, Johnson continued, "Let's go get 'em boys!"

The team carried the boat onto a floating dock, guided by Vales' squeaky voice. Holding the boat over his head, Alex could feel the dock sink beneath the weight. The team swung the boat away from their heads and, with a soft splash, placed it in the water. A few assistants brought the oars over to the scull, and Chief had carefully greased them in the area that would be hooked into the oarlock. The eight oars were slipped into the oarlocks. In perfect unison, the eight rowers, with their backs to the basin, entered the shell and sat down. The coxswain, facing the eight rowers, did likewise. "Pick up your oars!" Vales shouted, "Left foot in slide! Away!" With that command, the rowers pushed off from the dock with their right feet, placed them in the slides and drifted for a moment in total peace. The basin was filled with shells and sculls: some practicing their starts and turns, some just floating along enjoying the sights, and still others returning, exhausted, yet high from crossing the finish line, almost three miles away.

Alex closed his eyes and tried to remember the course. First, they would go under the black, steel railroad bridge. Then, they would be in the wide open, passing both the Riverside Boat Club and that of Northeastern University. They would go under four stone and three arched bridges over the next three quarters of a mile. Vales reminded everyone that, to avoid disqualification, they must row through the center arch of any bridge they pass under. Then it would be onward, past the Harvard Boathouse. The most difficult part would follow: for a quarter mile, the course made a sharp curve to the left. The remainder of the course would run perpendicular to the former. Finally, they would go through Eliot Bridge and past the Cambridge Boat Club's boathouse to the finish.

About five minutes before their scheduled start, the Princeton squad pulled as close as was permitted to the starting line, to watch some of their competition. The University of Pennsylvania was on the line. Their coach having drawn the lowest number out of a hat, they would go first. They were considered a strong contender this year. Yale was next, in for a long year since six of their starters graduated. University of Washington, always good. Dartmouth, no threat. Northeastern, possible threat since they scooped up some top freshmen from prep schools last year. Harvard. Goddamn Harvard. They were ranked first, nationally, two years in a row. They did lose one of their strokes and one from the bow pair, though, but there was a rumor circulating that the replacements were even better. Princeton would be next off the line, followed by the final team in the race, the University of Michigan.

Princeton soon found itself at the starting line. Vales faced the course, and Daley faced Vales, then Alex, Hartshorn, Simon, Haley, Jackson, Carr, and Johnson. The starter gave them little chance to focus, "Rowers are you ready?" For a split-second, Alex listened to the small ripples in the water slide off the outside of the shell. "Ready all? Row!"

"Get it up! Get it up!" Vales yelled, exhorting his teammates to bring the stroke count to the planned twenty-six per minute for the first 250 meters. A crew team usually starts out gaining speed as quickly as possible and then slows down into the planned stroke cadence. In this case, however, they would start substantially slower than they would in a normal two-thousand-meter race, because the Head of the Charles was an endurance test more than anything else. After about sixteen strong strokes, Princeton had the shell at the desired cadence. Shortly thereafter, the rowers awaited Vales next order. It came, "Settle in four strokes to twenty-eight." Four strokes later the switch was made without a hitch. Forty-five seconds later Vales commanded, "Settle in four to thirty." Bang. Thirty. There would be plenty of time later for sprinting. The team was definitely in synch.

Alex had a strong urge to look toward the riverbank to see the crowds, but he didn't dare. Concentrate on your stroke and only your stroke. One wrong move and you could send the entire team into the drink, Alex convinced himself. He could sense, by the sound of voices above him, that they were approaching the Railroad Bridge. "Bridge approaching!" Vales warned, "Stay the course! Stay the course!" A quick shadow and they were through. "I see the enemy, gentlemen!" Vales shouted, "About three boat lengths ahead. We're going to get 'em gentlemen and send a nice little message!" Alex felt the first beads of sweat forming on his forehead and upper lip. By the end of the race, his shirt and shorts would weigh a few pounds. "Passing River Street Bridge. Good rowing! Enemy at about two and a half," encouraged Vales. They were almost a mile into the race, so Alex knew the cadence would pick up slightly. He focused on the back of Daley's neck and breathed deeply to absorb as much oxygen as he could. "Here comes Michigan now, right behind us. Get ready for a pick-up," Vale instructed. In the silence, Alex could hear all sixteen blades slicing the water simultaneously. They were a finely tuned, human engine. "Settle in three strokes to thirty-one." Alex saw the back of Daley's neck redden. It was Daley's job to set the stroke and Alex's to hit it immediately. "Good! Enemy at two lengths. Here come the bridges." Alex could feel the boat move slightly to the portside as Vales adjusted the rudder. Again, Alex heard voices overhead, although this time louder than at the railroad bridge. Light. Shadow. Light. Vales had just veered them right through the center of the Western Avenue Bridge. Suddenly, Vales yelled excitedly, "Someone ahead must be rushing or crabbing; enemy one boat length and we're gaining." If a rower was out of synch with the rest of the crew, he was said to be rushing. This caused the boat to jerk and lose speed dramatically. As McGill could attest after his scull race with Alex, crabbing was worse. The rower loses control of his oar altogether. The news could not have come at a better time. Princeton was starting to tire, and the upcoming sprint loomed large. This was the boost they needed. Vales was smart enough to pounce on a weakening foe. "Power ten!" Vales yelled. A power ten was when the crew kept the same cadence, but they pulled as hard as possible for ten strokes, resulting in a burst of speed. "Excellent! Fifteen meters and closing!" Alex's heart was pounding. He had to get it under control. They had yet to hit the sprint. "Here comes the Weeks Bridge! Careful on turn to port." Coming into the Weeks Bridge, the course makes a ninety-degree turn to the left. Alex could feel the boat veering left. This long turn would require the utmost in concentration and skill to keep all sixteen oars hitting the water at the exact same moment. To his left, just off the course, Alex saw Pennsylvania's and Washington's boats, stopped, the result of a recent collision. This scene was all too common with so many shells over such a difficult course. "Halfway through curve. Keep it smooth boys, keep it smooth! Let's bring it in three to thirty-three." Again, Alex focused on the back of Daley's neck, now vein ridden and soaked with sweat. Alex could feel Daley increase the strokes, and Alex was right with him. The transition was perfect. "Enemy at six seats and closing. I want to pass those motherfuckers!" Alex could feel the shell pulling out of the curve. He felt as though someone could just blow on his arms or legs and they would fall off, but he knew it was about to get worse. To pass Harvard, though, would make it all worth it. "Going into Anderson Bridge, four seats behind! "This is it! Reaching two-mile mark. Four strokes to thirty-five. Let's do it!" Alex felt the shell pick up speed, and he vowed not to lose it. The plan was to pass

Harvard before the final bridge, Elliot, because that was a turn even more dangerous than Weeks. "We're gonna get 'em. Two seats and closing." Alex was puzzled by Harvard's rowing. He was dying to turn around and see for himself. It seemed to him that they just couldn't get it together. It must be a wonderful sight, Alex imagined.

"That's it boys! We should get them at the bridge!" Eliot Bridge was the last obstacle before the finish line, about seven hundred meters thereafter. "Bridge at forty meters. Do it! Do it! One more time, Power ten!"

To forget the pain, Alex focused on Daley's back as it moved back and forth in perfect rhythm. Fucking Daley, Alex thought, he's a goddamn machine.

"I'm moving starboard for the pass." Vales could not have come up with a better line. Alex could feel the boat surge forward as the team anticipated the oncoming annihilation. Alex felt the boat shift slightly to the right. "We're coming on them. They're trying to block us. I'm going more to starboard. Again boys, drive!" Although Alex's head was close to spinning from the strain, he could hear a huge roar behind and above him, and he knew they were rapidly approaching the bridge. He could usually block out most noise, but, here, the crowd seemed as loud as a jet engine. "We're almost onto their bowman. Here we go! Shit!" Suddenly Alex felt the shell jerk sharply to the right. Going from the bright light to the shadows, it seemed they were in total darkness and then Alex heard a loud pop, like gunfire. Then another. And another. His left hand jerked into his chest. Another pop. Alex lost control of the oar in his right hand. The confusion lasted only a second, then reality set in. Half the team had broken their oars on the side of the stone bridge. Without control of their oars, the shell careened haplessly along the stone, gouging a huge hole on the side. Slowly, the boat began to take on water. Alex heard laughter coming from outside the bridge. The Harvard team slowed to watch the spectacle. One of their crew seemed familiar to a stunned Alex. It was the asshole who had the drinking contest with Amanda. In unison, the Harvard team yelled, "One, two, three, go!" Then, laughing uproariously, they preceded to row to the finish line. The many Harvard fans on shore and on the bridge above clapped and whistled. Some of Alex's teammates jumped clear of the sinking shell. Others sat silent and stunned, somehow expecting that their oars would soon reappear, the leak would mend, and they would be on their merry way. Alex, still in the shell, stood up in disbelief. He stared at the ever-waning Harvard shell. He felt the chilly water rise up his thigh. The harassing bum from the previous evening popped into Alex's mind, and he half expected to look over at the shore and see him the middle of the crowd, laughing knowingly. As the water proceeded higher, Alex turned to Vales, who was in the water urging his teammates to help him save the boat, and said, "Why don't we just write dickhead on all our foreheads?" With that, Alex and the shell proceeded to descend into the water at a more rapid pace, as a forty thousand-dollar new home for fish made its way to the bottom of the Charles.

The ride back to New Jersey was not one of the more pleasant the team had experienced. Although the second team, the lightweights, and the women had all done very well, the trip was clearly overshadowed by the Eliot Bridge debacle. Everyone in that first boat would spend every day, until spring season, thinking about revenge on Harvard. It was going to be a long winter.

IX

Over fall recess, Boder got busted in Bermuda for buying weed from some local kids. The problem was, the local kids were young looking, undercover cops, waiting for some rich, well-connected American to snare. By the time word reached Boder's father in Washington, and by the time the U.S. Ambassador to Bermuda arrived at the Hamilton City Prison to get Boder out, the invented charges included: buying heroin, soliciting a minor, and vandalism. It took forty-eight hours, thirteen telephone calls, and forty-two thousand untraceable dollars for the ambassador to walk out of the prison with both Boder and all records on the matter. As the limousine left the prison, the Senator called to tell the Ambassador that he should inform the Governor that, rest assured, he would be up his ass about offshore tax havens. The Senator asked to speak to Boder and told him he what a dumb shit he was. Boder was shaken up, but not just because of what his father had said. While in the prison, a two hundred-pound, forty-seven-year-old transvestite with rotted teeth and body odor to match, thought that Boder was the cutest thing since Dorothy was reunited with Toto. Throughout his brief stay in prison, Boder was able to keep his various orifices from being violated, but not without some loss of his dignity.

*****

By Saturday night, a good portion of the student body had returned from fall recess. Many of the eating clubs were having Halloween parties. Over dinner at Conte's Pizza, Boder and Alex decided that they would go to Porch Club because the local cover band, Gatsby, would be playing, and they usually drew a large crowd. Porch was probably the only club on campus more off center than O'Neill. Most of their members were either extreme leftists or seemed to be rocketed to earth from another planet. It was no real surprise that they threw the best parties.

Alex, Boder, and some others, were busy making sure that they would fit right in. They were up in the X-room tuning up for the evening. BT burst into the X-room wearing white sneakers, white socks, extra-large white tights, a white turtleneck, and a white tail. BT slowly turned in a circle, his arms half outstretched. "Well, anyone care to take a shot at guessing who, or should I say what, I am?"

"My absolute worst fucking nightmare!" shouted Sheik, dressed like Alan from *The Hangover*.

"A rat!" suggested Javier, dressed as Donald Trump.

"Antonio's next meal!" added Boder, who was wearing a pair of bright red ski boots, a white union suit, and a motorcycle helmet, but who had yet to decide what the hell he was.

"OK, that's enough from the horse's ass contingent," stated a disgusted BT. He turned toward Ellie, who had stopped by. She was dressed as a nurse, in a costume that barely covered her ass. At every Halloween party Alex noticed, there was always one girl wearing a nurse's dress that barely covered her ass. "OK, Ellie," BT queried, "you must know who I am? Take a shot. I'll give you a little hint." With that, BT turned his back toward Ellie and started to shake his tail.

Ellie let out a little shriek, shoved the tail away from her privates, and laughingly said, "Tony, I have no idea what the hell you are, other than a sicko!"

BT threw his arms up in the air. Frustrated he said, "I give up. You guys are all brain dead. I'm a sperm, man! I'm a sperm!"

"You're gross." Ellie asserted.

"You never say that when I land on your chest." chided BT.

Appropriately adjusted, the group headed off to Porch. Coach Diriglia had given the team the following day off, so Alex was really looking forward to the evening. With the help of a friend in the Drama Club, he managed to get an old Albert Einstein costume that had been used in the 2012 drama group production, Oh Albie, if you were so smart, why did you help build the bomb? Alex felt just fine walking down Prospect Street in a pair of old brown shoes, no socks, baggy pants, an old green shirt, and an oversized black sweater. He also sported a bushy white mustache and a wild, tangled, white web of hair. Amanda was at an invitational tennis match in Philadelphia and wouldn't be coming back until Monday morning. It usually annoyed Alex that

Amanda missed out on so many good times at school, but for some reason, tonight, he didn't seem to mind.

When the group entered Porch, the band was playing, and the place was packed with a variety of interesting creatures. The Hulk was begging Cat Woman to whip him. Woody and Olaf were negotiating with Kim Kardashian, while Andrew Weiner looked on with great interest. John Wayne Bobbitt, his crotch still bleeding, and his darling wife Lorena, still holding the knife, were in attendance. Kidd Rock was drinking a Snapple, and Miley Cyrus, with one of her hands stuffed down the front of her satin short shorts, seemed quite amused. There was a six-foot purple condom that immediately started chasing BT around the club. Twisty the Clown, from *American Horror Stories,* stood alone in a corner with his hands behind his back and his eyes gazing up at the ceiling, apparently just happy to be there. Lady Gaga was talking to our last four Presidents, although she seemed to like Bill Clinton best.

As the evening wore on, Alex was having a blast. There were a lot of people there whom he knew, and he was talking and drinking up a storm. He danced a few numbers with Ellie, who, in

the nurse's uniform, looked outrageous. Fortunately, he was wise enough to realize that no one was going to forget who went home with that girl tonight. He was already anticipating having an argument with Amanda just for dancing with her. Alex wasn't too worried about Ellie. Every time they took a break, and Alex went to get a beer, she would immediately be surrounded by Jay-Z, Maxwell the Geico pig, Jon Snow, a cronut, and even Vincent Van Gogh. They were all dying to be diagnosed by Nurse Ellie. She would be just fine.

Shortly before midnight, Alex was tapped on the shoulder while talking to Zimmy, who was dressed as a large baseball with glasses. Turning around, he encountered a shadowy figure. It was clearly a woman, as the curves announced, but little more could be said. The individual was clothed in a long, black, flowing gown that completely covered her feet. Her matching black headdress covered her entire head, and descended to her waist. She wore black evening gloves that disappeared into the sleeves of her gown. Her face and hands were painted completely black. After a long silence, she spoke. "I have been watching you for some time now," she said.

"Uh-oh, please don't tell anyone what you have seen," Alex joked. The figure ignored his response.

"You should come with me," she invited.

"Do I know you?"

"You will, everybody does."

Alex was intrigued. "Your voice sounds a little familiar. Did we ever...."

"Enough questions." the figure said sternly. With that, the black figure offered her gloved hand to Alex, who reluctantly took it. She guided Alex through the crowded room, to the dance floor. The band had just finished a cover of Wes Walker and Dyl's "Jordan Belfort", and now broke into a rendition of Walk the Moon's "Shut Up and Dance". Alex considered himself better than acceptable on the dance floor, but he wasn't in the same league as his new friend. She turned, twisted, dipped, and spun with the utmost of grace and fluidity. She would make Beyoncé look clumsy, Alex thought. They danced the next three songs with few words spoken. Alex was still trying to figure out who, or what, she was impersonating. All the while, the figure danced with no visible emotion. Finally, with a break in the music, Alex intended to put an end to the mystery.

"All right, I give up. You win. Who the heck are you?" Alex pushed.

Continuing with no expression, the figure spoke, "I am dissolution. I am finality. I am extinction. I am the darkness."

"You are death?"

"Yes."

"Well, I didn't think death could be so sexy. Maybe it's not so bad after all." Alex realized that what he had just said was corny, but, in his condition, it was the best he could do.

"Thank you," she responded.

"Thirsty?" he questioned. Death nodded in agreement. "Shall we get a beer or something?" Death smiled and Alex saw the red of her lips shining through the black paint. The couple moved to a quiet corner in the hallway of the second floor, each with a plastic beer cup in hand. After some more small talk, Alex directed the conversation back to her costume, commenting, "Your getup is a cool idea. How did you come up with it?"

"I've always been into death."

"Oh, that's pleasant," Alex joked.

"See. That's just it. I just don't think it's a big deal."

"So, I assume you believe in some form of afterlife then?"

"Absolutely not. Did you ever hear of the poet, Wallace Stevens?"

"Of course, I'm an English major."

" 'The Death of a Soldier'?"

"Vaguely."

"There are a couple of verses in the poem that go

something like this:

> 'Death is absolute and without memorial
> As in a season of autumn,
> When the wind stops,
> When the wind stops and, over the heavens,
> The clouds go, nevertheless,
> In their direction.

"So, you think once we bite the dust, that's it?"

"Most certainly. We think too much of ourselves. How could we just fade away? Most people just can't buy that, but I think that's exactly what happens. In the overall scheme of things, we're just not that important. If all human time in the Universe were compared to the rest of time, it wouldn't amount to a nanosecond, comparatively speaking. This afterlife myth is just a psychological cushion."

"So, what's wrong with that? I mean, even if there is no afterlife, it can certainly help make some difficult times in a person's life a little easier. Don't you think that death becomes at least a little easier to handle if you believe that it isn't the complete end?" As Alex posed this question, he shook his head slightly in an attempt to remove an image of his father.

"In particular situations, possibly, but I think it messes up more than in helps. This belief puts us on a pedestal, as if we are the chosen beings. It makes us think we have permission to destroy the world around us, the trees, the water, the animals, because we believe some being that no one has ever seen, favors us over everything else in the universe. It fosters the belief that not only can we fuck up our own world, but, afterwards, we get to go to a better one." Even through the black covering on her face, Alex could see and feel her emotions growing more intense. Death continued, "What I mean is, you talked about belief in the afterlife helping us through our grief when we lose someone close to us. Did you ever stop to think that maybe there is more violence because of those beliefs?"

"I'm losing you now, babe," Alex said, the image of his father thankfully having faded from his consciousness.

"Take the witch trials. Witches were killed because they were believed to be helpers of the devil. What would have happened to those women if no one believed in any afterlife, good or bad? Answer: nothing would have happened to them. The Crusades. People fighting, and killing, over a belief about whose afterlife was better. Sounds familiar even today when we look at what's happening in Iraq, Syria, Afghanistan, and a few other places, doesn't it? And think about all the murders we see in the news. Unfortunately, most murders are committed in the heat of passion, by people who know each other. Maybe they wouldn't be so quick to pull the trigger, or plunge the knife, if they didn't think that the recipient was going to wake up in a heavenly version of a Ritz Hotel, or a terrorist-martyr ending, believing he will end up with seven virgins and a mule. And maybe cold-blooded killers, not too concerned with their own mortality, would be, if they knew that, after the lethal injection, no one would be waiting for them with bright lights, open arms, and forgiveness on the other side. All they would get was a wooden box and a pile of cold dirt."

"Interesting," Alex said, smiling. Alex was greatly attracted to this figure in black. She was clearly very bright, but the attraction had more to do than just her intellect. Why? he reflected. Is it because I'm drunk? Is it the music, the dancing, the heat? The allure of the unknown? Whatever it was, he wanted her.

"You don't seem to be taking me seriously," Death accused. Alex's smile vanished.

"Oh . . . no . . . I mean, you're reading me wrong. I'm absolutely taking you seriously. I'm smiling because I find you refreshing and interesting . . . in a lot of ways."

"Really?"

"Really."

"What do you believe happens after you die?" she asked.

"Well, let's just say my beliefs differ a bit from yours. You must realize, however, that you are talking to a guy who grew up with a lot of Catholic guilt, and one of his favorite works is *Paradise Lost.*"

"Oh, I see," said death, "So I take it you're into the whole gamut of afterlife imagery: heaven, hell, devils, angels, spirits, good versus bad, and all that?"

"No, not really. I mean, there's certainly a lot I question. Like you said, religions, whether Christian, Muslim, Jewish or whatever, are based upon stories never truly verified. Religion is based on a foundation of faith, but I don't see anything wrong with that. Even without religion, we rely on faith all the time. You are standing here, talking to me, because you have faith that I'm not a psycho who will throw you into one of these empty bedrooms here, rape you, and slit your throat. My mom keeps paying those tuition bills because, for some ungodly reason, no pun intended, she has faith that, somewhere down the road, I will make something of myself. And who's to say that just because humans dominate the world, they are the only creatures that go to heaven? Dinosaur's dominated this place a lot longer than we have. What about them? Odds are, that my old dog Billy makes it to heaven before I do. He's been much better behaved." Death laughed softly. "By the way," Alex continued, "I don't know if you realize this, but we've been talking, dancing and drinking together for over an hour, and we haven't even introduced ourselves. I'm Alex. Alex Williams."

"Rachel."

"Rachel . . .?"

"Just Rachel."

"OK, 'Just Rachel,' I need another beer, you?"

"Can we first pursue this death thing for a just another few minutes?"

"OK, but only for another minute. I'm having too much fun with you to be stuck on such a morbid subject, Halloween or no Halloween."

"I think you tilted this faith thing."

"Come again?" Alex requested.

Rachel responded, "Those examples you gave, like your mom having faith in your success, so therefore she'll pay for your tuition… pardon me, but that's absolute bullshit. Faith has nothing to do with it. She lived with you for seventeen years before you came here. She knows you inside and out. And since you had the brains to get into this place, she's by no means betting on a long shot. Real faith has to do with the totally unproven. You want to prove to me that your mom really has faith in providing someone with a successful education? Let her go blindfolded into New York City, pick someone from the street at random, and say 'Here's two hundred-fifty thousand dollars for four years of college. I'm sure you'll do fine. You can pay me back when you get out.' Now that would be faith. As for having faith that you won't slit my throat, don't flatter yourself, Freddie Kruger. First, let me inform you that I received my black belt in karate at age seventeen. Second, I am a champion equestrian rider. Third, I really don't think that some Princeton student dressed up in an Albert Einstein outfit is much of a threat. In short, faith has nothing to do with my lack of fear in you as a stranger. It's simply rational, common sense, and confidence in my ability to handle myself." Alex stood silent. Rachel was getting a bit emotional, and he didn't want the situation to disintegrate. Her chest heaved slightly.

"A ball," Alex said.

"What?"

"Don Larsen."

"I'm sorry Alex, but I'm totally lost. Either you're too drunk, or I am." Rachel raised her hands above her shoulders and shook her head.

"No," Alex said, "Let me explain. When my grandfather was in his early twenties, he got this second job selling sodas at Yankee Stadium."

"You are definitely drunk," Rachel accused.

"No, please, let me finish!" Alex asserted, slightly annoyed. Rachel put her index finger to her lips and nodded her head. Alex continued. "He had this job back in 1956. He was already married, and my dad was about four. He was always getting in trouble for watching the games while he was working. The supervisor would threaten to can him if he didn't hustle. Well, that year, as they almost always did in the fifties, the Yanks made it to the World Series. To add to the excitement, the Yankees were playing their arch-rival, the Brooklyn Dodgers. In the first series game, at Yankee stadium, even the fans were getting pissed at my grandfather for moving so slowly. The excitement, the crowd, every aspect of the event enticed my grandfather, so he couldn't keep his eyes off the field. At the end of the game, when each of the vendor's tallies was in, my grandfather had his lowest count ever—even though there was a full house. The vending supervisor was furious and gave my grandfather an ultimatum: he had to sell the most sodas of all the employees at the next game, or he was finished.

"In game two, my grandfather was working his ass off, selling rack after rack of Coca-Cola. Don Larsen was pitching well, but he paid little attention to the game. By the seventh inning, the crowd hushed and a low murmur started across the stadium. My grandfather knew the Yanks were up by about two runs, so he couldn't figure out what the fuss was all about. He looked onto the field and everything seemed normal. Then he looked up at the scoreboard in center field, and Larsen had not given up a hit, not one, single hit. In the history of the World Series, this had never been done before. But it got even better. My grandfather saw Duke Snyder come up for the Dodgers. A quick mental calculation of the batting order, and he realized that this was a perfect game. There wasn't even one walk, hit batter, or error. My grandfather was witnessing a perfect game in the World Series.

"My grandfather continued to sell sodas during the eighth inning, albeit much less aggressively. He knew that his reduced sales would cause him to fall behind others, and he would be fired. But witnessing this magnificent piece of history was more important. It was the top of the ninth. Although sixty-four thousand fans were now on their feet, the only sound to be heard in the entire stadium was the quick chatter of the Yankee infielders as Larsen prepared to pitch the final inning. My grandfather worked his way down to the front row near third base and crouched down in the aisle against the dark, blue, metal fence separating the seats from the field. Furillo grounded to Eddie Bauer, the right fielder. The crowd exploded. Then, silence. Campanella grounded out to McDougal, the Yankee shortstop. The following eruption bordered on mass hysteria. Again, miraculously, silence ensued. The first pitch to Mitchell was a ball. The crowd moaned in unison, like air slowly leaving a punctured tire. The second pitch was a strike. The sound of the ball popping into the catcher's glove could be heard in the bleachers. My grandfather recalled becoming sweaty and dizzy from the tension. From behind, he heard his name being bellowed, 'Williams!' My grandfather turned around quickly, knowing full well who sought him. At the top of the aisle, about eighty feet away, the supervisor was making his way down the steps, toward him. 'Williams,' he shouted, 'this is it. I want you out of here now!'

"My grandfather couldn't believe it. Who the hell in their right mind, other than this jerk, wasn't giving their full attention to the game at hand? Larsen pitched again. Strike two. This time when the crowd exploded, they didn't cease. Instead, they started to clap and chant, 'Strike! Strike! Strike!' My grandfather picked up the soda tray that was next to him and attempted to resume selling sodas, but it was no use. The supervisor went up to my grandfather, grabbed the tray away, and ordered, 'Follow me to the gate, you're done!' My grandfather hesitated, glancing back at the field. 'Now!' the supervisor roared.

"Larsen pitched again. Mitchell caught a piece of the ball and popped it foul toward third base. The slight breeze pushed the ball toward the stands. It drifted into my grandfather's vicinity. Everyone in the stadium watched the white rawhide with red stitches descend toward dozens of outstretched hands. Everyone, that is, except the supervisor whose eyes burned into the back of my grandfather's head, which was facing the field, looking up at the descending object. In that moment, my grandfather was probably more mentally and physically focused than any other time in his life. His gaze was on a foul ball hit by the last batter in a perfect World Series game, pitched by a New York Yankee. It had to be his. The ball was about twenty feet in the air, and heading right toward him. My grandfather could feel a crowd begin to close around him. A large, bald, cigar-chomping man joined the fray, knocking the supervisor on his ass, along with the sodas. The wind moved the ball ever so slightly and, as it descended the last few feet, it appeared the souvenir would not be my grandfather's. The crowd quickly shifted toward the cigar man who, with his legs slightly spread to avoid stepping on the supervisor's face, became the baseball's direct target. My grandfather crouched down and sprung up and over, as high as he could. The cigar man began to grin as he anticipated claiming his prize. Suddenly, fingers came out of nowhere and snatched the ball away, inches from the cigar man, whose hands grasped instinctively. My grandfather had caught the ball.

"There was no time to rejoice. In catching the ball, he had leaped as high as he could and was parallel to the ground.

With the grand prize in his hand, and about six feet in the air, his body was rapidly approaching the ground. The tightly wound crowd quickly drew back to avoid injury from this human meteorite. The supervisor was still lying on his coke soaked back, and in the direct line of fire from the missile that was my grandfather. Whoomp! My grandfather landed right on him, creating a perfect mirror, leg on leg, and stomach on stomach." Rachel conjured up an unpleasant image in her head. Alex continued, "Less than thirty seconds later, the tremendous roar of the crowd indicated that Larsen had put himself into the record books. The supervisor's screams were lost amidst the euphoric sound shield surrounding my grandfather, who, at the time, honestly believed if he died at that moment, he would die fulfilled. Instead, he was booted from the stadium, ball in hand, and told never to return.

Rachel looked intently at Alex, trying to figure out where he was going with his story. "That was a very interesting story, really." Rachel commented, "Please don't think I'm stupid, but I just don't get the relationship between that story and our previous our discussion."

"Well, believe it or not, despite my long-windedness, I haven't yet come to the point. Please, bear with me another moment, and we'll get there," Alex implored. "About ten years after that game, my grandfather, who was now the produce manager at a supermarket, recognized Larsen, who was in the store with his wife. My grandfather told Larsen that he was at that historic game ten years before. Larsen was so impressed by the foul ball story, that he offered to sign the ball if my grandfather would bring it by his apartment. He got Larsen to sign the ball, and, after that, it was displayed in a small glass case on a shelf in my grandparent's living room, next to a souvenir statue of the Virgin Mary my grandmother had purchased during the Pope's mass at Yankee stadium in 1965. My dad said he was never allowed to touch the ball without my grandfather's permission. My grandfather passed away from cancer a few years after I was born, and my grandmother gave the ball to my dad. My dad placed it on his desk in the study. I remember being lectured by my father about not touching that ball when he wasn't around. Of course, that's the wrong thing to tell a five-year old. One Saturday afternoon, my dad came into the study to find I had taken the ball out of the plastic holder and was playing a game of soccer with it on the floor. My father never spanked me, but he came close that day. I was forbidden to go near my father's desk, and especially the ball, ever again. I remember crying for the rest of the day. From time to time, I would glance at that ball from afar, but I never touched it.

"When I was fifteen, my parents were redoing my father's study. I was lying on my bed, listening to music, when my dad came into my room. He had the ball in his hand, out of the case. He proceeded to tell me the story, in detail, of how my grandfather got the ball. I had only heard bits and pieces before. My dad explained how the ball still made him feel connected to his father, even after all the years passed, and that was the main reason he valued it so much. I asked him if this ball of my grandfather's meant the most to him. He paused, put his head down, and then he lifted it up, smiling and said, 'Son, when I was your age, I thought this ball was the coolest thing in the world. As I got older, it meant even more to me. It was about the fact that it was so special to my dad more than it was about it being the ball from Larsen's no-hitter. I guess it helped me think about the good times I spent with your grandfather when I was growing up, something I hope someday you'll think about with me as well. But no, to answer your question, it certainly isn't the most important thing. I married your mother, and, now don't tell her this, but marrying her beat getting this ball by a country mile. You want to know something else? On the day you were born, from the very first moment I saw you, I only wanted to give the ball to you. I've been waiting for you to be old enough to take care of it, and I know you're old enough now.'

"With that, he flipped me the baseball and gave me a big hug," Alex said, pausing for a moment. Rachel stared at Alex, very taken by the story, but still confused over its relevance to their discussion.

"Alex, I still don't get the connection between . . ."

"That very same evening," Alex interrupted, "my dad took my mom to dinner in New York. He was killed in an automobile accident on their way home." Rachel found herself feeling that this was one of those awful moments where absolutely nothing you say could be the right thing. Fortunately for her, Alex continued, "What are the odds of my father choosing that particular evening to give me the baseball? I just can't believe it was coincidence. Sometimes, when I'm down, especially when I think about him, I take that baseball from my dresser and just toss it up and down. It helps." Alex forced a smile. He put his hands into the pockets of his baggy, woolen trousers. "Well, you probably think I am pretty corny, but you wanted to know my thoughts on the afterlife, religion, faith, and such, so now you know a bit about where I'm coming from." Rachel didn't want to pursue the matter anymore.

"Take me home," she ordered.

"I'm sorry, I didn't mean to bore the hell out of you."

"You didn't. I want you to come with me."

Alex took off his white moustache and wig, and they made out in her car for a while before driving to her place in relative silence. Hozier's "Take Me to Church" came on the radio, and they both laughed. Rachel lived in an old, two-bedroom apartment on Alexander Street. The building was once a single-family home but had been converted into several apartments. Upon arrival, Alex sat on a small couch in the living room while Rachel went into the kitchen. She returned with a half full bottle of red wine and two glasses. "Just what we need," Alex said sarcastically, "more liquor." As they drank the wine, the interaction became rather heavy. Alex suggested moving to a more comfortable place. Without saying a word, Rachel led him into her bedroom. For the first time, Alex noticed that Rachel had a slight limp. Rachel caught him staring and commented, "It was an equestrian accident." Alex, feeling a bit uncomfortable, quickly looked down at the floor. "It's all right," she reassured, "When I was nine, I was thrown from a horse and broke my femur and hip in two places."

Alex sat on the double bed in the middle of the room, while Rachel went to the dresser mirror to remove her costume. Looking over her shoulder, Alex could see the reflection of his face and let out a laugh. His face was smeared with black paint. "Wow, do I look like an idiot," He remarked. Rachel didn't reply as she removed her headdress. The hair underneath was short, choppy, and sweaty. Next, using make-up remover and several cotton balls, Rachel began to remove the black paint from her face. As the makeup came off, her pale white skin was revealed, marking a dramatic difference contrast. Rachel turned off the ceiling light, leaving only the small lamp on her dresser illuminated. She sat on the bed and asked Alex to help her with the zipper on her black gown. With some trepidation, Alex complied. Rachel stood up, raised her gown over her head, and let it drop freely to the floor by her feet. With no cover, Rachel appeared to be about twenty pounds heavier than Alex had initially perceived. At Porch Club, he had found her to be so attractive. She was mysterious, danced like a cat, and was intellectually stimulating. Now, however, this woman was a panty and bra away from total nakedness, expecting him to perform, and his desire was fading fast. To make matters worse, Alex began to think about Amanda. Right or wrong, Rachel's next few actions quickly diverted Alex's racing mind.

With the lights off, and experiencing Rachel's expertise, Alex's sexual desires quickly returned. In fact, Alex's senses had become finely attuned by Rachel's skills. Like on the dance floor, Alex felt he was out of his league with Rachel. Slightly embarrassed, he exploded rather quickly. With Rachel's hands, tongue, breasts, and crotch caressing him, he found himself up again in no time, and Rachel was riding him like the winning jockey in the final stretch of the Kentucky Derby. Alex felt the hot sweat from Rachel's thighs on the side of his hips. He came again. Jesus, he felt like a twelve-year-old staring at a vagina on his computer for the first time. Rachel kissed his wet forehead and went into the bathroom. Alex lay still in the bed, his hands folded behind his head on the pillow, feeling fully gratified, and even a little abused. Rachel returned with a glass of water and what appeared to be a little blue make up kit. She snapped it open, removed a tiny yellow pill, popped it quickly into her mouth, and swallowed. "Want one?" she asked Alex.

"Ecstasy?" Alex asked. Rachel nodded affirmatively and moved the make-up kit toward Alex's face. "No thanks," Alex responded, "I've had it once, and it wired the hell out of me. It's almost three in the morning. If I take it now, I'll be up until dinner."

"That's exactly the point," Rachel encouraged, as she gently rubbed Alex's penis and held the box even closer to his face. "Please," she urged, "I want to do it all night." It was tempting, but he knew if he took ecstasy, he would feel terrible for days after.

Thank God Boder isn't here, he thought. If she was feeding him that line, Boder would eat the whole box. "No thanks, maybe another time," Alex resolved. Rachel shrugged, put the box on the floor, rolled back onto the bed, and pulled Alex on top of her. She gently rubbed Alex's cheeks with her right hand and slowly whispered, "I want you to bang the shit out of me."

"What do you call what we've been doing for the last hour and a half?" Alex asked.

"Warmup," Rachel retorted as she smacked Alex's ass, stuck her tongue down his throat, and then whispered some of the nastiest things Alex had ever heard or imagined. To his surprise, he once again was standing at full attention. Rachel grabbed the prize, guided it into its proper position, and they were once again on their way.

At about six o'clock in the morning, Alex found himself

lying face down on a large feather pillow. Dazed, and very tired, he became aware of something moist and slightly bumpy on the back of his neck. Having fallen into a deep sleep not more than an hour ago, he was struggling to gain his bearings. "Yo!" Alex yelled, completely spooked. He turned around quickly. Rachel, naked and on all fours, was startled, and proceeded to put her tongue back in her mouth. Sober and with full sunlight streaming in the curtain less window, truth was staring Alex right in the face. To state it with political correctness, Rachel was not the prettiest girl with whom Alex had ever slept. Alex wondered, Was she really that good last night? Was I too drunk? Was it all just a dream? A dream that was becoming all too real and increasingly unpleasant. Rachel smiled and slowly began rubbing his crotch through the thin, blue bed sheet. Oh no, not again, Alex thought.

"Good morning," Rachel teased.

"Good morning," Alex replied. He couldn't believe he was growing again. He really didn't want it to.

"Sorry to wake you, honey, but I've got to be at the barn in about thirty minutes. Equestrian practice. If you want, I'll give you a ride back to your place," Rachel offered, as she put her face onto the bed sheet where her hand had just been and gave a playful bite. Alex, quite relieved and operating with about seventy percent of his brain cells sleeping or damaged, jumped out of bed to franticly search for his underwear, lest the situation take a turn for the worse.

"Oh, yeah, sure. A ride would be great," Alex muttered, walking around the room in a stupor while his semi-erect prick bobbed up and down like a fat finger scolding a dog.

"Your clothes are folded on the dresser. With the X, I

couldn't sleep, so, after you crashed, I tidied up a bit."

"You haven't slept?"

"Nope."

"Do you think it's a good idea to get on a horse and jump over things?"

"It won't be the first time," she assured him. Alex had a sinking feeling that he should have worn a rubber. Rachel rolled off the bed and headed to the bathroom for a shower. She opened the sliding glass door, adjusted the water, and went in.

"Care to join me?" She yelled.

"No thanks. I've got some more sleeping to do when I get back to my room." As Alex put his Einstein pants back on, he mumbled to himself, "Just get me the hell out of here."

Alex got in Rachel's car for the short ride back to the eating club. A light rain was falling, but, with colored leaves half on the ground and half on the trees, it was a pretty ride. Little was said in the car. "The Wrong Side of Heaven and the Righteous Side of Hell, Volume 1" by Five Fingers Death Punch played through the car speakers. Not a bad album, but it wouldn't have been Alex's choice at this moment. After driving up Prospect Street and arriving at his club, Alex told Rachel that he had a great time. "I'll call you," he bluffed.

"No, you won't," she responded, without the least bit of hostility.

"Why do you say that?"

"Hey, just don't sweat it, OK? Let's just say there's a very short list of guys who call me back. I get it. I don't mind. You shouldn't either." Alex wondered if he should kiss her goodbye but thought it best to just go. He opened the door while thanking Rachel for the ride. She didn't respond. Alex watched as Rachel drove off.

When he returned to his suite, he peaked in at Boder, who, sprawled and previously sleeping in his bed, opened one eye to check out the intruder. "Xander," he murmured, "Where the hell did you go last night? You look like hell!"

Alex put his hands in his pockets, looked at Boder, and, in a most serious fashion, said, "Bode, you know I've done a lot of crazy things in my life, but last night was the topper. For, last night, Bode, I fucked with death." Alex closed the door and left a puzzled Boder in the dark.

X

It had gotten cold early, and those November morning practices on the lake were almost unbearable. In the mornings, the fog was thick, and the air sucked in the last remnants of any warmth in the water. Alex could barely make out Daley sitting right in front of him. Alex's feet, inevitably encased in water-soaked sneakers, would be numb for hours after practice. His bones, especially in his hands, felt like he had been on the losing end of a tough fight. The mornings when it rained—that cold, almost frozen, goddamn rain that seemed to bite like tiny piranhas—were the worst. Those seven o'clock in the morning, cold, rainy days, sitting on a boat on a fog encased, man-made lake, had every member of the team working hard to convince themselves that they were not brain-dead dopes. The regattas were over until the spring, so Crew in November is all blood, guts, and no fucking glory.

Then there was Amanda. Word had gotten back to her that Alex had danced and talked with the black figure at Porch on Halloween night. She knew little else. It gnawed at her, but she didn't pursue it. Alex certainly cared more about Amanda than Rachel, and Rachel made it clear that they were not likely to meet again; that fact certainly didn't bother Alex. It was a one-night stand with an interesting person, nothing more, nothing less. Alex tried to feel guilty about it, but with little success. It was fun. It was exciting. In a way, both Rachel and Alex were probably a little better for it, each making a permanent, positive impression on the other. After all, Alex loved Amanda, or did he? He really wasn't sure anymore. How could he spend the night with another woman, if he knew it would hurt Amanda? Alex didn't have answers.

*****

The Friday following Halloween, Boder spent his entire first day back at school sitting on the edge of the drained Fountain of Freedom. The jagged edges of the brass sculpture were cold, harsh, naked, and dry. He was very unhappy. It wasn't about the Bermuda arrest, though, as he had done, and most likely would do, worse. Boder stared at the drained fountain. The paint was slightly chipped from the people and dogs that took dips in the fountain during the summer. Leaves had blown and littered the bottom. Boder remembered that when he was a child, when his room was painted the exact same color as the fountain: sky blue. Sometimes, he would stand in the middle of his bedroom and spin around and around, faster and faster, until he would finally collapse face up on his bed. The sky-blue walls would be spinning, and Boder would feel as though he was free falling thousands of feet through the air. He would pretend that the white ceiling was a cloud that he had just passed through on his way back to earth. Sometimes, when Boder would be lying on the bed, and his father would place his hand inside his underwear, Boder would look up at that ceiling, and it would become a cloud again. In those moments, he wanted so badly to drift into that cloud and be alone. He would pretend he was floating, while humming a song that would echo back distantly into his ears.

Boder's father, Senator Richard Boderman, III, was a child molester. Boder didn't block it from his mind, though he often wished he could, even if for just one day. It would be such a nice day. I might not even smoke any dope. Maybe I'd just walk around a park, or I'd ride a bicycle down a hill as fast as I could and feel the wind ripping against my face. Maybe I'd even close my eyes and not relive it. If I could spend an entire day without thinking about it, my brain would probably feel like a brand-new pincushion: smooth, velvety, with no punctures, nice. Boder thought about it more and more over the last few years. It seemed easier to chase it out of his mind when he was younger.

When Boder was thirteen, his father took him and his secretary's eight-year-old, son, Benny, to a Washington Nationals baseball game. Boder's dad hadn't touched him in over a year. They had so much fun that day, as they sat in the sun. Benny's head was nearly taken off by a line drive foul ball. It missed him by inches. The man who caught it came over and gave it to Benny. On the way home, with their pennants and souvenirs, Boder's father stopped at his Senate office to pick up a few things. His father told the boys to use the bathroom in his office before they left. Boder went first, then Benny. When Benny went in, Boder's father told Boder that he was going to go as well, "to save time." Boder waited longer than he expected outside his father's office in the hallway. He heard a faint, moaning protest from Benny. Boder's head started to rush, and he felt his face flush. He thought he was about to pass out. No, not Benny, he thought. He had to stop it. Boder returned to his father's office. Through the bathroom door, the lower half wood and the top half smoked glass, Boder heard another weak and muffled protest. "Stop it!" Boder yelled. There was no reply. He heard feet shuffling in the bathroom. Boder picked up the triangle Baccarat glass paperweight from the Senator's desk. It was inscribed with the words:

> With sincerest gratitude to
> Distinguished Senator Richard Boderman.
> Remember...People don't elect
> politicians...we do.
>   -The National Rifle Association

Through the glass half of the bathroom door, Boder threw a perfect strike. The glass shattered into hundreds of pieces, while the Baccarat paperweight continued its trajectory. It hit the Senator's left ear, knocking his head hard into the tiled wall. The Senator, already in a crouched position, released his hands from Benny's naked waist and fell, bleeding and dazed, onto the bathroom floor. Boder looked at the Senator and wondered if he had just severely wounded his father. Frightened, Benny looked at Boder for guidance. Boder, his heart racing faster than it had ever done, quickly stuck his left hand inside the area where the glass pane used to be and unlocked the bathroom door. Quickly, Boder helped Benny pull up his Spiderman underwear and pants. He grabbed Benny by the hand, and the pair raced down a corridor of the Senate building. About a hundred feet from the side exit, Boder came to an abrupt stop. There was a guard at the door.

Fortunately, it was Arty McDougal, a forty-five-year veteran guard, who was given the job by his Congressman after returning from Vietnam with one-less eye. Boder whispered in Benny's ear. Suddenly, Boder stood up straight and yelled, "Tag! You're it!" Boder took off, running down the hallway toward a startled Arty. Benny raced behind Boder, his right arm outstretched toward Boder's back. Attending to the situation, Arty realized it was just Senator Boderman's kid up to his usual hijinks. Nevertheless, when Arty saw Boder make a turn toward the door, he took the fact that his job was to prevent unauthorized exits seriously. He knew Senator Boderman would have his ass for breakfast if he let the kids get outside onto the Washington streets. Arty moved quickly—well, quickly for Arty— to block the exit. He spread his arms out and up high, and he spread his legs out into the door corners. "Hey, Kids!" Arty yelled, "Slow it down!" Boder completed his wide swing toward the center of the exit door, lowered his right shoulder, and laid it right into Arty's groin. Arty crumpled like a snapped toothpick. Boder's force caused him to flip over Arty and land on his ass on the walkway outside. Benny simply ran right over Arty, leaving a Nike For Kids footprint on Arty's cheek. Job-loss or not, Arty decided not to pursue. He was way too old for this bullshit.

Boder and Benny roamed the streets of Washington for hours, talking and laughing. At some point, however, fear set in. Was Boder's father dead? Was Arty dead? Where should they sleep tonight? Soon, these thoughts were interrupted as an unmarked FBI car careened around a corner, stopped, pulled the kids into the back seat, and jetted onward. One of the FBI agents told the kids that Boder's father was OK. They also shared that the fat old guard was fine as well, but he was last seen huffing and puffing toward his car, mumbling something about disability and goddamn kids. The agent in the front passenger seat turned around in his seat to face Boder and Benny. He smiled a warm smile. He reassured the kids that everything was going to be just fine. "Well, it could be just fine," the agent shared, "except maybe for one possible little problem." The agent explained that Boder's father knew an awful lot about America's secret space defense systems. Apparently, there was a group of foreign spies whose mission was to kidnap the Senator in an attempt to extract this valuable information. These spies would go to any lengths, including spreading vicious rumors about the Senator that could cost him his seat, and ultimately enable an easier kidnapping. "Now," the agent warned, "if this little misunderstanding in the Senator's bathroom got out, it could really give the advantage to the bad guys. In fact, these spies might even do something terrible to you two, just to make it seem like the Senator is a madman." They pulled the car into a deserted alleyway. The engine was shut off. Both the driver and the agent, who had been doing the talking, stared at the two boys. They wanted to be sure that the boys comprehended the enormity of the situation. Benny's mind raced faster than his eight-year-old brain had ever done. Sexual assault and national defense all in one day was just too much to take in. Benny was fully in favor of forgetting everything that happened. He reasoned that maybe the Senator saw some dirt on it or something.

A voice from the backseat replied, "What a bunch of bullshit!" Benny froze in stunned silence.

The agent in the passenger seat spoke in a polite but strained tone, "What did you say, son?"

The voice repeated, "It's a bunch of bullshit!" This was getting to be more than Benny could handle. Benny peed himself. Embarrassed, humiliated, and more than a little bit confused, Benny looked over at Boder, who was engaged in a stare down with both agents. Collectedly, and calmly, Boder began, "My dad likes to touch little boys . . . my dad hits my mom . . . I've answered the telephone and talked to my dad's girlfriends. There are no stupid foreign spies, only a sick, albeit influential, man." Even at thirteen, his Princeton potential was shining through. Benny wasn't exactly sure what Boder said, but, looking at the agents' faces, it was all he could do not to pee himself again. The agents briefly whispered to each other and then sped off.

Eventually, they drove back to Boder's house. One of the agents walked up to the front door. Boder's father answered, his head wrapped in a white bandage. He appeared angry and tense during the conversation. The agent returned to the car, looked at Boder, and said, "Son, sometimes it just pays to forget certain things." With that, he removed Boder from the back seat and brought him inside the house. The FBI agent followed. For all the Senator's shortcomings, he had never been physical with Boder. That evening, however, the Senator beat the crap out of his son. A black eye, a bloody nose and several various blows later, the Senator warned, "Never, ever mention this day to anyone." The Senator stared into Boder's eyes, and then he looked toward the FBI agent who was standing nervously against the wall. He continued, "If you do, may God help you, because no one else will." The Senator nodded to the agent, who promptly returned to his car and drove away.

Before bringing Benny home, the agents made a stop at the McDonald's drive-thru, purchasing some burgers and a Kid's Meal. Still nervous, but hungry, Benny wolfed it down. About a block from Benny's house the car pulled over and came to a stop. The FBI agent in the passenger seat turned and spoke softly to Benny, "Son, you seem like a nice young boy. Understand that Senator Boderman is a very powerful man. If you would like to grow up and go to college one day, and if you care about your mommy and daddy, you should forget about everything that happened after you left the baseball stadium today, OK?" A crotch-soaked Benny nodded quickly in agreement. They drove to Benny's house and pulled into the driveway. The agent walked Benny to the door. Upon seeing Benny's mother, the agent explained that the Senator had been called away from the ball game on a matter of national security, and, therefore, they were returning Benny home. The FBI agent complimented Benny's behavior. As a relieved Benny walked through the door way into his house, the agent patted him on the head and remarked, "He's a fine young man." The hair on the back of Benny's head stood up. He closed his eyes and repressed a strong urge to throw-up. About a week later, Benny's mother was fired from her job as the Senator's secretary for the past fifteen years "for failure to pay attention to detail." Benny and Boder never saw each other again.

XI

Alex sat in his Shakespeare course 311, the last of the Shakespeare courses Princeton offered. Alex had taken them all. When reading Shakespeare, he felt as though he was in the story; in the cave with Lear, the tomb with Romeo, or at the wedding of Claudio and Hero. Perhaps even more beneficial to Alex, he had ingratiated himself with more than one female friend by enclosing a sonnet in a letter or Valentine's Day card. Long live the king.

Alex thought the ultimate tribute to a life well lived was one that could appropriately call for the following epitaph:

> His life was gentle, and the elements
> So mixed in him that Nature might stand up
> And say to all the world "This was a man!"
>
> -Caesar 5. 5. 68

On the other hand, it is unlikely that Shakespeare would have permitted that phrase to be used. Shakespeare wrote his own epitaph, and it had a much more basic concern:

> Good Friend, for Jesus' sake forbear,

To dig the dust enclosed here.
Blessed be the man that spares these stones,
And cursed be he that moves my bones.

Long live the fucking king.

After class, Alex walked into the Chancellor Green Student Center to grab lunch. He rarely ate there, instead opting to eat at O'Neill, but lunches at the club always took much longer with all the socializing, and Alex was already in a hurry to get to class. Opening one of the large oak doors at the entrance to the Gothic style cafeteria, he immediately recognized a twosome eating lunch. It was Amanda with a blonde-haired guy whom Alex thought he recognized but couldn't quite place. As Alex ordered a BLT with chips, and grabbed a Mango Madness Snapple, he didn't think much about Amanda's lunch partner. He was more concerned about Amanda being there at all.

Things had been unstable between them of late. They strained to show elements of normalcy. Their nightly calls were much shorter recently than usual, filled with totally non-confrontational topics and surrounded by a lot of dead air. Texts were much less frequent than the fifty or sixty on a usual day. They still went out together, at least once a week, but almost always enjoying activities that involved other people. Amanda had cut back on having dinner at Alex's club, citing an increased workload. The sex was still good, but their mornings did not include the intellectual banter with which they had become accustomed. Alex preferred to study at O'Neill rather than Firestone, and he was no longer walking Amanda home from the library. Alex knew he was about to be forced into an emotional lunch, one that he would have preferred to avoid at that moment. Amanda turned Alex's insides upside down when things were going well between them, never mind when things were uncertain.

Alex paid for his meal and went to the condiment section for mayonnaise. He figured that Amanda was sure to spot him there. When Amanda waived to him, he would pretend that he saw her for the first time. When invited over, Alex would join Amanda and her acquaintance for lunch. The games people play, he thought. Alex took two packets of Hellman's and looked up, focusing in the direction of Amanda's table. Alex expected to see her smiling and waving. Instead, Amanda was intently focused on her conversation. Alex thought it would be best to walk over. "Oh, Hi!" Amanda exclaimed, "Wow, where did you come from?"

"Condiments."

"I didn't even see you."

"I noticed."

"Sit down. Robby, this is Alex. Alex . . . Robby."

"Hey, Alex. Amanda told me quite a bit about you."

Alex wondered if the guy was being nice or conveying another message. "Anything good?" he asked.

"Not at all," Robby quipped in a very disarming manner and held out his hand. He looked familiar, but Alex couldn't place him. Alex shook Robby's outstretched hand and sat down.

"What are you doing here?" Amanda asked.

Alex wasn't thrilled with the question. He answered flatly, "Eating." Alex thought he sounded overly sarcastic and tried to rectify. "Actually, I'm running a little late, so I thought I would stop in here rather than go back to the house."

"Yeah, that place can be a hellhole sometimes," Amanda replied, taking a bite of her shrimp Caesar salad.

Alex maintained his forced smile and reacted, "What is that supposed to mean?"

There was a silence while Amanda finished her bite. Then she responded, "You know, noisy. A lot of the guys are rude, a lot are weird, and the women are even worse."

Alex's voice became a little tense as he commented, "Funny, I've never heard you mention any of this before."

Amanda smiled and said, "You never asked." She took another bite.

Robby joined in, trying to lighten things up, "I think O'Neill is a great place. If anything, you guys throw great parties!"

For some reason, Alex didn't really appreciate the support. He questioned, "You in a club, Rob?"

"No, I'm only a sophomore. Plus, I'll probably stay along my political lines . . . independent." Any positive reaction Alex was trying to bestow on this guy was rapidly diminishing. "But if I did, Alex," Robby continued, "I can tell you, I would give O'Neill serious consideration."

"Glad to hear it," Alex replied. Fat fucking chance, he thought, as he turned to Amanda,
"Can we be friends again?"

"I'll think about it."

Switching his attention, Alex asked, "Rob, we've met before, no?"

"Clairvoyant too. Very impressive," Rob confirmed.

"Moliere?"

"Come again?"

"Moliere, *The Miser*?"

"Yes! Now I remember. Last year, Amanda was in the Triangle Club play. Harpagon, you played Harpagon, right?"

"Very good! And Amanda played Marianne." Rob put his hands to his heart and looked up at the ceiling. "But alas, no matter how I tried, I just could not steal her away from my selfish son, Cleante." Rob smiled. Alex had met him opening night, when Amanda had taken him backstage for the after-party. Alex had taken little notice of Rob that night, except that the other women in the show, a.k.a. Elise and Frosine, were flirting with him. Amanda had introduced Rob as "the guy who helped me get my lines down." When they met, Rob was still in costume, so his face hadn't fully locked into Alex's mind. Now, as Alex thought about it, he remembered seeing Rob once or twice at library when he would meet Amanda to her walk home. Could he be the unknown friend, Alex wondered, who drove her back to Chicago last May?

Alex realized he needed to remain calm. There was nothing worse than jealousy to create ridiculous fantasies that gnawed at his mind. Alex put his sandwich down; he was no longer hungry. His blood felt like it reached one thousand degrees. He tried to shake it off. "Yeah Rob, I remember you. You made a great Harpagon," Alex complimented, and abruptly followed with, "Well folks, it was great chatting, but I've got a class to attend."

Amanda looked confused. She fretted, "Are you kidding? You just got here. You hardly touched your food."

"Yeah, I guess I didn't realize how late it was," Alex responded as he stood up. He felt like he was watching himself, as though his body was separated from his mind. He said politely, "Rob, nice meeting you." *You fuck*, Alex added in his head. He walked over to Amanda and gave her a kiss on the cheek. Her lips tightened. "I'll call you later," he offered.

"Please," Amanda responded, though she knew it was too late.

Alex left the cafeteria, his mind racing. People passed by in unrecognizable blurs. Over the past year, Alex didn't think he cared about the times Amanda mentioned doing something with an unnamed friend. Now, to his surprise, he remembered each incident in all too graphic detail. He needed a minute by himself. On his way to McCosh Hall, Alex walked into the University Chapel. Walking through the vestibule and into the nave, Alex looked around at the large, beautiful stained-glass windows. He stood below four windows of the great Christian epics: Dante's *Divine Comedy*, Mallory's *Le Morte d'Arthu*, Milton's *Paradise Lost,* and Bunyon's *Pilgrim's Progress.* The colors streamed through the glass like a giant prism. They softly coated the caramel colored pews and the white marble floors. In particular, Alex loved the window of the *Divine Comedy*. The window was divided into three parts: "The Inferno," "Purgatory," and "Paradisio." In each of the three tiers, was at least a dozen panes in amazing complexity. Alex's favorite part was on the lower right-hand section of the window, where the likeness of Dante was fast asleep. Dante held an empty scroll in his hand, awaiting the writing of his favorite poem. Above Dante, written in Latin, were the opening words of his epic:

When halfway through the journey of our life
I found that I was in a gloomy wood,
Because the path which led aright was lost.

The chapel was so quiet, one could hear himself breath. Alex's mind kept racing forward, focusing and refocusing, like a human iris honing in on the eye of a needle. She fucked him! Alex closed his eyes. The reflection from the window bathed his face like a warm washcloth. *The truth*, he wondered, why do we search for it so?

*****

The next few weeks were not among Alex's favorites. Amanda and he were barely speaking. His coach continually harassed him for missing practice when he went to the beach with Boder and Zimmy. Thanksgiving came and went. He'd spent it with his mother's relatives in Long Island, and it was nice to see family, but that was about it. Alex took the GRE's. Luckily, he was very good at taking those tests, because his head certainly wasn't in it. He was also supposed to be completing graduate school applications, but, unfortunately, that was the last thing on his mind. He was stuck on his senior thesis as well, having not written a word in more than ten days. Amanda was clearly the reason. Both knew what was coming.

"Hello?" came Alex's greeting.

"Hello," responded Amanda.

"Hi."

"Hi."

"We have to talk."

"I know."

"Want to come over for dinner?"

"Sure, Alex. Perhaps you could give each of us a microphone, so we can discuss things for the benefit of everyone else while they're eating? It would be more private to have our discussion on CNN."

"OK, maybe you're right; that was a stupid suggestion."

"Thank you. Maybe we can talk tomorrow afternoon. I have an accounting quiz in the morning."

"I can't believe you can even think of studying tonight."

"I'm sorry, Alex, but for some strange reason, I don't think my accounting professor gives a damn about us."

"Fuck the accounting quiz, Amanda. I've got to talk to you."

"Alex, don't do this to me. I'm very upset as it is. My body is shaking," Amanda confessed. Hearing this, Alex took some comfort.

She continued, "Stop thinking about yourself all the time. I need a little more time to get myself together."

No matter how much he tried to shake it out of his head, in that moment, Alex wanted to hug her. He could never stand it when she was upset.

"I'll meet you at the football stadium at noon, unless you want to eat lunch first."

"I won't be hungry."

"Fine, I'll see you at noon."

"Alex?"

"Yes?"

"Remember, I love you."

"Let's talk about it tomorrow." There was silence. He put his head down and put his phone back in his pocket. He stood up, grabbed a mason jar half filled with lose change, and shattered it in a single throw at his bedroom wall.

That night, Alex couldn't sleep. The minutes ticked slowly, the same way they might when one has a toothache and must wait until morning to see a dentist. Alex heard Boder stumble in at about two o'clock, and, predictably, he lightly tapped on Alex's door. "Xander, you awake?"

Alex considered not answering because he really needed to sleep, but the chance to talk was comforting. "No," he responded.

The door opened, light clicked on, and Boder rejoiced, "Ah, you're up! Well, at least half way. You missed it, man! A couple of us went to the opening hockey game. We got the shit kicked out of us, but it was still fun. Then, one of the players, Timmy Vandover, had a party in his dorm. I'm telling you, every girl worth a shit in this goddamn school was there, not to mention a few imports. I finally had to leave because I was tired of walking around with a boner." Alex grinned, his first in a while. Fucking Boder, Alex chuckled in his head. God how he loved life.

"Hey, Bode . . . " Alex said quietly.

"Oh no, it sounds like you're still in a state of mourning."

"Tomorrow's D-day."

"Well then, there's only one thing to do."

"What's that?"

"Smoke some ganja and forget about it."

"Well, I can't sleep anyway. Can we smoke and talk about it?"

"I can deal with that. Let's get the good stuff though." Boder left the room and came back moments later holding a thin, white joint in his hand. "Chocolope strain. This will fix your anxiety and insomnia. Dr. Boder guarantees it." Boder lit the joint, and Alex sat up. They smoked in silence for a few moments.

"I don't know, Bode, this one is throwing me for a loop."

"I bet."

"I didn't think I would feel this way. I mean, things weren't going great between us, but, for some reason, I always thought they would fall back into place. Somewhere. Sometime."

"But it's not?"

"It's not."

"Because she fucked someone else?"

Alex paused. "I don't know, Bode. You know there's a lot behind that."

"Hey, you fucked around."

"Yeah, but that was different. And I don't mean that it's OK for guys to fuck around or anything."

"Yes, you do."

"Listen, I don't know about other people, but I do know about Amanda and me. Yeah, I screwed around, and maybe I wouldn't have if everything was perfect between us. If Amanda ever wanted to leave me because of that, I couldn't blame her. But I can tell you this: my fling didn't mean much. I did it just to see what it was like—kind of like the one time I did Molly with you. But Amanda . . . . Amanda wouldn't do anything like that on a whim. For her, that's a well thought out decision." Alex took a long hit off the joint and passed it to Boder. Slowly, he let the white smoke release toward the ceiling.

"You think Amanda screwing around puts more of the cerebral and emotional aspects into play?"

"Most definitely."

Boder took one last hit of the joint and snuffed it out on the bottom of his shoe. "Too much more of this, and we'll sleep for two days," he warned and put the remnants of the joint into his shirt pocket. "I don't know, Alex, but I think you're reading into Amanda's behavior a little too much. While I don't know her as well as you do, I know that she isn't a robot, nor an emotional ball of Jell-O."

"Come again?"

"I just wouldn't put so much into her sleeping with that Rob guy, that's all. Listen, I love ya, but if I were a chick, you wouldn't be the easiest guy in the world to go out with. You're smart as shit, a tremendous athlete, good-looking, and funny. As your roomie, though, I've got to tell you: you are a tough act to follow. To boot, you've been known to fool around once or twice."

"I don't think she knows about that."

"Don't bet on it. Going to this school is like living in a little glass fish bowl."

"What are you getting at?"

"What I'm getting at is, the girl was probably feeling a little insecure and felt good about the attention she was getting from this guy. OK, maybe she went a little too far—"

"A little! How much further could she go?" Alex asked in exasperation.

Boder put his hand on Alex's shoulder. "You're too hung up on this thing."

Alex paused, "Maybe you're right, but, I'm sorry, I just can't help it."

"I know. Easier said than done. But, in the words of a

Persian medieval adage, 'this too shall pass.' " With that, Boder stood up, shut out the light, and suggested, "Get some sleep, my friend." Alex fell into the deepest sleep he had in weeks.

When Alex woke up, he was in that peaceful place where the realities of life have yet to arrive. Slowly, a mesh of thoughts started to come together. Alex jumped out of bed. He grabbed his clock radio, as if it were a poisonous snake about to bite him, and just stared at it. Six fifteen, fuck, it seems much later than that. Alex went to crew practice, which included a two-hour lecture on destiny and the importance of this season. He didn't hear a word Coach Diriglia said.

After the meeting, Alex went back to O'Neill for breakfast, but he could only put down a cup of coffee. He skipped his Shakespeare class. By 11:30, he was sitting on a wooden bench at Princeton Stadium. He waited on the fifty-yard line, twenty rows up. Too bad that he was going to be part of the game being played. It was very cold and windy, even for November, so he kept his hands buried deep within his pockets. There was a sole jogger running around the adjoining track in a jogging suit, gloves, and a ski mask. Alex could hear the gentle echo of the jogger's shoes hitting the track. After a few laps, the jogger ran across the football field and disappeared into a tunnel. Totally alone, Alex thought about what he was going to say. He was bothered by the fact that he couldn't get his mind to properly focus on what he wanted to accomplish. In fact, he wasn't totally sure what that was.

A figure appeared out of the tunnel. She was wearing brown leather loafers, pink socks, jeans, and a white turtleneck with only the collar visible. Over the turtleneck, she wore a grey, hooded, Princeton sweatshirt with the hood down, and a blue jean jacket with a leather collar. She wore absolutely no makeup but had on a pair of gold earnings with small pearls that Alex had given her for her last birthday. She spotted Alex immediately, put her head down, and walked across the field. Her red hair, much longer now than when they first met sophomore year, blew across her face in the breeze. She walked up to the fifty-yard line and arrived at the four-foot cement wall that separated the field from the seats. "A little help?" she yelled to Alex. She winced as the sunlight got in her eyes. She smiled. Alex stood up instinctively. He ran down the steps, looking at his shoes. It would be easier if he didn't look at her too much. He grabbed her by the hand and helped her over.

"Hi."

"Hi."

Amanda smiled at him nervously and asked, "Do we have to talk here? I'm freezing just from the walk over."

"It's the wind that's making it so bad. Let's go into one of the entrance ways," Alex offered, stretching out his hand to help walk up the stairs to the narrow corridor.

Amanda shook her head, declining, "That's OK, I can manage." Inside the corridor, the wind ceased, providing at least some relief. "Well?" Amanda asked.

"Well what?" Alex heard himself say. Be firm, but not an asshole, Alex reminded himself.

"You're the one who wanted to see me, Alex."

"Do you think that was a bad idea? Don't you think things are getting out of hand?"

"Out of hand?"

"Come on, Amanda! Be real. We hardly see each other alone anymore. We don't talk much. This relationship has been headed in the wrong direction for some time, but I always thought we could save it. Then I put the pieces of this Rob Bracken thing together . . ."

"Oh, I didn't realize that you were a detective too. What about this Rob Bracken thing?"

Alex was going to put an end to the bluff right here. He pleaded, "Amanda, don't make me say it."

"That I slept with him?" she jumped in, "Is that what you don't want to say? OK, Alex. I slept with Robby Bracken. I'm sorry. It was a mistake. I shouldn't have done it. It was last year, and it only happened once. OK? What do you want to do to me?" Just because you know something to be true, it doesn't necessarily sting any less when you hear it from the horse's mouth.

"Is that supposed to be it, Amanda? You tell me it was a mistake, and we leave here arm in arm and go to P.J.'s for some pancakes?" Alex mocked.

"Alex, I don't think there is anything I could say that would change your mind about what you've already decided to do." Amanda looked into Alex's eyes and tried, unsuccessfully, to hold back her tears as a few trickled out. "I love you, Alex. That's all I know. And I'm not perfect. I never will be. But like most human beings, I learn from my mistakes."

"It doesn't take a genius to know that you don't fuck around on somebody you care about," Alex accused.

Amanda was growing more visibly upset. She fired back, "And I suppose you never have? I'm not stupid. I hear things. Your friends think they're so cute with their little jokes and innuendos."

"Jokes aren't always true," he shot back.

"Oh please, Alex. You can do better than that," she provoked. Amanda wiped her nose on her sleeve and continued, "I'm the laughing stock of my friends. But you know what? I didn't care what they said. I mean, it bothered me and all, but, when you love somebody, everything is not always perfect. You wanted to get drunk and fuck around? Fine. I know you well enough. I felt you would outgrow it."

Alex put his hands up in the air and turned his back on Amanda. Incredulous, he yelled, "I can't believe what I am hearing!" He turned back quickly. "Listen Amanda, this is about you, OK? You want to make presumptions about me, fine. But let's keep this about you. The simple fact is, you fucked around. But you know what's really killing me? You fucked around with this guy last year, when things were absolutely the best between us. At least, I thought they were the best— I mean, I thought we were so happy then . . ."

Amanda grabbed Alex's arm and said, "Alex, we were happy. I was very happy, and we can be that happy again. Please listen! I know you're hurt, and I don't want to belittle your feelings, but you must believe me when I tell you it was a mistake that means absolutely nothing to me."

Alex wanted to believe her. The problem was that every time he thought of Amanda sleeping with Rob, he almost lost it. He probed, "If it meant nothing to you, why did you do it in the first place?"

"I just don't know."

"You're going to have to do better than that."

"Am I on trial here?"

"Amanda, as far as I'm concerned, the trial is already

over."

Amanda, her face reddened, glared at Alex. For a few moments, she tried to prevent words from coming out of her mouth. Then she exploded, "I can't believe you. You're trying to put yourself on a little pedestal and make me feel like a piece of shit. Well congratulations, you've succeeded. But do you know what? You screwed yourself. I loved you Alex. I've loved everything about you. It may come as a surprise to you, but you're not perfect. But I didn't care. And do you know what I loved about you the most? You're a dreamer. Even if you don't get everything you want in life, I know you'll have fun trying. And I wanted to be part of that. But this thing you are trying to do with me. Accusing me of being the betrayer of our bond, a liar, a fucking whore or something. You've gone too far, Alex." Amanda backed away. "I would have been good for you," she added as she turned and walked away. Alex knew that when Amanda turned away, it would be forever if he didn't stop her. Amanda always thought through decisions quite carefully. She didn't bluff. Alex's thoughts were a mess of logic and emotion. His first reaction was to grab her, to kiss her, to forget what he was upset about. She walked further away. He wanted to yell, "NO!" at the top of his lungs. He stood there like a mute. Alex turned around and. kicked hard at the old and cracked cement wall. The only thing he accomplished was a few sore toes.

XII

Christmas time at Princeton was as nice as one would imagine, and Downtown Princeton was the prettiest location during it all. This area consisted of eight square blocks, covered with two and three-story buildings that generally contained a merchant on the first floor and apartments or small businesses on the others. The merchants prided themselves on their holiday decorations, and all the storefront windows were decorated in various holiday themes. The Presbyterian influence lingered. Large wreaths with red ribbons, and a few with gold or silver bells, adorned the entryways of buildings. Decorated trees cheered up lobbies. Fresh evergreen adorned all the lampposts. St. Nicholas, dressed in long, nineteenth century, velvety garb and a waist long beard, walked the streets. At the dead center of town, across the street and slightly south of Nassau Hall, was Palmer Square. In the middle of the square, there was a large, grass plot, surrounded by stone buildings with slated roofs. In the center of this plot stood Alex's favorite holiday symbol, an enormous evergreen tree, at least seventy feet tall, covered with thousands of snow-tipped lights. Behind the tree, was the Nassau Inn—an eighteenth-century tavern and hotel. Two reindeer ice sculptures stood by the entrance to the Inn, and the area lights reflected off the ice, enhancing the artwork. On that early evening, Alex watched a five-year-old running around and around the tree, chased by his laughing, three-year-old sister. Alex smiled, remembering his own similar holiday episodes played out with his sister Jennifer.

Alex, slightly enlightened, walked back to his eating club for dinner. Twinkling lights adorned dormitory windows. It snowed early; five inches on the sixth of December and another four on the eighth ensured that the grounds would be white until winter break. With exams not scheduled until January, calmness pervaded the campus. It had been almost two weeks since his fall out with Amanda. It was quiet walking across the front of Nassau Hall. He could hear the snow crunching under his feet. O'Neill looked nice, as a great wreath hung between the two outside columns. Inside, a finely decorated tree, albeit much smaller than the one in Palmer Square, stood in the foyer. White, twinkling lights ran along the edge of the ceiling in the smoking room. Alex walked in and popped open the humidor, which Javier had recently filled with fresh Cubans. Javier, you've done it again, Alex thought as he grabbed one. He found the cigar cutter in the end table drawer, cut off the end, licked the cut like a cat with a sore paw, and placed it in his mouth. A few members sat at the bar, enjoying a pre-dinner liquid appetizer. He walked over near Zimmy, who obliged him with a lighter. The two female hockey stars, Betsy Linsinksi and Sydney Marrow, were having vodka on the rocks. Sheik was smoking a cigarette over a glass of white wine. BT nursed a bottle of beer, and Zimmy drank club soda but was clearly stoned. Alex took a slow drag off the cigar. "Man, these are great," he exhaled, "Javier really has me hooked. I couldn't think of anything else I would rather be doing than smoking this cigar at this particular moment."

"More than anything else?" Zimmy asked in astonishment.

"What are you getting at, Zimmy?" Betsy O'Hara jumped in, "That no one craves anything more than sex?"

"No, not sex. Food," Zimmy corrected.

"What?" O'Hara asked incredulously.

"That's right," Zimmy stated matter-of-factly, "If I had my druthers, in any particular moment, I would prefer one of my favorite culinary dishes to a willing female."

"Zimmy, get the fuck out of here!" BT admonished.

"Zimmy, you've got to be putting us on," O'Hara interrogated, "I know guys. I don't think about it all the time, but I have yet to meet a guy who doesn't."

"Well, you just did," Zimmy responded with utmost seriousness, "I'm not a metrosexual or anything. I just like food a little better."

Sheik shook his head in a futile attempt to disengage his state of shock. To Sheik, Zimmy was challenging sacred ground. Compelled to address this, Sheik looked down at the bar and waived his right hand in the air. "Just wait a minute," he demanded, "Zimmy, are you telling me . . . that if you went up to your room at this very moment and a beautiful, luscious, naked woman, with legs longer than any you had ever seen, was lying on your bed longingly, calling your name, you could ignore her if your favorite food was on the bedside?"

Zimmy stared long and hard at Sheik. It was clear Zimmy had the image. Everyone waited for an answer. He finally replied, "OK…OK… I can see a compromise in that case. How about eating a pizza while she's blowing me?"

*****

Alex spent the last few days before winter break wrapping up some schoolwork, attending indoor crew practices, and trying to decide what he was going to do after graduation. Besides considering a master's in English, he was also interested in journalism school, though not sure what that meant given the prevalence of the Internet. He was starting to think he really needed a break. Counting nursery school and kindergarten, he had been going to school for the last eighteen years. If it wasn't time for a complete change, it was at least time for a pause. "But what to do?" he wondered out loud. The discussion about hitchhiking across country, that he'd had with Amanda when they first met, had to be tempered by the reality of needing money to eat and sleep. On the other hand, despite his love for his mother and sisters, he knew he couldn't live at home again. A compromise was in order, but he just couldn't figure out what the hell it was. He sent away for information about jobs overseas, considered Teach for America, and wondered if he could get an entry-level editorial job for a magazine or blog in New York. Most people viewed Alex as generally calm and one to take things in stride, but Alex had to work at that facade. In many ways, he was actually wound a bit tight. It used to drive Amanda crazy that, no matter how drunk or hot and heavy they were getting, Alex had to stop and brush his teeth before going to bed. By the end of their relationship, Amanda considered it a major accomplishment to get him to at least wait until after sex. The idea of being out of school for the first time since he was four, without any certainty of what he was going to do, even if it was temporary, absolutely frightened the shit out of him.

*****

After much deliberation, the day before winter recess, Alex left a Christmas card at Amanda's door. He put more thought into the selection of that card than of any card he'd ever bought before. It wasn't that he was looking for something very specific to say. In fact, it was just the opposite. He didn't want the card to say anything that could be interpreted with even the slightest innuendo, hidden or otherwise. After about forty-five minutes at the stationary store, he found a card that was, at least, passable. It was a white card with a balsam Christmas tree on the front. The tree had some old-fashioned decorations on it, but no lights. There were no presents under the tree. Inside, in red print letters on white, it read, simply:

ENJOY THIS HOLIDAY SEASON.

Perfect, he thought.

On December sixteenth, winter recess began, but Alex wouldn't be going home until the twenty-second because of crew practice. Nearly everyone was gone, making it a strange time to be on campus. Despite the festive lights in many of the windows, nobody was home.

Before heading back home to Washington, Boder was planning to head to Delaware to see Tina. Alex talked him into staying the night of the sixteenth. Alone at O'Neill, the two scrounged around for supper, sitting at opposite ends of one of the long dining tables for hours, drinking beer, dipping into Javier's humidor and talking. With thoughts about what he would do after graduation weighing heavily on his mind, in addition to his recent break up with Amanda, Alex was really cherishing this moment with Boder. Alex knew he and Boder would be friends for life, but probably never this close again. They had lived together for three and one-half years, really lived. They would always remain in contact with each other, but not quite like this. Alone in their club, in a smoky dining room, surrounded by a deserted, cold, snow-covered campus, they were absolutely on the same plane. It wasn't like they were talking about anything earth shattering. They spent an hour discussing which Hoagie Haven sandwich each liked most and another hour on best episode of *The Wire*. That was probably the point. It was just so comfortable, like talking to your own soul. At about eleven o'clock, they walked outside with half a bottle of red wine and proceeded to the fountain. The lights on the sides of the empty fountain reflected off the footprint covered snow. They threw snowballs at the brass sculpture in the center and laughed until bedtime.

The next morning, Alex awoke to music playing on his clock radio. After the events of the previous night, it seemed magnified to a decibel many times its actual volume. Springing up, he moved into the shower like a robot. He got out shivering, dressed, and went downstairs for some orange juice. He drank it straight from the container, gulping it down with his eyes closed. He reveled in the almost sensual pleasure derived from ridding his mouth of its alcohol and cigar-induced parchedness. Back upstairs, he checked in on Boder, who was sprawled across the top of his sheets, still fully clothed. Putting on his suede coat, a scarf, and a Princeton crew stocking cap, Alex headed for the boathouse. Other than the crew practices and lunch with his teammates, he spent the next week in solitude. It was very strange to spend a lot of time alone at college. It just isn't meant to be experienced this way, he considered. The sidewalks and corridors were empty, footsteps of the walker echoed in the courtyard, music didn't blare from dormitory windows, and nowhere was the drone of endless conversation.

Coach Diriglia went easy on the team during that week. Maybe he was in the holiday spirit, or maybe he felt sorry for the fifty-four poor slobs, who were giving up most of their break to practice rowing in rowing tanks or spending hours on the ergometer. The coach allowed a bit more fooling around, spent a lot of time discussing the importance of teamwork, and even took the entire team out for dinner a few times. Alex was glad he decided to row that year. He felt the team growing closer, and they knew they were good. In addition, it helped him take his mind off Amanda.

When Alex pulled into his driveway for winter break, he felt an odd mix of emotions. The house was fully decorated. A Christmas wreath, albeit plastic, was hanging on the door, lights ran around the entrance, and Alex could see the Christmas tree inside, glowing through the bay window. The big evergreen in the front yard didn't have lights. He and his father used to hang those together, so Alex would make sure to do it before Christmas day.

Six years earlier, Theodore "Ted" Williams was killed in a car accident while driving home from a charity dinner in New York on a crisp, clear February evening. Alex's mother was with him. He was driving on Route 95 near Port Chester. A drunk driver heading the other way, eager to reach the New York bars with their later boozing hours, jumped the divider, depositing the grill of a Toyota Camry into his chest. Alex's mom suffered only minor scratches from the shattered front window. The contents of the ashtray floated through the car, as if in slow motion. Illuminated by the still operable Toyota headlights, Mrs. Williams clearly saw the bloody, mangled, and strangely peaceful remains of the one adult human being she had loved dearly.

As a skinny, almost runty kid, growing up in one of the last poor Irish-Italian neighborhoods in the Bronx during the fifties and sixties, Princeton was out of his dad's reach. He had the brains, but not the money, and certainly not the connections. For more than the better part of the twentieth century, if you had the money and connections to get into Princeton, they would give you the brains—or at least enough brains to let you know that your money and connections would be more important to your future than anything they could ever teach you.

Alex's father entered Fordham University in 1971, shortly after being discharged from the Army for having his right kneecap blown off by shrapnel from a hand grenade during training exercises in Biloxi, Mississippi. This incident left him with a slight limp and the need to use a cane, which, although he threatened on a few occasions to use on Alex's "little ass," he never actually did.

After graduating college, Alex's father entered Columbia

Law School, taking advantage of a program for veterans. The program was developed and administered by the Dean of the Law School, partly a result of losing his own son during the Vietnam War. In 1968, the army informed the Dean that his son had been killed while dragging an injured soldier to a temporary Red Cross shelter. They were victims of a direct hit from a Viet Cong mortar attack during a fierce battle for the South Vietnam village of Tam Quan. Closer to the truth, is the rumor that the Dean's son was killed with a single bullet to the forehead, shot by a nineteen-year-old, pimply kid from Alabama, who correctly assumed that the Dean's son was making a pass at him while at a US camp outside Binh Dinh, about sixty miles south of Tam Quan.

Following law school, Alex's father went to work at the New York law firm, Kroger & Whitman. It was an old-line, waspy law firm, which, by the late seventies, conceded to admit an occasional Irish-Catholic into their ranks; but it was a good decade away from admitting a Jew, and certainly not even in the thinking phase of females.

It was at the law firm that Alex's father met his mother, then known to the world as Carol Anne Young, a Presbyterian girl who was ten years younger than Ted. Miss Young came from a single-parent home on the Upper West Side of Manhattan. They lived about as Upper West as a white person would dare to live at the time, without crashing into the southern reaches of Harlem. Alex's mother was the newly hired secretary to Todd Kroger III, grandson of the founder and managing partner. Alex's parents' courtship appeared to be rather commonplace, except possibly the exception of Alex's conception. As the story was told to a large gathering one Thanksgiving, Alex was conceived on the Thomas Sheraton English Desk Chair that resided behind the large solid mahogany Thomas Chippendale desk in Todd Kroger's office. Needless to say, Alex's mother was not very happy with that disclosure. "What's the big deal? Beats getting conceived in the back of a Hyundai for Christ sake," Ted retorted, while he finished the last spoonful of stuffing on his plate.

Recognizing Alex's intellect at an early age, and with his own keen eye to practicality, his father tried to push him into medicine. Alex liked science and was very good at it. He even entered Princeton with the intention of studying pre-med, however, that didn't last long. What would his dad have thought about that? They certainly would have argued over its usefulness. His dad likely would have shouted, "What the hell am I doing? Spending sixty thousand dollars a year, so you can be a high school English teacher?"

"But dad, there are plenty of things you can do with an English degree."

"So, you want to be a writer? I hope you do what F. Scott Fitzgerald did when he attended Princeton and drop out. At least he saved his old man a couple of bucks."

But for all the imagined attacks, Alex knew his father would have wanted him to be aware of all the aspects of his decision more than anyone's opinion. In the end, his father would acquiesce, "Well, whatever you do son, don't be a lawyer. I've been doing it for many years now, and you don't want to be in a job where no one is ever happy to see you."

Alex's mother was one of the unfortunate few who never got that lucky break, the fifteen minutes of fame, the moment in the spotlight. She took everything that was given to her in life in stride: her father leaving at age seven, the death of her younger brother to leukemia when she was ten, the beatings from her alcoholic mother for as long as she could remember, and the sexual advances of unpaid landlords. Wearing second hand clothes given to her by her cousin, the daughter of her mother's younger sister, his mother sucked in the difficult events of her life and spit them out with grace. From the time he was little more than a baby, Alex was aware that his mother had been through more than he would ever know. She was one of those people for whom life's experiences necessitated a tough exterior but left her eyes whispering a slow, consistent message of pain and sadness. The eyes. The traitors.

Alex unconsciously provided her with moments that all humans need—moments that allowed her to feel on top of the world—if only for the briefest of time. It was Alex who had given his mother the pleasure of telling Martha Mason—their loud, five foot one, two hundred forty-three pound neighbor with the mustard yellow tights—that her son had been named valedictorian of his high school. It was Alex who permitted his mother to tell the Wilton Woman's Club—for which she was treasurer for seven years running—that, not only was her son going to Princeton University, but he won a student writing contest and was going on a scholarship given by the New Yorker Magazine as a promotion for its eighty-fifth anniversary. His winning essay, "How Come Trickle-down Economics Never Trickled to Me? The Continued Decline of the Middle Class," can still be read at the Wilton Public Library; although the demand for this publication may have been distorted by the amount of times Mrs. Williams checked it out.

Alex enjoyed Christmas break, even though it was a little

melancholy. It made him aware that, someday, Christmas with the family, in the house he had spent so many Christmases, would come to an end. It might not happen next year, but soon enough. In the meantime, it was awfully nice. Other than seeing a few old friends, Alex tried to spend as much time with his family as possible. He wanted to do everything within his power to postpone the inevitable. His seventeen-year-old sister, Jenny, wasn't around much. Boyfriends, girlfriends, shopping, and cheerleading occupied her time. There was so much for the suburban girl to do. Thirteen-year-old Madison, however, was available, and Alex really enjoyed his time with her. He noticed that she was changing fast. Madison was no little kid anymore. She and Alex went to the movies, the Mystic Aquarium, and even to one of the mega malls that Alex had always despised. On the way home from the mall, Madison confided in Alex a disturbing incident of a man who had exposed himself to her on the side of the local Seven-Eleven. Alex was unaware that Madison had any problems, other than maybe growing out of her clothes too fast. For a moment, Alex could think of no hardship, pain, or tragedy too harsh for that exhibitionist.

Alex managed to save a couple of hundred bucks from tutoring a freshman student from China that semester. He bought his mother a pair of emerald earrings, her birthstone. He wasn't even going try to figure out what to get for Jenny, so he purchased her a gift certificate to Urban Outfitters. For Madison, he bought a light red dress with dog prints. He knew Madison would love whatever he bought her, yet it took Alex over half a day to find just the right one. Alex had even stopped at the supermarket to purchase oxtail bones for his eleven-year-old Labrador, Billy. He had done this every Christmas since Billy was a puppy.

At Christmas morning church services, Alex's mother caught him looking at her. She had tears in her eyes but forced a smile. Holidays always made losing her husband worse for her, and maybe that was okay. He had only hoped that he would be fortunate enough to find someone he could love as much. After mass and breakfast, Alex drove the family to his aunt's house in Garden City, Long Island. Alex had made this trip every other Thanksgiving and Christmas for as long as he could remember. As with every other trip to Long Island, they got stuck in traffic, and Alex had wondered, since a young child, why anyone lived there.

XIII

"How the hell are you supposed to study, and retain for a test, weeks in advance?" Boder would ask Alex every year at this time, before heading out for some inebriated fun. Reading period for examinations began after New Year's. It lasted for ten days, then exams another ten.

"Yeah Bode, like it would make any difference to you if the test was tomorrow," Alex usually responded. To some degree, Alex knew that Boder had a point. Even students who had much more academic drive than Boder did little work during the first week. Instead, there was a lot of partying. Fortunately, three hours of indoor crew workouts each day helped keep Alex away from the more serious fiestas.

Workouts usually began with a jog from the boathouse to Jadwin Gymnasium, where crewmembers lifted weights. They would then continue back to the boathouse for a workout on the ergometer. After that, the whole team got into the rowing tank—a shallow pool with water that continuously flowed. On concrete, just outside the tank, was a simulated boat. When the oars went into the water, the pressure in the water fluctuated to simulate various rowing conditions. Practice usually ended with a strategy session and another jog to the football stadium, where the team climbed up and down the long flights of stairs that divided the various sections. After practice, Alex would walk back to his room for a few hours of sleep. Besides crew practice, Alex had spent the examination period working predominately on his senior thesis. He also completed papers for his philosophy class, Twentieth Century Philosophical Analysis, and his Shakespeare class. All in all, it was quite uneventful.

After exams, the week between semesters was always a big one for the crew team. Frozen lake or not, the intensity climbed. All rowing took place in the indoor tank. As the head rigger, Freddy Lewis told Alex on more than one occasion, "Rowing in that tank is a little like playing with yourself . . . feels good for a while, but, when you all done tuckered out, you realize it was nothing close to the real thing." Alex had thought of sex in many ways, but never relative to a lake, or lack thereof.

That week the team did everything but sleep together. They met for all their meals at the dining hall in Whitman College. They had two workouts a day, watched films of their upcoming opponents, and talked about strategies at night. Even The Cruiser flew in to give the crew a pep talk. He pulled Alex aside and encouraged him to always feel free to ask for advice during the season, regardless of the situation with Amanda. "Alex, you know I love my daughter to death, but we're talking about a man's destiny here. I expect to hear from you weekly about what's going on in them boats." Alex would always admire The Cruiser for that.

Alex was glad that he had stuck with crew that year. Putting aside the embarrassment of the catastrophe at the Head of the Charles Regatta, there was no doubt that Princeton was showing a lot of promise. Everyone on the team was in their best shape, destroying previous best times and records on the ergometer, weights, and runs. The team was also becoming close knit. Even Alex, who was traditionally one of the most distant, looked forward to spending time with his teammates. The expectation that something special could happen was growing. On the back of their practice jerseys, they conveyed the sentiment rather bluntly, with the credo: *To err is human, not to err is Princeton Crew*. Deep underneath the still waters of Carnegie Lake, a bubbling euphoria was beginning to rise.

*****

It was second semester, senior year, the last one, no mas, finite, au revoir. Academically, Alex was all set. Other than his senior thesis, which he was beginning to make a substantial dent in, he had met all the requirements for graduation. He registered for one English class, Contemporary Drama, primarily to help with his own play writing. He'd missed the deadline on applying to graduate schools for the following year, but he really didn't mind. He was twenty-one years old and had no clue what he wanted to do when, and if, he grew up.

Boder didn't show up for the first few days of the new semester, and It was starting to concern Alex. He did say he was going to spend a few days with Tina in South Beach, but Alex thought he would be back by now, and he wasn't answering Alex's texts or calls. Alex thought that maybe Boder had stopped home on the way back to New Jersey. Trying not to sound alarmed, Alex called Washington one morning and, although Boder wasn't there, Alex's concern about scaring the family appeared to be unwarranted. Mrs. Boderman didn't seem too concerned. Alex decided to contact Tina, who was back at school in Delaware. She told Alex that Boder had dropped her off a couple of days ago and was planning to go to New York City for a couple of days to sort some things out.

"Sort what out?" Alex questioned.

"I don't know really," She replied. "He said he had a few things he had to clear in his head. I'm not supposed to tell anyone, but, since it's you, he's staying at the Essex House."

"Thanks, Tina."

"You going to call him again?"

"I'm going to do better than that, Tina."

About ten minutes later, Alex was driving on the turnpike, headed toward the city. Alex had known Boder for a while now, and he knew Boder did a lot of crazy things. Most of the time, Alex could blow them off, thinking of Boder as just being Boder, but something just wasn't right here. In the past, whatever Boder did, he never did quietly, and this New York thing was just too quiet.

It was early in the evening when Alex drove out of the Lincoln Tunnel, proceeded east to Eighth Avenue, and then North to Fifty-Eighth Street. Miraculously, he found a parking space one block from the Essex House. Thank God I parked close, Alex thought, as the weather was windy and cold as hell. He buried his gloveless hands deep inside his jacket, bowed his chin toward his neck, and headed in the direction of the hotel lobby lights.

At the front desk, Alex handed the clerk Boder's expired driver's license. He had found it in Boder's desk drawer and brought it along hoping the clerk wouldn't notice the expiration date or that Alex bore no resemblance to Boder. It worked; Alex received a new key for the one he claimed he lost. He took the elevator to the 5th floor, walked down the hallway, and knocked on the off-white door of number 515. There was no answer. Alex yelled through the door for Boder. Still, silence. After debating a bit in his mind, Alex used the key to enter the room. No Boder found. He headed back to the elevator intending to return to the lobby. The elevator door opened, and from inside the mahogany space, a casually dressed, half-intoxicated Boder emerged. He didn't seem the least bit surprised to see someone he knew standing before him.

"Xander! A small world or what?"

"Not that small Bode. What the hell are you doing here?"

Walking past Alex and down the hallway, Boder justified, "I have a room on this floor, and you?"

Alex didn't move from near the elevator, "I came here to ask you what's wrong with your room in Princeton? I'm especially curious since the semester has already started without you."

Boder stopped in the hallway, but he didn't look back as he remarked, "I don't think we have to worry about that."

Alex didn't like the sound of that and urged, "Boder, for Christ's sake. Talk to me."

Boder turned around. He looked at Alex and smiled. He reached into the inner pocket of his long, navy, camel hair coat and pulled out a crumpled piece of white paper. He held it aloofly. Although he couldn't tell from Boder's expression, Alex knew that whatever was in the letter wasn't good news. He walked briskly to Boder and looked at him. Boder looked toward the wall. Alex slowly reached for the letter. He opened it, immediately noting the familiar orange and black shield in a circle within a circle. In the outer circle were written the Latin words: *Sigilum Universitatis Princetoniensis.*

The letter read:

Dear Mr. Boderman:

As you were made aware through past letters of academic warning, any sophomore, junior, or senior student who receives a failing grade in two or more courses, in any term, will be required to withdraw from the University. Unfortunately, you have received a failing grade in all three of your fall semester courses, and your senior thesis advisor has indicated that your work has been negligible. You are hereby required, under the rules and regulations of the Committee on Examinations and Academic Standing, to withdraw from the University, effective immediately.

Readmission to Princeton is not guaranteed to a student required to withdraw. It should be noted, however, that it is within the Committee's jurisdiction to grant a second opportunity to a student who has demonstrated readiness to resume acceptable academic work. The definition of readiness varies from student to student. It is a definition set for each individual by the Committee.

After careful review of your record, the following are required for readmission:

> 1.) A demanding work experience for six months immediately following your withdrawal;
>
> 2.) Disaffiliation from the eating club environment, specifically, O'Neill; and
>
> 3.) Monthly meetings with an academic probation officer after readmission;

Readmission can be considered no earlier than the January, 2016 semester. You must contact the Dean of Student's Office by October 15th to be considered. For additional details, please do not hesitate to contact my assistant, Felicia Kurtz.

Please note that any action taken by the Committee can be reconsidered at the request of the student. However, such a request is reconsidered by this same Committee and reversals are unlikely.

Good luck.

Sincerely,

Frederick D. Ruffington, III
Chairman
Committee on Examinations and Academic

Standing

Alex didn't know what to say, not that it was a complete shock. Boder was always living on the academic edge. He had been put on probation every year. He had done less work than ever last semester, but he'd come so far. Boder wasn't Snow White, but the school hadn't done much to help matters. An occasional letter sent, telling him that he was being watched and needed to do better, wasn't terribly effective for Boder. The use he had for those letters was purely in the event that he ran out of rolling papers. Alex thought long and hard about what to say. Not much came to mind, so he uttered, simply, "What are we going to do?"

Boder placed his hands in his pockets and forced a smile, saying, "Hey, it's no big deal. I was getting tired of the dump anyway. I could do more up here in a week than I could do at Princeton in four years." Alex couldn't stop looking at Boder's face. There was a lot going on, and, for the first time, Alex saw real sorrow and fear. They were hidden only slightly by that Boder smile. Alex never told anyone because he always thought it would sound so corny, but at that precise moment, Alex realized how much he cared for Boder. The boy was the genuine article. Boder's smile began to fade, his face turned toward the floor, his body began to shake. Alex hugged him.

"Oh man, I've really screwed this one up, haven't I? I just couldn't get into it. The routine, you know? The studying every night, the same classes, the same cookie cutter teachers that wouldn't last a day outside that place."

"Yeah Bode, you've always had trouble with routine."

"Yeah, but you know what's fucked up? I loved that

place. I mean, I really fucking loved it. You get me away from that place for a couple of days, and I get the shakes. I'm not sure how I'm gonna handle not going back."

"Boder, what the hell are you talking about? I'm not graduating without you, man. You've got to stick around for the next couple of months and have some fun. Bode, you're the president of our club for Christ's sake!"

"That doesn't sound like a demanding work experience and no affiliation with O'Neill to me."

"Screw that letter Bode. You're making too big a deal out of this thing. Not that I am trying to trivialize it or anything, but, Bode, you just weren't ready. You needed a little more time to get some things out of your system. You didn't make the grade this time around, so they were forced to suspend you. Bode, you think they wanted to do this? Your father's a U.S. Senator, and you're a legacy, man. When you're ready to commit, they'll let you back in, no matter what. You could spend your time off smuggling drugs from Colombia, it doesn't matter."

"You think he really cares what the hell happens to me?" Boder protested, "The only two things he cares about are the latest Gallup Poll results and how he looks on television."

That response alarmed Alex; nevertheless, he felt this was not the time to get into it. He persisted, "I don't care if your father is Genghis Kahn; he still spent two hundred fifty grand on your Princeton education. You're crazy to think he's not going to want you to finish."

"What if I don't want to go back?" Boder pursued, "That's the thing, man. It can never be the same. First, if I go back now and watch the rest of you guys go through graduation, while I lie around with my finger up my ass, it'll just kill me. Second, if I do go back in a year or so, it will be entirely different. None of you guys will be there, I can't be in the eating club, and they'll be looking over my shoulder." Waving the letter in the air, Boder added, "What the hell is the point?"

"The point is to finish something you've started. Now, Bode, you know me. I'm not the biggest fan of our future alma mater. I've certainly had my issues, but you must admit: we're privileged to have been able to go there. Bode, I don't want to get all parental on you or anything, but it's important that you finish this, even if you want to drive a bus when you're done. I just can't see you quitting when you're so far over the hump. It's not for you? Fine. Finish it and move on. The degree will get you a job, and it'll help pay the rent while you decide what you really want to do.

"Now about it not being the same without the guys and me around, first, even if you did graduate with me this year, I'm not going to be around you next year anyway, so what difference does it make?" Alex smiled as the next thought popped into his mind and out of his mouth, "And as for just hanging around watching us graduate . . . how would that really be any different from what you've been doing since you got there?" Boder's serious demeanor crumbled, and they both had a good laugh.

Boder and Alex then spent the night in the city. They ate dinner at a small, cheap, Latin American restaurant in SoHo, called Comodo. Amid the ajiaco soup, the poblano pepper pasta, churros, and margaritas that would knock the shoes off a clown, Alex and Boder talked and laughed as if it was just another night at their eating club.

Heads buzzing from the margaritas, they Uber-ed

uptown, sharing a joint with the driver on the way. They stopped at the Sugar Bar on the Upper West Side, where a window of opportunity with two stunning blondes arose. These women were not the ordinary stunning, rather, they were a level of stunning that normally could only be found in New York City. Sadly, Alex and Boder failed to connect, as the ill effects of alcohol and pot were obvious, but nothing could get the duo down. Boder and Alex hit about half a dozen bars on the West Side, before grabbing breakfast at the Utopia Diner in the early morning hours. Alex ordered a western omelet, home fries, tomato juice, and coffee—lots of coffee. Boder ordered a cheeseburger and chocolate milk. Boder lifted his glass in Alex's direction, "To you, bro . . . thanks. I really mean it."

"Bode, let me tell you something. When I'm eighty years old, and my memory is going, and there's only one thing from my college days that I'll remember, it's going to be you."

The exhaustion of the past twenty-four hours was closing in on them. Boder noted that he still had not checked out of the hotel, and it might be a good idea to catch a few winks before heading back to Princeton. "Wait a second. I've got a call to make," Alex replied. He gave ten dollars to the hostess in exchange for the use of a place where he could have some quiet. The hostess led him to a closet in the back of the diner. He made a call to Diriglia at the boat house. Alex closed his eyes and tried to pull himself together, as he waited for the telephone to connect.

The phone didn't even complete one ring, "Diriglia."

"Coach, hello. It's Alex Williams."

"Alex. Where the hell are you? You should have been

here half an hour ago. The rest of the guys are out running. Get your ass down here!"

"That's going to be hard to do, sir. I have a bad case of the runs."

"You got the shits?"

"Yes, sir. I went out for a late snack, and I probably had too many buffalo chicken wings."

"I've told you guys to stay away from that crap. It's like eating motor oil for Christ's sake. I had Henderson call you about twenty minutes ago. He said there was no answer. Where the hell were you—on the throne?"

"Precisely."

"Get some Kaopectate 1-D, not the regular Kaopectate. Get the 1-D. Works like spackle. It'll feel like someone is vacuuming your ass from the inside. Get some rest, drink plenty of water, and I'll expect you here for the afternoon practice."

"Will do."

"And cut out the junk food. At this point in the year, before you eat or do anything, you should ask, 'Is this going to help me row? Help my conditioning?' Spicy Chicken wings? Hell no! Come on, Williams, I always thought you were smarter than that. Got to go. See you this afternoon."

"Yes sir," Alex sighed in relief as he hung up the telephone. His forehead had beaded up with sweat. He decided that being on the crew team provided excellent practice if he ever decided to be a politician.

XIV

On the first day of the last semester of Alex's college career, he went to the only class on his schedule, Contemporary Drama. Alex knew immediately that he was going to enjoy it; it was like that with some things. Professor Thadeus Zinkel was barely more than five foot five, sixty-ish, and about forty pounds overweight. There was more than a hint by the redness in his face that he drank daily, and he smelled horribly of mint-flavored tobacco from his pipe smoking. Zinkel had a problem with the idea that contemporary drama considered anything written from the twentieth century forward.

"Back in the fifties," he said, "there were a great many outstanding plays. But you dialed a telephone, paid fifty cents for a movie, and watched one of six stations on a black and white television—changing channels by getting up off the couch. There were no iPods, never mind Snapchat. You heated food in an oven, did your term papers on a manual typewriter, and spoke on a telephone attached to a wall. Not very modern now, was it?"

The professor continued, "We will be looking at plays

from the early seventies, including *Equus,* by Peter Shaffer. It has all the elements we have come to love in film and television: sex, violence, and perversion. Can you really beat that combination? We will end the semester looking at a relatively recent play by Edward Albee, *The Goat or Who is Sylvia.* For a little perspective, however, I suggest that there is no better place to start than in the middle with *Angels in America,* by TB Kushner. Sometimes, when you start in the middle, you can see the beginning and the end. Please read it for the next class. Thank you, and have a marvelous afternoon."

After crew practice and dinner, Alex lay on his bed and perused the plays he was assigned to read. Alex was knowledgeable about a lot of plays, but his expertise wasn't nearly as strong for those more recently written. Virtually, all the plays Alex had read in college were written before 1950, with the majority from previous centuries. It would be nice, for once, to read something without using a glossary. Alex flipped through *Equus.* He read the playwright's description of the set. Minimal would be an understatement. He began to read the play, and, an hour and twenty minutes later, Alex closed the book, mesmerized. It was a great feeling to read something that really hit home. It was like Shaffer had been reading Alex's mind for the last year or so. Alex wondered if he was like the psychiatrist, Dysart—a typical, educated human, whose wildest adventure was a well-planned vacation. Or was he the patient, Allen, whose spirit was closer to that of a wild stallion. In truth, Alex knew which character he was more like, and he wasn't too happy about it.

*****

It was Saturday afternoon, Valentine's Day. After an all-morning crew practice, Alex left the boathouse and went to meet Boder. They were going to attend a hockey game at Baker Rink. He walked across Faculty Road and took a shortcut down a dirt path. Alex walked past the Lenz Tennis Center, where he had watched Amanda play on numerous occasions. He hadn't seen her at all since their breakup in December, but he'd heard that she had become more absorbed in her schoolwork and tennis. Those close to her said she didn't seem to be even a bit interested in the progress of the crew team. Since the Lenz center had strictly outdoor courts, Alex wondered if Amanda was practicing inside at Jadwin Gym. Curiosity overtook him. He turned and walked back toward Jadwin. Alex wasn't sure what his reasons were, only that he had a tremendous urge to see her.

Inside the gym, Alex made his way down a level to the tennis courts. He spotted her instantly. Amanda was on a far court, practicing her backhand with an automatic ball machine. Leaning cautiously against a door at one of the entrances, Alex watched Amanda work. She was flawless. As soon as the ball was shot from the machine, her left hand dropped onto her right, clutching the racket tightly. With her legs set in preparation for the approaching rubber and felt attack, her arms and racquet moved back and away from her body, as if they were trying to get away from the fight. Suddenly, her arms reversed course, and hard, toned muscles appeared in her upper back and shoulders. She moved the racket forward with perfect, linear motion—her eyes were the only part of her body not moving. Alex thought that if a stare could dissolve a ball, Amanda's would. Next, the racket connected with the ball with a loud thwack. The force of contact lifted her entire body upward and forward. The yellow ball and racket moved in unison for a nanosecond, before the ball shot off the cat gut like a cannon, rocketing to the exact spot where the tip of her racket was pointing. It was beautiful to watch. Alex believed that Amanda was so good that she could go professional; after all, she had The Cruiser's genes. But she was more dedicated to her schoolwork than to the sport, and Princeton gave little leeway for anything other than academics. There, potentially great tennis players would remain potentially great.

Alex noticed that Amanda's backstroke said a lot about her personality. *Focused.* Alex was a little jealous of that. If her backstroke was not just the way Amanda wanted it, one could be sure that the ball machine would wear out before she did. *Determined.* In her quiet, please-do-not-mind-me way, she got what she wanted. *Successful.* Amanda was a winner. That was why Alex knew their relationship was over the moment she walked away from him at the football stadium. "I would have been good for you," she had said. She had closed the book. She was not coming back. There is something rare about the individual whose mind and body are perfectly sharpened. *Beautiful.* Alex turned around and walked away. He had really fucked up this one.

Alex made one more stop on the way to Baker Rink. At Bloomberg Hall, a dormitory, he found an empty study room and called The Cruiser in Illinois.

"Hello?"

"Hello Mr. Fallon, Alex. Alex Williams here."

"Alex! Good to hear you! Coach Diriglia tells me you

guys are really shaping up."

"There's a good chance we'll do very well, Mr. Fallon."

"That's good, son. You keep practicing hard. Ninety percent of the winning takes place before the season starts. Did you call me about the team?"

"Not exactly, but it is always great to hear your point of view."

"Well, enough shop-talk then. How can I help you?"

Despite an outwardly gruff exterior, Alex found The Cruiser to be the most comforting guy on earth. The guy eked of trustworthiness.

"It's something a little closer to home."

"Ah . . . Amanda," he assumed. "She has spoken about you guys on more than just a few occasions. She loves you, Alex. I told her to give you some time, but you know Amanda. Since she was born, everything had to be in its place. She was the only baby who cleaned up her own nursery. Amanda can't live with uncertainty. It's just not in her nature.

Alex laughed, "Sounds like she hasn't changed much."

"No, she hasn't, but she's the greatest. She's my daughter, so, of course, I am going to say that, but I have to tell you, Alex, even compared to my other kids, and I love them all, Amanda is one special human being."

"I know.

"And if she is behind you . . . well, you have no better partner in the world."

"I know." Alex paused for a moment before continuing, "Mr. Fallon?"

"Yes?"

"Are we done? I mean Amanda and me."

"Jesus Alex, I hate to answer that one. You're like a son to me. But maybe so, kid. Once her mind is made up, you know what that's like. You have to admit, it was your call."

"Don't remind me."

"To be frank, in her twenty-one years on earth, I can't recall her ever changing her mind, but, hey, maybe reuniting with you will be the first exception."

"I doubt that, sir."

"Alex, what I've told your team about crew has some application here. To be the champion, there is no second place."

"I'll try to remember that."

The Cruiser could sense Alex's depression. He encouraged, "Anyway, you can't change what you can't change. Your final season is approaching. Put your mind on the water!"

"I'll give it a shot," Alex said, not even convincing himself.

"Good." The Cruiser forced himself to say, then added, "Now listen, you ever need to talk about this again, you give me a holler, OK?"

"Sure."

"Take care of yourself. I'm flying down to Annapolis for your opener against Navy. I'll see you then. So long and good luck."

"Bye Mr. Fallon. Thanks."

"Alex…"

"Yes?"

"Don't ever say thanks to someone who gives you bad news." There was brief pause, and then, click. Alex put his phone back in his jacket and walked outside. He looked up to the sky. It was crystal clear, and the air was brisk. A streetlight shone directly into his eyes. After rubbing his hands together, he pulled them toward his mouth and blew his warm breadth into their center. Alex thought of a childhood poem his mother used to read to him:

> Have you ever been to The Land of Happy,
> Where everyone's happy all day,
> Where they joke and they sing
> Of the happiest things,
> And everything's jolly and gay?
> There's no one unhappy in Happy,
> There's laughter and smiles galore.

Alex shook his head as he recalled the end of that poem and recited out loud, "I have been to The Land of Happy—What a bore!" Land of Happy, my ass, Alex thought.

Alex finally arrived at old Baker Hockey Rink, and Boder was there waiting. Since his forced withdrawal from the University, Boder listed a friend's off campus apartment as his new address, but he hadn't left his room at O'Neill. "Hey Alex, where the hell were you? I was just about to call it quits."

"Sorry. I hit an unexpected roadblock on the way. Come on, I need to get inside."

With only seven rows of stands and a small balcony, the old rink wasn't much warmer than the cold February air outside. Almost immediately after sitting down, Boder slipped out two cans of beer from inside his jacket. "I would have left them in the fridge longer if I knew you were going to dilly-dally," Boder teased.

A Cornell player got to the puck first but was quickly pressed, face first, into the surrounding plexiglass wall. To the onlookers, he resembled a grouper fish in pain. He fell to the rough ice, as Princeton skated away with the puck. Alex watched the dazed Cornell skater slowly rise to his feet, his nose bleeding profusely. Looking up at the old, white, wooden ceiling, with ninety lights dangling over the ice, Alex shivered. "Bode, why would anyone in their right mind want to play this game?" In the end, Princeton lost five to two. Alex turned to Boder as the final buzzer sounded, "Well, at least the cool air kept the beer cold."

"At least," Boder responded.

After the game, Alex and Boder went back to the eating club to take a nap before attending a Valentine's Day dinner and party. Tina couldn't make it up to Princeton for weekend due to a bad case of the flu. She had, however, Federal Expressed a perfumed, red G-string to Boder, with a note that read:

Dear Richie,

Please hold onto this in my absence. My current physical condition leaves me unable to put it to proper use—that is, firmly positioned on your face!

Happy Valentine's Day, Sweetie!

Hugs and Chugs,
Tina

P.S.

Please bring the enclosed

article of clothing—and
your face—back to me
next weekend! Luv ya!

Alex didn't ask anyone to the dinner either. Ellie had called a few days earlier, asking what was on his agenda for the weekend. Alex just wasn't into starting any sort of relationship on Valentine's Day, though. Talk about the kiss of death. Alex and Boder decided that they would be each other's date for the evening, although they agreed that corsages would be excluded.

A candlelit dinner was held in the main dining room. Everyone was dressed in tuxedos or gowns. A three-piece, classical trio played in the corner. The main course included Chateau Briand and fine wine. Boder was in a good mood. Despite being dateless, out of school, and in total violation of his terms for readmission, he appeared happy. In fact, Boder had been in a good mood since he and Alex returned from New York a little more than two weeks ago. Conversely, Alex realized he was in a funk, but he was trying hard not to let it show. He wasn't doing a very good job, though. "You keep that face on for the rest of the evening," Boder stated, "and I'm sorry, but I'm just not going to be able to sleep with you tonight." It was all Alex could do to force a smile. He stared out a large window onto Prospect Street, where the light from the lampposts illuminated evidence that it had begun to snow. Suddenly, Alex was drawn in by the sound of piano music. It started softly, then became very demanding. My God it's beautiful, Alex thought as he turned his attention to the classical trio in the room. Some club members had persuaded Sophia Yao to play. She replaced the hired pianist, who then picked up a violin, forming a quartet. They played Tchaikovsky Piano Concerto Number One. No one in the room uttered a word. When the tempo of the music picked up, so did Alex's heartbeat. Alex wasn't sure if it was due to his emotional state, but, at the time, he felt that this was the most beautiful piece of music he had ever heard.

The after party in the Smoking Room took on an entirely different tone. The DJ blasted electronic music, and they were four deep at the bar. The TV screen showed homemade club movies in silence, and Zimmerman was kicking ass at the dartboard. Alex watched with amusement as unsatisfied couples flirted with others. All the while, the fireplace flickered in the background. This would be the last Valentine's Day in Sheik's Princeton history and people had high expectations. He couldn't make it to dinner because his date had previously scheduled a function in New York, but he promised to make it to the after-dinner party.

Rumors had been circulating that Sheik might be bringing twins. This year, however, Sheik out-Sheiked even himself, walking in with none other than model Alyssa Miller. Alex had to lean against the wall to keep from falling. If not for the blaring music, there wouldn't have been any sounds in the room. As fate would have it, Sheik spotted Alex and walked over. Alex had always wondered whether magazine models looked as good without significant photographic touch-ups. As Sheik approached with his date, Alex realized the answer was a resounding ab-so-fucking-lutely!

"Hey Alex. What's going on?" Sheik was speaking to Alex as coolly as he would if he had just run into him on the stairs, heading for class. Alex just stared at the pair. "Oh, excuse me. Alyssa, this is my buddy, Alex. Alex, Alyssa."

"Very nice to meet you," Alyssa said politely, "I have really been looking forward to meeting Charles' friends." It took a few moments for Alex to figure out who the hell Charles was. He had never actually heard Sheik called by his first name.

Alex heard his own voice say, "Very nice to meet you as well."

Sheik could feel the presence of other males gathering around behind him. He smiled politely and said, "Well, we better make the rounds. Talk to you later." Alex nodded at Sheik and looked at Alyssa. Alyssa smiled a full, toothy smile with lots of lip. Alex thought he had died and gone to heaven. Since he was thirteen, Alex had spent the greatest amount of his time thinking about women, talking about women, and trying to go out with women. Here, right in front of him, at a college eating club in the middle of New Jersey, was quite possibly the most beautiful woman he had ever seen. Ab-so-fucking-lutely.

As the evening wore on, over one hundred people packed the Smoking Room. Javier went over to Alex and whispered "Hey Hombre, I have something special for you, man." Javier pulled a perfect looking, Cuban cigar out of his pocket. "These are the actual cigars made for the Castro family: Cohiba, Corona Especial. Please enjoy."

"Javier, that looks fantastic, but I can't accept, it's too much."

"Alex, don't be an ass. My father sent me a handful, so they cost me nothing. You're one of the few people in this school who has always treated me as an equal, rather than a minority enrollment statistic. I appreciate it."

Javier cut the tip off the cigar, pulled a cigarette lighter from his that had belonged to his grandfather, handed the cigar to Alex, and said, "Now please, don't insult me." Alex smiled as he puffed rapidly on the cigar to get it going. The rose-colored smoke ascended slowly and gracefully toward the ceiling. Alex became melancholy, as he began to realize how much he was going to miss that place. He didn't know where he was going next, but he knew it would never feel like this again.

Alex's last memory of that evening was that of sitting under the Marilyn Monroe statute in the X-room with a half-dozen others who were even more toasted than he was, and they were debating everything from the war on ISIS to whether boy bands should be illegal. At five forty-five in the morning, Alex's alarm clock went off. It was still dark. This low was much lower than the highest high of the past evening. If hell was worse, it could not be by much. Alex didn't remember when he went to sleep, but it couldn't have been more than two hours earlier.

The bare floor was cold. Peering out the frosted window, he could see that it was still snowing. He made his way to the shower where he stood with his eyes closed, as the water hammered on the back of his head. Shivering and achy, Alex put on his sweats, coat, and hat, and headed toward the stairs. Passing the X-room, he heard voices behind the closed door. Alex paused for a moment, then continued toward the stairs. On the first floor, partially filled glasses of beer and wine were everywhere. The stale smell made Alex slightly nauseous. Alex's feet stuck to the floor as he made his way to the kitchen for some juice. On his way out of the club,

Alex peered into the Smoking Room. On one of the couches, an unidentified male was asleep. His pants were off, there was a huge pile of shaving cream on his head, and there was something shoved up his shirt made to look like breasts. The danger of being the last to leave.

Alex walked outside. The dark eastern sky was beginning to give way to a dull light. It was so quiet, you could hear the snow falling. It had been snowing for about twelve hours, and at least eight inches lay on the ground. Alex debated whether he should change his sneakers to boots, but he wasn't motivated to go back inside at this moment. He put his chin to his neck and moved on. The fresh air felt good, or at least as good as it could feel given his present condition. The streets hadn't yet been plowed, so Alex passed on jogging to practice. At the end of Prospect Street, about to turn onto Washington, he turned back to look at the snow-covered eating clubs. The light from the smoky glass streetlights was beginning to fade into the coming dawn. The thick, wiry elm limbs were bent under the weight of the snow. Parked cars looked like snowdrifts. It all looked so peaceful. If I had a pillow and a blanket, Alex thought, I could curl up right here and go into a deep and happy sleep.

He walked on; left on Washington Road, down the hill, right on Faculty Road. A chain link fence surrounded the boathouse. The gate was pushed open just enough to allow an individual body to slide through. Preceding footprints had all but disappeared at the behest of the breeze blowing off the frozen lake, pouring snow into crevices like sand into footprints on a beach. The lights from inside the boathouse reflected dimly onto the white docks and lake.

Once inside, the awakening effect of the fresh air rapidly

wore off. There had been a lot of Valentine's Day parties the previous evening. No one on the team looked especially spectacular that morning, but, as usual, Alex went that extra mile. One look at him and it became obvious that he drank more and slept less than anyone else in room. This was not lost on Coach Diriglia who queried, "Hey, Willaims! You feeling OK this morning?"

"Sure, sir."

"Well, you look a little rough around the edges."

He heard himself respond, "The club had a little Valentine's Day party last night, so I was up a bit later than usual." As the words come out of his mouth, he knew it was a mistake. In this situation, honesty, even if only partial, was not the best policy.

"Is that right?"

Yes, you big dickhead, Alex thought to himself. I'm too hung over for this nonsense, and I am about to puke on your shoes. So, please, stuff an oar in it. "Yes sir, that's right," he uttered.

"Mr. Willaims, you look like hell."

"No, I am OK."

Coach Diriglia raised his voice and addressed the team, "Everyone now hear this. Mr. Williams attended a Valentine's Day party last night. You will all be happy to hear that he had a grand time. He may have stayed up a bit too late, but not to worry, he says he is OK. Looks like a dead dog warmed over to me, but, hey, we all know that looks can be deceiving. In celebration of the fact that Mr. Williams is OK, he is going to lead us on a three-mile run around beautiful, snow-covered Princeton this morning." A large groan rose from the group. "Now, now boys. Let's not insult

Mr. Williams. If he says he's OK, then he's OK. In fact, no one passes Mr. Williams. When he finishes, we all finish. The faster he goes, the sooner we will warm up. Gentlemen, you know the route. Coach Diriglia approached the large doors through which most of the boats entered and exited the boathouse. He opened the doors inward. The cold and fine swirling granules of snow filled the room. Coach Diriglia gracefully pointed his hands to the outdoors, inviting, "Mr. Williams, if you please . . ." As Alex slowly left the boathouse, he wondered when he would wake up from the nightmare. As the cold hit his face, and the snow whirled up in his eyes, he realized that his hope that it was a dream was not to be. Alex jogged up toward Princeton Stadium with a very unhappy group of fellows behind him. He didn't dare look back.

The normal three-mile run called for a quarter-mile run to the outdoor track where they would complete four laps. Next, they would go into the adjoining football stadium, where they ran up and down the steps twice, then, continuing up Washington Road, and through a variety of side streets, for a mile. They would then turn left onto Alexander Road, run through the University golf course, and finally return to main campus through a couple of paths, cross Faculty Road, and back to home sweet home: the boathouse.

By the time Alex got to the track, he was exhausted. He fell twice on the way, once attempting to jump over a snowdrift and once going down a hill near the stadium. On the second fall, he rolled to the bottom and looked back at his teammates. They were expressionless. Snow covered, Alex got up slowly and stared at them. He turned around and continued running. What was that old adage? he thought.

Never let them see you sweat.

Running on the track was nearly fruitless. It was worse than running uphill on a sandy beach. Alex thought about seeing Alyssa Miller the night before, and that got his mind off the pain for a minute or two. By the third lap around the track, the team had created a nice little groove in which to run, albeit very carefully. If the team thought running in the stadium steps was bad, they discovered downtown was worse. Although the main roads were in the process of being plowed, the snowplows created mountains of the white powder they had to climb over to get through to each block.

Alex couldn't believe that he was sweating so profusely in such weather. His sweat smelled like alcohol, and his mouth felt like cotton balls. Periodically, he would scoop some snow into his hand and put it in his mouth. Alex's sneaker-covered feet were cold and wet, and his toes were beginning to hurt. Running past the Small World Coffee Shop, the scent almost made him quit right there, but he kept going. He ran up Witherspoon and made a right onto Nassau. On the left side of Nassau Street was the main entrance to the University, behind it, Nassau Hall. The white snow was a dramatic contrast to the black wrought iron fence that separated the University from the town. Alex wondered, for the first time, what the graduation scene would look like on that first Tuesday in June. In his mind, he conjured images of warmth, joy, and happiness.

Alex continued down Nassau and made a left onto University Place. The university campus continued on the left, absent of the black wrought iron fence. Thick stone buildings stood close to the sidewalk like a fortress. There was little opportunity for observation within. Finally,

University Place curved to the right, away from the main campus, giving way to the town train station and the busiest Wawa Convenience Store in the land. Directly across the street was Forbes College, one of the five separate undergraduate "colleges" within the University. Forbes stood alone, separated from main campus, and the other four colleges, by Alexander Street. Immediately behind Forbes College was Springdale, the University golf course. Now, covered in nearly a foot of virgin snow, it bore little resemblance to its purpose. Looking straight ahead, Alex bolted into the knee-high snow without hesitation. This leader-maniac ran like a sinner who had managed to slip into heaven. The other team members watched Alex in exhausted amazement. After about thirty yards, he stopped short like a hiker coming face to face with a grizzly bear. He was cold; his toes tingled, his nose and ears burned, his throat was dry and swollen. The rest of Alex's body was feverish and sweating, and he had the awful feeling of wanting to puke but not being able. Slowly he turned to his teammates. There was no silence quite like that of a snowy, early morning. Alex looked at the puzzled faces of his teammates. A smile came across his face, as he wondered how smart people could be so stupid. He yelled, "This is crazy." His voice echoed into the silence and disappeared into the trees. "I mean," he went on, "what the hell are we doing this for? Because I had a little too much to drink last night? You really think that's why we're out here? I don't think so. We're out here because some screwed up masochistic asshole thinks this will set some fucked up example of how we're all for one. How we need to operate as one. Personally, if I hear him say 'Be one, win one' just one more time, I may have to kill him on the spot. Don't get me wrong; I have nothing against Coach. He wants us to succeed just as much as we do. But in this instance, with my legs frozen up to my ass, I think the best thing for everyone is to fade back to that Wawa over there for a nice warm breakfast. Then, we can cut across the railroad tracks to Faculty Road and back to the boathouse. No one but us will be the wiser, and the only difference is that maybe we won't get sick." Alex took a wet glove off his right hand, reached into a pocket, and pulled out his bankcard. He held up the card. "Well gentlemen, what do you think?"

Everyone went from staring at Alex to staring at their feet. Alex's heart sank. Suddenly, a voice from the middle of the pack spoke, "Let's get the fuck out of here. I'm freezing." It was Jim Daley. Alex couldn't believe it, Mr. Mum himself led the way.

"Yeah, this is ridiculous. If Alex's buying, I'm flying," Neil Johnson chimed in. Receiving the proverbial "yeah" from Daley and Johnson, the rest were a shoe-in. Soon they were yelling, whooping, and racing to the Wawa. They ate, had some warm drinks, told stories, and laughed. Alex realized he had spent more time with these guys than anyone else in his life, except his immediate family, and this was the first time he had seen them all with their guard down. He watched with a smile as individuals, who had hardly said a word to one another, yapped away like best buddies. After about half an hour at Wawa, they walked a shortcut to a wooded area about 100 yards from the boathouse. They had a hearty snowball fight and, once appropriately cold and snow covered, ran the remainder of the distance back to the boathouse. Indirectly, Coach Diriglia's objective had been achieved, and to a degree he never could have anticipated. In that morning, the team was forged into a unit that would, in the upcoming season, put on a show greater than anyone had ever seen before.

XV

Although Boder wasn't even supposed to be living at the club, he was thriving there. Officially, when Boder was removed from school, Alex took over as President of O'Neill. In reality, though, it was still Boder's show. To the surprise of most, he was really taking care of things. Boder straightened out the long-awry financial books, oversaw major house repairs, and did some small ones himself. This was no small feat for a guy who thought a monkey wrench was a zoo animal with a sore wrist. He also planned a few spring parties, as well as other social events. "You keep this up Boder, and we'll actually be organized and reputable like all the other clubs," quipped one member.

Alex about fainted when Boder informed him that he'd taken a part-time job at the Princeton Record Exchange, just to keep himself busy. Alex and Boder spent quite a few late-night hours talking about what courses Boder would take the following year, and what he was going to do when he finally got out. They hadn't talked in a couple of nights, though, and

Alex had not seen Boder at all the previous day. As usual, Alex had gotten up early for crew. He rarely checked in on Boder, and wasn't sure why he did on that morning. He opened Boder's door with a smile on his face, expecting to see Boder either lying face down, in his underwear, with last night's clothing strewn across the floor, or no Boder at all. But Alex would see neither. Instead, Alex was startled to see Boder lying on the floor, unconscious, his skin a mixture of white and blue hues. He was on his back and fully clothed. Boder still had on his ragtag army jacket, of which he was so fond. His clothes were sweat-soaked and the smell of vomit rapidly crawled up Alex's nose. Panicked, Alex begged, "Hey Bode, you OK? Bode!" Nothing. "Answer me, please!"

Alex ran to Boder's side and shook his unresponsive body. The cold sweat from Boder's shirt seeped onto Alex's fingers. A nervous soft cry escaped from Alex's throat. Putting his ear to Boder's chest, Alex could hear a faint heartbeat. He ran out of the room, down to the next floor, and banged on BT's door. Alex knew that BT would remain calm in a situation like this, and keep his mouth shut. There was no answer. Alex banged with greater intensity. Finally, the door opened, and there BT stood, all two hundred eighty, almost naked, pounds. BT was a sight to behold in his yellow bikini briefs. "No thank you, little girl. I already bought Girl Scout cookies," BT joked.

"We've got to take him to the hospital, right now!" BT immediately sensed the gravity in Alex's words, as well as who he was talking about.

"Let me get my clothes."

"There's no time for that."

"We owe it to the world for me to get dressed."

"Fuck it man. Just put a coat and shoes on and let's go."

Seconds later, BT returned with a thigh length suede coat and high black Nike sneakers. He could have been in a 1950's low budget sci-fi flick. Even in this urgent situation, Alex stared for a moment and shook his head. Within minutes, they were carrying Boder to Alex's car and were on their way to the hospital. Halfway there, Boder puked again. Alex pulled over to make sure Boder's mouth was clear, so he wouldn't choke. "How fucking disgusting," BT said as Alex checked the inside of Boder's mouth with his forefinger.

"Yeah, but at least he's breathing."

Alex drove his car right onto the sidewalk in front of the emergency room door. Alex and BT jumped out and pulled Boder from the back seat. Carrying Boder into the emergency room, Alex was struck by how bright it seemed, like the visual sensation of waking up in the middle of the night and turning on a lamp. "Any doctors? I need a doctor!" Alex yelled. Two nurses came running over. One called for a gurney.

"Do you know what's wrong with him?" the other nurse asked.

"We're not sure, maybe an OD!" said BT.

Two aids brought the gurney, put Boder on it, and quickly rolled him into another room. Alex and BT tried to follow but were prevented by one of the nurses. "I'm sorry, you can't come any further."

"But maybe I can help," Alex pleaded.

"You can help by staying out here and letting us do our job," the nurse said tersely, disappearing behind the swinging doors. Alex and BT could see a group circle around Boder's limp body. Alex's heart skipped a beat, feeling the pain of the situation.

He turned toward BT in a rage, "What is wrong with you?"

"What do you mean?"

"What do I mean? Are you kidding me? Where do you get off telling these people about an OD?"

"Where do I get off? Get real, Alex! Do you think Boderman passed out in his own puke because he overdid it on the Mexican food? Come on man, this guy's life is in danger here. This is no time for pretenses."

Staring eye to eye, Alex realized that BT was right. What else could it be? In this area, Boder had skated on thin ice many times before. Alex wondered if he was trying to hide this fact from the hospital or from himself. "I'm sorry BT, just upset I guess. You have no idea what it was like finding him like that. Christ, for a minute, I thought he was dead."

"It's OK, man. Listen, take the car and get to practice. This is going to take a while. I'll hang."

"Are you crazy? How the hell am I supposed to practice with this on my mind?"

"Listen, from what I've heard around the club, Diriglia is really on your ass. You don't need any more shit. Besides, you know there's nothing you can really do here right now. If you get kicked off the team because of another missed practice, Boder would never forgive himself."

"I just don't think I can . . ."

"Go! Keep your phone on you. I will text you if I hear anything."

*****

The team met in Jadwin Gym to perform some running and endurance tests. Alex was so angry with Boder that he could not contain his energy, running with better times, lifting heavier weights, and performing better on the ergometer than he ever had before. Nevertheless, the three-hour practice seemed to go on forever. After practice, still dressed in his workout clothes, Alex hopped in his car and drove like a maniac back to the hospital. BT was asleep, cuddled on two seats in a corner of the emergency waiting room. Alex shook BT more violently than he had intended. Startled, BT fell right to the floor on his ass. BT held his chest. "Jesus Christ, Man! What the hell you trying to do? Make me a patient as well?"

"Sorry. I'm a little uptight. How is he?"

"Meth, but he's going to be OK. Doctor said it was good you found him. Another hour at best, and . . . well, it would have been a different story." After a short silence, Alex sat down, put his head in his hands, and began to cry. He hadn't done that since his father died. A little later, Alex tried to see Boder but was told to come back the next day. He did and was relieved to find Boder in better shape. He had an IV in his arm, wires attached to him and machines all around. He had deep black circles under his eyes. Half awake, Boder caught sight of Alex out of the corner of his eye. "Xander, como esta?"

"Hey, Bode."

"Scared you, eh?"

"Hell no, I knew you were just goofing."

"While we're at it, what gives you the right to barge into

a sleeping man's room like that?"

"Sorry. It won't happen again."

Boder smiled. "It better not."

After a brief silence, Boder's face grew more serious, "I guess I owe you an explanation."

"Not really."

"I appreciate the gesture, but I do," Boder said coughing roughly. "Walking home from work the other night, I cut across the campus like I usually do. It was really cold, but, other than that, everything was fine. I mean personally, I felt good, you know? Then, as I approached the library and saw people going in and out, I got a bit depressed… about being out of the loop and all . . . not that I ever spent any time in that hole or anything, but you know what I mean. I guess I just started feeling sorry for myself, like that time in New York but on a much grander scale. Pretty pathetic, huh?"

"No."

"I really don't know what clicked. Anyway, I needed a pick me up, and fast. My emotional state was crashing. I turned around, left campus, and proceeded to the apartment of a local yokel who stops in the Record Exchange regularly. He works as a landscaper and is always stoned. I mean, compared to this guy, I could be the head of the DEA. Every time he comes into the store, he invites me over to his pad to imbibe. I figured, 'now is as good a time as any,' so I headed over with the hope of destroying the unpleasantness buzzing around my mind. I smoked a little. Alex, it was absolutely the best ever, and you know I've spared no expense when it comes to that stuff. I mean, I was flying. We were listening to music, hanging out. It would have been all I needed. Then the dude goes into his bedroom and comes out with a chewing tobacco tin. But I know it's not tobacco. He opens it up. The only thing the guy says after he opens it is, 'I use to cut it.' This cowboy was a trip. I looked into the tin. He said it was crystal meth. I mean, pure Hawaiian Ice. I'd heard of this stuff, but I never saw it before. I swear it looked just like rock candy. I remember the dude putting a good size crystal into a glass pipe, heating the bottom with his hand over the top and then me taking a few hits. Then the space shuttle took off, and the lights went out. I mean, I remember nothing. The next thing I know, I wake up with a tube up my nose and one motherfucking headache. The doctor said that, when I got here, my heart was only blipping a couple of times a minute. Thanks for checking in on me. . .." Slightly teary eyed, Boder stared at Alex and continued, "Xander, I need some help, man. Real help."

It hurt Alex to realize that Boder was right. This was going to be a bigger job than helping a buddy get over a bad date. "We all need help, Bode," Alex said, musing that he should be valedictorian for that statement.

Boder turned his head away and closed his eyes. "Thanks for coming bro," he whispered.

"Sure. You need anything? Magazines from downstairs or whatnot?"

Boder just shook his head no, as he slowly nodded off.

"Bye, Bode," Alex whispered.

Alex left the room quietly, went downstairs, found a restroom in the lobby, and screamed at the top of his lungs.

*****

Alex was leaning against a bicycle rack in front of

Firestone Library. He was eating an apple, biding his time, while waiting for his eleven o'clock drama class to begin over in McCosh Hall. Since the abrupt slap in the face from life Alex had received at Boder's door a few days earlier, he had really been focusing on his surroundings. It's a funny thing, this college thing, Alex thought.

Boder was fine now. Two days after the OD, Boder's father came to take him home from the hospital. Boder told him to fuck off. He said he would rest just fine, "thank you," on the third floor of O'Neill. It became Alex who felt a little tilted. To say the least, it was unpleasant when real world issues invaded the campus. Fortunately, it didn't happen very often. No one worked nine to five. In his four years, the most serious disease Alex had seen was the flu. The biggest potential problem was students having trouble coming up with spring break money. There were no wars, no unemployment. Academically brilliant teachers were preparing students for a real world that many, themselves, couldn't survive in. A funny thing, this college thing.

But there was more about the college trip that made it unique, Alex realized. On the first day, you walked into a ten-foot by ten-foot room and introduced yourself to a stranger. Maybe you'd had a few exchanges on Facebook, but now you were going to live with that person. After meeting the stranger, you'd trudge off to a large dining room where you'd eat average food off plastic trays with hundreds more strangers, some whom you would never actually meet. You would buy your books and check your schedule, which would dictate that you would get up at different times every day and go to different places. You would pause, look out the window, stare at the grass and brick courtyard, and realize that the goal in the whole college process was to out-perform all the people with whom you ate dinner. A funny thing, this college thing.

As he finished his apple and threw the rough core into a wastebasket, Alex mused that the funniest thing about the college experience was the strong feeling that, in the final analysis, this would be the best experience of your life. What is so great about reality, anyway? Alex wondered, The nine to five job? Good morning boss. Bills? Wake up early . . . and tired? Make sure your tie isn't too risqué . . . you don't want to offend anyone. Car needs to be fixed. The kids are sick. The wife's pissed because you came home late again last night and smelled like beer, smoke, and perfume. The smell of perfume isn't really there, but your wife insists she can smell it. If only you were so lucky. Hope this business deal goes through so I can pay the mortgage. Jesus, I didn't think credit card interest would be so high. What is so strange about college is exactly what makes it so appealing. Fuck reality.

What's wrong with serious concerns like a shortage of cash for spring break, or the need to get a pass into a club party? Most important, however, is the closeness you get to true freedom. There is no complete freedom, no one gets that, but in college you can get darn close. The truth is, you're absolutely on your own. Yes, if you have a couple of bad terms, grade wise, you could have some people to answer to, but otherwise it could be some ride. Alex smiled and agreed, Sure was a funny thing, this college thing.

*****

About a week after the overdose, Boder was up and about, as if nothing had happened. Boder was back to just being Boder. This concerned Alex. A few days prior, the guy was lying in a hospital bed, begging for help, following a near death experience. Now, he was relaxing on his bed, smoking a joint, and acting like he had just successfully completed years of psychotherapy. "Hey, Bode, don't you think you should take it a little easy?"

"Doesn't get much easier than this, Xander," Boder said as he took a slow hit off the joint.

"Come on, man. You know what I mean."

"You mean the OD thing?"

Alex was incredulous, "Yes, I mean the OD thing."

"I know you won't believe me, but I've done a lot of thinking about that whole episode, and I've figured it out."

"Pray tell, Dr. Boderman, just what did you figure?"

"I've been carrying a lot of excess baggage from my past. Everybody has it, to some degree, but I let mine get to me, eat at me, fuck with me and almost kill me, so you know what I did?"

Alex was almost afraid to ask, "No, what did you do?"

"I realized that there was absolutely nothing I could do to change it. I could whine, hide, OD, whatever, and my background would remain the same. In conclusion, I've decided I'm starting my life all over again. The point is, that my past is my past, and I've got to live with it. The best way to do that, is not to let it interfere with my life now."

"I don't know, Bode," Alex responded, "Don't get me wrong, there's a lot of truth in what you are saying, but I'm not a psychiatrist. You might be simplifying things a bit here." Alex knew there was more going on than Boder ever let on and had to ask, "And anyway, I've been wondering what's so bad about your life? You come from one of the most prominent families in the country, have plenty of cash, and anyone who knows you thinks you're a tremendous person. I know your relationship with your folks isn't the greatest, especially with your dad. He doesn't always appear to have a lot of time for you, and I am sure that could be a problem." He continued, "But then again, he is a U.S. Senator, and I am sure his time is limited. Not that I am condoning it, but since I've been here, I've met plenty of students whose parents . . ."

"He raped me."

"Excuse me?"

"Played with me since I was four. Maybe earlier, but I really can't remember further back. Had me suck him when I was about seven. For the grand finale, he shoved it in my ass when I was nine. Have you met plenty of students with parents like that, Alex?"

Alex did not know how to respond to that. Almost from the day he met Boder, three and one-half years earlier, Alex had known the relationship between he and his father was strained, but Alex never expected anything like this. Alex thought of his own father. The thought of him doing something like what Boder's father did was inconceivable. Alex started to feel lightheaded, and his skin grew warm. "Geez, Bode, I'm sorry. I had no idea . . ."

"Don't worry about it," Boder said as nonchalantly as he could, considering the topic of conversation. "You had no idea because I never told you. Call me odd, but I never felt much like discussing it. But even if I told you, what difference would it have made?"

Was he right? Alex considered, Does it really make a difference if he dwells on the past? Maybe we should just forge ahead. It would be better not to mention, less of a burden to others as well as ourselves. What a minute. Get a grip. Alex blurted out, "Boder, that is just ridiculous."

"What is?"

"That we can just turn ourselves off like a light switch. Wish it were true, Bode, but it's not. Fortunately, my dad didn't screw around with me like that. But when I was fifteen, he left me in an instant. Do you know how many times I tried to get the thought of his death out of my mind? How often I just couldn't get to sleep? All kinds of messed up thoughts would run through my mind. Was thinking about him going to bring him back or change what I had to go through? Of course not. But I'm a human, and something happened to me that hurt. It hurt badly, and I had to deal with it. My mom sent me to a shrink. I began to realize my mind and body are interconnected, and so are my emotions. What I feel impacts both my mind and body, sometimes one more than the other. But when you're hit with something so serious in your life, like we both have been, it can wreak havoc on all systems. And you know what, Bode? You can't shut that out. Sometimes it may appear as though you can, but that's only a symptom of the problem. When you ignore your emotions, sometime down the road, your body, your mind, or both, will explode. It needs to be worked out. If we injure our bodies, it is easy to see, but our minds, that's another story. I guess the point I'm trying to make is that it's not that simple; separating the body from the mind, the past from the present, emotional from physical. Sometimes, we should work through it. It is just the nature of the beast.

We're all different, so maybe you can do it faster and easier than I did, but, Bode, don't turn your back on it. It will tear you apart."

"What are you suggesting? That I spend a few hours with a shrink and my problems will go away? What can they really do but tell me to go on with my life?"

"Maybe they can help you realize that what happened to you in the past isn't your fault and how to deal with it. I can tell you from personal experience, Bode, that understanding that distinction makes the difference between surviving day-to-day and living."

"Xander, I know what you're trying to do, and I really appreciate it. I know you have my best interest at heart. I'm no Freud, Jung, or Skinner, but I'm feeling pretty good. The main reason is that I know what I've got to do. If it doesn't work, well, then I'll take your advice. But I believe everything's going to be just fine."

Alex looked deep into Boder's eyes. A reading lamp on a nearby desk bathed one side of his face in a soft white light, while eclipsing the other half. With utmost sincerity, Alex said, "I hope so, Bode. I really hope so."

*****

For a few days after their talk, Boder appeared fine, yet Alex continued to be concerned. Boder had seemed fine after the New York incident too, but he wound up in the hospital shortly thereafter. Alex wondered if the next crash would be worse. He knew the guy wasn't going to seek help on his own, but asking Boder's parents for help was out of the question. Apparently, they could use a good dose of help themselves. Alex decided he would call Shirley Lewis or Mary Robinson, Boder's beloved housekeeper and cook, and ask their advice. Those two probably knew Boder better than anyone.

"Boderman residence," came the greeting. Alex wasn't sure who had picked up the phone, but he knew by the accent that it wasn't Mrs. Boderman.

"Mary?"

"No."

"Shirley?"

"Who's askin'?"

"It's Alex. Alex Williams. Richie's roommate from school." The tone at the other end of the line shifted dramatically.

"Why Sweetie! How is y'all doin'? We miss you and our boy Richie down here. You gonna come down and visit us soon?" They call him Richie, and Alex thought it was interesting how a person can have many first names, given at different periods of their life.

"I hope so."

"Good! Anyway, neither the Mr. nor the Mrs. is here right now. Can I leave a message for you?

"Thanks Shirley, no message. I was actually hoping to speak with you, if you wouldn't mind." There was no response from the other side. "I wanted to speak to you about Richie."

"He's alright, isn't he? He's not hurt now, is he?" Shirley's voice had quickened.

"No Shirley. Boder . . . uh, Richie is fine. Nothing is wrong. At least, not right now. But I wanted to talk to you about Richie while everything is OK with him. It might help me a little bit when things get more confusing. Am I making any sense?"

"Alex, I love that boy like he was my own. You understand? Since I found out he was in the hospital a few weeks ago, I 'bout got no sleep. But to tell the truth, I kind of expected it to have happened earlier."

Alex realized he might have been too specific too fast. "Shirley?"

"Yes, Honey?"

"You know how you just said that you loved Richie like he was your own?"

"Yes, I do. Might as well have shot out of me like a Pop Tart from a toaster."

"I love him like a brother, myself."

"I know you do, Honey. He speaks the world about you all the time. Like you walk on water or somethin'."

"No, Shirley. I just row on it."

"What you saying?"

"Just something stupid. Pay me no mind. I love Richie dearly, and I am very concerned about him. It seems that lately he has all these high points and then low points. Recently, they seem to be accelerating, and becoming more extreme. I don't know what's happening or how to help. That's why I'm calling you. You may know him better than anyone." Alex paused and then confided, "Shirley, I want you to know that this call is just between you and me. I'm just looking for some answers to try and help Richie."

"Alex, for all the money, he never had it good here. The father drinks, plays around and worse. The mother just lives life as a high brow, looking the other way on issues concernin' her husband's indiscretions. And the boy, he is so damned gifted! If it weren't for Mary and me, he might have grown up deaf, dumb and blind."

"Wow."

"Well, maybe I'm pushin' it a bit, but not too far. I mean, he saw things most kids only dream of. He met presidents, kings, and the like, but Mr. & Mrs. Boderman never let Richie inside them, and that's what he wanted most."

Alex inhaled, held his breath than slowly released it, "Shirley, was it really that bad?"

"Alex, if it weren't for Richie, I would have left this place a long time ago. His father is just plain no good. Me and Mary always suspected he was doin' disgusting things with Richie, though we never saw it firsthand, but that ain't all. Mary once caught him with one of little Richie's friends in the third-floor bathroom. Before Mary caught him, he had always been so nice to her, but, after that, it all changed. The Senator told her if she ever told anyone what she saw, she would disappear forever. Mary believed it to. She didn't confide in me for about three years after that. But, by then, I knew from firsthand experience what a snake he was."

Alex felt a little queasy, but he had to go on, "What do you mean?"

"I mean, he got me to."

"Sexually?"

"Yes."

Alex wondered how much uglier this story could get. Shirley continued, "Once, when Richie was about eight, the Mrs. was away in California, visiting her sister. The Senator had been out all evening. At about two in the morning, I heard a knock on my bedroom door. I put my robe on and opened it. He asked me if I would make him something to eat. Now this was not altogether uncommon. Many nights, he'd work past midnight with no dinner or nothing. Mary usually went to bed early, so, when he finally came home, I'd fix him somethin'. But this time was different. He was standing there stone drunk. He smelled of whiskey and was slurring his words. I smiled, walked past him and went down into the kitchen to fry him up a small steak and some potatoes. In a stupor, the Senator sat behind me on one of them wooden stools at the kitchen counter. He sat exactly where Richie used to sit every morning for breakfast. He started talking about how no one realized how hard he worked and the sacrifices he made. He mumbled a lot of other stuff too, but he wasn't making much sense. Suddenly he starts talking about what a fine woman I am, and how he can't understand how I never remarried after my husband died. Went on about how good my body looked considering my age and everything. Then he says, 'with that beautiful ass, Shirley, you should have them panting at the doorstep.' I'm telling you Alex, the sound of his voice, as much as what he was saying, made the hair on my neck stand straight as a proud peacock's tail. Next thing I know, Mr. Boderman is behind me, grabbing me at the waist, and pulling me in toward him. I asked him to please stop, but he wouldn't."

"Shirley, this is unbelievable."

"I wish that was so."

"If you don't want to go on, I understand."

"Child, I ain't come this far to stop now. But I must admit, here is where it gets a little heavy. You understand what I am saying?"

"Unfortunately, I might." Alex began to feel a little queasy.

"I was getting very nervous, so I elbowed him in the stomach. Maybe I shouldn't have, but it just came to me. He stepped back, and I turned around to face him. First time in my life, I came face to face with the devil. His eyes were so angry, they were shining like on coming headlights. His face was as red as a fire truck, and he screamed just as loud. His nostrils got very wide. He pointed a long, bent finger, inches from my nose. I could hardly breathe. I don't know how I stayed standing. 'Bitch!' he said, 'Who the hell do you think you're fucking with? I could certainly crush some little piece of shit like you. I pay you good money, and I suggest you do what the Senator wants.' With that, he lurched and gave me a big wet kiss. And it wasn't just on my lips either, but all over my face. This time, I gave him a hard right to his cheek, just like I saw Mike Tyson do in the ring. The Senator fell to his knees like someone pulled the floor out. We stared at each other. I don't know who was more shocked, him or me. I guess I should've run, but I just stood there, leaning against the counter like someone had put super glue on my butt. Jesus, there was a photo opportunity, eh Alex?"

"The *Washington Post* may have shown some interest."

"Well, like I said, maybe I should've run. The Senator got up very slowly. He looked at me and smiled. I can still remember the sound of the clock ticking on the wall and the friendly hum of the refrigerator. All of a sudden, whack! Pain rippled across my face, and I fell flat on the same kitchen floor that I'd cleaned so well earlier in the day. The Senator stood over me, the angry face now back in full force. 'Now you listen to me and listen good. What we need around here is just a little more respect for authority. And do you know what, Shirley? I am the authority! If you and Mary want to continue working here, or anywhere else, I suggest you become a bit more receptive to my complements.' Now, let me tell you, I've been around this house an awful long time, and I knew the Senator wasn't bluffing. He has an awful lot of power. I mean, I've seen him ruin people's lives for next to nothing. When the Senator told me that he was going to make it hard for Mary and me if I didn't oblige, I knew he could, and I knew he would. It was especially true in my case because, before I got the job with the Boderman's, I had a brush or two with the law. And then I started thinking about the boy who slept upstairs and what would happen to him if Mary and I left. I know I'm rambling on here a bit, and I apologize. I guess what I'm tryin' to say is, I obliged."

"Obliged?"

"Laid right across the cooking island, turned my head to stare at the damn clock, and let him have his way."

"I can't believe you did that! The guy is an animal. I don't care what his job is!"

"Alex, women have been lying on their backs for men when they didn't want to for things much less serious than this, let me tell you… myself included. There were a couple of times I did it when I was much younger and broke, just for a warm place to sleep. But, with the Senator, I did make one thing clear to him when he was finished."

"What was that?"

"While he was zippering up his pants, I got up on my elbows and looked him straight in the eye. 'Mr. Boderman,' I says, 'I hope that took care of it. The only reason I want to stay here is because Mary and I are good for your son. I'm not gonna say a word to anyone of what went on here tonight, but I got to tell you, because I always try to be honest, that, if you ever try this again, I will kill you. I don't care if they hang me off the Washington Monument.' The Senator didn't say nothing, but I could tell by his face that he knew I meant it. He never touched me again after that, and you are the first person I ever told about it."

"Shirley, I don't know what to say."

"Don't say anything. Just help Richie. He's a good boy."

When Alex hung up the telephone, he was trembling. He sat on the edge of the bed with his head in his hands. Alex wanted to get the first train to Washington, burst into the Senator's office, and tell him he knew the whole sordid thing. He wanted to tell the Senator that he better keep his dick in his pants and get Boder some help and quick, or he would blow the lid sky high. You stupid, scum bag, fucking jerk off. Look at all the problems you've caused. You molested your son and his friends. You even fucked the nanny for Christ's sake! Then, reality set in, as it tended to do. Shirley told Alex that horrible story in confidence. In addition, Shirley was right, that guy was powerful. Who knew what he would do, if threatened. Considering what he had done to his son, to Shirley, and to others whom he was presumably "close to", who knew what he was capable of doing to someone he was hardly acquainted with. The fact remained, though, he had to be stopped. Alex knew in his heart that Shirley's story probably wasn't the worst in this guy's repertoire. Alex went to the refrigerator, put some ice in a glass, and poured some of Boder's Chivas. Then he lay down and tried to take a nap. Alex needed to shut his mind off, if only for a short while. Before drifting off, he thought about the poem "The Human Abstract," by William Blake:

Pity would be no more
If we did not make somebody Poor;
And Mercy no more could be
If all were as happy as we.

XVI

The last Friday in March was a glorious day. That fact had nothing to do with the weather, as, in fact, it was raining like hell. That afternoon, the crew team gathered at the boathouse to board the bus that would take them to their first meet of the season against Navy. While upstairs packing his gear in the well-worn locker room, Alex stared out a large window overlooking the lake. The rain and wind couldn't disguise it. He knew that lake inside and out, as if he and the lake were an old married couple, together longer than he could remember. He had laughed on it, cried on it, been angry on it, and joyous on it. He had ached and grown up on it. Put Alex in the boat blindfolded, start rowing, and at any point he could tell, within inches, where on the course he was. The smell was the thing. Sitting in a boat in the middle of the lake, away from the din of thousands of people and their cars, radios, smart phones, and other invading noises, Alex's senses relaxed and became heightened at the same time. The air carried the sweet scent of the trees from the shoreline. They changed with the seasons like a woman changing her perfume. But it was the smell of the water that Alex connected with, a deep cool smell, echoed in vision by the darkness of this water. Standing by the cracked open window, the faint odor of the lake was unmistakable to this duckling. He knew it always would be.

Someone yelled from the ground floor that the bus was ready. Jolted out of his semi-trance, Alex went to his locker and picked up the black canvas bag with the large orange P. He hustled down the mahogany stairs, ignoring the framed black and white pictures of teams from years past. On the bus, Alex took a window seat toward the middle. The team had two buses, so there was ample room. Alex threw his bag onto the seat next to him. The pickup trucks pulling the trailers that held the team's expensive, sleek, white boats were long gone. The buses were filled with nervous chatter, as they made their way down Route 95 South. It was beginning to sink in that being the preseason favorite wasn't necessarily the most comfortable position. They knew the difference between being expected to win and winning.

On most road trips, the team stayed in a hotel near the school they were challenging. Annapolis provided an exception. Two midshipmen met the bus in the parking lot. They politely greeted and escorted the team to the guest quarters, announcing that they would return in twenty-eight minutes, at eighteen hundred hours, to escort the team to dinner. Alex had been at Annapolis as a sophomore. As it had then, this politeness and efficiency made him a little uncomfortable. He couldn't separate from the sense that big brother was keeping tabs on the strangers in their midst. The team was housed in a dormitory. Alex was driven nuts by the ten toilets, no stalls bathroom. There seemed something peculiar about having no stalls. Alex wondered, What the hell do you say to the guy loudly passing gas three seats down?

At exactly eighteen hundred hours, the midshipmen returned, and the team was escorted to King Hall. Alex was quite sure that this mess hall was the largest dinning room he had ever been in and figured it seated at least five thousand people. The midshipmen were all dressed in dark blue pants and shirts, with shoes so shiny they looked plastic. Alex was amused that anyone with eye glasses stood out because they all wore the same, standard issue, thick, black-rimmed glasses. The poor bastards looked like they came right out of an old *Revenge of the Nerds* movie. Princeton's crew team, overdressed anywhere else, appeared as though they were extras from an MTV rap video. Alex and the team took their filled trays to their reserved table. Not one midshipman looked over at them while they ate their meal, never mind coming over to talk. Cutting an overcooked pork chop served on a plain white plate, Bob Carr looked across the table at Alex and remarked, "This is not reality. It's just not reality."

"Bob, I'm not sure I've seen reality in quite a while," Alex replied.

*****

Early the next morning, Alex awoke to a loud wake-up knock on his bedroom door. Jim Daley's bed was empty. Alex smiled, thinking that the communal showers would preclude Daley from his washing and wanking ritual. A freshly showered Daley came into the room a few minutes later. Unusually not talkative, he questioned, "Alex, I just don't know how you can lay there like that. I woke up at four o'clock with butterflies. Never did go back to sleep."

"Oh, don't you worry about me, Daley, the butterflies will

be coming soon enough. In fact, talking about it doesn't help much. What time is it?"

"Ten to six."

"Ten to six! Who the hell are we rowing against, goddamned roosters?"

"Breakfast is over by six-thirty."

Alex put the blanket over his head and mumbled, "I hope that there's never another big war, because, if I were ever to get drafted, I know I'd get court-martialed. I have a very hard time with mornings." Alex knew it was too late to go back to sleep. He began having visions of himself on the starting line. This was the first meet of his last season, and so much was expected. "Fuck!" Alex yelled as he jumped out of bed. Wearing nothing but his jockey shorts, he ran down the hall and found himself hugging the toilet bowl for the next fifteen minutes.

Weather wise, it was a much better day than yesterday. The sun was shining, and the sky had only a couple of small clouds traveling quickly by in the late March breeze. Alex had breakfast with the team, and, as he watched through a cafeteria window, he was amazed to see midshipmen, in full uniform, doing exercise and marching drills on an open field. Even early Saturday morning, they never get a break. God bless them, Alex thought.

A van gave the team a ride to the boathouse. A beautiful brick building, Hubbard Hall, was named after a crewmember from their 1870 team. The building was a tribute to Navy athletes, with a room that contained accolades to all past Navy sportsmen. The Annapolis boathouse was nicer than the Princeton boathouse, but that didn't bother Alex or his crewmates. They usually beat the whoop out of Navy. While these guys could shoot a nuclear missile into a chimney from fifteen hundred miles, they weren't much at paddling on a lake. There would be quite a few races, first the men's lightweights, then the women, followed by be five men's heavyweight contests—two freshman and three varsity. Alex's boat, Varsity 1, would be the last to race. By the boathouse, Alex sat on the grass near the dock on the Severn River and watched the second freshman team prepare to row. For some on this boat, especially those who hadn't attended prep high schools, this would be their first real race. As if he had just crossed the finish line, Alex remembered his first race. Seven months prior to that race, he had seen a scull for the first time and, unless counting the two or three times he had been in a rowboat at a lake near their house, Alex found himself rowing for the first time. It was a whole new experience, like learning the piano without any prior musical knowledge, or learning Chinese having never spoken anything but English. It was a new world and not always a particularly pleasant learning experience. After some instruction, Alex made the final spot in the second freshman boat. The race against Navy was at home on Lake Carnegie. Alex had been so nervous prior to the race, that he puked for two straight hours. To get into the boat, Alex had to persuade the coach that his green skin was caused by medication he was taking for a stomach virus. Competition breeds good liars. About one thousand meters into the race, Alex's throat and mouth were so dry, his tongue felt like an oversized sandbag. With each row of the oar, Alex felt certain his arms were going to snap off like dry branches on a dead tree. He was almost right. As rowers say, Alex "caught a crab" when, exhausted, he over slanted the oar and placed it into the water. The handle was ripped from his hand, ripping open blisters in the process. Alex fell back as the oar flew over his head, into the rowers behind him. The boat had come to a complete standstill, as if someone had thrown a three hundred-pound anchor over the side. As Alex laid sweating and gasping on the soaked floor of the stalled shell, the target of sixteen angry eyes, he wished he could cut a hole through the hull and swim deep into the mud at the bottom of the lake.

Recalling that day, Alex smiled. He was somewhat amused by the fact that things that seemed a matter of life and death at the time, later looked like just another life learning experience. From his grass seat, Alex watched the second Princeton freshman boat lose badly. Feeling dejected, they'd rowed back in, carried the upside-down scull to the trailer with their heads obscured more than necessary. Alex was tempted to share his story with the freshmen to keep their spirits up. He knew, however, that only two or three of these guys would continue to the highest varsity level. Most would quit or be content staying in the second or third varsity boats. Some wouldn't even make it to the end of that season. So, Alex stayed seated on the grass, but he hoped that there might be one goofball like him, and that the guy would hang on through the agony. There would be a lot of agony.

High school graduates from places like Andover, Exeter, Groton, and Haverford filled Princeton's first freshman boat. They easily beat the outclassed Navy squad. Princeton won the third varsity boat race and Navy the second. Then, it was time for the big show. A good-sized crowd covered the area around the start and the first hundred meters of the Severn

River course. Everything was still on the starting line. Alex could hear his heart knocking loudly on his rib cage and the slow dripping of water from the waiting oars. He stared straight ahead at Jim Daley's back, just like he had done hundreds of times before. The call came, "Rowers, are you ready? Ready all? Row!" Mercifully, the gun went off. Immediately, Vales wildly exhorted the rowers to increase the rowing cadence. At that point, Vales didn't need to say a word as the rowers pumped their oars as hard as they could, like robots from a mad scientist's laboratory. The team to Alex's right, in yellow and dark blue shirts, did the same. Within thirty seconds, Princeton was rowing at forty strokes per minute.

"Settle in four strokes at thirty-eight," Vales ordered. Sometimes, very early in a race, a team can tell whether they are on or off. On this day, Princeton was on. At about two hundred yards, Alex could see that Navy had started to fall behind. Vales smelled an early kill and ordered, "Let's pick it up! Three strokes at forty-one." Sixteen arms rowed in unison. Two giant scorpions couldn't have done it better. Vales encouraged, "That's it! That's it! We almost got 'em by a full boat. Keep it going! Keep it going!" Alex felt beads of sweat building on his neck. "We're at five-hundred-meters. Great job! Long way to go. Keep it steady at forty-one."

Alex didn't remember much more about that race, beyond the fact that it was one of the few times rowing became truly fun. Early in the race, it had been obvious Princeton would win, but it would mean a lot more. Princeton just might live up to the preseason hype. Granted, Navy wasn't one of the best teams, but, still, orange and black was kicking ass and taking names. Alex could almost feel the tension leave his body as he rowed. Through each finger it exited, trickling down the laminated wooden oars and into the cool, dark water. Late in the race, the Navy boat was easily three boat lengths behind. Carr let out an exalted scream, "Yahoo!"

Vales immediately shouted, "It's not over yet. It's not over yet! Focus! Focus! It's not over!" Again, Carr let out a yell. Hartshorn, Johnson, Alex, and Haley followed suit, then everyone— even Daley. Vales was yelling something about control, but his voice was drowned out by the exuberant team. Alex felt the boat move faster as each member, in unspoken unison, increased his speed. Soon the scull was over fifty strokes. Everyone was howling like mad dogs. Even Vales had given up his attempt to regain order and joined the pack. They whisked past the finish line with a collective howl. If you had been in the Navy boat, you would have wanted to kill them. Diriglia thought about reprimanding them, as they rowed and splashed their way to the shoreline, but he was also relieved that the doubt he felt over the past few months, despite his attempts to shake it, were finally put to rest. Princeton Tiger Crew was for real.

With one fist in the air, Diriglia joined the howling as the team rowed the final ten yards to the dock. Once on shore, with little hesitation, the team threw the coxswain into the cold river. Seeing the coach's happiness, the team decided to take advantage of the moment and threw him in as well. Alex's face hurt from smiling. He had been smiling continuously since early in the race. He finally realized that, despite how hard he tried to fight the notion, it was a lot more fun to win. Fuck how you play the game.

XVII

When Alex announced that he had stopped smoking pot, Boder became annoyed.

"I haven't totally quit, Bode," he explained, "I'm just taking a break." Alex wasn't about to tell Boder that he quit smoking for the crew team. He could hardly believe that one himself. It was a selfish thing, really. This team had the potential to be a big winner, and Alex had never experienced a feeling like that before and might never again. While he was growing up, he had won many academic awards in grammar and high school, but the only ones who really gave a damn about those were his parents, maybe. The Olympic team had already talked to Carr and Johnson about tryouts for the upcoming games, and there was a rumor that they had their eyes on other members of the team. Things like that never happened to kids who won the sixth-grade spelling bee. Alex doubted he could accurately express his feelings about this to Boder. After all, Boder was the only guy he knew who subscribed to *High Times*. The thrill of victory was not Boder's thing.

Boder was no fool. He could see through screen doors as well as anyone. He questioned Alex, "Instead of giving up pot and ruining your fun, why don't you give up paddling the puddle with the crew of the Pequod?"

"Crew has little to do with it, Bode."

"Yeah, and I've just been appointed the new Dean of Students."

"OK, maybe I am concerned about its effect on my performance, but I think it might be affecting a lot of other things too. We always talk about your problems, but I don't exactly have the world on a string."

"Example?"

"Okay, how about the fact that, in less than three months, I'll be out of school, possibly forever, and I have absolutely no idea what I'm going to do next. And you know what's even scarier? I have hardly given it any thought."

"So?"

"So!"

"Echo?"

"What the hell am I doing here Bode? This wasn't a free ride. I owe it to my family, and to myself, to make the most of it."

"I think you owe it to yourself to live a little bit and experiment with life."

"Experiment? How about this for one: my senior thesis project? Most people in my major are writing spectacular, analytical essays. What do I end up doing? A one-act extravaganza about bowling! What am I, out of my goddamn mind? I'll be lucky if they don't laugh me out of here."

"Hey, they did it to me, and it's really not that bad."

"It's not just school, either. I'm not dating anyone. I mean, not even casually."

"That's why God gave you hands."

"I'm so depressed about things lately, I don't even do

that. But seriously, I miss being close to someone. I miss Amanda."

"God forbid you should tell her."

Alex ignored Boder's last comment as he continued, "Besides, I do the same thing day in and day out. I row, I go to class, I eat, and I sleep."

"Boy, I wish I didn't have to take a shit every day."

"Yeah, thanks for taking me seriously, Bode. I need to make some changes. I don't think I've had a spectacular existence over the last few months. Hopefully, this is one of many changes I'm going to make. I don't feel like smoking pot for a while, so what? We don't need to make a federal case out of it."

"I think that rowing in the sun has gotten to your brain. You've always been too serious about things, but it's been extra noticeable lately. And I don't mean to compare you with me. I mean, compared to me, Bart Simpson takes life too seriously. But speaking, rather, in comparison to the general population, you have just got to lighten up."

"I guess it's my nature."

"I'll give you fifty-bucks if you miss this afternoon's crew practice."

"No."

"One hundred."

"Bode, I just . . ."

"Two hundred. That's my final offer. Come on, be crazy."

Alex was starting to become angry. He thought it best just to leave. He quickly packed his practice bag and headed out the door. "You know, Bode," Alex remarked, "sometimes I wish you had a little more understanding for the way other people deal with things."

"Xander, if you want to spend your days and nights rowing in a little boat with seven sweaty guys and a midget, that's your prerogative. I was just giving you my point of view. Don't worry, I still love you!"

Alex stared at Boder, tried unsuccessfully to think of a good retort, and then slammed the door as he left the room. To make matters worse for Alex, earlier that day, his faculty advisor read him the riot act about falling behind on writing his play. He hadn't completed a first draft yet, and the completed play was due in five weeks, no exceptions. Alex had to be at the boathouse at seven the next morning for the bus ride to New Brunswick, but he woke at about three am in a cold sweat. He opened his laptop and began typing.

*****

The Princeton - Rutgers meet was always a highlight of the season because of the proximity of the two schools. A mere sixteen miles, straight up Route 27, separated them. Princeton would win the meet—both parties knew it. Rutgers had only won twice in the previous fifteen years, and this year was not going to be the exception. It would be crowded, and more than just a little rowdy.

Rutgers students generally disliked Princeton, much more so than vice-versa, but, when tuition at one school was three times as much as the other, there were bound to be some disparities. The students at the less expensive school were not so fond of the disparities. That year, the crew races were held at Rutgers along the Raritan River, and Princeton was blessed with even nicer weather than they had had at Annapolis. More importantly, there was a northeasterly wind on the lake, giving both teams a bit of aid. As the morning wore on, Rutgers proved to be a more difficult opponent than anticipated. They won the 3V race and, after the seventh man on Princeton's 2V lost grip of his oar with a hundred meters to go, Rutgers won that race as well. There was some mumbling in the crowd that Rutgers might have a chance at winning in the first varsity boat race. Prior to the race, the Rutgers captain cornered Neil Johnson outside the boathouse and warned, "You guys pull any of that hooting and hollering bullshit that I heard about from Navy, and I'll personally shove my oar up your ass, so help me God."

"We'll be as quiet as church mice," Johnson promised.

When the gun went off, Princeton immediately jumped to a quarter boat length lead, but after that, Rutgers was hard to shake. At the halfway mark, Princeton maintained the same lead. Alex was growing concerned. The team's timing was off. The strokes weren't in unison. Alex sensed they were right on the edge of disaster. He knew that if any one of them went further off stroke, that scull was headed for a tailspin. Vales was cool as he tried to get the crew back in rhythm, "Keep it steady. Unison, guys. Unison! Let's get a nice thirty-eight, strokes at three. Here we go, boys! That's it! Better! We got this one!"

The rowing became a little easier. Alex felt the scull pick up speed. Then Alex felt a sharp muscle cramp in his lower back. "Not now!" he moaned. Alex squeezed his eyes shut. If he was alone he might have dived into the water to get away from the agony, but he was not alone. He knew that the pain simply had to be gutted out. Cramping went with the territory. They learned that they just had to row through it, but that was easier said than done. Alex likened it to sitting in a chair reading a book while someone hits you all over with a club. He groaned after each stroke in an effort to release the pain.

Vales wanted to put Rutgers away. "Bring it up, boys! Forty strokes in five!"

For a moment, as Alex increased his stroke, he thought he might pass out. Almost as quickly as it had come, the pain seemed to subside. Alex felt relief and his sweat soaked body could now focus on the task at hand. He heard the rhythm of the oars hitting the water simultaneously and with a clear sense of urgency. Although Alex kept his eyes glued to Daley's back, he sensed they were doing better by the more relaxed tone of Vales voice, "Yes! Yes! Keep it going! We got 'em by six seats! I want to lose these guys!" Alex knew what was coming. It didn't take long. Vales pushed, "How about a ten boys? Let's try and put 'em away. Ready? Two strokes and let's do it! Go!" That was what training was all about. Hours upon hours, days upon days, weeks, months, years, all so the required elements would be in place in those few seconds of intensity. That was the main reason Alex rowed, to test his limitations. For a few seconds in the middle of the power ten, with the veins ripping out of his neck, he would be amongst the most efficient rowers in the world. Vales yelled loudly into the microphone, "Excellent! We got 'em. One and a half lengths! Keep it steady at forty. We are going home!"

The Princeton boat crossed the finish line over two lengths ahead of Rutgers. The cheers from the winning boat were much more subdued than those expressed when they beat Navy. In part that was due to a smaller margin of victory, but, in larger part, to the less than gracious comment made by the Rutgers Captain prior to the start of the race. There was no sense going home with an oar up your ass.

*****

Waking up the next morning, Alex wasn't sure he would be able to get out of bed. Every muscle in his body ached. It was a significant effort to move in the slightest. Nevertheless, he smiled as he remembered the race against Rutgers. He pulled himself up, hunched over, and staggered out of bed and into the hot shower. That was a quirk about the old eating clubs and dormitories on campus: however antiquated, they all had water hot enough to fry a chicken. Alex stood motionless for at least fifteen minutes while the steaming hot water careened off his neck and back. He could almost hear his muscles moan, it felt so good.

It was a little after noon by the time Alex made it downstairs to the dining room where the remnants of what appeared to have been a good brunch were being finished off. He was starving. Since there was no bacon or sausage left, he piled cold scrambled eggs onto his plate and grabbed a bagel upon which he spread the last bit of remaining cream cheese. There were about a dozen people in the dining room, either still finishing brunch or just talking. Javier was sitting alone in a corner, an empty plate and a half-full cup of coffee on the table beside him, reading the sports section of the *New York Times* on his iPad. Alex walked over and asked, "Sticking around awhile?"

"Sure man, take a seat. I heard you guys smoked Rutgers yesterday. Excellent!"

"Yeah, but I'm paying for it today. Feels like I've been

mugged."

"You going soft on me, Man?"

"I'd like to see you try rowing."

"Hell no! Once we row over from Cuba, we're done with that nonsense."

Alex laughed and considered, "Do you ever wonder what it must be like?"

"What are we talking about?"

"Cuba. I mean, you once told me that your grandfather and your dad left in the late fifties by a rickety boat, and that it took a few more years to get your mom and grandmother over. Does it bother you living so close to your parents' homeland, but you've never seen it?"

"Boy, you're really brightening up my Sunday morning."

"Sorry, I've just always wondered what it must be like never being . . ."

"Able to go home?"

"Yes."

"If I was born in a bathroom stall on the New Jersey Turnpike, would I have a desire to go back to see it on a regular basis?"

"Que?"

"The American definition of home is much different than most of the world. Americans are born at home. For many other peoples, home is a place for which they search. Some never find it, while some are more fortunate. Why would I want to go to an island where an eighty-something relic of a dead dictator's baby brother presides, with an iron fist, over people so poor that most have never seen as much food as you have on your plate? My father's family had a home there, once, but it is long gone. His home is Miami. He is happy. I'm not sure where my home is. I don't think I've been there yet."

"Well, the US has started to release sanctions. What if democracy comes back to Cuba?"

"Do you see Americans flocking back to Britain? Perhaps I'll visit someday, as I would Aruba or any other vacation island. You Americans are very susceptible to becoming attached to inanimate things, like where they live and their possessions."

"You think that is a bad thing?"

"I envy it."

Alex looked over at the Mexican help cleaning the table next to them. He ate in silence for the next few minutes.

*****

Alex spent Sunday afternoon finally reading a previous assignment for his drama class. Technically, it was to read two plays by Tony Kushner: *Angels in America, Part One: Millennium Approaches* and *Angels in America, Part Two: Perestroika*. It was obvious that Kushner didn't write this play between college classes and crew practices. This is some damn compelling writing, Alex reflected. What would be the odds, back then, of a play featuring homosexuals and aids winning the Pulitzer Prize? After Alex finished both books, he went downstairs and left them on a coffee table in the Smoking Room. He knew he would never read them again. He didn't have to, because he would never forget them. As the character Harper said in *Perestroika*, "Nothing's lost forever. In this world, there is a kind of painful progress. Longing for what we've left behind and dreaming ahead.”

XVIII

As April progressed, spring took hold. Alex was headed to the center of campus, and the forsythia Alex passed along the stone path were sporting bright, canary-yellow flowers. A small flock of field sparrows, finally heading back to the warming north, pecked at the soft, wet ground in search of a snack.

It wasn't going to be a normal April for Alex. First, he had to finish his thesis by the eighteenth. Then, after a handful of drama classes remaining and a ten-page paper due the first week of May, he would be done, really done. There would be no course cards to complete for the following year, no lotteries for a room at the eating club. Alex's mother had suggested law school or journalism for an advanced degree, but he felt that choice was about whether to become an asshole, or to write about how everyone else is. Regardless, Alex never completed a single graduate school application, which was probably the main reason he was headed to career services to check out job opportunities. In truth, that wasn't going to be any easier than deciding on graduate school. Alex had no idea what he wanted to do.

Zimmy landed a job in the investment banking division of Goldman Sachs. He had attended the on-campus interview, as well as the more intense second interview in

New York, wearing beat up Nikes, wrinkled khaki shorts, a white T-shirt, and a Pharrell-type hat. Maybe his hiring had more to do with the fact that Zimmy could read a company's annual report in under thirty minutes and then recite it back virtually word for word, including the balance sheet and income statements, while pointing out errors and inconsistencies.

Alex bounded down the steps to the entrance of the career services building. It was by far the ugliest building on campus, exemplifying typical, early sixties, bland architecture. Its blandness was only exacerbated by the numerous examples of Collegiate Gothic architecture that surrounded it. Alex entered a small lobby. On the wall, written in small silver letters, was CAREER SERVICES AT PRINCETON UNIVERSITY. Except for a couple of Apple computers, there was nothing dating after nineteen eighty. All drab brown, the waiting area had one small couch and two well-worn chairs. The old, white, stucco ceiling had half a dozen brown stains from leaks. A woman in her fifties was sitting at an oak desk. She was on a telephone call and seemed surprised to see a visitor. She smiled, whispered into the telephone, and hung up. Addressing Alex, she said, "Hi, my name is Ms. Myerson. Can I help you?"

"Maybe. I came to look around."

"Are you a junior?"

"Senior."

"Oh. And you haven't been here before?" There wasn't a hint of consternation in her voice. He could see in her eyes that she was asking these questions to see if she could be of any help, nothing more.

"To be frank, I've kind of blocked the job thing out of my

mind until now."

"Well, considering the date, I've got to say that your mind is a very fine blocker," she smiled.

"Are you going to ask me what type of job I'm looking for?"

"Well, considering that you're a student who walked into my office, and I'm the Assistant Director of Job Placement, it might be something I would think to say."

"I have no idea."

"Come again?"

Alex felt his mind begin to race. He felt like the words were about to spew out of his mouth like an excited three-year-old. He began, "About what I should do, I mean. You see, I'm still undecided about what I want to do. I was thinking of graduate school, but I never got around to the applications. I still might, but not for at least a year or so. So, I'm not sure if I should look for something permanent or temporary. Should I attempt to do something in tech or seek old school? If I . . ."

"OK, I get the picture," Ms. Meyerson interrupted. "You basically have no idea what you want to do or for how long. Correct?"

"Exactly." Alex imagined that this woman must be a perfect mother.

"You've finally come to the right place. This is the epicenter."

"Excuse me?"

Ms. Meyerson smiled and leaned against the corner of her desk. "Why do most people come to Princeton?"

"To get an excellent education."

"Let's have a reality check. Want to try again?"

"To get a good job."

"Close, but they don't want a good job, they want a fantastic job. Whether Princeton is the end of the line, or graduate school is on the agenda, people come here to get a fantastic job. I can list a hundred places where you can get an excellent education, but I would be hard-pressed to name one that carries greater weight with employers than the school you currently attend." Alex thought about Zimmy getting the Wall Street job while dressed in shorts and a T-shirt. Maybe she had a point.

"You're saying that I can get a job anywhere?"

"Let's not get carried away just yet. Are your grades in the top third of the class?"

"Probably top ten percent."

"OK, now we can get carried away. You can get a job anywhere."

"But don't you see, that doesn't really solve my problem. I have absolutely no idea what I want to do."

"I wish I had that problem."

"Come again?"

"You know what I wanted to be when I graduated college? Keep in mind, I didn't attend Princeton. There weren't many women here when I was applying for school, and my family wouldn't have been able to afford it anyway. I went to a small, liberal arts school in Upstate New York, Wells College. I bet you never heard of it."

"True."

"I certainly am rambling on here. Anyway, take a guess at what my ambition was."

Alex couldn't help himself. "Assistant Director of Job Placement?"

"Very cute," she responded, "I wanted to be an architect. The environment was a big issue when I was in school, and I thought I could be a new breed of environmentally conscious builder. My dad wasn't so hot for the idea, especially since it meant graduate school. I think he was hoping I would meet some guy and settle down in a house, not build it, but he never complained. I went to Berkeley for grad school. Although I had majored in architecture in college, graduate school was much different. There was very little altruism involved. Most of the students wanted to build things for profit, not save the world.

"In one group project, I oversaw designing the bathrooms in a fictional new football stadium. My presentation included ideas on recycling the toilet water, river safe hand soap, and reduction in toilet paper usage. The field guy, the seat guy, and the concession guy got rave reviews from the professor. The professor had only one comment after my presentation. He told me to go spend twenty hours in a stall at the Oakland-Alameda County Coliseum and to come back with a 'bathroom that's not a fantasy.' He said, 'We go in there to do our duty, nothing more and nothing less. Just build a stall, Miss Myerson. Just build a stall.' That moment devastated my ambitions in the architectural field. I tried to hang on for the year because I didn't want to tell my father, who worked six days a week in the deli of a supermarket, that a large part of his savings had been wasted, but I wasn't that good of an actress. My grades plummeted, and I flunked out.

"And?" Alex asked, seriously curious.

"When I had the courage to go back home I was convinced my father was going to read me the riot act and serve me a litany of 'I told you so's.' Instead, he said nothing for a while, then finally, after what seemed like hours, he spoke. 'Fantastic!' was all he said. 'Excuse me?' I replied. 'My life is in ruins, I fully expected you to take my head off, and all you can say is fantastic?' 'Yes, my lil' darlin',' he always called me his lil' darlin', 'it is fantastic. For one thing, and it is an important thing, you are sitting here in front of me, still living and breathing. Second, and almost as important, you saved yourself a lot of grief. You caught on that architecture was not what you thought it was. I know you don't like to hear this, but you're just a baby. You could make three or four more mistakes like that, and it would not matter.' My father was, however, quick to note that the next three or four mistakes would be on my tab. 'But somewhere down the line,' he continued, 'it will matter. At some point, if you're unhappy you won't be able to do anything about it. Believe me, I know.' "

"I've met a lot of smart people, academically speaking, since my father said that to me thirty years ago, but, to date, no one else has told me anything so brilliant. Leave it to my father, a man whose biggest daily problem was too much fat on the top round, to straighten me out. I'm not going to take up your valuable time with what I've done over the years but, apart from the last few months, it hasn't been spent in this dungeon-turned-employment-office. I thought I would spend some time here to let kids know it is a big world out there. I apologize for using the word "kid," but that's what you are. I don't mean it as an insult, rather, as a tremendous asset. Try something different, maybe something you have no idea about. If it doesn't work out, try again, and maybe again, while you can. Forget about the permanent or temporary job distinction. Something you try as a part-time lark may become your lifelong passion. Something for which you go to graduate school, may become only a blip on the screen of your life."

Ms. Myerson suddenly stopped talking and put a hand to her mouth, her face in a state of an exaggerated exclamation. "I am sorry," she flushed, "You didn't come here for a lecture. Goodness knows there are plenty of those around here."

Alex smiled. He felt as if he had known this person a long time. "No, it's OK," he insisted, "You are very helpful. If I want to poke around and see what's out there, how do you suggest I start?"

"Try one of those computers on the desk over there. It will give you a listing of employers seeking Princeton graduates. You can also find information on virtually every company in the U.S., as well as many abroad. That way, if they have not come to us, you can go to them." Alex stared deeply in her face. Her eyes were a fiery blue. He could see that there were a thousand stories held within, each worth listening to. While she had a lot to give, there would be many to give to. Alex thought it best not to be a hog.

"Thanks."

"If you need me, just holler."

Ms. Myerson went back to her desk. A little less daunted, and much more comfortable than when he first walked in, Alex went over to a computer. The number and quality of jobs offered to Princeton seniors, even at this late date, were remarkable. There were jobs listed from Wall Street to Wakayama. Businesses from all over the globe were beckoning for the best and the brightest. Alex's eyes caught a job description from Facebook, personally written by Mark

Zuckerberg, looking for the company's next superstar. He may have dropped out of college, but he sure knew where to look for help.

After about an hour, Alex was going to call it quits for the day, when clicking the enter button brought him to a job description very different from the rest. Previous descriptions ran for pages. They listed the company's history and philosophy, the job opening and required qualifications. They were so detailed they practically included the number of urinals at corporate headquarters. This description, if it could be called that, was certainly different. In fact, it contained only five sentences:

Former Princeton graduate seeking
recent Princeton graduate
for employment. Maximum job
length: eighteen months. Substantial
travel required. Must have some photographic
ability, knowledge
of computers, and a loud voice (former
Princeton grad hard of hearing).
Apply via regular mail to: Mr. George Applegate,
167 Bygone Road,
Sewickley Hills, Pennsylvania 15143.

Alex printed the screen, walked over to Ms. Myerson, and handed it to her. "Any more to this?" Alex asked. Ms. Myerson checked her records. She pulled out a file with a page or two in it.

"Doesn't appear to be much else. Just that this Applegate fellow is an alumnus, Class of 1958. If you're interested, he also has the BK code after his name."

"The BK code?"

"Big Kahuna. A heavy hitter. A significant contributor. Get it?"

"I guess so. What do you think about this job?"

"I don't know what to think about the job. I can see that it has obviously caught your attention, though, and that would be enough for me to find out more. I suggest you sit down and write Mr. Applegate a brief description about yourself. We'll mail it out and see what happens."

"Don't you think I should put a resume together?"

"I think you should let him know who you are. Why don't you take the time to write him a letter?"

Alex couldn't remember the last time he had written a letter. "I've got nothing to lose, right?" he pondered.

"Except maybe ignorance," Ms. Myerson shot back.

Alex sat back down at the table and stared at the computer screen. About twenty minutes later, with the screen still empty, Alex realized why people emailed resumes instead of offering more personalized descriptions. It was easier. Finally, in a hail of impatience and frustration, Alex quickly typed the following:

Dear Mr. Applegate:

I am a graduating senior at Princeton University. I read your job description while in our placement office. Your brief description indicates that the employment includes computer work, photography, and extensive traveling— all of which I have a great interest and enthusiasm in. Details beyond that are absent, thus I am without full understanding as to exactly what type of job you are offering. Finding this intriguing, I am interested in pursuing the matter further.

I will start by saying that I am not afraid of demanding work. I am hopeful that the job you are offering can give me an opportunity to "get myself together" regarding my future. As you likely know, it can sometimes be difficult to grasp the real world within the ivied walls of this great University. If a mutual fit, I can assure you that I would perform the duties of the job to my fullest ability.

I can tell you that when it comes to career planning, I am more ignorant than most around this campus, many of whose careers have already been well-charted. I'd like to convey, in a manner that does not sound too pompous, that I am very bright, love to learn, and can follow directions quite well

It has taken me quite a while to write this brief description, yet, suddenly, I feel as if I could go on for hours. With that thought, I think it best to leave you my contact information:

Alexander T. Williams

c/o O'Neill Eating Club
53 Prospect Street
Princeton, New Jersey 08540
(609) 683-7777
alexander.t.williams@princeton.edu

Thank you for your time and consideration. I hope to hear from you soon.

Sincerely,
Alexander T. Williams
Princeton University '15

Alex placed the letter in an envelope, addressed it, and handed it to Ms. Myerson.

"Please take this before I actually read it and change my mind."

"I'm sure it's fine."

"Thanks. I want you to know that I'll remember our meeting for a long time."

"So will I."

Ms. Myerson held out her hand and Alex shook it. Alex left the office and cut across the center of campus on his way back to O'Neill. He found himself on Canon Green, just behind Nassau Hall. In the center of the green was a revolutionary war canon. It was buried up to the breach to prevent Rutgers students from stealing it as part of a long-standing fight for its possession. Opposite Nassau Hall, across Cannon Green, were Clio Hall and Whig Hall. They were built over one hundred twenty-five years ago in the Ionic Greek style and were home to the debating societies.

Additionally, West College, Dodge, and the majestic Gothic Chapel were within view. During his nearly four years at the University, he had never felt as much a part of it as he did at that moment. It was beyond beautiful. Before, he often felt more like an outsider looking in. Now, Mother Princeton was offering her hand, and Alex realized that he would never be able to totally let go. He was a tiger.

*****

One evening later that week, Alex sensed that Boder was up to something, as he had sat through dinner with a smirk on his face. Even Zimmy, who never notices anything, noticed. "Hey, Boder," Zimmy baited, "what gives with the secretive smile?"

"No Zim, my boy. I was just imagining that I was one of the few lucky women in this world who had the once-in-a-lifetime opportunity to touch your schlong."

"Bode," Zimmy continued, "as a close friend, I'd let you be one of the few males whom I would indulge."

Alex interrupted, "Bode, I've noticed it too. You're looking a little bit smug."

"A guy isn't even allowed to be happy around here? OK, I'll be as morbid as the rest of you walking dead." Boder finished his meal with the most serious of faces, despite the laughter and various small objects being thrown in his direction.

Later, upstairs in their suite, Alex questioned, "OK double-o-seven, what gives?"

Sitting on the couch, Boder offered Alex the same sly smile he had on downstairs in the dining room. He reached into his pocket, pulled out a set of keys on a plain gold ring, and jangled them over his head. "Just call me Bilbo Baggins," Boder said playfully.

"Why is that?"

"I have discovered the magic ring."

"Listen, Bilbo, I'm not Gollum, don't worry. Give it to me straight. I can keep a secret."

"I was walking behind Sophia Yau on the stairs this afternoon. She was on her way to a rehearsal at the Academy of Music in Philly. The keys fell out of her open pocket book. Guess she was in a rush. Anyway, I picked them up."

"And . . .?"

"And I figured, why deter the musical genius from her train of thought. When she comes back late tonight, I'll just have them by her door with a note that I found them on the steps."

"You're not thinking of . . ."

"Like a tracking bloodhound, my friend."

"Have you gone wacko? They'll have your head, not to mention a couple of other parts."

"How will they know?"

"I have five good answers to that question: Rena, Rebecca, Elaine, Stephanie and Suzanne, or have you forgotten the roommates?"

Boder slowly rose from the couch. "Xander, you disappoint me. Just because they kicked me out of school, that doesn't imply I don't do my research. It just so happens that Sophia invited the entire 'we-don't-need-any-penis' team to go with her in the limo to Philadelphia. So, shall we begin our journey?"

Although he was trying to show restraint, Alex had to

admit that he was very curious about what lay beyond THE door. Alex's thoughts were broken by a knock. Zimmy walked in before being acknowledged.

"Hey, dudes."

"Come on in!" Boder said facetiously. "Please, don't make us get up to answer the door."

"What are you guys up to? I'm bored."

Boder held up the keys, teasing, "This should un-bore you."

"Keys to Hannah Davis' swimming pool?"

"Better."

"Keys to Hoagie Haven?"

"Um, close, but I still have to say better."

"Wow, better than models and munchies. This must be really good."

"I hold in my hand the keys to the impenetrable tomb."

For a few moments, Zimmy was lost in thought. Suddenly his eyes opened wide. He made a fist and pointed his thumb in the direction of another suite on the third floor. He marveled, "You don't mean you've obtained the keys to the lesbo lounge?"

"Precisely!"

Zimmy bowed down. "You are my god! My one and only god."

Alex had had just about enough of both. "Hey, will you two please get a grip. You guys need to bring your imaginations back from Jupiter."

"Don't you think it's been a little weird living next to them all this time?" Boder asked.

"Boder, what the hell have we seen?"

"Nothing. That's my point."

Alex shook his head. "Bode, if this is about our discussion last week on not smoking pot, I must admit, you're doing a decent job convincing me to start again. Right now, I feel like rolling a fat one and trying to forget about this conversation. "

Boder continued unperturbed, "Don't you think it's unusual that we have six chicks living in there, forty percent of O'Neill's live-in, female population, and nothing ever goes on in there?"

Alex stared at them in disbelief, trying to catch some glimmer of rationality, but it was useless. "You're talking sex here, aren't you?" he asked.

"Unless it's a good pizza, what else is there?" Zimmy asked. Boder nodded his head in agreement.

Alex took a deep breath and began, "Okay Masters & Johnson, hear me out. I'll admit that it's a little odd that we never see anyone but the actual occupants go in or out of the suite, but we also must admit that we're talking about a highly unusual situation. These girls are all unique. They're superstars in their respective fields of study. Might it be possible that they've all agreed to keep their personal lives private? Would that be such a terrible thing?"

Boder and Zimmy stared at each other in apparent deep thought. After about twelve seconds, Zimmy broke the silence. "I think they are all carpet munchers."

"So do I," Boder replied.

With that, Boder hopped off the couch and proceeded with Zimmy out the door.

"Damn!" Alex moaned, and followed.

Boder quietly opened the door, and all three peeked inside, their heads stretching through the door as if from an old Three Stooges movie. Once inside, Zimmy slipped on the carpet runner in the narrow hallway, falling flat on his back and evoking nervous laughter from the others. Halfway down the hall, they came upon a door, half ajar—the entrance to the first of three bedrooms. Glancing inside, Alex concluded that the Chinese and Japanese books and artwork belonged to Susan Reilly. There was no clear theme emerging from the knickknacks that occupied the other half of the room. Alex figured the other roommate must be Rena Satz, the anthropology major. Continuing down the hallway, past the bathroom, they entered the living room. On either side were bedroom doors. "Ah, mission control!" Boder exclaimed. The living room contained a couch, two chairs, a flat screen and an old, inexpensive coffee table. The only things that could be considered personal were two photographs that hung on the wall. One photo featured Sophia Yau with President Obama after a White House recital. The other featured Elaine Freedman and Mary Cheney hugging at some March in Washington. A book entitled *Catalogue of the Andrew Alpern Collection of Drawing Instruments* laid on the coffee table.

"Not much going on here," Boder said. "Onward, gentlemen."

Boder led the way into one of the adjoining bedrooms. In sharp contrast to the orderly bedroom off the hallway, in this room, paintings and sculptures, in various stages of completion, were scattered about. A blouse was draped over the lampshade of a floor lamp, and a dusty, brass statue of Vivaldi was prominently displayed on a desk cluttered with musical scores, many handwritten. "Sophia and Stephanie's room, no doubt," Zimmy stated the obvious.

"Gentlemen we have to check out the certified lesbo room before we do anything else," Boder replied.

Even Alex nodded in agreement. The trio crossed the living room to the other door. A bumper sticker on the door read, "Don't blame God . . . She had nothing to do with it." With great anticipation, they opened the door. They walked in and looked around. Alex sat on the bed covered by a plain, dark red bedspread. There wasn't even a single picture on the wall. On Rebecca Harrison's desk, there was nothing but a five by seven framed picture of her and a boyfriend on some beach. On a shelf near Elaine Freedman's desk, hanging by a piece of scotch tape, was a small, yellow paged reprint of the Emily Dickinson poem, "There Is Another Sky." Boder opened and closed each draw of the dresser on Elaine's side of the room. Zimmy opened the closet, unsure what he was looking for. He found clothes hung on hangers, and shoes covering the floor. Alex looked at Boder, who had the expression of a teenager whose mother found beer bottles underneath his bed. Alex wasn't going to let him off the hook. "Hey, Bode, you think they carry on human sacrifices in here?" He quipped.

Zimmy joined in. "Yeah, Bode, this place is freaking me out!"

"Don't let anyone fool you. There is more than meets the eye my friends," Boder replied, still trying to appear upbeat.

Suddenly, footsteps were heard outside the room. The three stared at each other, frozen in utter terror. Silence ensued for a few seconds. Then, ever so slowly, the bedroom door opened. The individual at the door wore brown leather shoes, no socks, blue jeans, a black and white striped polo shirt, with the buttons unbuttoned and the back of the white collar up. "Sheik, you fuck!" Boder said in a louder than intended whisper. Alex fell back on the bed.

"Christ!" Zimmy said. Still standing, he put his hands on his knees and bent his head in toward his feet, breathing deeply.

"Ah! I had an idea something was up," Sheik commented. "I noticed the door to this suite cracked open. I'd never seen that before, so I couldn't resist taking a peak."

Boder turned toward Alex and admonished, "Well, Mr. Ethics, you seem to be the only one around who had any sense that a little visit in here wasn't a promising idea."

"Yeah, Bode, I guess I was wrong," conceded Alex, "but it sure was funny how we all crapped ourselves when we thought Sheik could have been one of the girls."

Sheik interrupted the banter, "Dudes, what did you find?"

Alex stood up, walked over to Sheik, and placed one of his hands on each of Sheik's arms. He teased, "Sheik, it's unbelievable! Possibly even too vulgar and disgusting to explain." Alex walked over to Elaine Freedman's desk, pulled the Dickinson poem off the wall, and returned to Sheik. "Just look at this filth." Sheik looked at the poem and then looked back at Alex as if he had two heads.

"Just ignore him, Sheik," Boder interrupted, "he's going through a morality crisis."

"But no action, eh?" Sheik asked.

"Well, we didn't really explore the other rooms too carefully," Zimmy asserted.

"Forget it, gentlemen," Boder resigned. "I'll give it to Alex . . . there's nothing here. It would have been more interesting to break into a convent." Just then, they heard a basketball bouncing in the hallway. Alex would always remember that precise moment because it was the only time he'd ever seen Sheik lose his very high level of composure. He looked like he'd come face-to-face with Satan, and there was no way out.

"Excuse us! Anyone here?" BT's voice echoed.

Boder exhaled and called, "In here, asshole!"

BT appeared in the doorway, dressed in a bright yellow sweat suit. Javier appeared behind him, dressed in jeans and a ripped T-shirt. "Hey, thanks for the warm welcome!" BT said.

"Christ, did we put ads in the paper about this?" Alex asked. "What the hell are you two doing here?"

"Why? Are we in your way?" Javier retorted.

"Actually," BT added, "we were going out to shoot some hoops and came up to see if any of you sneaks wanted to join us. The suite door was wide open, so we figured something was up. So, you guys find anything nasty?"

As everyone shook their heads in the negative, BT and Javier appeared puzzled.

"People," Zimmy said, "this is one potential Broadway show that is closing on opening night."

"Amen," Alex agreed.

On the way out, Zimmy tripped again over a locked trunk in the corner of the living room. A six-volume book set entitled *The Story of Juliette,* and a small, black, onyx statue of the author tumbled off. Zimmy hastily placed the books and the statute back on top of the trunk. Neither he nor the others noticed the three-inch tip of a leather whip sticking out of the side.

XIX

Graduation was creeping ever closer, and Alex had already submitted his gown measurements. He had also received a letter back from Mr. Applegate. The letter was handwritten in as neat a handwriting as Alex had ever seen. It read:

April 10, 2015

Mr. George Applegate has reviewed your application, brief and rather confusing as it was. Enclosed, please find a plane ticket to Pittsburgh, American Airlines Flight 1929, leaving Tuesday morning, the 18th, at 8:00 am, and returning that evening, flight 437, at 10:35 pm.

It is understood that you row a boat or something of that sort. Your coach will be notified, and you will be excused from practice.

Mr. Applegate looks forward to the pleasure of your company.

Very truly yours,
Mrs. Mildred Stone

Executive Assistant to William Applegate

P.S. A jacket and tie will be proper attire for dinner.

Alex looked at the postmark to see if maybe one of his buddies got wind of his job application and sent this letter as a joke. Although it was marked "Pittsburgh, Pa," Alex didn't fully believe the authenticity of the letter until later that afternoon when Diriglia pulled him into his second-floor office. "Williams," he boomed, "early this morning, I got a call from President Delectus about you."

"The President of the University? About me?"

"Am I speaking Chinese here?"

"Sorry."

"You're excused from practice next Tuesday. Seems that the biggest alumni honcho of them all wants to see you."

"You mean the Applegate interview?"

"President Delectus did mention some kind of fruit. All I know is that I've never had this happen before. We're going for a national championship here, and I'm getting demands from above that screw me all up!"

"Sorry, coach. If you want, I'll call Mr. Applegate and see if I can re—"

"No! The way Delectus sounded, if you're not on that plane when you're supposed to be, we'll be rowing in a paddleboat for Christ's sake. Most importantly, keep your mind totally on Penn and Columbia this weekend.

"Don't worry sir, I will." Alex left Diriglia's office smiling and thinking about the small world the coach lived in.

That Saturday, the team headed for the University of

Pennsylvania. Princeton would compete against Columbia and Penn in the Childs Cup Race. When held in Philadelphia, this was one of Alex's favorite races. Known as Boathouse Row, fifteen boathouses lined up along the Schuylkill River, none less than one hundred years old. The river provided a much more challenging current than Carnegie Lake and a spectacular view of the city. The race would begin north of the boathouses, and there would be one bridge to contend with, the Strawberry Mansion bridge, but, otherwise, it was a straight shot. The race would end in front of a large grandstand, which, due to the beauty of the surroundings and the deep race history of the river, normally drew a larger crowd than one might expect for a regular season, college crew event.

The early portion of the race went as anticipated. Within the first five-hundred-meters, both Penn and Princeton quickly outdistanced Columbia. The Penn team was a little harder to shake than Princeton had anticipated. As the boat approached the final leg, Alex could hear the crowd along Boathouse Row getting louder. Out of the corner of his left eye, Alex could see that Penn appeared to be neck and neck. Alex caught a glimpse of his water-soaked sneakers. His ankles were blue. It was a strange feeling to have cold feet while the remainder of his body poured out sweat, but Alex felt good and he was ready for the closing sprint. Alex's introspection was broken by the shrill yell of the coxswain, "It's all even! Come on gents, we want this one! In three strokes let's bring it to forty-one!" Alex could vaguely hear the Pennsylvania coxswain barking similar commands. This is it, he thought. Alex felt confident. The movement of the boat was smooth, increasing its speed with no ill effects.

"Come on, boys! They're still with us! Drive!" For a moment, Alex thought about how good it would feel to throw Vales into the drink at the end of the race. Alex felt the boat surge forward, as though they were hardly touching the water. "I have their stroke!" Vales yelled, meaning that the rower in the stroke position of the Pennsylvania boat was directly across from him. Penn was winning. Alex's heart pumped even faster. Princeton had not been behind yet this year. Alex nervously wondered how his mind and body would react to defeat. He must not have been alone in this thought, because the entire boat seemed to pause. Even Vales grew quiet.

"Fuck Penn!" Alex heard a voice yell. It was his own.

Vales took the cue. "This one is ours! Forty-five in three. Let's do it!" The boat surged forward with increasing speed as if on autopilot. "We're even! Give me ten tough ones! Drive!" Alex dug in for the ten hard strokes, his shoulder muscles now screaming. Grunts of pain echoed throughout the boat, and Alex's eyes blurred. "Way enough!" Vales called out, the signal that they had crossed the finish line. Alex had no idea who had won. He glanced toward the Pennsylvania boat. It was about a quarter boat length behind. "Yes!" an exuberant Vales exclaimed. Then Alex leaned forward, hugged Daley's sweaty back, and yelled with joy. Even amidst the exaltation, Alex felt sympathy for the Pennsylvania team, as their boat cruised, aimless, with their members' heads hung in utter exhaustion and despair.

As Alex was walking into the boathouse, wanting to take a shower, a sportswriter from the *Philadelphia Inquirer* approached and asked if Alex felt the team had a good chance at finishing the season undefeated. In disbelief, Alex looked at the reporter, who was holding a small pad and pencil and eagerly waiting for a reply "I think we can do it," Alex claimed. After appearing on page eight in the next day's sport section, Alex's genius comment would be the subject of more than one remark at the following Sunday brunch.

*****

Later that evening, Alex received a telephone call from A-1 Limousine, asking him what time he wanted them to arrive on Tuesday morning. "How do you know I'm going away on Tuesday morning?" Alex asked. "I never called you guys."

"It's been requested by the office of a Mr. Applegate."

Alex had a feeling of happiness mixed with concern. He feared that this guy, Applegate, might not be so impressed with the product of his efforts. Applegate was spending quite a bit of time and incurring quite an expense, while arranging for Alex's delivery. "The plane leaves at ten after seven, so I guess six o'clock is fine."

"Six o'clock! Who do you think we're sending, Jeff Gordon? We're gonna need at least an hour to get the airport, not to mention that you need time to check luggage, clear security, and getting to the plane. Five-fifteen at the latest."

"One of these days, I'm going to get some sleep," Alex mumbled into the phone.

"Excuse me?"

"Five-fifteen is fine." Alex hung up in disgust.

Tuesday morning the alarm went off at four-thirty, an hour earlier than his normal wake up for crew practice. It was painful. He had barely tied the yellow, Vineyard Vines necktie that Amanda had given him and was putting his arm into a recently dry-cleaned jacket, when the doorbell rang. He hurried to answer the door before someone else woke up and wanted to kill him. The caller from A-1 Limousine had been right: New Jersey might be the only state where you can hit traffic at five-thirty in the morning. Alex made his flight with little time to spare.

"Would you like some coffee?" the stewardess asked.

"Can I have it intravenously?" Alex teased. The stewardess didn't find his attempt at early morning humor the least bit funny. Alex wondered what the applicants who didn't get that job must have been like.

When the plane landed at Pittsburgh International, a chauffeur was waiting for Alex in a Bentley Mulsanne. Whatever happened from this point on, Alex was confident he would at least have a story to tell. The car drove northwest on Ohio River Boulevard to Sewickley, about twelve miles outside of Pittsburgh, proper. It seemed to Alex that this understated downtown, comprised of expensive stores and restaurants, surrounded by rolling hills and very large homes, was Pennsylvania's answer to his home state's Greenwich.

After taking a maze of turns, the Bentley finally approached a wrought iron gate that slowly opened as the automobile approached. After driving about a quarter mile on a cobblestone road, the car turned a corner, revealing the most spectacular house Alex had ever seen. The Bentley pulled into a circular driveway and stopped in front of the portico. At the center of the portico was a large fountain, featuring a statue of Venus. The facade of the house, made entirely from hand-cut blocks of Laurel Hill sandstone, was enormous. The dark grey of the English, hand-sawed, slate roof, complimented by periodic German copper domes and gutters, thrust itself against the blue sky as far as Alex's eyes could see.

As the driver exited the car with the intention of opening Alex's door, Alex yelled that he would get it himself. The driver nodded in agreement but rushed to open the door anyway. They went to the humongous, dark oak doors, and the chauffeur knocked. After a brief time, a man wearing a black tuxedo appeared. An honest-to-goodness butler, Alex thought, almost wetting himself with amusement. Alex had never met an actual butler before. If he introduced himself as "Jives," Alex decided he was simply going to turn around and run home to Princeton. It was starting to be too much.

Alex entered a short hallway that led to a marble foyer, where the butler asked him to have a seat. Alex looked around. On the walls hung paintings, some of which he recognized from his sophomore art class. There was a Monet, a Renoir, a Gauguin, and two Degas. Alex swallowed hard as he suspected these were not reproductions. From his left, he heard the clicking of heals approaching. Arriving at his side, he found a redheaded woman in her late sixties, short, heavyset, sporting glasses, and wearing quite a bit of make-up. She smiled warmly, held out her hand, and greeted, "Mr. Williams, we're so glad you could make it. My name is Mrs. Stone, Mr. Applegate's assistant. How was your flight?"

"Right on time."

"Excellent!" replied Mrs. Stone without any evidence of the phony interest Alex assumed had to be there. "Please, follow me. Mr. Applegate is awaiting you on the patio."

Mrs. Stone led Alex through a maze of hallways. Each room they passed looked more spectacular than the last. Finally, Alex found himself in a study, which was at least fifty by seventy-five feet. Thousands of books filled dark mahogany shelves. With a quick glance, Alex noticed that quite a few of the books were about anthropology and geography. Scattered throughout the room, were items from around the world. Alex felt as though he was in a museum, not someone's home. His feet sunk deeply into a large thick Aubusson rug. Mrs. Stone pressed one of many buttons on a small, black panel atop a large, mahogany desk. White, satin curtains that hung behind the desk opened immediately. The curtains had hidden two floor-to-ceiling windowpanes, which were separated by matching, glass French doors.

Were Alex not preoccupied with what would come next, he would have noticed that the view was nothing less than spectacular. Beyond the glass windows, were at least fifty acres of meticulously landscaped and groomed property. A stream, a small lake, and even a humming waterfall glistened in the early day sun. About six acres, smack in the center of the yard, contained various floral gardens that would have done any botanical garden proud. The patio, which stretched beyond both the left and right windowpanes, was made entirely of white, Yugoslavian travertine marble and encompassed two levels. To the right, it ended, finally, at the light blue waters of a large oval infinity pool, accented by an exact replica of Michelangelo's statue of Bacchus.

Alex noticed little of this for, just outside the French doors, seated next to a small glass table shaded by a white umbrella, littered only with a pitcher of ice water, a half-full glass, and a pad and pencil, was a white-haired man in a wheelchair. A tartan wool blanket covered the man's legs. He wore a navy-blue sport jacket and a yellow, cotton shirt, buttoned to the top. Thick, tortoise shell, horn-rimmed glasses decorating his wrinkled, charcoal grey eyes. Oddly, Alex remembered seeing a recent picture of Johnny Depp wearing a similar pair. The man's white hair, whatever was left, was slicked back. Some strands ran wild, a testament to an old man hell bent on doing things for himself. Amidst the grandeur of what had to be one of the most opulent homes in the country, Alex could do little more than stare at the cripple seated on the porch. In his heart, from the minute his eyes locked onto that tired body, Alex knew that this would be a most interesting meeting.

Mrs. Stone opened one of the doors to the patio. She motioned for Alex to follow as she guided him to the table where Mr. Applegate sat. As she approached from behind, she began to speak, "Mr. Williams is here for his appointment, sir."

"Thank you, Maggie, but I'm not blind yet," he retorted.

"Yes, sir."

Maggie stopped short, and Alex almost bumped into her. "Well, come around son, come around. It will take all day to meet you if you make me turn this wheelchair around." Uncomfortably, but quickly, Alex moved directly in front of Mr. Applegate. Mrs. Stone walked briskly to stand behind Alex.

"That's enough, Maggie. The boy doesn't need a shadow. We can handle it from here."

"Yes, Mr. Applegate. Shall I bring the boy something to drink, sir?"

"Maggie, for Christ's sake, the boy came here to interview for a job, not for a drink." He turned to Alex, "You want a drink, son?"

Alex didn't think it was in his best interest to answer in the affirmative.

"No, thank you, I'm fine."

"Maggie, are we satisfied? May I get on with this now?"

"Yes, Mr. Applegate. I'm leaving," Mrs. Stone acquiesced. Her tone clearly indicated a slightly annoyed understanding.

Mr. Applegate shook his head, but not without a slight smile, as Mrs. Stone walked briskly back into the house. His smile gone, Mr. Applegate looked at Alex. "That woman takes care of me like I'm her own son, but sometimes she just doesn't know when to quit. Take a seat, sir. Please! Take a seat!" Mr. Applegate gestured dramatically with his right hand. Alex was almost mesmerized as he slowly sat down on the wrought iron chair. Suddenly, he popped up again, realizing he'd made a critical error. Alex thrust his right hand out.

"Excuse me for the omission. My name is . . ."

"For God's sake, I know what your name is, Mr. Williams. I'm not that far gone as to forget with whom I'm meeting, although I realize that time will be here soon enough. Probably before you leave, if you and Mrs. Stone have anything to do with it. Now, please, sit, and let's get on with it!" Red faced, Alex sat. "Can I ask why you're here?"

"For the job, sir."

"The name is Applegate. What job?"

"The one for which you placed an ad at Princeton's Student Placement Office."

"What job?" Applegate repeated.

Alex was determined not to get flustered, at least not this early.

"The job with a maximum eighteen-month lifespan. The job with substantial travel. The job that requires some photographic and computer skills, in addition to a loud voice. Other than that, Mr. Applegate, I have absolutely no idea what job."

"In other words, you don't have a job and school is about to end. You have no idea what you are going to do with your life, and you are scared to death. So scared, in fact, that you'll go to a job interview hundreds of miles away, with little idea or concern for what the job is, if you can get something to take the pressure off. Am I right?"

"Not exactly…well, I guess I am more than a bit concerned. I've been going to school for the last sixteen years. I'm slightly terrified of what September will be like, not sitting in a classroom, but I'm also excited. I'm not here because I need this job, Mr. Applegate. I'm sure that if I applied myself over the next few months, I could get some decent job offers. But, to be frank, your ad seemed to offer a little breathing space, and that's what I'm looking for right now. I'm in no hurry to buy black oxfords, dark blue suits, white collared shirts, and sit on a train each morning next to a guy with the same briefcase and haircut. I'm told that may appeal to me some day, but not now. It's hard to explain, but I think I just need to get out and look around awhile."

Mr. Applegate stared at Alex and kept nodding his head. "Maybe Maggie was right," he consented, "have a drink with me."

Alex relaxed. "Coffee would be great, thanks."

"A real drink."

"Alcohol?"

"What other type of real drink is there? Scotch, to be precise."

After living with Boder for four years, no one was likely to shock Alex when it came to the partaking of intoxicants at unusual hours. On more than one occasion over the past few years, Alex had indulged in a few early morning drinks. These were mostly a result of not sleeping and continuing a good party from the previous evening. Certainly, he could have a morning shot or two with an old man and at least a few hours' sleep under his belt. However, the question at this moment was how to properly answer Mr. Applegate's question. Alex didn't know whether he should play the straight arrow or go with the flow, but this question only plagued him for a moment. His immediate thought was to say "no thank you," but he heard the words "why not?" leave his lips.

"Atta boy," Mr. Applegate said as he smiled widely. From the pocket of his robe, he pulled out a gadget that contained a handful of multicolored buttons. Mr. Applegate pressed the green one. There was no sound, however, moments later, the butler, who had answered the door when Alex arrived, appeared. The butler, black and not much younger than Mr. Applegate, nodded slightly in Alex's direction before focusing his full attention on the man in charge. "Maurice, a bottle of Macallan Forty and two glasses, if you please." Maurice nodded and left the room. Even given the somewhat formal nature of the situation, body language made it obvious that there was more than a fleeting relationship between the two men. Mr. Applegate confirmed Alex's observation.

"Met Maurice in 1972. Actually, Maurice met me. I was driving home from a Rotary function in downtown Pittsburgh late one evening, three sheets to the wind. They say that after I fell asleep, I veered off Allegheny Avenue and took out two lampposts, six garbage cans, and a fire hydrant. I also sideswiped the legs of some poor drunk before finally crashing into the first floor of an apartment building. The wino managed to crawl to the burning car and pulled me out before it exploded. I woke up in the hospital about two days later with about two hundred stitches, three broken ribs, and a punctured lung. I had my people track down the poor bastard who saved my life. A few days later, a very unkempt guy, in piss stained pants, was brought up to my hospital room. Although I questioned myself after seeing the him, I kept a vow made to myself. I offered the guy a job for the rest of his life, plus a couple of million dollars for retirement or when I croaked, whichever came first—as long, of course, as my death was not by his hands."

Maurice came back with the scotch and two sparkling glasses.

"Ah, here is that poor bastard now!"

Maurice looked at Mr. Applegate with mock discontent. He spoke in Alex's direction, "This old coot telling stories again?"

"Don't 'old coot' me, you black, old fool!"

Alex tried not to let his worry show. He could feel his muscles relax when both Maurice and Mr. Applegate broke out in laughter. After Maurice left, Mr. Applegate poured two good-sized drinks and continued, "Maurice has been taking care of me ever since that day, but he got the raw end of the deal. I've lived too long, and I'm not the easiest guy in the world to be around, you know?"

"Never would have guessed that," Alex replied in fake sincerity.

"Glad to see that Princeton is still teaching that polite bullshit, Mr. Williams. It will take you a long way." Mr. Applegate raised his glass in salute. Alex did the same. Mr. Applegate quickly downed the amber colored liquid and, with a look of quiet satisfaction, placed the empty glass on the table. Alex mimicked Mr. Applegate. The whiskey was so smooth that the anticipatory cringe on his face proved totally unnecessary. Surprised by the superior taste, Alex smiled as he placed his glass on the table. "We aren't drinking Wild Turkey here, you know," Mr. Applegate laughed as he poured them both another round. "Enough idle chit chat. Quoting Sir William Schwenck Gilbert, who found some fame in the musical theatre business, 'The meaning doesn't matter if it's only idle chatter of a transcendental kind.' So, first, let me say that I appreciate you coming. Although I'm old, and Princeton was mighty different when I was there, I do have some idea of what goes on there today. I have always maintained very close ties with the University. You are a product of where you've been, you know. I know that you are one of the best and brightest amongst the best and brightest." Mr. Applegate picked up a manila file that was sitting on the empty chair next to him. He waved it briefly in the air and continued, "Your academic record is truly impressive." Mr. Applegate noticed that Alex appeared taken aback by the fact that a copy of his Princeton record was in a stranger's hands. "Mr. Williams, please, don't be alarmed. Someday, give a hundred million dollars to a

University and you, too, will be able to call in a favor."

"To be frank, Mr. Applegate, I find it a little disconcerting that someone can look into my background without my explicit consent."

"Disconcerting?" Mr. Applegate let out a low laugh. "Well, Mr. Williams, I apologize for making you feel that way, I sincerely do. But, unless you get used to it, you are going to be disconcerted most of your life. TRW already knows more about you than your mother does. Bank of America? Google? Facebook? They could write a better autobiography about you than you. Become famous, or powerful, or make a remark against the government, and someone will have a file on you thicker than the Bible. Don't kid yourself. In any event, take the complement. You did a superb job at Princeton."

Alex decided to let the matter drop. Besides, Mr. Applegate was right, he was kind of flattered. "Thank you, sir."

"So, you belong to O'Neill?"

"Yes, sir."

"That place was a shithouse when I went to school there. I was in Elm. Elm was tops at that time, and I understand it's still doing very well."

"That is a matter of opinion, sir. Besides, O'Neill has come a long way since you were there," Alex said defensively.

"You mean, since Hershfeld gave your club all that money?"

"More or less."

"He was a piece of work, that son of a bitch, Morty."

"You know of him?"

"Know of him? Son, Morty was my roommate during my freshman and sophomore years, '50 to '52. He was one of very few Jews who we had in the school back then. Being Jewish and poor at Princeton in the fifties was about as common as being a black Grand Wizard in the KKK. No way was he getting into Elm, or most other clubs for that matter. But he was a good Jew. Smartest person I ever met, and I've met thousands of very smart people. He had a big heart, too. He would have given you anything he had . . . if he only had anything. I'll never forget the first day of school. I called my father and told him about my new roommate. When he heard the name Hershfeld, he told me to get a new roommate or get the hell out and come home. He said he didn't send me to Princeton to sleep with a bagel. I was upset and didn't know what to do, as I had never disobeyed my father. Embarrassed, I told Morty I was going to have to request a room change. He laughed and told me, 'well you know, I can also be known as Richard Huntington, III.' I smiled back.

"Over the next two years at school, every Thursday evening, I would call my father from the one telephone in our building. I would always put Huntington on the line to say hello. Sometimes they would spend hours talking about politics, sports, or whatever. It amazed me because, in my life, I don't think I'd ever had more than a ten-minute conversation with my father. My father didn't catch on until graduation weekend when he came for his first and only visit. He was really interested in meeting 'that Huntingdon fella.' It became obvious to me that no amount of excuses for Morty's absence was going to discourage him. I arranged a breakfast meeting, between Morty's family and mine, at a long-gone restaurant named the Baltimore Dairy Lunch. We called it the Balt. It wasn't Kosher or anything, but, if Morty's family wanted to eat that day, there was not much choice in Princeton back then. I had never met Morty's family, either. They hadn't visited the campus before. Never called or wrote much. When we walked into the Balt, it was all I could do not to faint on the spot. First, I must tell you that you can't get much more Jewish looking than Morty. I mean, his face screamed Jew, but at least he dressed half way like the rest of us. True, his clothes were cheaper and more worn than most, but at least they were of the same fashion. On that day, I remember he was wearing a brown wool suit and a tie. His parents arrived with at least six brothers and sisters, and they were all dressed in orthodox Jewish garb. His father and brothers wore cheap, black suits, plain black loafers, white shirts, open collars, and black hats. They each sported two long locks of dark brown hair, dangling in curls in front of each ear. The women wore black skirts and white blouses, all made by Morty's mother. I watched as my father looked at my face, squinted his eyes slightly, and turned to look at Morty and his family. My father's face turned red as a tomato, and his eyes opened wide like two silver dollars, as if something had gotten hold of his short hairs."

Mr. Applegate paused and then began to laugh, his old skin growing red. He went on, "That crazy Morty didn't miss a beat. He walked over to my father with an air befitting the highest aristocrat. Morty held out his hand and my father reluctantly grabbed it. 'Mr. Applegate, I presume. Sir, I have looked forward to this meeting for many years. I am Morton Francis Hershfeld. Known to some as Richard Huntington, III.' Even Morty's parents looked puzzled. In that moment, I was hoping someone would pull out a gun and shoot me.

My father stared straight at Morty as he began to talk to me. 'Andrew, dishonesty is precisely why I didn't want you associating with this kind during your stay at Princeton.' My father pulled his hand away from Morty and looked directly at me. 'Hopefully,' he admonished, 'the damage that has been incurred here can be undone.' My father headed for the door, demanding, 'Andrew, it is time to leave now.' There was dead silence for at least twenty seconds. It could have been twenty years. 'I'm staying right here, dad,' I told him. Although the words came out of my mouth, even I looked around the restaurant to see what horse's ass had the balls to say that to my father. My father stopped short at the door, turned around, and walked toward me. It was about that time that I decided I was not having a very good day. The scene kind of reminded me of a gun duel in a cowboy movie. My father walked within inches of me, and his voice cracked with anger when he spoke. Trying desperately to maintain his composure, he said, 'Andrew, I am leaving. If you do not come with me, you are on your own.' My father didn't have to go into greater detail. I knew exactly what he meant. My postgraduate job as Chief Financial Officer of Applegate Steel would be history. I looked my father straight in the eye—I am not sure I had ever done that before. 'Morty is my friend, Dad. I'm staying,' I managed. My father nodded, forced a smile, and walked brusquely out the door. My mother and he did not stay for graduation. In fact, I would not have any contact with them for years."

Alex was genuinely impressed. "Mr. Applegate, that is a very interesting story. Given the time and the place, I must confess, I'm not sure I could have done the same thing. I hope I'm not being too forward by asking you what you did after your father walked out on you?"

"I had breakfast with Morty and his very surprised family."

"No, sir. I mean for the long run. You said you didn't talk to your father for years after that, so I presume that the job at the family business was out the window?"

"It was out the window, all right. I was very upset about the whole thing. I loved my father, dearly. I always had the most profound respect for him and always tried to model myself after him. But after he walked out of that restaurant, I realized that he was an ignoramus. Someone who my father had talked to over the telephone for years, someone my father insisted on meeting in person, was now a pariah because of his religious background. It can be very upsetting when your hero dies. I didn't know what I was going to do. For my first twenty-one years, I was groomed to be like my father. At that moment, I was lost. He was intelligent and successful, but I realized that I didn't want to go through life that ignorant. I took heart in the words of the philosopher David Hume. Are you familiar with him?

"Yes, he was the basis of a course I took, entitled Early Modern Philosophy."

"Did you study his work, *A Treatise of Human Nature*?"

"That all our knowledge is derived from experience and observation of human nature."

"Very good. Do you see where I am going with this Thomas?"

"I guess that you decided to become a student of human nature. You might have felt that the more you knew about people, the closer you would be to ultimate truth." Applegate smiled and nodded slowly. "But how does one become such a student?"

"There are many ways. I decided that I would throw myself into the pits. I would travel the world to see what a Frenchman was like. A Nigerian. A Filipino. An Aborigine. I wondered, if a picture says a thousand words, what would actually being in the picture say? Anyway, I collected what savings my parents hadn't pulled back, spent a few months working at a local food store in Princeton, and then set out on a trip around the world. My first stop was Guadalajara, Mexico. From there, I drove through Colombia, Venezuela, Guyana, Suriname, and, finally, down to Sao Paulo, Brazil, where I caught a plane to Madrid. Thirty-eight countries in eighteen months. Sometimes I was entertained in palaces; sometimes I slept in the streets. I had dinner with a countess in Paris, slept with two whores at once in Bangkok, had a seventeen-course meal in Bombay, was robbed and beaten in Stuttgart, laughed at the clowns in the Moscow Circus, and cried in front of the Sphinx."

"Did the idea work?"

"Well, my calculus got rusty, but my knowledge of the human condition certainly grew. Mr. Williams, you must never stop wanting to learn. I never allowed my mind to close. Over your life, things will happen that will define you, some things will not be in your control. What you believe in, what you discover, will have little bearing on what you must do to survive. For example, many in your generation are going to business school. Of all the things we can do to educate ourselves, does anyone truly want to sit in on a class, entitled Aggregate Economic Analysis? Of course not. We whore ourselves. But that's OK. We do it for a reason, a means to an end. There will come a point in your life, sooner than later, when the search for truth and knowledge will take a backseat to more mundane matters."

"I am very curious to ask you more details about your trip, but pardon me if I jump ahead for a moment. What happened when you got back? Did you make amends with your father?"

"Sometimes, Mr. Williams, when a cord is cut, you can tape it back together. It might work, but it will never be what it once was. I showed up at my family's house, not too far from here, in Pittsburgh. It had been two years to the day since my Princeton graduation. To my relief, my parents treated me very cordially, but it became apparent, after two or three days of my stay, that things would not return to the old way, and I was happy for it. My father asked me if I wanted my job at Applegate Steel, and, when I said 'no thank you,' he didn't rant and rave. Rather, he simply nodded his head in understanding. We had developed respect for one another. I don't think it was the best way to close a father and son relationship, but I guess there have been worse endings."

"You became successful without help from your family?"

"Nobody becomes successful without some kind of help, but if you're asking me if I inherited my money or created it, I created it. I spent the next six years looking for alternative materials to steel and wood. After World War II, universities were teaming with scientists who were taking their alternative ideas ever further. I started to study the experiments of two scientists in Europe, a German and an Italian. The German created this thing called Polyethylene, the Italian, Polypropylene. I thought they had something there. I bought the rights to a ten-year period of exclusive manufacture of these materials in the United States. These guys ended up sharing the Nobel Prize in 1963. In 1967, after a few years of ridiculous profits, I sold my manufacturing rights to DuPont for one hundred fifty million dollars. But believe it or not, they got the better end of the deal. Plastic was here to stay."

"That's a fantastic story!"

"For someone like you, maybe. But I'm not done yet. I had one hundred fifty million dollars, not to mention another dozen or so in the bank. What the hell was I going to do with that much money? What could I do to get a thrill that would be comparable to the average Joe betting two dollars of his hard-earned dough on a spin at the roulette wheel? We didn't have a legal casino in the Pittsburgh vicinity, so I decided on the next best thing . . . I put a hundred million in the stock market. The market wasn't the greatest in the sixties, but I was fortunate. I put a good chunk of change into a former typewriter company that was fooling around with this new computer thing. I fell in love with computers, and you should too. History will show technology to define your generation. I got bored with IBM by the seventies, so I switched to a new company of computer misfits whom IBM rebuffed. Needless to say, Mr. Gates and the rest of his merry men have done well for themselves, but probably not as well as me. I recently got bored with Microsoft as well, and, if I hire you, I might just tell you where I'm playing now." Mr. Applegate picked up his glass and, with a salute only half as high as the first, quickly downed another whiskey. Alex followed suit. Mr. Applegate poured another.

"Mr. Applegate, excuse me if I am being too forward here, but I must ask. What exactly is the job?"

"Remember that your time here on earth is short. You can never be too forward. I am very old now, Mr. Williams. I am ill and will not be around very much longer. I know I'm supposed to tell you that it's OK because I lived my life, etcetera, but that is a bunch of bullshit. No one wants to die. But dying is the one thing in my life I have yet to figure out how to beat. When death is walking slowly to your side, you begin to think about the things you've done with your life. By other men's standards, I have had some great successes. With three marriages ending in divorce, and my only child dying of a drug overdose when he was nineteen, I have certainly had my share of failures. But when I look back upon my happiest times, and the most important and interesting parts of my life, I find it was when I was a pimply-faced, whack-off artist, traveling around the world." Mr. Applegate stared Alex right in the eye and said, "I want to do it again."

"You want me to take you around the world?" Alex asked.

"Not in the physical sense, I'm no longer up to that. But I want to experience it through you. I want to be inside you when you view the Himalayas for the first time. I want to watch you barter with a Pakistani street peddler. I want to understand what has remained the same and what has changed since I was there. My idea is to send someone equipped such that he can communicate both visually and verbally." Mr. Applegate grinned and winked, "Unless, of course, you meet up with those two whores in Bangkok." Mr. Applegate laughed loudly as he lifted hid glass and swallowed his third whiskey. Alex smiled and looked down at his feet.

"Mr. Applegate, that sounds like an unbelievable trip. I've been dying to travel abroad. I haven't been to Europe since I was ten and with my parents. Not that I minded my parents per say, but what could you really do at ten years of age, in Paris, with your parents? It's not like I was going to close down the Moulin Rouge or anything. On the other hand, regarding the applicant you are seeking, I might not be the right guy for the job."

Mr. Applegate did not even blink. "Explain."

Alex was about to speak, paused, polished off his third whiskey, and began, "I understand that when you work for someone, you play by their rules, but, in this case, with what you are trying to accomplish, which, again, is a neat idea, it won't work. When you did your trip, you probably had a very broad itinerary with little, if any, day to day planning. Whatever happened was spontaneous. Now you are trying to recreate the trip from over fifty years ago, which can never really be done. Even more important, the main premise of the trip, a quest for truth without concern for time or space, would never exist. I would be more worried about catching a train or a plane to get to the next place on time." Silence followed. Alex poured both another round.

"So, what do you suggest?" questioned Applegate.

"You give the individual resources and you send him out."

"Period?"

"Period. The computers and stuff are fine. Probably not much different from carrying a Kodak camera in '61. But I think the key to this idea is the same as it was fifty years ago: to keep the mind of the traveler open and free. Every rule and regulation that you add, even those that are necessary, distorts an individual's perception to some degree. You can't experience the absolute truth."

"Example?"

Alex thought for a moment, "Well, if a town imposes a midnight curfew on its citizens, no one will really know what goes on at two in the morning, will they?"

Mr. Applegate spoke quietly, "Mr. Williams, I am impressed. You are correct, the traveler will need much more leeway than I had considered. However, we must also keep in mind that the main beneficiary of this whole idea, or at least the man paying the bills, is me. Therefore, my needs must be met as well. Any suggestions?"

Alex was feeling good, and not only from the whiskey. It was a kick being asked advice from someone so successful. "Well, Mr. Applegate, I believe it's important that you hire someone who understands the feelings behind, and purpose for, the trip, just like you did when you went. There's nothing wrong with having the candidate discuss where he is planning to go and why. But I wouldn't want you to sway or suggest too much. And I don't think it would be too much to ask for reports, but it shouldn't be too regulated. If I was doing the traveling, I would suggest a small laptop for me, with some applications and knickknacks for sending writings, photographs and even some live video via Go Pro to your desktop back here in Sewickley. Of course, you could send your thoughts and desires to me as well. I would imagine that, sometimes, we might spend a couple of hours communicating, and, at other times, we might not connect at all for a couple of days. It would depend on the flow. I don't think I would have any trouble getting you into the feel of what I was experiencing."

Mr. Applegate looked up at the sky, his grey eyes darting in all directions, like a hungry hunter looking for a stray goose. Finally, he remarked, "The feel of what you are experiencing. I like that." He picked up his last whiskey of the morning, sniffed the top of the glass gently, and offered, "Well, Mr. Williams, would you like to join me for this adventure? You are the man for the job."

Startled, Alex uttered, "Are you sure you don't want to interview any other candidates, sir?"

"Don't try to get me to kiss your ass, Mr. Williams, as you would be pushing your luck. I don't have enough time left on this earth to interview any more snot-nosed kids to whom I can give away a trip around the world. If you don't mind, I would like an answer."

Alex didn't have to think long before answering, "Absolutely, sir. It would be an honor." Alex knew this was the beginning of a relationship that would run very deep. Mr. Applegate smiled, recognizing the thoughts running through Alex's mind.

"Splendid."

Mr. Applegate pulled the gadget out of his robe pocket once again, this time pressing a yellow button. Mrs. Stone quickly appeared. "Maggie, good news, we have our man."

"Splendid," Mrs. Stone replied in a similar tone.

"How about some lunch for me and my new employee?"

"Would you like lunch out here or in the dining room, sir?"

"We have had too much whiskey for moving around, Maggie. Out here would be fine."

"Don't you think it would be wise to ease up on the drink so early in the day, sir?"

"Maggie, I called you out here for a couple of sandwiches, not a lecture. If I want to be lectured or scolded, I'll marry you, OK?"

More annoyed than she sounded the last time she had left, Mrs. Stone retorted, "Sue me for being concerned, sir!" She turned and briskly walked back into the house.

"Sweet old shrew, eh, Mr. Williams?"

"She seems very nice, sir."

"Maggie is a lot of good things, but, when it comes to deliberately annoying me, she is more effective than a mosquito bite on my asshole."

*****

Over lunch, the two eased into a discussion of the differences between the current environment of Princeton University versus Mr. Applegate's undergraduate years. Mr. Applegate concluded that it was still basically a collection of boorish snobs, but that the advent of coeds made it easier to get laid. Alex assured Mr. Applegate that it was still not that easy to get laid. Alex asked, "Don't you think the student population has shifted from a privileged class to one more intellectually inclined?"

"There are simply more smart rich kids today," Mr. Applegate responded. "The fact remains that, although Princeton may severely lack in social reality, it provides the finest academic education in the world. When it comes to instruction, no one does it better. Some of the most important research in the world—be it economics, science or technology—is being conducted right there on Nassau Street. That's why I give so much. I disagree with much about the University, but I wouldn't be where I am without it. When you leave that school in a few short months, you will find that no peer, outside those who were Princeton trained, will be as intellectually prepared as you. But keep in mind, you may have to work on the spirit."

After lunch, Mr. Applegate excused himself for a nap. Alex was provided with a bathing suit and a towel. After a brief, invigorating swim in the indoor pool, Alex lay on a lounge chair and softly slept away the effects of the morning's imbibing. "Excuse me, Mr. Williams . . . Mr. Williams, sir . . . you may want to change, sir." Opening his eyes, he saw the silhouette of a face and upper body surrounded by bright light. The silhouette slowly came into focus. It was Maurice. "Good afternoon, Mr. Williams. May I suggest a shower and change of clothes before dinner?" Much cooler than Alex recalled, the chill of the air scattered goose bumps across Alex's body. Alex's eyes widened, as he realized where he was. He sat up quickly and tried to act as normal as one could when, on a job interview, waking up by a strange pool in a borrowed bathing suit after sleeping off four scotches in the home of one of the richest men in the world.

"Maurice, excuse me! What time is it?"

"Quarter past five, sir."

"Quarter past five! I've been out here for over three hours?"

"Yes, sir."

"Where is Mr. Applegate?"

"Oh, don't worry about him, sir. After his afternoon nap, he usually retires to the library upstairs and reads until we call him for dinner."

Suddenly there was a loud voice from an open window on the second floor of the house. "About time you got up, Mr. Williams. I hope you don't sleep away your time on the Serengeti!" Alex looked up to see the old man leaning out the window. Applegate was wearing white cotton pajamas and a silk purple robe with the initials WA embroidered in scarlet across the left breast pocket. He had a hardbound book in his hands.

"What about the freedom to do my own thing?" Alex said, smiling.

"Better to do it when your five thousand miles away."

"And why is that, sir?"

"Because I won't be able to hit you with anything!" With that, Mr. Applegate threw the book at Alex, who reflexively clutched the book. Mr. Applegate roared with laughter. "Now get dressed, boy. I'm hungry!" Slamming it closed, Mr. Applegate disappeared behind the window.

Alex's father had been an avid book collector, and Alex wondered if the book could be an original edition of an old book, like Dostoevsky's *Crime and Punishment*. Before following Maurice into the house to get dressed, Alex looked down at the book in his hands. The title was *Confederacy of Dunces*, by John Kennedy Toole. The book didn't seem that old, and Alex had heard of this book but had never read it. Later, he would find the book so good, so funny, that he would finish reading it later that night on the plane and in the limousine, despite being completely exhausted from the day's events.

*****

Dinner was served in the dining room, which was significantly larger than the one at O'Neill, which sat ninety. The room was so splendid, it was almost farcical. The walnut table was at least forty feet long. Three Baccarat chandeliers hung overhead. Two eight-foot high, Calcutta marble fireplaces, adorned with various gargoyles that had both human and animal characteristics, roared. Original artwork, much from the sixteenth and seventeenth centuries, hung on the Mahogany walls. A Persian carpet covered most of the floor. Alex doubted a larger or more beautiful one could exist. Along the walls was a collection of George I chairs and tables. Alex was particularly amused that he and Mr. Applegate were the only two eating dinner in this behemoth room. The pair sat in the middle of the enormous table, across from each other, and Alex was dressed again in his original interview clothes. "Do you eat in here often, Mr. Applegate?"

"No, Mr. Williams, I usually take dinner in my bedroom closet." Mr. Applegate smiled. "What kind of question is that? This is a dining room, isn't it?"

"Don't get me wrong, this is really spectacular. It just seems like it would be a lot of space to eat alone."

Mr. Applegate's mood became decidedly more somber. While looking down at the table, he began to speak, "My last wife died back in ninety-nine. I finally get the marriage thing figured out, and she left me way too soon. Breast cancer. We had recently completed building this home, and Nancy did virtually all the architectural work. I knew she would do a superb job, as she had the best of taste. From what you've seen of my home so far, I'm sure you would agree." Alex nodded emphatically. Without even noticing, Mr. Applegate continued, "Nancy loved dancing and music. She was one of the best ballroom dancers you've ever seen. And classical music . . ." Mr. Applegate's voice grew lower and more distant, "she would listen to for hours and hours. This was her music room. We would invite guests here to listen to piano concertos or, perhaps, dance the rumba. Her face would always light up when she was in here. Many times, I was too busy with my work to join her at her functions. I realize now how much that disappointed her. After Nancy's death, I planned to keep the house exactly as it was, but, every time I came in here, my heart broke. There would never be any dancing in here for me. I would never have any musicians. No, not without my Nancy. It just wouldn't have been right. I had this room converted into the dining room. I know Nancy is in here, and I enjoy eating with her. Being the party girl that she was, I make sure there's enough seating for anyone upstairs she may care to invite."

Alex said nothing. He was beginning to like Mr. Applegate a lot.

The rest of the evening was spent engaged in typical small talk, mixed with much laughter. They agreed to plan the trip in more detail soon. The Bentley pulled up at nine o'clock to return Alex to the airport.

"Sometimes, life is good," Alex sighed to himself.

XX

Alex's senior thesis project was due in just a few days, and he had spent virtually the entire previous week working on it. Alex tried to figure out what possessed him to write a one act play centered on bowling, as Princeton University and bowling had about as much in common as Queen Victoria and the Duck Dynasty clan. Early on, he had nixed his advisor's suggestion to revolve the story around a water polo team. Not much to do about it now, he conceded.

As Alex's father once told him, "if you must step in shit, at least try to do it gracefully." He would get that paper done this week, no matter how painful the process. Come next Monday, Alex would hand the paper to his advisor like he was handing him the Hope Diamond.

Working until at least three in the morning each night that week, Alex was busy rewriting and editing the first four scenes of his play. Whenever he was asked how he was doing, Alex replied, "Rowing and writing. Just rowing and writing.'"

The completion of the senior thesis, though, had Alex rethinking his desire to be a writer. He was mentally spent. He had to get up early so he could drop the play off at the printer before heading to the boathouse for the race. Alex needed to get some sleep, but he was just too wired. It was Friday night, and there was still some activity in the club, although it was rapidly winding down. Alex decided to go down to the smoking room to see if he could grab a glass of wine to help him relax. The doors were closed and, when he opened them, he found a couple he didn't recognize making out on one of the couches.

Wineless, Alex closed the door, made his way to the entryway, and walked outside. For a late April night, it was warmer than usual. Alex's heart was beating fast, and he felt funny. He decided he needed to let off some steam. Alex cut behind the club, across the baseball field, to the track. He took off his Docksiders and, in bare feet, sprinted a lap around the track. Still wired, Alex ran another lap, and again, and again. Sweaty, and at least a bit more tired, he headed back to the club.

Alex had still hoped to get a glass of wine from the bar after his run, but he could still hear the couple inside talking in whispers. He knew it was just too late to deal with that scene. Before returning to his room, Alex checked on Boder. Since that fateful January night, when he had to rush Boder to the hospital, he was always fearful of a repeat. Boder was sleeping on the top of his blankets, fully clothed, with his shoes on. Alex went into his room and set his iPhone alarm for a few hours later. It seemed like he blinked and the alarm went off.

Alex sat up quickly, disoriented. It didn't take long for reality to set in. It was race time. The Harvard Crimson were in town. He jumped out of bed. Should have gotten more sleep, dammit. This thing is hard enough to get through on a full engine, he thought. Alex took a quick shower, put on sweats, picked up his bag and completed screenplay, and headed out the door. Alex was running so far behind schedule, he didn't even have time for his usual pre-race vomit jitters, as it was ten minutes to eight. Races started at nine. The heavyweights were scheduled to go off at about ten-thirty. Despite the appearance of plenty of time, Alex knew he was supposed to be at the boathouse by eight. There was no way that was going to happen. The bookbinder was nowhere near the boathouse. For a moment, Alex thought about skipping the binder, but decided that graduating on time might be a worthwhile cause.

When Alex entered Smith-Shattuck Bookbinding, it was packed. These were everywhere and in various stages of completeness. Some were done, some were being redone, and others were pouring in. Some authors milled about, exhibiting various stages of anxiety. He waited in line for about ten minutes, but the line wasn't moving very fast, and Alex became considerably concerned about his lateness. He politely excused himself to the front of the line and interrupted the clerk. He asked for immediate help, explaining that he had to get to the crew meet. The female student whom he interrupted became more than a little annoyed. For a moment, she considered protesting but politely kept silent. Alex nodded to her in a gesture of gratitude.

Due to the relatively uniform binding requirements of all senior thesis papers, there was little to discuss with the clerk. The English Department required two copies and Alex figured he would get two more; one for his mother and one for himself. "Can I please get four copies of this bound?" he requested.

"No problem, we can have it ready by Tuesday afternoon."

"I need it by tomorrow morning," Alex urged.

"As you can see, we are really overloaded."

"How much?"

"We are doing at least five hundred papers and . . ."

"No, I mean how much to get it back by tomorrow morning?"

"It would entail rush charges."

Alex smiled patiently, although he felt as though a cold sweat was about to burst out of every pore in his body. "Look," he insisted, "I know it's not your fault, but I'm in a huge hurry. I really can't spend any more time here. Whatever it costs to have it back by tomorrow, do it!"

"No problem!" The clerk reached under the counter and pulled out a long form with many lines and continued, "Let me just get some information and we'll be all set."

Alex slapped his right hand on the counter, forced a smile, and started to back away. "There's a page in there that provides directions as to what I want on the binding. Any questions, my phone number is in the book. Thanks!"

"Hey!" the clerk shouted, but it was too late. Alex ran across Nassau Street and made the long cut across campus to the boathouse. Out of breath, he arrived at the boathouse at eight forty-five. He went through the back entrance, and was about to go up the stairs to his locker as the Captain spotted him from the boat bay.

"Hey, Williams! Coach been lookin' for you. He says, if anyone sees you, to send you to his office right away!"

Alex stopped short in his tracks. "Thanks, Captain."

Alex moved slowly upstairs to the coaches' office. Through the glass panel in the door, Alex saw Diriglia's profile. He was on the telephone. Assistant Coach Henderson was also in the office and spotted Alex approaching. Henderson said nothing but winced in Alex's general direction, indicating that it was not going to be pretty. Alex knocked on the door. Diriglia looked up and quickly waived Alex in.

"Never mind! We found him!" Diriglia slammed down the receiver.

"Williams, where the hell were you," he exploded, "you're almost an hour late! I should be outside prepping the 3V boat; their race is going off in ten minutes. Instead, I'm in here trying to track your ass down. What's going on?"

"Sorry coach, I had to bring my senior thesis to the printer and it took longer than …."

"Your senior thesis to the goddamn printer?"

"Yes, coach."

Diriglia took a deep breath. "Mr. Williams, may I ask you something?"

"Sure."

"When were you given approval on your senior thesis project?"

"November."

Diriglia nodded his head. "November?"

"November, Coach."

"And when is it due?"

"Monday."

Again, Diriglia nodded his head. "Monday?"

"Monday, Coach."

Diriglia stood up and turned toward Henderson. "Did you

hear that Coach Henderson? Williams gets his thesis approved six months ago, scrambles around at the last minute to get it done, and he puts a national title in jeopardy. Isn't that interesting? There are seven other rowers and a coxswain in that boat, who have poured their hearts, souls, and sweat into this goal nearly every single day, for years. And on one of the handful of days that we get to prove that point, Mr. Williams decides to tell his team to kiss off, to run an unannounced errand he had months to do!"

"I'm sorry, Coach. I should have done it earlier. The project took me longer than I expected, and I didn't think I would take so long at the printer. Besides, sir, if I may say so, our race isn't for another hour and fifteen minutes, and I'll be more than ready."

Diriglia kept up his conversation with Henderson. "I just don't think he gets it, Coach Henderson."

"I guess he doesn't," Coach Henderson replied. Judging by the look on Henderson's face, Alex wasn't sure he got it either.

Diriglia looked directly at Alex. "Mr. Williams, there are two basic parts to my job here at Princeton Crew. One part of my job is to train young men to be responsible team players. The other part of my job is to teach young men that it is better to win. Showing up late for such an important race demonstrates to me that, with you, I have not done my job correctly. I'm taking you off 1V today and replacing you with McGill."

"But you can't do that!"

"I just did."

"Don't you think making that kind of change at point in the season might jeopardize our chances to go undefeated?"

"Yes."

"But you're still going to go ahead with it?" Alex replied, exasperated.

"As I said earlier, if you were listening, part of my job is to teach responsibility and teamwork."

Alex could see that Diriglia was serious. In fact, Diriglia was as serious as Alex had ever seen him. For one weird instant, Alex both despised and respected him more than he ever had before.

"Then what am I supposed to do today?"

"Do whatever you like, but I hope you will do whatever it takes to help your team win."

Alex was at a complete loss for words. He just nodded his head and walked out the door as though someone had tied twenty-pound lead weights to each leg. Alex closed the door to the coaches' office in a state of complete shock, which soon changed to deep embarrassment. He was a traitor in the ranks, Judas amongst the apostles. The coaches' office was near the locker room. There weren't many places to hide in the boathouse.

Alex hadn't been this upset in years, and it was all he could do to fight back tears. He tried to think about what he should do. He rubbed his face back and forth with the top half of his fingers. For a few minutes, he thought about blowing out of the boathouse and never coming back. He had given so much of himself to this goddamn thing. With all the stuff going on in the world, and in Alex's own life, for that matter, he wondered if he really should have to worry about getting there over two hours before it was his turn to row? Maybe Boder was right about the bullshit, he thought. Alex put his head straight back, looked up at the wood-beam ceiling, and took a deep breath. Who is kidding who? Alex chastised himself. Diriglia can certainly be an asshole, but, this time, he has a point. It's about more than rowing a boat. The Cruiser had once told him, 'If you're going to lose, lose to a team that beats you fair and square, don't beat yourself.' Alex knew that he did have a responsibility to those guys. If they were at the boathouse at eight o'clock, even if they did nothing but sit on their asses, he should have been there as well. Alex had to admit that, when someone showed up late for practice, he would get aggravated, even though he never showed it. Goddamn prima donna, Alex reasoned, but now what? Even if the guys think that Diriglia went overboard, won't they be pissed at me for tempting fate? His mind was racing at a thousand miles a minute, as Alex went back downstairs and headed outside. Most of the first team was standing in a group by the lake, cheering 3V as they left the dock to begin their race. As Alex walked over to the group, he knew by their looks that they had been informed of the change. He spotted Neil Johnson and stopped in front of him. There wasn't a normal high-five of greeting. In fact, no one spoke.

Alex broke the ice, "Gentlemen, I guess you heard."

There were a couple of slow nods.

"Neil, can I see you for a minute?"

Johnson's sullen appearance didn't change.

"Sure," Johnson said. The pair walked north along the bank, away from the group. They stood awkwardly, face to face, in silence.

Alex spoke first. "I want to say, I'm really sorry. I fucked up. I could have planned things better, and I shouldn't have been so late. To be frank, I didn't think it was that big a deal.

But, after getting my ass chewed out by Diriglia, I can see his point. I want you to know that I would never intentionally do anything to hurt this team. If only from a selfish point of view, I've put too much into being part of it. But it's more than that. It sounds a little corny, but after all these damn years around this boathouse, I have a certain fondness and respect for every member of our team." Alex tried, unsuccessfully, to force a smile. "I know it doesn't mean much. I'm sure McGill will do just fine. Hell, probably better than my ass! I just hope I haven't screwed you up too much. If there's anything I can do to help the team out today, let me know."

Alex tried to smile again. Though nervous, he was slightly more successful than he was previously. Johnson stared back, expressionless, turning his head to look out onto the calm lake. He shook his head slightly, turned his back on Alex, and headed back to the team, who were torn between watching the 3V race and eavesdropping on the discussion between Johnson and Alex. When Johnson rejoined the group, they listened closely as he spoke. When Johnson finished speaking, the team, including McGill, nodded their heads in agreement. Watching the interaction from a distance, Alex felt he would be more comfortable at the bottom of the lake with a rock tied around his neck. Johnson nodded back to the group, turned, and walked toward Alex. Although Alex tried hard to appear complacent, he looked more like a Ken doll with a broomstick up its ass. "You're in," Johnson said.

Alex was puzzled. "I'm in what? The only thing I know I'm in right now is hot water."

"You're part of 1V. You earned it. We don't believe we'd

be in the fortunate position we're in today, if it weren't for each one of us, you included. Barring an injury, we all row or none of us row."

Alex paused, stunned. "Do you think that's the wisest thing to do given how pissed Diriglia is at me?"

"Listen, Alex, a few of us owe you, I certainly do. Since I was nine years old, my father has been grooming me to succeed in this sport. Right now, I'm on the best collegiate boat in the country, and I have a decent shot at the next Olympics. For most of my life, rowing has taken center stage. You and I have never really done much together, outside of rowing, but you've helped me more than you know. Remember that day Diriglia had us run through town during that blizzard when you showed up for practice tired from a party?"

"Please, don't remind me."

"If it wasn't for your leadership, I probably would have trudged through the whole thing like a horse's ass. But you had the balls to stand up to everyone and convince us how ridiculous we were being. Besides bringing the team closer together, you helped teach this horse to take his blinders off."

"I appreciate that, but you are giving me too much credit."

"No, I'm not. I did a lot of thinking after that blizzard day. I finally admitted to myself that I really don't like this sport that much. Problem is, I can't quit just yet. To be frank, I'm too damn good at it." Alex nodded in agreement. "I want this national title, and then I'm skipping the Henley Royal Regatta. I'm going to try out for next year's Olympics, and that's a little more than a year of rowing. After that, I'm done. I recently realized that I have too many other things I want to try. After the Olympics, I will have taken this as far as I can."

Alex exhaled deeply. "Thanks!" he responded. "I'm glad I had that impact, but I still think you are giving me too much credit. What's your plan for getting me back on the boat?"

"I'm going into Diriglia's office to tell him the rest of the team thinks you should row. I'll tell him that we respect his stand, but we believe that your academic well-being should have taken precedence over the sport. I'll remind him that this premise is one of the main cornerstones separating us from most other college institutions in this country. I don't think the alumni would appreciate his explanation that a national championship was forfeited because a member of the team had to finish his senior thesis and was punished for it." Johnson didn't wait for a response. He immediately turned away from Alex and, quite deliberately, walked into the boathouse. Alex, feeling a bit like a putz standing there alone, walked over to the team and thanked them for their support. In particular, he thanked McGill, who was giving up a big opportunity. Alex wondered if he would have done the same.

Alex's wondering was cut short when Johnson reappeared in relative short order. With a serious face, he approached the group. He looked directly at Alex, smiled, and held up his hand to offer a high five. The group cheered. Empowerment filled the air. After the group calmed down, Alex spoke, "Neil, you are incredible. To be honest, given his ill-temper when I left his office, I didn't give you much of a chance."

"It was quite simple, really. I told him what I told you I would say: that you are important to our boat, that we think academics take precedence over rowing, that the alumni wouldn't like a forfeit, etcetera, etcetera."

"And he bought that?"

"No, not at all."

"Then what happened?"

"I told Diriglia that if he put you back in the boat, I'd guarantee we would break the course record."

"Come on, what did you really say?" Johnson didn't respond. "Wow, you're serious, aren't you?' Johnson nodded in the affirmative. "And what if we don't?"

"Then, next week, 1V and 2V trade places."

Everyone in the group started to speak at once. The tone wasn't exactly positive "Hold on!" Alex exclaimed. The group slowly quieted down. Alex continued, "Listen, taking that stance on my behalf took a lot of guts. You were willing to forfeit to the competition this week. With Johnson's offer to the coach, the worst-case scenario is that we don't row in 1V next week. There's not much of a difference, right? And, anyway, why can't we break the course record? We are supposed to be the best team Princeton's ever had. We're undefeated, and it is the middle of the season, when we should be in our best shape."

"I can think of one reason," said Haley.

"What is that?" Alex asked.

"1983 National Champs, Yale. 5.24.7."

"If you ask me, that's even more incentive," Alex replied. "It's a little embarrassing that Yale has held the course record, at our own school, for over thirty years! We owe it to ourselves to give this one our best shot. Look at whom we're racing against today! Does anyone here recall sinking into the Charles last October, only to watch those snickering asses wave and laugh as they rowed by? Don't you think that gives us a little extra incentive to get things done?"

"Hell yes!" Someone yelled. Chants of support followed. There wasn't any time to waste. With all the complications of this morning, the team certainly had a lot to do. Additionally, they all knew in their hearts that beating Harvard, the only other undefeated team on their schedule, was not a guarantee, never mind beating the course record. They had to check the equipment, listen to the coach's final words, get their boat out of the boathouse, and Alex, still dressed in his jeans, had to get changed. It wasn't long before the team found themselves on Carnegie Lake, slowly rowing north to the starting line.

It was a still, cool morning for that time of year. The shoreline and bridges were lined with more than the usual spectators. The team rowed quietly and methodically, not even disturbed by Vales' lack of a request for a practice sprint. The team knew there was no need. They knew exactly what they had to do. Alex felt more than the usual tension in the boat, and he wasn't sure if that was good or bad.

The Carnegie Lake course was a 2000-meter, straight shot. Nearing the finish line was evident because the Kingston Damn was right behind it, making it imperative that a team pay close attention to avoid disaster. As they approached the starting line, Alex looked toward the western shoreline, which contained some of the nicest mansions in Princeton. Many were holding parties on their back lawns, as they watched the festivities.

The plan was to bring the strokes per minute into the forties as fast as possible. Once the desired speed was reached, the cadence normally slowed to between thirty-six and thirty-eight strokes per minute. To break the record, they knew they couldn't reduce the starting cadence by much. This was something they had never done before. For Alex and the other seniors in the boat, it was now or never. That was their last race on mother Carnegie. Before we go old girl, Alex thought, we're going to give you one last ride. Alex stared down at his reflection in the calm water. The starter pulled in front of the two teams in a powerboat. He held a megaphone in one hand and a red flag with a white X in the other. Through the megaphone, he yelled, "Ready all…Go!" As he waived the flag, the teams took off.

Princeton need not have worried. Vales brought the team to forty-four strokes per minute in about thirty seconds. After that, they never looked back. Instead of reducing the cadence, they kept it just the way it was. Harvard was a boat length behind within the first hundred yards and more than two boat lengths by the halfway point. Princeton's only real competition was the clock. Alex had never felt such burning in his arms, but he wasn't going to fold, especially since he had one foot in the doghouse already. "Gentlemen, history in the making! We are history in the making!" Vales screamed.

The cheers from the sidelines were getting louder which meant they were nearing the finish line. The western shore, at that point, had the largest parking lot on the lake. On game days, it filled with spectators, their tents, picnics, and pets. Occasionally, Alex would sneak a quick glance at the festivities, but not today.

"Drive brothers! Drive!"

Drive? Are you fucking crazy? Alex thought. He could literary feel the veins pushing against his forehead. Nevertheless, he drove…and drove.

After crossing the finish line, Vales informed the crew of what each of them already knew. The course record had been shattered. There were a few yelps of joy, but the boat was, in fact, quieter than it would normally be after a victory. Absolute exhaustion prevented any overly exuberant celebration. It was all Alex could do to hold onto his oar while his head lay between his knees. For about a half-minute, he blacked out. Regaining consciousness, his body jerked in dry heaves, spewing a few drops of his insides onto his water-soaked sneakers. A few of the rowers had let go of their oars, causing the boat to circle slowly and precariously toward the damn. Alex prayed that the boat not tip over because he didn't think he had the strength to swim to the shore. Assistant coach Henderson and a few other members of the team were dispatched to the flailing crew in a small motorboat. "Gentleman, grab your oars!" Vales screamed. Alex squeezed his stick weakly. Suddenly, Alex felt the boat stop turning, and he slowly looked up. Almost as exhausted, a member of the Harvard boat was holding onto the starboard side of the Princeton boat, trying to stabilize it. Alex sat up as straight as his condition would allow. He saw that the whole Harvard team was doing the same thing along the entire length of the Princeton boat.

"Thanks," Alex called weakly.

"Hey, that was one hell of a race. Well done," came the reply from the rower nearest him.

At that very moment, Alex decided he would throw away his Harvard Sucks T-Shirt.

*****

Alex took a long, hot shower, drank about a half-gallon of Gatorade, and rallied enough energy to join a boisterous celebration in the locker room. Even Coach Diriglia came in. He said it was not only the best rowing performance he had ever seen, but that the day had taught him a few things about priorities as well. As Alex left the boathouse, he received pats on the back from many crew alumni acting like they, themselves, had won the race. It caused Alex to worry a bit about growing old. One of the alumni offered Alex two hundred dollars for the Harvard crew shirt he collected from the losing team. Although tempted, Alex politely declined and walked happily outside onto the sunlit parking lot. Since the cool of the morning, it had warmed up quite a bit.

With the race finished and his thesis at the printer, he had little to do for a change. He considered that a little nap, and maybe some playtime with Boder, might be in order. Most of the cars in the parking lot were gone. Johnson pulled his car by Alex and asked if he needed a ride, but Alex declined. He wanted to leave the scene slowly and savor it.

"That was a great race," a voice in the distance called. Alex knew it wasn't an alumnus. He knew exactly who this was. Alex turned toward the voice. Leaning against a log-rail fence that separated the parking lot from the lake was Amanda.

"Hi," Alex said, a little stunned.

She looked as beautiful as Alex had ever remembered. Her hair was longer than when he had seen her at the tennis courts. Her face looked relaxed, yet alive. She wore a black leather jacket, light brown sweater, blue jeans, and black leather boots. Amanda was one of those girls who could look classy in army fatigues. "Hi," Amanda replied, running one of her hands through her hair. "Really, that was a great race. My dad was right. He said you guys were going to do some serious damage today."

"I'm a little surprised that he wasn't here today."

Amanda looked down at the ground. "Dad's in the hospital." Alex knew by the tone of Amanda's voice that it was no small matter.

"Amanda, I'm really sorry. Is he going to be OK?" Amanda was still looking down and her body started to shake uncontrollably. Reflexively, Alex moved in and hugged her. "It's fine, Amanda. It's fine."

"He has cancer, Alex." Alex felt his heart sink.

"Hey, they can do a lot with that now."

"No, it's in his pancreas, and it's stage four. He was so stubborn; he wouldn't go to the doctor until he passed out in the kitchen a few weeks ago. My mom told me he might not be here to see me graduate." Amanda sobbed, and her knees buckled under her. Alex felt tears welling in his own eyes, but he fought them back. He knew that wasn't the time. Alex leaned her gently against the fence post. He caressed her hair and face. He didn't say anything for quite a while. He had been in Amanda's situation, and knew that nothing he could say would really help. Sometimes fate comes down and rips out your beating heart. He knew the best that anyone could do was be there and give you a place to lean while you're bleeding. After about five minutes, Amanda slowly pulled away from Alex and wiped her eyes. "I'm sorry," she said, forcing a weak smile. "Probably one of the best days of your life, and I come swooping in from nowhere and drop a bomb on it."

"If you hadn't told me, I would have been more hurt."

Amanda looked up and smiled. Alex slowly rubbed the rest of her tears away.

"How about some coffee?" He offered.

"You making it?"

"I wouldn't wish that on my worst enemy. Let's go to P.J.'s."

Alex and Amanda walked up Washington Road to the center of town. Although little was said, Alex's mind was racing. He felt so many conflicting emotions in his body, he felt like tearing his skin off. Alex hadn't spoken to Amanda in months but had been thinking about her often. She was a great person, he reasoned. Why is it that, when a love relationship breaks off, the friendship goes with it? Not in that phony, we-can-still-be-friends way, but maintain the attraction that put you together in the first place. Alex had to admit, he still felt the attraction with Amanda, but these weren't the best of conditions. Her father, Alex's mentor, Mr. Princeton Crew, was dying. Alex felt very sorry for Amanda. He knew it was going to be painful.

Over coffee, Amanda spoke quite a bit about growing up with her father. Alex had heard most of the stories before, but he didn't mind. Since they had broken up, there had been times he missed her, but it wasn't until this point that he realized how much. Alex began to speak while Amanda was in a mid-sentence, "Amanda, I'm really sorry."

"About what?"

"About us. I was stupid that day at the football field. I was an immature jerk."

Amanda smiled. "That's true. But it's part of what I loved about you. You had your feelings, and you were not afraid to express them, no matter how childish they may have been." They both laughed.

"You're talking about me in the past tense. I'm not dead you know."

"I meant as it relates to us."

"Wow. That sounds so final."

"Well, you were quite final that day at the football stadium."

Their thoughts were disrupted by the sound of a teaspoon dropping on the floor, landing by Alex's feet. He picked it up and handed it back to the woman who dropped it. Alex continued, "I thought I just stated my regrets about that."

"And what, exactly, does that mean?"

"I really don't know. I don't think either of us know."

Alex knew Amanda well enough, though, to sense that she wasn't going to let him off the hook that easily. "Does it mean you're sorry that you broke us up, or just sorry for the way you did it?"

"You really need to learn how to stop skirting issues," Alex joked. Grinning, Alex stared at Amanda for a few moments, hoping to ease the tension. "I'm not just sorry for the way I did it. Do you think it's easy walking away from someone like you? Let me tell you something, it's a lot harder than I could have imagined. I can't tell you how many times I wanted to call you or stop by your room." Alex elected not to tell Amanda about watching her play tennis. He felt she might construe it as a little too voyeuristic, if not actually creepy. "But I never did call or visit. Was I a coward? Or was I just trying to keep on a path that I thought was right? That day in the stadium, I thought I was going to put our relationship to rest. All I succeeded in doing was lighting a slow fuse to an emotional bomb in my head."

"That's not all you succeeded in doing," Amanda said calmly. "You hurt me very badly, Alex."

"I'm certainly not proud of that."

"Are you still confused?"

"Yes."

Amanda made a face.

"What was that for?" Alex instigated.

"Cop out."

"I can't be unsure about this issue?"

"First, we are not an issue," Amanda began. "You can be unsure about abortion, gay marriage, or whether the remake of *Ocean's Eleven* was better than the original. But when it comes to loving somebody, to wanting to be with somebody . . . that is not an issue. It's either there or it's not there. Period." Amanda realized that Alex was getting upset, for she quickly resumed, "Now don't let your shorts get too tight. I'm not upset about it anymore." Amanda paused and looked up at the ceiling. "Well, that's a lie. But what I'm trying to say is, I have come to terms with it." She forced a short laugh. "You don't have to worry about getting a bullet in the back."

Alex laughed back. "Well, that's reassuring."

"But you're still coping out."

Alex grew more serious. "I might be. I really don't know. But as you said, one of the reasons you were attracted to me in the first place was because what you see is what you get. I know that I do stupid things, but, at the time, I believe in what I'm doing. Yes, I was out of line at the stadium, but I couldn't stand the thought of you sleeping with another guy. I really couldn't handle it. If I had pretended everything was OK, it would have been a lie. Call me immature. Call me a

Neanderthal. At that moment in my life, I couldn't continue the relationship."

"And now?"

"I miss you like crazy, and I just don't know."

Amanda put her face down toward her lap. Alex was sure she was about to be upset, but it was just the opposite. "Alex, I know you do what you believe is right. And yes, I was always attracted to your candor, but I don't want to argue about it. I know you still care. For the past few days, I really needed somebody to talk to. When I was standing outside the boathouse, waiting for you to come out, I knew it didn't matter that we ended on bad terms and hadn't spoken in months. I knew you would be there for me. I think when things settle down a bit, we should have a deep conversation about us." With only a slight smile on her face, Amanda pointed her finger at Alex, warning, "Just remember what I told you on that fateful day, when you made the biggest mistake of your life."

"You would have been good for me," Alex responded quickly.

"Yes. And I'd like to make an addendum to that."

"And that is?"

"I'm not one to wait around, cowboy."

"To be frank, I'm surprised you're not with someone else."

Amanda grew a bit more serious. "Actually, I am." She took a sip of her soda. Alex felt a new rush of emotions, but, for the time being, decided to let the last comment sit.

The subject of the conversation eased over the next few minutes, as the pair called a truce and began discussing graduation and future plans. Alex had heard through the grapevine that Amanda had been accepted at Stanford for graduate studies in architecture, she confirmed the rumor. She told Alex that she wanted to delay a year because of her dad, but The Cruiser would have none of it. Alex told Amanda about his job with Mr. Applegate, and Amanda thought it was the greatest thing she ever heard. When they left the restaurant, Alex offered to walk Amanda back to her room, but she declined, saying she had a few errands to run. They both knew that was best. They were both aware that the next step could get complicated.

Alex went back to the club, grabbed a sandwich, went to his room, and laid on his bed. His mind raced, What a day. Rushing to get the thesis bound. Late for crew. Kicked off first team. Back on first team. Course record. Meeting with Amanda. The Cruiser isn't going to make it. Alex felt like an over stimulated infant. If the rest of the day was anything like the first half, Alex was afraid he might spontaneously combust. But it was all worth it, he mused, if only to kick Harvard's ass and speak to Amanda again. He reached into his bag and pulled out the dried, sweat encrusted, crimson shirt with the white H to his nose. How could something that smells so terrible be so sweet? Alex smiled. He would mail the shirt to The Cruiser, dry sweat and all.

XXI

Alex spent a good portion of that afternoon in bed. He woke at four-thirty and felt as if he had been beaten up. He lay awake in the bed for twenty minutes, wondering how he was ever going to get out of it. Then he heard the hallway door open and the sound of keys landing on the coffee table. "Hey, Bode!" Alex yelled weakly.

"Yo!" came the reply.

"A little help please."

Boder came rushing in. Alex lay flat on his back, staring at the ceiling.

"Xander, what's the matter bro, someone superglue you to the bed?"

"Might as well have." Weakly, Alex raised his right arm. "Can you give me a hand in getting up?"

Boder went to Alex's bedside and slowly helped him up. Once on his feet, Alex was hunched over. Slowly, he straightened up, releasing a slow moan along the way.

"Seriously, what happened to you, man? You look terrible!"

"I feel terrible." Alex said, heading toward the shower. "It's from the race this morning. Pushed it a little too hard, I guess."

"I heard about that. You guys beat Harvard."

Alex turned the shower on. "And the course record."

Boder leaned against the doorframe. Clapping his hands together, he asserted, "Bravo! Bravo! What do we do for an encore?"

"Take a very long, hot shower, get some dinner, and probably go back to bed." Slowly, Alex moved under the steaming water. Almost immediately, he felt his sore muscles begin to relax."

"Nonsense. The year is closing in on us fast, my boy. You can count on your fingertips how many Saturday nights we have left. There are none to waste." One thing about Boder: even when he was talking nonsense, he'd get you thinking.

Alex stuck his face directly into the stream of water. "What are you proposing?"

"I met these two chicks last night at the Triumph Brewery. Very cute. They live in New Brunswick and invited me to a party. My instincts tell me this is going to be a must-show."

Alex thought about his earlier encounter with Amanda. "I don't think so, I'm really hurting."

"Nothing a chick likes better than a wounded jock. Especially these two."

Alex took the bait. "OK, why these two?"

"Med students."

Alex stuck his head out of the shower. "Med students?"

"Get the water out of your ears. Beautiful students from Rutgers Medical School."

"What would two med students want with us?"

"Probably an examination of our extra-large sexual organs."

Alex shook his head and put his face back in the shower. He was intrigued. "What about Tina?"

"Unfortunately, that fizzled out, bro."

Alex was a little surprised by that comment, but decided not to pursue it at this point. "OK. Let me take a short nap after dinner, and I'm in. But just to tag along."

"Atta boy! That's the Xander we all know and love."

Alex felt cold water hit his back, causing him to arc forward as though he had been shot.

"Boder, you fuck!"

Boder dropped the plastic cup in the bathroom sink and ran out of the room laughing.

Some of us never grow up, Alex mused.

*****

After dinner and a nap, Alex put on a fresh pair of kakis, a navy polo shirt, and his Docksiders. It wasn't long before Boder came into the room. "I hope you're ready for some fun. I'll drive. You almost ready?"

"Sounds good to me. I'm ready."

"You're going dressed like that?"

"Like what?"

"Like you just stepped out of a photograph in the Princeton admission's bulletin."

"What is wrong with it?"

"Why don't we just paint a bright orange P on your forehead?"

"You've never said anything before."

Boder smiled. "I've been kind. Listen, what you're wearing is fine for around here. Goes well around my Georgetown neighborhood as well. But I want to let you in on a little secret." Boder lowered his voice to a whisper. "The average college student, especially a state school graduate student, doesn't wear J. Crew khakis and Ralph Lauren shirts to a party." Boder walked over to Alex's bureau and pulled out a pair of blue jeans and a plain grey sweatshirt. He held them out to Alex. "Trust me on this one." Alex was about to raise his voice in protest but stopped. He took off his shoes, pants, and shirt, and grabbed the jeans and sweatshirt from Boder. After putting on the new choices, he held up his Docksiders for Boder's approval. Boder gave the thumbs down, smiled, and pointed to a pair of work boots in Alex's open closet. Alex threw the Docksiders down and grabbed the boots.

They stayed on the two-lane Highway, Route 27, for about seventeen miles and drove straight into New Brunswick. Boder made a left onto Easton Avenue, driving under the railroad tracks that run from Boston to Washington. They stopped at a red light at the intersection of Easton and Somerset. Bright, multicolored, neon lights advertised one-of-a-kind fast food restaurants, numerous bars and clubs, as well as book, comic and drug paraphernalia stores, all hawking their wares. The streets screamed with youth. Students walked in pairs, foursomes, and even packs of ten or more. "Man, this town seems so much cooler than down our way," Boder remarked. "Tell me again why we didn't go to college here?"

"Because we wanted to be guaranteed an elitist job when we graduate."

"Oh yeah, right," Boder replied, lighting up a one hitter he had pulled from his pocket. After a few blocks, Boder made a left off Easton Avenue driving into a neighborhood of row houses long in need of a facelift. The city ordinance, prohibiting three unrelated people living in the same abode, was apparently widely ignored. Boder made a series of left and rights.

"Boder, how the hell do you know where we're going without GPS?"

"One of the girls told me, and you know I've got a memory like a steel trap."

"But this is the third time we've passed by this same corner."

Boder stopped the car in the middle of the street and pulled out his smart phone. "OK, I surrender." Soon, the pair pulled onto a dead end. It was packed with cars. Boder parked the car in the only available spot on the street, the one right in front of the fire hydrant. Over the past four years Boder had parked in worse places and had never been towed. Perhaps it had something to do with his U.S. Senate license plates.

Boder knocked on the door of the house. No one answered, so they walked inside. There were two different doors off the hallway and stairs leading to another door on the second floor. What was once a single-family home, was now three individual apartments. Alex and Boder could hear jazz music coming from the upstairs, so they ventured in that direction. They knocked loudly on the only door. Some guy opened it and nodded at the pair as they walked in "Beer's in the kitchen." He then turned his attention back to the girl with whom he was having a conversation.

The apartment included the entire upstairs, so it was large for a typical student abode. The space was crowded, but the party was more subdued than they'd anticipated. Throughout the apartment there were numerous small groups of two to six people engaged in private conversations. "Do the girls live here?" Alex asked Boder as they made their way to the kitchen, smiling at curious onlookers.

"No. The place belongs to some guy from the med school."

As the pair located the kitchen, they heard a voice of recognition, "Richie!" The voice came from a group near the kitchen counter. It was from a woman in her mid- twenties, wearing grey sandals and a denim shorts and a green tank top. She was tall, thin, and cute. The only jewelry she wore was a small, silver bracelet. She wore little makeup and had a nice smile. Boder smiled back in recognition. The woman waved the pair over to join her. The woman gave Boder a quick kiss on the cheek. "I'm so glad you made it. You must be Alex. Richie told us a lot about you." The woman held out her hand. "I'm Rachel." Alex had never actually met anyone named Rachel. She gave Alex a weak handshake. "Wow, it's such an honor to have two Princeton men in our presence," Rachel said, more than a little sarcastically. Alex forced a polite smile and then excused himself to get a couple of beers from the keg in the kitchen.

"Where's Renee?" Boder asked.

"Oh, Renee might be stopping by later, she started getting nervous about this gross anatomy test we have next Tuesday.

She's a real worry wart." Boder looked over at Alex. Rachel noticed his gaze and reassured, "Oh, don't you worry about him. There are plenty of girls for him to talk to. There's a group in one of the bedrooms splitting up some DMT. Would you like to join them?"

Boder put his right hand behind his back. "Ow! You're twisting my arm!" Rachel laughed. The pair disappeared through the living room, down a hallway, and into one of the bedrooms.

Not at the party five minutes, and Alex found himself stuck near the beer keg with some overweight guy in a New York Giants hat. Alex had a sense he was in trouble when he noticed he was about to be talking to the only person at the party not otherwise engaged in a conversation. Alex filled the first of two red plastic cups from the keg and placed it on a nearby counter. As he filled the second cup, the fat guy began pumping the keg. Were it not for the appearance of the man at the pump, his action might have been considered sexual.

"You like this beer?" Fat Guy asked.

Alex smiled back. "I haven't had one yet, but I'm sure it will be fine."

"It's Coors Lite. Fucking future doctors watching their calories. Regular Coors is definitely better for drinking from a keg. I told them to call me before they ordered. I probably drink more beer in a week than everyone at this whole party would in a year."

"I would believe that," Alex replied.

"Of course, regardless of the container, neither of them can hold a candle to Sam Adams Triple Bock. Now that stuff will kick your ass, man. It contains about three hundred percent more alcohol. If you watch for a sale, you can pick it up for about twenty-five a case. And we're talking bottles!" Fat Guy slowly shook his head up and down, eyes opened wide. He anticipated that Alex would mirror with a look of astonishment. Seeing little change in Alex's demeanor, Fat Guy plowed ahead saying, "What do you think?"

Alex was getting a little depressed. "Hey, no arguing with that logic."

Fat Guy held out his hand. "Wayne Rotini."

Alex shook Wayne's hand. It was clammy. "Alex Williams," Alex replied, as politely as he could muster. Alex had to ask the question that was burning inside him. "So, you're a med student here?"

"Nah, I'm not putting my fingers in someone else's asshole. I live in one of the apartments downstairs. Went to undergrad here for a year, though. Played football. They gave me the heave-ho for shitty grades. Probably should've stayed away from engineering." Wayne shook his head in agreement with himself, chugged most of his glass, and asked, "So Alex, what's your favorite beer, man?"

Alex was about to go into his discourse about why he usually drinks, Yuengling, but stopped himself as the first word was coming out of his mouth. He just couldn't do it. Wayne was too mind numbing. "I like them all," Alex said happily as he picked up the other beer he'd placed on the counter. "Good talking to you Wayne, but my buddy gets upset if he's without a beer too long. I'm sure I'll talk to you later."

Alex quickly walked across the kitchen and into the living room, fully hoping to find Boder and Rachel to see if there was an update on Renee. They were nowhere to be found. Instead, he discovered four guys on the couch, talking in whispers. One of the guys spotted Alex looking at them and stopped whispering. The rest of the group looked up and did the same. Alex smiled awkwardly and turned away. Alex continued through the living room. In one corner, a couple was talking seductively, leading Alex to deduce that the pair wasn't long for the party. In another corner, five people were talking shop. Alex could hear bits and pieces of their conversation about the stages of testicular cancer. He almost stumbled over a group sitting in the middle of the floor playing truth or dare. The loser was required to consume a shot from a rapidly dwindling supply of Grey Goose. Alex quickly drank his beer. Not seeing empty cups anywhere, he placed the full one in his empty and continued. The hallway must have been designated the smokers section. Upon entry, Alex found six people talking and laughing, four puffing on cigarettes and the other two sharing a joint. "Excuse me," Alex asked, looking directly at the guy in the brown shirt who was taking a long hit off a very thick joint. "Any of you seen Rachel around?"

Brown shirt smiled and said, "She's probably about three thousand miles south of Saturn about now!" The rest of the group laughed. Brown shirt, very proud of his own joke, bent over in forced hilarity and pointed down the hallway.

Stupid bastards, Alex thought. They hadn't even offered him a hit. He had given that habit up, but he thought good manners should be universal. Alex nodded, forced a smile, and proceeded down the hallway to the last door on the left. When he got to the doorway, he could hear mumbled conversation beneath the music of Bruno Mars' "Locked Out of Heaven." He put his hand on the doorknob, then pulled back. Nothing worse than being among a bunch of fucked up people when you're the only one sober. Especially when you don't know most of them, Alex considered. As for Boder, Alex had seen him intoxicated so many times; there were no new surprises in that act. At least, that is what Alex thought.

Alex walked back up the hall. As he passed the smokers, the guy in the brown shirt quipped, "What's the matter? Forget your space helmet?" Once again, the group broke into laughter.

Alex pointed his thumb and index finger at the questioner like a gun, smiled, and said, "Exactly!"

Alex returned to the living room, wondering what the hell he was going to do. He didn't usually mind meeting new people, but he felt awkward there. But for boring Wayne, it didn't seem to be the friendliest group in the world. Everyone seemed lost in their own little click. Alex would have been happy to try a conversation with a new woman, if there were any free, legitimate prospects. Boder had certainly made the right choice with Rachel. The rest of the women at the party made Alex a little less keen on attending graduate school. Standing alone in the living room, wondering what to do, Alex felt like a mannequin in a store window. Finishing his second beer, he made his way toward the kitchen and peeked inside. Wayne was nowhere in sight. Alex quickly walked to the keg to get another beer. No sooner had he begun to fill his cup then he heard a flushing sound and the door to the adjoining bathroom open. Wayne walked out, still zipping his fly. "Hey bro! Back for another! Good man!" Wayne held up his hand for a high five. Alex lightly slapped it, trying not to think about what that hand

booth at the other side of the bar. With its payphone long gone, Alex reasoned that the proprietors must have kept it to provide space for a cellphone call away from the noise in the bar. Alex squeezed his way through the crowd to the glass doors of the booth. He entered and closed the door behind him, the music now only a dull thud against the glass. Alex closed his eyes, took a deep breath, and dialed the number. With each ring, he grew more anxious. Maybe this wasn't such a great idea, he nervously wondered. After six rings and almost relieved, Alex was about to press end. "Hello?" Alex pulled the phone back to his ear.

"Hi. It's me." Alex closed his eyes. He felt a little dizzy.

"Alex? What are you doing?"

"Technically I am alone in a bar in New Brunswick. But in actuality, I've been thinking about our meeting this morning. To be frank, I can't get it out of my mind. I really enjoyed it. Probably more than anything I've done since we broke up."

"Are you drunk?"

"Yes. Did you ever drink when you were by yourself? I have to tell you that, when you're not talking to anyone, you tend to drink a lot more."

"Alex, I don't think you know . . ."

"Wait a second, Amanda. This is not the beer talking, although I will give credit on assisting me with the courage to make this call. You put me in a real dilemma this morning."

"How so?"

"Well, I always knew I cared about you, but I never realized how much. After this morning, I realized it was a lot. It really bothered me when I found out you fucked that

Robby guy from that play."

"Alex, we've been through . . ."

"Anyway, you fucked him, and I couldn't stand it. But the scary thing is, although it really bothered me, after this morning, I realized it really didn't matter. I love you anyway. Walking away wasn't the answer."

"What are you saying?"

"You're not going to make this easy, are you?"

"Should I?"

"I think I would like to give us another shot. It's obvious we really care for each other. If we break up, it has to be over something more than jealousy."

Alex waited for a response. A brief silence on the other end of the line was followed with laughter.

"What's so funny?" Alex asked.

"Nothing." Amanda laughed again. "Did you hit your head on the sidewalk or something? You couldn't possibly have grown up this fast."

"I am capable of amazing things, you know."

"I'll give you that!" Amanda said both warmly and sarcastically.

"Well?"

"It's not that easy, Alex. A lot has happened over the last few months. Dad's dying, school is ending, I'm going to Stanford next fall, and you're going around the world starting this summer. Not exactly the greatest foundation for starting over. Don't you think?"

"Amanda, we would have had to face those issues if we had never broken up. We can deal with them now."

"It gets a little more complicated. With everything else, we didn't have a chance to really get into it this morning."

"Hit me."

"I'm seeing someone." Alex's heart sank; he had forgotten, or maybe he had wanted to ignore, that she had briefly mentioned that over their coffee. He clearly remembered that fateful day at the football field when Amanda said she would not wait around. This was going to be a tough one. Alex swallowed hard.

"Is it serious?"

"It's getting there."

"Well, I don't want to mess that up." Alex said. *Yeah right*, he thought to himself. Continuing he said, "But is there any possibility of me getting onto the playing field?" There was no immediate response. "Amanda?"

"Oh, Alex."

Alex didn't like the sound of Amanda's voice. He braced for some unwelcome news. He need not have.

"I know I am going to be messed up for saying this…but I'm really glad you called." During the phone conversation between them that night there were no pretenses. They knew if they took the road Alex was suggesting, it would not be smooth. "So how are you getting home tonight? What if Boder split the party?"

"I'll manage. There's a fat guy who lives downstairs, and who is in desperate need of a friend. I might have to spend the rest of the night discussing the subtle differences between Old Milwaukee and Old Milwaukee Light, but I'm sure I can crash with him. Then I can grab a train in the morning."

"You're not staying at some stranger's house. What's wrong with you?"

"A lot of things," Alex joked.

"That's certainly true, but I don't want you sleeping with a stranger . . . I want you sleeping with me." Alex couldn't imagine hearing anything better.

"That's great Amanda, but you have that tennis match tomorrow. I'll manage. I've been drunker and further away from home than this."

"Alexander Williams, don't start another fight with me just yet. Now where the hell are you?"

"I'm at this place called the Scarlet Pub, but I have no idea what street it is on. If you hold on, I'll ask someone."

"Don't worry about it. I'll find it. Don't move. And one more thing."

"Yes, ma'am?"

"I love you."

"I love you, too."

Alex hung up the telephone and let out a yell so loud most people in the bar heard it, despite the closed glass door and the loud music. Alex smiled as they stared at him. Alex swung open the door and screamed, "She's back!" A few people next to him drunkenly clapped and cheered, though they had no idea what he was talking about. Alex bought everyone around him drinks until he ran out of money. Considering he only had sixty-one dollars on him, it didn't take long. But this act of kindness didn't go unnoticed, and Alex didn't go thirsty during the hour he waited for Amanda to walk in the door. When she did, Alex immediately turned away from the conversation he was engaged in. She wore white corduroy jeans and a grey turtleneck sweater. Around her neck hung the gold locket inscribed with both of their initials and the date they first met. Alex had given the locket to her the Christmas before last. She had trouble spotting him at first. Alex waved at her, catching her eye. She waved back and proceeded toward him. Given the late hour and the predominately drunk crowed, she made slow progress. Alex got up and forcefully headed toward her. "Hi." Alex yelled to be heard above the din.

"Hi."

"Want a beer?"

"Let's go home."

"I can live with that."

A light rain began to fall as the pair drove home. After they arrived at Amanda's room, they probably would have made love for hours, like they do in the movies, except Alex had been up since six that morning. The combination of the morning crew race, meeting Amanda, the party and drinking, and the emotion of their late-night telephone call took its toll on Alex. Amanda turned out the light in her bedroom and waited quietly in anticipation of Alex's caress. Instead she heard a growing snore. Amanda wasn't angry. On the contrary, she was happier than she'd been in quite some time. She turned to him, placed her naked body against his, and joined him in deep sleep.

*****

A gentle breeze knocking the Venetian blinds against the window woke Alex mid-morning. He looked around the room and remembered waking up alone in Amanda's dormitory room the very first night they met. Amanda now lived off campus. On her desk, she still had pictures of her German Shepherd who humped everything in sight, the unhappy cat, and members of her family. A new picture of

The Cruiser, taken last fall when he came for a visit, smiled at Alex from the end table. Alex could barely look at it. He was going to be missed.

The CD jewel box of Mozart's *Le Nozze di Figaro* lay on top of the stereo. It was Amanda's favorite. As the unpleasant thought of Amanda's ill father faded from his mind, Alex focused on the light-yellow wall with a poster of Van Morrison, another of Amanda's favorites. It had been her dad's favorite as well. Amanda had told Alex, "My dad would sit me on his lap when I was no more than two and play Van. I would clap and sing, and he would call me his brown-eyed girl."

On her dressing table was a small picture of Amanda with her arms around someone, in front of the snow-covered entrance to Firestone Library. He recognized the guy as someone from around campus. He vowed not to make an issue of it. If Amanda was recommitting to him, he knew she wouldn't be two-faced about it. She was a big girl and would set the record straight for everybody involved. Alex lay back down and fell asleep. A few hours later he woke to sweaty kisses on the back of his neck. Amanda had returned from her tennis match. "Well, how did we do?" Alex asked, dazed, but aroused.

"We kicked some ass," said Amanda as she pulled the sheets off Alex and bit his shoulder. Turning over to face Amanda, Alex did the same. In a few short minutes, it was a love-all. Afterwards, Amanda tried to talk Alex into having something to eat, but Alex said he had to get to the printer to review his thesis. They agreed to meet at Alex's club for dinner.

It had been a long twenty-four hours. The combined odors

born from parties, bars, smoke, sweat, sleep, and sex, while wearing the same clothes, had Alex smelling less than appealing. Alex returned to the club and waved to Javier, who was having a cigar in the smoking room. "Alexandro! Come join me!" Alex kept walking toward the stairs.

"Maybe later, Jav. Right now, it's best for both of us that I go upstairs and shower. Have you seen Boder this morning?"

"Nada," came the reply. It didn't appear to Alex that Boder had been home since the night before. Boder's room looked exactly as it did when the pair left for New Brunswick. Alex looked out the window, and Boder's car wasn't in the parking lot. This wasn't the first time Boder was out all night, but Alex was having a problem shaking off a feeling of uneasiness.

After his shower, Alex went downstairs to the dining room where Sunday brunch was winding down. He drank a glass of milk, made a baloney and cheese sandwich to eat on the way, and headed across campus to pick up his thesis. The store was even more crowded and chaotic than it had been the day before. Alex got in line behind Abby Siegleson, a woman he knew from his freshman year dormitory. She was a certified genius, albeit neurotic. "Hey, Abby."

"Alex! Alex Williams! Long time no see. So, tell me. Is this ridiculous or what? You would think they were selling Taylor Swift tickets or something!"

"You would think."

"So, when is yours due?"

"Tomorrow."

"Tomorrow! Wow! How can you breathe? Mine is due Friday, and I'm about to have a heart attack. This is the fourth time I have had to make revisions at the printer. I really hope this is it. I haven't had a night with more than three hours' sleep in weeks."

"Maybe it's me Abby, but there's something about a fourth final revision that seems a bit redundant. You're a science major of some sort if my memory serves me right."

"Molecular Biology. I know you're an English major. I remember you in that American Lit. class I had to take to satisfy the writing requirement. Closest I ever came to not getting an A. I hated you, Alex Williams. If that professor picked one more of your papers to read during class, I thought I was going to kill myself." Abby laughed and continued, "Only kidding! So! Here we are at the end of the line literally and figuratively. Quite something, eh? Originally, I was going to do my thesis on Mammalian Genetics, but I wanted something with a little more definition. You'll never guess what I finally chose as a topic."

"I bet you're right," Alex said, realizing why he never stayed in touch with Abby.

"The Contribution of ACYL Amides to the Toxicity of the Damaging ALGA Prymnesium Parvum. What do you think?"

"Sounds like great summer reading to me."

Abby lightly poked Alex in the chest. "Still the wisenheimer! Well, smarty pants, what is your thesis on?"

For some reason, Alex was glad she asked.

"Bowling."

"Come again?"

"Bowling."

"You mean the game with the ten pins, the alley, and the

ball with the three holes?"

"Exactly. I wrote a play about bowling."

Abby's expression was both one of amazement and puzzlement. "I bet that's never been done here before."

"Abby, the more time I spend here, the more I realize that there are a lot of things that have never been done before." Abby's look of bewilderment vanished, as it was her turn at the counter. The clerk, a part-time student at the local community college, knew Abby by name.

"We've been expecting you," said the clerk, somewhat apprehensively.

"I know!" exclaimed Abby. "I've spent so much time and money in here lately. I should have invested in the place! So, what have we got?" The clerk reached under the counter and pulled out one black leather, round back binding. It was rather thick, especially for a science topic, which usually involved more research than written pages. Abby carefully picked up the book preparing for a close inspection. She mouthed the words on the cover as she read them. She placed the book back on the counter, took a six-inch, white, plastic ruler out of her pocketbook and measured the distance between the words and the edges of the book, as well as from each other.

The clerk, well versed with Abby's attention to detail and with how long the process would take, suggested, "you can take it home and go through it, and then let us know if it's OK." Abby snapped out of her trance.

"Oh, sure, sorry. I see one or two things I may to have to change. Unfortunately, there are probably more. Hopefully, when I come back this afternoon it will be the last time."

"I hope so," said the clerk, barely biting his tongue.

"When I come back, can you let me know how much it will be to print and bind one hundred copies?"

"One hundred copies?" asked the astonished clerk.

"Job interviews, friends, and you never know when else you might need one."

Like when you need a doorstop, Alex thought. Alex was amused by his own wit for a moment, but recognized that he felt some concern. Granted, Abby took things a little overboard, but he wondered if he had been a little lackadaisical about this project. He wasn't here for last review and revisions; his paper was due the next day, and he was basically just making sure nothing was severely out of whack. If it looked all right, Alex was going to order right then and there. Maybe leaving more time for a thorough review wouldn't have been a bad idea, he considered. On second thought, maybe that is what separates the science majors from literature majors. Science demands exactness, no room for error. Literature leaves plenty of room for interpretation, opinion, and artistic license.

Alex and Abby said goodbye, promising, with little conviction, to get together before graduation. Alex approached the counter, now feeling some trepidation. "Name?" asked the clerk.

"Williams, Alexander."

"Bowling guy, right?"

"Uh, yeah," Alex replied, more than a bit perturbed.

The clerk looked on one of the shelves behind him. Somewhere between the theses "The War on Poverty: What the American Government Can and Can Not Do to Improve," and "Detailed Origins of Economic Growth in China," was a copy of "The Bowler." It was one of the thinner books on the shelf. Certainly, it was no match for another student's political science thesis, "Corruption in Illinois Government, Vols. 1&2." The clerk handed Alex his thesis. Alex read the title as he reached into his back pocket for his wallet. Mid-action, he stopped dead. His last name was spelled wrong on the cover. Alex thumbed through the pages and noted that page eight was missing. Alex began to feel very warm. "My name is spelled wrong," Alex said with more than a little concern. The clerk looked at the name and compared it with to the yellow invoice sheet taped onto the back of the book.

"Spelled the same way as you requested it. A-L-E-X-A-N=D=E=R W-I-L-I-A-M-S..."

"I know how it is spelled! How many Williams's do you know who spell their name with one L for Christ's sake?"

"I'm certain we would have given you a copy at the time of drop-off, for verification." Alex remembered that he had been in a rush when he dropped the paper off the day before, but he had printed a copy of what he wanted on the binding.

"May I please see the instructions I left with you yesterday?" The clerk must have intuited Alex's request, because he placed it in front of Alex before Alex finished his question. Alex had been in such a hurry to get to the crew meet, that he never even looked at what he printed. Looking at the paper in that moment, he saw it, plain as day: "Alexander Wiliams".

Alex tried to regain some dignity. "Well, what about page eight?" he accused.

"What about it?" asked the clerk, clearly annoyed but use to a process bringing out the most neurotic behaviors.

"It is not fucking in here," Alex articulated, his ability to be patient rapidly disintegrating.

"We bind what we are given, no more, no less," said the clerk, returning to an amazing level of calm.

"After spending months writing this thing, do you actually think I would be so stupid as deliver it to be printed without all the pages?"

"You wouldn't be the first, nor, I would wager, the last. And keep in mind, you did spell your own name wrong."

"Excuse me," came to voice of a student standing in line behind Alex. "I can't wait here all day, you know."

Alex turned around, took a step closer, and put his face within inches of the commenting student's face but, after a few moments and some rational thought, he pulled back. "It's all yours," Alex heard himself say as he walked past the incredulous student and out into the bright sunlight.

On the sidewalk, Alex took a deep breath. He knew there was work to be done. He crossed Nassau Street and headed to a study hall in Holder. It was a quiet little room tucked away in the basement corridor. Alex hadn't set a foot in that room since one morning, about three years ago, when he did some last-minute cramming for a calculus test. Calculus was a course he hated, but it had fulfilled a requirement. In the morning before every exam that year, he would huddle in that study hall with a carton of orange juice, coffee in a thermal cup, and a handful of protein bars. In the latter years, Alex preferred to spend exam mornings relaxing on his bed and always waited until the last possible minute to head over to the examination room. Alex hated the feeling of tension in a room filled with stressed out peers. The nervous talking, the tapping, and the desperate last reviews of notes made him feel uncomfortable. "Screw that," Alex always thought,

"Give me the test, and let's go."

The room in Holder had served him well, so, after receiving his misprinted thesis from the printer, he called on it one more time, sans snacks and beverages. The air was slightly moldy. Alex sat in one of the old, cracked, leather chairs. It still felt familiar. For about ten minutes, he stared at the cover of his thesis. As for the missing page, Alex's face turned red as he remembered printing some revisions and leaving them on top of his computer early Saturday morning. That was probably the first time Alex had read his play from beginning to end in one sitting. He was aghast at the spelling and grammatical errors, even though he had used his computer's spell and grammar checks. He pulled a pencil out of his backpack and first changed the title from "The Bowler" to "Confessions in the Alley." Then Alex began making extensive changes.

Almost five hours after Alex had entered the room, he finished. Now what? he wondered. How in the world am I going to get these changes made, copied, and back to the printer to be bound before the end of the day? I'm just not that fast. As Alex left, he turned around to take a good look at the study hall, then raced out for the last time. Alex ran back to his room and quickly transferred a copy of his play to his USB drive. Despite his frenzied pace, Alex noticed that Boder hadn't yet returned to his room, but had no time to deal with it then.

At about four-thirty, Alex jogged down Nassau Street to an old Victorian house in need of some work on the outskirts of downtown. A small sign, much newer than the building, hung over the center of the porch: EXECUTYPE - WORD PROCESSING, RESUMES, LETTERS, MAILINGS. In

smaller print below that: Leave the Drudgery to Us. Alex
walked up the several stairs, through the front door and into
the foyer. The tapping sound of fingers on a computer
keyboard could be heard coming from an adjoining room.
Alex entered quickly. A woman in her late twenties, with
short jet-black hair and a look of concentration, continued
tapping away.

"Hello!" Alex interjected. The woman, clearly startled,
jumped back in her roll away chair, her hands on her chest,
letting out a short shrill. She stared at Alex in wide eyed
silence.

"I'm sorry," Alex said. "Did I scare you?"

The women breathed deeply. "No, I was just trying to see
what it felt like to have a heart attack."

"I'm really sorry, the door was open, and I thought you
heard me, so I . . ."

"What can I do for you? Alex got the impression that the
woman was not one for small talk, regardless of the situation.

"I need a final draft of this thesis typed."

The woman held her hand out. Alex gave her the play.
She leafed through it quickly.

"What's the matter?" she asked. "Couldn't do the last go-
round?"

"Not enough time."

"Don't fret. This isn't more than two hours work. I'm a
bit backed up, but I can have it back to you by Thursday."

"That's great, but I really need it sooner."

"How much sooner?"

Alex looked at his watch. It was almost five o'clock. The
printer closed at seven.

"Oh . . . let's say . . . in about an hour and forty-five

minutes."

The woman laughed.

"I'm glad somebody finds this funny," Alex commented.

"I'm sorry, but you've got to be kidding. We close in ten minutes."

"Haven't you ever heard of free lancing?"

The woman got up and turned off her machine. "Haven't you ever heard of I've-got-a-life? I spent about eighty hours here this week. Normally, we aren't even open on Sunday."

"How much do you get an hour? I'll double it!"

"Hey, don't go crazy," responded the woman, more than a little sarcastically. "I wouldn't want you spending the movie money your parents gave you."

The woman opened the bottom draw of her desk and pulled out her pocketbook.

"Name your price!"

"Believe it or not, sometimes money isn't the only issue."

Grabbing her keys off the desk the woman continued, "Now if you don't mind, we are about to close."

With a forced, but polite smile, she stretched her arm toward the door, inviting him to leave. Alex neared panic. He took a deep breath.

"Listen... uh . . . may I ask your name?"

"Diane," came the rather terse reply.

"Diane. Beautiful name. Mine is Alex. Alex Williams."

Diane rolled her eyes, forcing, "Your name is great too. Can we go now?" Alex stared deeply into the woman's face and saw nothing. He felt there was only one alternative left and he hated to use it. After all, as a negotiating tactic, it was used infrequently in our society. But Alex was desperate. He knew it was time for the absolute truth.

"Listen, I know you don't know me, but if you don't help me out with this, I am totally screwed."

The woman's eyes grew larger.

"Excuse me?"

"If you don't help me out with this, I . . ."

Diane held her hand up in a stop signal. She forced a smile.

"OK, I got it. I guess you'll learn the valuable lesson of starting earlier next time." Diane took a few more steps toward the door, looked at Alex, and rattled the keys in the air.

"Did you ever do something different?" Alex pushed.

"Eh?"

"Did you ever do something unusual, knowing it would be scrutinized by your peers, or people you respect? Maybe they'd even think it, or you, a little weird? But you didn't give a damn. In fact, that expected response was half the reason you did it in the first place." The woman thought for a moment. She smiled.

"Where are we going with this?" she asked.

"Well I'm not exactly your typical Princeton student, and I don't think this is a typical Princeton thesis. I was wondering if sometimes you ever felt like an outsider looking in."

The woman looked down at the ground and was quiet or a few moments before looking back at Alex. "I grew up in Beaumont, Texas. Ever hear of it?"

"It's somewhere near the gulf in East Texas is all I know."

"It was a lower middle-class town at best, and the black and Hispanic population grew a lot while I was there. Everyone kept to their own kind. Even if you thought a black or Hispanic could be your friend, you didn't dare explore it for fear of being beaten up by either your group or theirs." Alex reflected on how different that was from his high school, where the biggest controversy on any given day was what to eat for lunch. "I'm not sure why I did it," she went on. "At first, I thought it was because I'd just been through a rough break up with my, then, boyfriend. Now I'm not so sure. Anyway, one weekend, while getting my haircut, I had it braided into those cornrows, just like the black girls did. Sometimes, you see black girls wearing cornrows now, but, back then, it seemed like they all did. I'll never forget my mom's face when I walked into the kitchen. She almost choked on her sandwich. She tried to get me to change it, but when my dad split a few years earlier, the authority in the house seemed to go with him. I thought she was overreacting, but, after a few days at school, I could see she wasn't.

"What do you mean?" Alex asked, much more interested in Diane's response then he thought he would be when he initially asked the question.

"Well, the student body had four clear-cut opinions. The white girls thought it was cool, though no one else dared try it. I realized later that the real reason they liked it was because it lowered my standing in the competition for the white boys. The white boys didn't take kindly to the look. When groups of them passed me in the hall, I'd hear things like 'white Jemima' and 'nigger fucker.' And the black guys thought I was sending out some screaming signal that I wanted to get more than friendly. I mean, they were all over me. But it was the black girls that were really something. I mean, they were pissed with a capital P. On the fourth day of wearing my new hairdo, a group of black girls cornered me in the girl's bathroom. The spokesperson asked me, point blank, what I was up to with the hair. I told her I just liked the way it looked. She looked at me for a second, then pushed me hard into the stall door. To say she spoke frankly would be an understatement. She told me that I better not be making fun of them, like I was some white girl imitation of Alicia Keys or something. Then the biggest girl put her face right in mine, grabbed me by the sweater, and told me that if any of them ever saw me come onto a black guy at school, I would be one dead bitch. With that, she gave me a good shot in the stomach, leaving me crouched over on the bathroom floor."

"Wow! What did you do?"

"Do I look that stupid? I ran home and practically ripped the braids out. After that incident, I looked at life a little differently. I realize now that there are very few, if any, times in our lives when we truly do what we want." Alex and the woman stared at each other. She looked puzzled.

Diane asked, "So how the hell did we get into this discussion anyway?"

"I was going to try to guilt trip you into helping me, but after hearing your story, mine is embarrassing.

"I don't follow you."

"If you don't help me, I'm not going to get beat up in a bathroom or anything. The only consequence will be a lower grade for turning the paper in late. I'd like to think that I've done things a little differently while here. Keep in mind, we are talking about Princeton, so being different doesn't necessarily mean running head on into sexual and racial barriers. My defiance was a lot tamer than yours."

"Well?" Diane said sounding quite disinterested.

"I wrote my thesis on bowling."

"What?"

"I'm an English major. For my senior thesis, I wrote a play about bowling." Diane instantaneously broke out in laughter. It became apparent to Alex that she wasn't going to stop quickly. "Is it that funny?" Alex asked.

Diane tried to compose herself. It was no use. Screaming out, "BOWLING," she covered her mouth with her hands and quickly looked down at the floor. Her shoulders heaved. Alex waited impatiently for her to calm down. Alex attempted dialogue three or four times before she wiped her eyes, and apologized. "I'm really sorry," she sniffed. "I guess I got carried away, but you guys are really something. I've been working here for five years now. I've done work for hundreds of you Princeton people, both students and professors. Sometimes, I feel like I'm working at a cloning center. Everyone's so bright, most are good-looking, and more than a few of you have some serious cash. I don't think I've ever remembered the name of a single person who came in here, and I can't tell you how many times I've mixed up assignments. I understand what you are saying, that you consider it radical to write a play about bowling for your senior thesis. I think you either should laugh or cry about it, because it's either very funny or very sad. I chose to laugh."

Alex thought about that for a moment and nodded his head in agreement. "Does any of this mean that I'll get some help?"

"Three hundred dollars," came the reply.

Alex almost said something about the price, but he bit his tongue. In any event, he reasoned, the story she told was worth at least half the price of admission.

They spent almost two hours inputting Alex's changes. Diane was good at her job, and, having processed hundreds of theses over the years, she also made some excellent suggestions. "If Joyce Carol Oates listens to me, you should too," Diane quipped. Finally, at about six forty-five, it was done. "You said the printer closed at seven? You better hurry." Diane smiled. Alex paid her with a wrinkled check he kept in his wallet for emergencies. He thanked her, grabbed his jacket, and was about to hurry out.

"Hey," she said, "I enjoyed helping you. Earlier, I told you that I never remember any of you once you walked out of here. I don't think that's going to be true any longer."

"I appreciate that. You did more for me than you could imagine."

"Any possibility that, after things slow down a bit, you could take me for a drink or a movie?"

Alex stared at Diane. He felt that she deserved not to be led on. "I'm sorry," he said, "I just got back into a pretty heavy relationship. I don't think it would be a smart idea at this point. But if I hadn't, then I would have been happy to see a movie with you."

Diane forced a smile. Unconvincingly, she said, "It's OK. Maybe if things don't work out."

"Maybe," Alex said in the same tone. He stiffly shrugged his shoulders and repeated, "Thanks again." Diane nodded in acknowledgment, and he left the building, thinking about what might have been. Resuming focus on the matter at hand, Alex hurried to the printing store, making it with just seconds to spare.

Having not eaten a thing all day, Alex went to P.J.'s and ordered two bacon cheeseburgers with fries and a large milk. He ate so fast, it seemed he had finished everything before the plate even hit the counter. Fully contented, Alex headed back to O'Neill. He was tired, so he went upstairs to call Amanda. As the phone rang, Alex realized he had completely forgotten that he was supposed to meet her for dinner. To his surprise, Amanda didn't seem mad at all. "Hey, aren't you pissed that I stood you up?"

"Alex, I've learned a few things in my old age. I stopped by your club and BT said he hadn't seen you. I figured you got caught with your thesis."

"You figured right. Want to come over?"

"I hope you don't mind, but, after last night and my match this morning, I feel like someone shot me."

"Understood. I'll be here tomorrow, so come over for lunch, or else."

"Or else what?"

"Or else you will be in big trouble," Alex joked.

"Or else you are going to have go down on me," Amanda said very matter-of-factly.

Alex was stunned for a moment. It wasn't that Amanda was a prude, but there was a bedroom Amanda, and then there was an everything else Amanda. She was a real example of why judging a book by its cover was a bad idea. "Ms. Fallon," Alex said in a mock stern voice, "that was uncalled for. Upon our next meeting, you will be punished."

"Is that a promise?" Amanda responded. Their relationship was clearly entering a new phase, and Alex smiled to himself at the thought as he and Amanda said goodnight.

Alex grabbed a coke from the refrigerator and sat down on his bed. He was still quite concerned that no one had seen Boder since Alex left him at the party in New Brunswick the night before. For all he knew, Boder could still have been partying, or perhaps he was shacked up with Rachel somewhere. Alex texted Boder but got no reply. He decided that, if he didn't hear from Boder by the next morning, he'd drive up to New Brunswick and see what was going on. Comforted with this idea, Alex fell asleep, the freshly opened soda falling out of his hand and spilling onto the floor.

XXII

Alex was never exactly sure what happened after he fell asleep. Perhaps he had a freaky bad dream, but Alex thought he felt a rough kiss on his lips. He awoke in darkness to the sound of the hallway door closing, so he put on a light and walked into Boder's room. No one was there. Alex went back to the living room. He was alone. Suddenly, something clicked in Alex's head. He returned to Boder's room and found a pair of soiled, wrinkled pants slung over a desk chair. Alex recognized the pants as those worn to the New Brunswick party. He looked at the clock on Boder's desk. It was two thirty on Monday morning, one of the rare times O'Neill was totally quiet. Alex sat down on Boder's bed. Maybe Boder was on some drug and sex binge with Rachel, he guessed. No, after all, she was a med student. Maybe she goes off occasionally, but not for days at a time. Alex recalled her saying that she had a test early in the week. Alex searched the common rooms of the club, no Boder. "Goddamnit, Boder," Alex whispered to himself, "Where the hell are you?"

Alex walked over to a window in the dining room. The sky was crystal clear, and the full moon cast distinct shadows along the ground. Looking south, beyond other eating clubs,

Alex could see the sky illuminated behind Benheim and Corwin Halls. The illumination was from the fountain lights. In honor of the warmer weather, the fountain had been reopened that previous day. Alex's eyes widened. He knew Boder never missed the opening of the fountain. Alex ran to his room, put on a pair of black sweats and sneakers, and ran outside.

As Alex approached the steps between Robertson and Fisher Halls, which lead up to the fountain, he could hear the rush of the water. Going up the stairs, Alex began to see sparkles of water shooting up from the fountain that was still blocked by the building to his left. Reaching the top of the stairs, Alex walked quickly, rounded the corner of Robertson, and came to the promenade. Now in full view, Alex gazed at the blue pool of water shining brightly in the clear night air. The wind pushed a cool mist onto something standing in the water near the fountain. Facing away, clad only in boxers and a tee shirt, Alex knew exactly who it was. As Alex slowly approached, he remembered coming here at the very beginning of the school year, where he found this person in the middle of the water, lying on a chase lounge chair, reading a book, and having a wonderful time screwing with people's heads. "Well, if it isn't the Bodster!" Alex announced in the same tone he'd used that late August day. Boder didn't respond right away. "Hey, did somebody stuff a couple of squid in your ears?" Alex asked in as lighthearted a tone as he could muster. Boder slowly turned around. Alex could see instantly that he was high, very high. Alex swallowed hard and tried to stay non-confrontational, commenting, "Wow! Guess you had a little fun after I left the party last night, eh?"

Ignoring Alex's inquiry, Boder asked, "How did you know I was here?"

"Hey, it's opening day at the fountain, where the hell else would you be? Besides, some queer kissed me on the lips about fifteen minutes ago, and I think I need to hunt him down and kill him." Boder smiled slightly.

"Did you ever have a tree house when you were a kid?"

"What?" Alex asked.

"A tree house. Did you ever have one?"

Alex remembered the tree house his father had helped him build with some scrap wood from a house addition. For weeks, Alex took the scrap wood out of the garbage until his father finally caved in and let him build a tree house in the only large tree in the whole yard. "Yeah, when I was about nine or so."

"Did you like it?"

Alex's dad had teased him, saying the view from the house looked like a junkyard, but Alex loved it. "Yes. Very much."

"I always wanted a tree house." Alex wasn't sure where the conversation was going, but he didn't like it. "Obviously, the townhouse in Georgetown wasn't very conducive to a tree house, but our home in Virginia had acres of land. Not that we really spent any time there. It wouldn't have mattered, anyway. Once, on a trip back home from one of my dad's many fundraisers, I asked my father if we could build one. You know what he said, right in front of Shirley and Mary? He said, 'What the hell do you think this is, kid? A ghetto? I don't want any press coming around here finding some shack blocking the view of the roses. Cost me a pretty penny to get that garden in shape, and you want to go and ruin it with some goddamn tree house. Next thing you know, you'll be asking for a trailer home. Sometimes, I think you're spending just too much time with the help around here.' Even my mother joined in. 'Richard,' she said, 'your father is right. Well, not about the remarks concerning the help, but in general. You have a beautiful home, son. I really don't think you need another one.' I ask you, what the hell are you supposed to say to that?" Boder looked down at the rippling water and then back at Alex, continuing, "I mean, Jesus Christ, all I wanted was a fucking tree house."

In the silence that followed, they both knew Boder wanted something much less tangible than a tree house. Alex wanted to take this one step at a time. "What do you say we continue our little chit chat back at the club? It's not the warmest of spring evenings." Alex exaggerated the chill by bringing his arms close to his body and moving up and down.

Boder's eyes grew large and excited. "Are you kidding? It's great here!" With that, Boder ripped off his undershirt and fell back into the water, laughing. Alex stood uncomfortably at the water's edge as bubbles rose to the blue and white surface at the point where Boder had been standing. Suddenly, Boder's head, eyes closed, hair back, and mouth open, resurfaced both coughing and laughing.

"Come on in, bro!" Boder, again, dived under the water and resurfaced with a yell of exuberance.

"Bode, I'm too goddamn cold. Let's go back and grab a beer."

"Fuck going back. Never go back, Alexander. It's not a good thing." Boder had never called him Alexander, but Alex would wonder about that later. Boder continued to swim in the water, and Alex paced.

Boder stood up and, without a word, began to take off his underwear. "What the hell are you doing, man?"

"Getting butt naked. What does it look like I'm doing?"

"Bode, you must be stoned out of your mind. You'll get arrested. We're in clear view of Washington Road, and there has to be security cameras around here somewhere."

"Have I ever been concerned about consequences?"

"No, you certainly haven't. While I usually admire that characteristic in you, I wonder if it's such a good thing in this circumstance. Bode, don't do this, man." Alex took off his sneakers and stepped into the chilly water. "You get arrested on campus, when you're not even supposed to be here, and they'll never let you back."

"I'm not coming back!" Boder sang out. As Alex approached, Boder threw his underwear over his shoulders and retreated into the brass sculpture, where the water spray was heaviest. Alex was more than a tad annoyed.

"Bode, don't be a baby. You're not thinking squarely. Now please, let me help you out." Boder smiled and waved to Alex from the safety of the sculpture. "Fine, then just stay here with your dick sticking out. Just don't call me from the police station tonight, because I am not coming to bail your ass out. Totally disgusted, Alex proceeded to walk out of the water, slipped his sneakers back on, and determined he'd go home alone. About twenty steps away from the water's edge, Alex was surprised he hadn't heard a response to his declaration. Peeking back, Alex saw Boder trying to climb the jagged edges of the brass sculpture. Alex ran to the edge. "Boder this is ridiculous. You're going to get hurt."

While continuing to climb, not looking in Alex's direction, Boder yelled through the water spray, "I thought you were leaving."

"I am, but not without you."

Boder stopped climbing. Water dripped off his nose and down his face. "When I went back to the room tonight, I got a text message. It was my father asking me to call him right away. There was a tone in his voice that I knew meant there was a problem. I was so stoned and scared, that I could hardly dial the goddamn phone. Guess what it was?"

"He found out you were kicked out of school."

"Bingo! Give that kid a prize!

"Well we knew that was going to happen. I mean, even he knew you were supposed to graduate this June."

"Some jack-off in the press, doing a little sniffing around before the election primary next month, found out. I heard it made page seven of *The Washington Post*. You know what he told me?" Boder took one hand off the sculpture and wiped his eyes. He didn't wait for Alex to respond. It didn't matter. Alex knew it was bad. "He told me I was an embarrassment to the family. He told me he couldn't risk jeopardizing the welfare of him and my mother. . . Do you know what it's like to be called a risk to your parents by your own parents?"

Alex looked down at his shoes, feeling the uncomfortable combination of leather and wet feet.
"No, Bode, I don't," Alex said honestly. "I'm sure it's no bowl of cherries."

"It's not even the pits," Boder said, as he began to resume his climb.

"Hey!" Alex yelled. "So, your father is an asshole. So what? You're not the only one in this world who has an asshole for a father. At least you had a rich one. Think of the poor kid who gets a whipping every day in some trailer home. The fact is, you're anything but an asshole, and that's the most important thing. I love you, Richard Boderman, and I am not the only one."

Boder smiled. "Alexander, I appreciate your support. I always have. You are a friend, Mr. Williams, of the very first order. You helped me more than you will ever know. I believe, however, that there are a few things that even a friendship of our magnitude cannot rectify. One of them is blood. It is a very strong thing, and I hate that fact. You hear stories all the time, about people abandoned at birth by biological parents. They get raised in a super loving home by adoptive parents, who were willing to bring a total stranger into their home and love him and take care of him, as if he was their own. And what do these adoptees do? They search the world for their birth parents, the ones who threw them out in the first place. My parents kept me, but I don't think I fall into the fortunate category on that one. It wasn't a love thing. I was a part of the happy family charade designed to better enable Daddy to get ahead."

"Bode, you might be taking it a bit too far. I will give you that your father seems to be the living incarnation of every bad politician joke. He's no Dalai Lama, but he is concerned about you." Alex swallowed hard. "I think he loves you."

"He does not love me," Boder immediately responded through tight lips.

"I think you're being unfair."

"He does not..." Boder couldn't finish his sentence. He began to weep. Alex did not know what to say. Boder continued, "Did I ever tell you the story of my friend, Benny?"

"Benny?" Alex asked, drawing a blank.

"The kid at the ball game in Baltimore that my father diddled?"

"No, Boder. I don't think this is such a promising idea right now." Alex knew what the answer was going to be, and he thought it best to stay away from this topic. Unfortunately, he also knew he had little choice.

"Benny wasn't the first. I'm not sure who the hell was first, but I was in that club." Boder began to cry more heavily. Alex felt a cold sweat seeping through his upper torso. He was at a total loss as to how to diffuse that situation but knew he had to try. He walked back into the water without bothering to take his sneakers off. When he reached the sculpture, he began to climb it. He felt the sharp edges and almost immediately saw blood gushing from a cut on his hand. The blood mixed with the water to give it a pinkish hue, and Alex wrapped his hand in his shirtsleeve before continuing the painful climb. After another few feet, he could place a hand lightly on Boder's right calf.

"Bode!" Alex yelled up, gasping as the downward tide of the water hit his face. "I'm not going to lie and tell you everything's going to be OK. You're too smart for that. I know you are in some terrible pain, and it's not going to go away overnight. Maybe it will never go completely. But, Bode . . . man . . . we're all dealt some good hands and some bad hands. This hand you lost, but it's a long game. We've only just begun to play."

As he paused, Alex could hear the echo of water being pumped up the veins of the sculpture, pouring out to the waiting body below. His cut hand was throbbing, the pace of the blood flow increasing. Suddenly, Alex felt Boder pull his leg away from Alex's good hand. Boder climbed to the top of the sculpture. When he reached the pinnacle, he sat down precariously. Alex tried to follow but the pain in his hand was too much. After almost falling twice, Alex stopped, looked up at Boder, and said, "Well?"

"Well, what?" Boder asked.

Alex tried desperately to lighten things up. "Are we leaving, or should I have a pizza delivered?"

Boder looked up at the sky. "No, we're not leaving." Alex's brief sense of levity once again turned to fear. Boder continued, "I know what you're saying Alex, about it being early in the game. But I don't think you understand what it's like to be me. Remember when you were a kid, and they chose teams in the sandlot? You're very athletic, so you were probably always picked early. I sucked. I was always picked last."

"I didn't think you gave a shit about sports."

"Don't you see? I never had the chance to give a shit. Having teams fight over who's not going to have you doesn't exactly give you the incentive to maintain interest. My parents are like the captains of those teams that didn't want me. I grew up as a necessary evil. To them, I was great for the family angle around election time, but I was shitty when they had to hunt down a babysitter. Growing up, I always felt like a spectator in my own life. So, yeah, it may be early in the game, Alex, but I never really was in it from the start."

Suddenly, Boder's expression changed from one of depression to what seemed like utter joy. He stood on top of the sculpture. Alex's heart raced, and he thought he might pass out from just looking at Boder. Boder was weaving, slightly, back and forth, assaulted by the wind and shooting water. "But it is here, Alex . . . here, at this one place on this great big earth, that I always feel good. I'm not exactly sure why that is. All I know is that I'm at peace here." Neither party spoke for a few moments. To Alex, the sound of the water shooting up and over Boder, then back to the water below seemed almost deafening.

"Hey, Alex, remember the Robert Frost poem, "The Road Not Taken"?

Alex forced a smile. "How could I forget it? You had it taped to the wall of our room freshman year."

Boder nodded in agreement and began to recite the last verse of the poem:

I shall be telling this with a sigh,
Somewhere age and ages hence Two
roads diverged in a wood and I—
I took the one less traveled by,
A road that has made all the difference.

Boder outstretched his arms.

"Boder!" Alex yelled. "Come down! It's very dangerous!"

"No, Alexander, this is not dangerous. Life is dangerous." Boder raised his face toward the sky and, while laughing loudly, arched his back. Alex forgot about the pain in his hands and scrambled up the sculpture to grab Boder. It was not to be. Boder fell backwards over Alex.

With a chilling voice, Alex screamed Boder's name. Everything seemed to move in slow motion. Ironically, Alex felt what Boder had just described, as if he was watching the world from the outside. Alex looked down as Boder hit the shallow water almost flat on his back. He felt as though he had time to count each of the hundreds of individual droplets jumping out of the water, before they crashed down again. Alex looked at Boder's face and noticed he was smiling. It wasn't a large smile, rather a peaceful one. Boder disappeared into the water.

Alex looked up at the sky, moonlight reflecting off the water on his face. An agonized utterance came deep from within. It was a sound he had never heard come out before. Boder's body, spread eagle, eyes open and head surrounded by a growing red cloud, began to rise to the surface. Making nonhuman noises, Alex climbed a few feet down the sculpture and jumped off, landing on his feet and then falling into the water near Boder's body. "Boder!" Alex yelled as he hurried to stand up, lifting Boder up by his back, and finding Boder's face still and sullen, his brown eyes staring, while blood trickled out of his mouth. Alex dragged Boder to the side of the fountain and onto the ledge. Between desperate attempts at CPR, Alex would yell, almost angrily, at Boder to wake up. Boder's expression didn't change. Alex's cries for help echoed helplessly against the surrounding buildings. Alex softly placed his head on Boder's chest, held him tightly, and began to cry.

At the fountain, Alex had stayed with Boder until help finally arrived. Another student had heard Alex's screams on her way home from a lab and notified campus security. The paramedics tried to convince him that there was nothing to be done. They encouraged Alex to stay behind and talk to the police, then go home. Alex insisted on going in the ambulance. He stayed at the hospital for hours after the doctors told him that Boder died of a cerebral hemorrhage. At first, the cops were pestering Alex with questions about the drugs found in Boder's body, and then they stopped abruptly. They'd received a high-level call that originated in Washington, went to the Governor's mansion down the road, and then to the small police station in the center of town.

*****

The services took place in Washington. The wake, even though he was there for only a very brief time, was the worst part for Alex. Alex hadn't seen a dead body since his father died. This was much worse. This was a bypass of the normal course of nature. When he walked into the Devol Funeral Home on Wisconsin Avenue, made his way through the crowd of people, and came upon the body of his best friend lying dead in a blue suit in a casket, the urge to vomit became uncontrollable. Alex dashed out a fire exit, into the back of the parking lot. For nearly ten minutes, in a light rain, he coughed and puked violently next to a shiny new hearse. Sweat dripped down his face and off his nose and chin like it did after a crew race. He thought about leaving and coming back the next day for the funeral, if he could muster the courage. Suddenly, someone wrapped an arm around his upper back. Alex looked over his shoulder at the face in the shadows. A voice spoke softly, "It's gonna be all right, honey. It's gonna be all right." It was Shirley. Alex turned around and hugged her. They held each other tight, as Alex cried hard into her shoulder. Finally, Alex regained enough composure to speak.

"I'm sorry, Shirley," he began. "I didn't mean to impose

on you like that."

Shirley rubbed his cheek lightly with her hand. "You ain't imposing on no one, honey. Richard was a good boy. He deserves some tears." Alex looked at Shirley's face. She had gotten older since the last time he had seen her. Her hair was mostly grey. Alex considered what a terrific addition she would make to Princeton's philosophy department. Wanting to ask a question, Alex almost stopped himself, but decided that there was no need to be bashful with Shirley.

"What's it going to be like at the Boderman's now that Richie is gone?"

"I'll never know, Alex. About time I get back to Arkansas. I'm leaving right after the funeral. Haven't been back there in twenty-two years. Richie was my job here. He's why I stayed. Once he finished college and moved out of the house for good, I was good as gone anyway. I can't take that father of his for another minute. If I stay any longer, I'm seriously afraid I might kill him."

Alex looked deeply into Shirley's eyes. It was no joke. "What about Mary?"

"She's coming with me. Says she's been listening to me talk about Arkansas for so long, feels like she was born and raised there herself." The pair stared into each other's eyes, feeling each other's pain. "I just can't stay here no more."

"I know Shirley. I know."

Alex went back inside. He walked through the crowded viewing room, nodding in acknowledgment to classmates and Boder's friends whom he had met over the years. He wanted to pay his respects to Boder before talking to anyone. Within ten feet of the casket, the crowd thinned out. Boder's mother sat in one of the wing chairs in the front row, teary eyed, wearing something from the latest Vera Wang Collection. Boder's father stood nearby, somberly talking to a pair of men wearing the same black suit and black tie. Mary was sitting next to Mrs. Boderman, wearing her wool overcoat. From the look on her tired face, scarred by the marks of dried tears, it was apparent that she had been there for a long time.

Amidst a few dozen allergy inducing floral arrangements, Alex found himself looking again at his best friend inside a mahogany casket. A little dizzy, Alex knelt on the kneeler in front of the casket. Alex smiled. He had rarely seen Boder in a suit. Even at the eating club formal events, Boder always managed to forgo the required tuxedo "You're still here," Alex whispered into the box. "Bet you're dying for a blunt." Alex looked into Boder's face, whiter now than when he turned him over in the fountain. Alex stopped joking. Once again, he fought back the tears and began to whisper, "Bode, I'm sorry, man. I knew you were going through tough times. I should have paid more attention. I get so caught up in the shit around me. I thought it was all so important. I already lost my dad. You'd think I'd have learned what's important. Getting kicked out of school, your father's abuse, the drugs . . . Jesus, it's amazing you lasted as long as you did."
Alex rubbed his eyes with his right thumb and forefinger. "I just wish you knew what you meant to so many people, Bode. I don't think you had any idea how many people cared about you. Behind that crazy front you put on, it was obvious to everyone that you had a heart of gold." Alex took a deep breath and looked up at a small brass cross tucked into a corner of the inside top of the casket. "I wish that heart hadn't stopped." Alex bent over and kissed Boder on his

cheek. "I'm going to miss you, Richard Boderman. So long old friend. I hope what they say is true and we get to meet again."

Alex made the sign of the cross, something he had not done in a long time. He took one last look at his best friend and turned to walk away. As he did, Alex's eyes met the gaze of Boder's mother. Her look was almost apologetic, as if she was asking forgiveness for what she knew was a terrible wrong. Alex, who was afraid he would say something awful in a fit of anger, felt sorry for her. In that one instant, he understood that she was a puppet on a string. She had about as much control over her life as Boder had over his. Either dinner at the White House, casting a blind eye to mistresses and an abused child, or no dinners, no White House and, probably, no child. She was in serious pain, realizing she had played the game too long. Alex could see in her eyes the knowledge that he knew, the secrets of her messed up family. He wanted to give her a hug, to tell her it was all right, but she seemed so fragile, as if she would fall to ashes on the spot if she was touched, fancy dress and all. Instead, Alex offered a warm smile, nodded at Mary, and walked away.

Unaware of Alex's presence, the Senator kept talking. Alex decided not to intervene. He hoped to deal with the Senator on another occasion. He knew that was not the time. For once in his life, Alex thought, let Boder be the center of attention.

There were a couple of classmates whispering and nervously laughing in the lobby, but Alex wasn't in the mood to engage. He walked into the Washington air, where the rain was falling more heavily. He stopped at the corner store and bought a cheap umbrella. He walked aimlessly for a while, out of the Georgetown area, across the Potomac, onto Pennsylvania Avenue, through Washington Circle, and found himself in Lafayette Square. He stood, staring through the black wrought iron fence at the White House across the street. Every window was lit up. Could there possibly be something going on in each room? Behind the White House, Alex could see the top half of the Washington Monument awash in bright, white light, against the black and rainy sky. Probably the most famous penis symbol in the world, Alex thought, allowing himself the opportunity to authentically smile for the first time all day.

Alex walked up Seventeenth Street, around the side of the White House, and into the National Mall. He faced the monument, and looked up, taking in all five hundred fifty-five feet, five and one-eighth inch of marble and aluminum, and the red blinking light that appeared hazily at the top. Alex turned to look back at the city, and he smiled. It was like a history book had come to life. Out there were The White House, the Lincoln Memorial, the reflecting pool, the Jefferson Memorial, the US Capital, and other familiar buildings. That was Boder's town. Alex was disturbed by a noise. Two rats, much larger than those from high school biology, were moving along the edge of the garbage can about six feet away. Looking around the base of the Monument, Alex saw a few more scurrying about, no doubt searching for treats left behind by long departed tourists. Alex watched one, perhaps weary of the rain, scurry under a barred, windowless entrance of the monument, now dry inside America's most famous piece of architecture.

*****

The funeral was held at the National Presbyterian Church on Wisconsin Avenue. The church was filled with dignitaries from the various branches of government. Members of O'Neill, as well as other Princeton friends, were scattered in the pews. Amanda was unable to attend the wake because of a tennis match at Brown, but she had taken a very early train and was now seated next to Alex in the back of the church. Alex reasoned that, if Boder's spirit were present, it would be hanging out in the last row, watching the fiasco.

Alex heard a muffled commotion in the vestibule. He turned around and saw a half dozen solemn but watchful men enter the church. The President of the United States followed them. As he began his procession into the church, the President nodded at Alex as if he knew him, but proceeded to make the same gesture to people on both sides of the aisle as he passed. He made his way to the front of the church, whispered solemnly to Boder's parents, then sat in the pew immediately behind them. "Well, Bode," Alex whispered. "They even got you the Big Cheese. I'll be really impressed if the Pope comes strolling in."

Alex heard another commotion in the vestibule a few minutes later. Alex would never learn that it had been Benny, Boder's childhood friend. He was yelling about it all being the old man's fault. Benny never made it further inside.

There was a television camera recording from a corner of the church. For a moment, it almost made Alex ill. The old man never can pass up a publicity opportunity, can he Bode? Alex's thought was interrupted by music coming from a gallery above the nave of the church. A choir began singing the choral from Beethoven's Ninth Symphony, an interpretation of Friedrich Schiller's poem, "An Die Freude"/ "Ode to Joy." Boder loved that piece. Alex felt himself drift from the activity within the church, as his mind invoked memories of Boder so vivid, Alex was almost convinced he was being transported back in time. Maybe a last gift from Boder. He recalled their first meeting in Holder Hall, so much more boyish then. There was the big fight at Lionhead, the parties at O'Neill, road trips, sitting around drinking or getting stoned, lying around their room talking. They were kids having fun together, learning together, and becoming men together.

The altar was filled with white violets. The minister, in his sixties and with a British accent, read the Gospel. Alex had heard it before. It was about the two criminals crucified with Jesus. One criminal felt that, if Jesus was really their Messiah, he should save them. The second criminal scolds the first and asks Jesus to take him to heaven when they die. Alex thought the second criminal really had his stuff together. He doubted he would have been as composed in that situation.

After reading the Gospel, the priest closed the red leather book and delivered his sermon. Alex expected a sermon about death and the afterlife—the usual story about how the deceased was now happy in heaven and could always look down on everybody on earth—but it was quite different. The priest told a story about a guy who was a blue-collar factory worker living just outside Livonia, Michigan. The guy worked very hard for some company that made hand dryers for public restrooms. He was never late for work, and he rarely socialized, just did his job and went home. For enjoyment, his favorite activities were smoking and drinking. The guy was a bit high strung. He would curse a blue streak if someone cut him off on the highway. If dinner was late or his shirt wasn't clean enough, he wasn't averse to giving his wife a good one across the kisser. He took his family on vacation one time, to Disney World, and complained about the expense of it for years.

On their twenty-fifth wedding anniversary, he bought his wife a new vacuum. On his retirement, after thirty-five years with the same company, the firm gave him a blue rain jacket with the company logo—a pair of dry hands on the pocket— and a weekend in the Poconos. After retirement, he sat around watching talk shows on television and waiting for his monthly social security check to arrive. Every time a check arrived, he made a mental note that it was one more for him and one less for them.

In his late seventies, he became sick. His doctor had told him he had Alzheimer's. A progressive disease, he knew he would end up in a nursing home, not knowing where or who he was. He spent his remaining lucid time hiding his few assets, so, when he needed services, he would become a ward of the state. One more plus for him, he thought. Sure enough, he did become a ward of the state, drooling and defecating on himself until he died in a state of ignorant bliss just short of two years later.

Initially, Alex had absolutely no idea where the story was going, but then realized that was the whole point. There were millions of people out there in the world like that guy. Maybe not all of them were wife beaters, although there were probably more than people would like to admit, but millions of people who drone through life and then die. The priest made it clear that he thought heaven was a much better place than earth, but he did not think it wise to squander away the human years. He called it "the experience of living." Alex liked that. Boder had experienced life, albeit not for as long as most would have liked. He not only tasted life, he bit into it. Boder had experienced more of what life had to offer in any given month, than the guy from Livonia, Michigan had in his entire lifetime. Alex smiled to himself as he stared down the center aisle at the casket at the foot of the altar. Richard Boderman, Alex thought, you were some piece of work. I'll always love you, man.

*****

  A few days after Boder's death, Alex would walk into Boder's room, convinced that Boder would be in his bed taking a nap. Alex hated that feeling of grief that swept over him when reality would set in. It was spooky and sad. He'd had the same feelings for almost a year after his father died. Afterlife or no afterlife, death sucked.

XXIII

The remainder of the year brought more mental stress than Alex had envisioned on that early September day when he drove on the New Jersey Turnpike, ready to begin the last hurrah of college. Certainly, Boder's death was mostly to blame, but writing his senior thesis, chasing the national crew championship, and completing the graduation checklist, had Alex more on edge than he would have liked. That weekend was no exception. Saturday morning, the crew team would race against Cornell and Yale in Ithaca, and the Spring Ball at O'Neill was scheduled for that evening. Going to the Spring Ball would mark Alex's first official date with Amanda since they began talking again. No one at the club, or anyone else for that matter, knew they were together again. He anticipated a barrage of nosey questions. Just human nature, Alex tried to reason.

The team rode up to Ithaca Friday evening. Alex had been reluctant to go—not sure he was ready so soon after Boder's death. Amanda told him how she hated the thought of walking onto the tennis court knowing her father's condition. She also knew that her father would be more upset if she didn't, no matter what his condition. They agreed that Boder would have felt the same way about Alex's crew meet. Still, that did nothing to soothe Alex's unease.

The next morning, Princeton had an easy time beating both Cornell and Yale on Lake Cayuga. It was becoming clear that, barring an unforeseen disaster, Princeton would go into the National Championships at the end of May undefeated. At about two o'clock, the team left Ithaca for what was usually a four-hour ride back to Princeton. On that day, however, traffic was brutal. Alex was anxious to get back for the Spring Ball. He texted Amanda to apologize in advance that he might be late, and the bus finally pulled into the boathouse house parking lot just after seven. Throwing his equipment bag to Daley, Alex asked that he put it in the locker room for him. He jumped off the bus and jogged back to O'Neill.

With the rigors of the race still wearing on his body, Alex put his ear to the front door of O'Neill, pausing before he had the strength to continue. He could hear music and voices coming from various rooms. The cocktail hour had already begun. Alex decided to go around back and enter through the kitchen. He waved to Antonio who, upset and testy with the caterers who had taken over his kitchen, didn't even see him. Alex raced upstairs to get dressed and call Amanda to tell her he would be over to pick her up shortly.

Alex flung open the door to his suite, only to find Amanda sitting on the couch. She was impeccably dressed in a black velvet evening gown and wore a Mikimoto pearl necklace that The Cruiser had given to her on her twenty-first birthday. In an empty flower pot Alex had bought with the best of intentions at the beginning of the year, Amanda had iced down a bottle of Dom Perignon. Alex closed the door behind him, leaned back, and smiled. "Sorry, I'm late," he said.

"It just makes the champagne colder," Amanda replied without a hint of emotion.

"We won."

"As The Cruiser's daughter, I would expect nothing less." Amanda brushed her right fingers through her hair.

Alex, still sweaty and out of breadth, walked over to the couch and sat down. "Is that so?" he queried.

"Damn straight." They stared at each other with mock seriousness, but only for a few seconds before laughter broke through.

"I'd better get dressed for this shindig," Alex said, as he began to get up from the couch. Amanda grabbed his belt loop and stopped him in his tracks.

"I don't think that will be necessary," she said, as she crawled onto his lap and gave him a kiss. After their fun on the couch, the floor, and the coffee table, they both took a much-needed shower. He put on a used Tuxedo he had purchased from a fellow eating club member who graduated two years earlier. By the time Alex and Amanda walked into the dining room, dinner was over. Looking at the remnants of the spectacular feast, displayed on discarded plates, Alex wondered whether skipping the third go-round upstairs might have been a better idea. Amanda looked at Alex and, recognition of the absence of more food being served, gave him a mock pout.

The pair went through the smoking room and onto the back patio, where the party was in full swing. A reggae band was playing on the back lawn, and illuminated ice sculptures of famous people adorned the landscape: Winston Churchill, John F. Kennedy, Bono, Nelson Mandela, Albert Einstein, the Princeton Tiger, Saddam Hussein, and Brian, the dog from *Family Guy*. Alex looked around at all the people. He had come to know most of them well over the past few years. Even with the good times surrounding him, in fact, because of them, Alex couldn't help feeling a bit melancholy. Something inside was telling him that whatever was ahead, it would never be quite as memorable as this part of his life. College, good and bad, takes the cake, he confirmed.

Javier came over to the pair and patted Alex on the back. "Compadre! The end is near!" Usually reserved, Javier was louder that evening. Alex wondered if he was seeing Javier drunk for the first time. Javier looked at Amanda, arched his back, and offered a look of astonishment that said he was surprised to see her with Alex. He smiled and gave Amanda a big hug and a kiss on the check. "Welcome back," he shouted, "I always knew this guy couldn't be that stupid!" Alex didn't have to wonder anymore; Javier was three sheets to the wind

Zimmy interrupted their conversation when he came over to the group holding darts. "Hey, Alex!" he greeted, "Some of the boys from Cabin Club are coming over to play 501. Twenty bucks a game. Want to team up and kick some anus?"

"Tempting Zim, but not tonight." Alex glanced over at Amanda. "I have some entertaining to do." Zimmy shrugged his shoulders. It was easy to see that Zimmy was not as enthralled about Alex and Amanda getting back together as Javier was.

"Come on four eyes!" offered Javier, "I'll throw with

you."

"But you suck at darts, Javier."

"I suck? Bet you ten bucks I can hit you between the eyes, blindfolded."

"I'll bet you ten bucks you couldn't hit me in the head without a blindfold!"

Javier playfully smacked Zimmy in the head.

"I just did!"

"Javier, I'd tell you to fuck off, but there's a lady present."

Zimmy placed the darts in Javier's hands and commented, "I must be a masochist. Come on, let's go get the crap kicked out of us." Zimmy shook his head and walked dejectedly toward the dartboard with his newly acquired partner. Amanda laughed.

"I bet you're really going to miss them," Amanda said.

Alex looked around. "Yes, I am going to miss all of them." Bowing his head, he continued, "Especially the ones who have already left." Through their silence, Alex and Amanda could hear the loud murmur of a hundred conversations below, and the band playing Jimmy Cliff's "Many Rivers to Cross." Alex reflected, "It has been great, really great, but it's time to go. Maybe it's been since Boder died, I don't know, but things have changed. I feel detached."

Amanda smiled and nodded understandingly. "Things change and life goes on, and sometimes that sucks. Boder's gone. My father is almost gone. Ditto for college. Things don't always get better. You just learn to live with it." Amanda looked down at her black, suede Louboutin shoes. They weren't making her as happy as they usually did. She bit her lip and pushed the bad thoughts away, as there would be plenty of time for those later. Amanda looked up at Alex, smiled, and gave him a quick kiss. Alex smiled back, and she thought he looked quite happy, all things considered. They talked with friends and danced on the lawn, with the melting ice sculptures, until daybreak.

In the morning, when other revelers gathered in the dining room for breakfast, Alex asked Amanda if she minded if he went to sleep. "What? An early morning crew race, a few hours of sex, a dozen drinks and an all-night party, and you're ready to call it quits? What kind of man are you?" she joked. Amanda helped Alex to bed, and he fell asleep before she could kiss him goodnight. It was Sunday at about eight in the morning. The sun had already bathed the campus in a soft illuminated glow, but Alex wouldn't be a witness to its glory.

Alex awoke and looked at the clock. It read three minutes past eleven. His swollen tongue felt like it was filled with warm sand. He raced to the refrigerator and pulled out an open and flat bottle of Coke, but it didn't matter. He drank it down in a few seconds. As his other senses came to his attention, he braced for what he thought would surely be a severe headache. A lot of drinking with only a few hours of sleep was a great recipe for one. Surprisingly, Alex felt quite good, except that he was starving. He remembered that he and Amanda had skipped dinner in favor of a sack attack, and he realized he should have had breakfast before he went to bed. He wondered if they would have the normal Sunday brunch downstairs. As Alex walked to the shower, he prepared for the sharp aches he normally felt the day after a crew race. Strangely, he felt nothing. "I should stay up and drink more often," Alex thought.

Alex showered and dressed. While combing his hair and looking in the mirror, he smiled as he thought about the sex Amanda and he had engaged in the night before. Sometimes, thinking about the sex he had was almost as good as when he had it. Almost.

Alex went downstairs. Looking around, he thought the crew in charge of cleanup had done one hell of a job. He went into the dining room and was surprised to see it set up for lunch instead of brunch. Alex thought that was odd. He wondered if maybe it was simply easier to throw sandwiches together after a big night like the one before. Suddenly, Alex's eyes grew wide. He ran into the smoking room, spotted a copy of the *New York Times*, and picked it up. It looked awfully thin for a Sunday. Under the header, he found the date: Monday, May 5, 2015. What the fuck. Did I have a run in with the Greek God Hypnos? Coach Diriglia is going to love this one.

Alex was disappointed in himself. Very early that morning, six sevenths of the best collegiate crew team in the nation got up to practice to become indisputable champions. Meanwhile, one cog was sleeping. He wondered what the others were thinking of him, especially after the team went to bat for him when he showed up late for the Harvard meet. He seemed to be the only one who was ever late, or missed practices. Alex could still hear his old man saying, "Don't do anything you do not want to do. But whatever you decide to do, don't do it half-assed."

Alex walked to the boathouse. He looked at the dock where the boats and equipment were laid out clean and perfect, ready for the afternoon workout. Alex went upstairs.

He knew he had to explain to Coach Diriglia, but, as that moment neared, Alex wouldn't mind if the coach was not around. Alex walked down the short, narrow hallway to Diriglia's office where the door was open. As Alex poked his head in the room, the coach must have heard him because he looked up from his paperwork before Alex said a word. "Ah!" he boomed, "The missing link! What brings you to the boathouse on such a lovely day?" No one said it was going to be easy.

"I came to talk to you about missing practice this morning."

"I'm all ears." Diriglia stood up, walked around to the front of his desk, placed his buttocks on the outside edge, and folded his arms across his chest.

"I have no good excuse. I overslept, pure and simple."

"Is your alarm clock broken?"

"I didn't set it, coach."

"Forget?"

"No, sir. I just didn't think it was necessary."

"Excuse me for being presumptuous, Mr. Williams, but if history is any indicator, you just don't seem like the early riser type."

"I'm not, coach. I just thought I'd have plenty of time to set my clock when I got up."

Diriglia shook his head and said to no one in particular, "I must be missing something."

"I slept a lot longer than I thought I would."

"I think we both realize that."

"I mean that I went to bed very early Sunday morning."

"You mean early Sunday evening."

"No, morning. I slept for twenty-eight hours."

"Straight?" Diriglia showed honest amazement.

"Probably as close to dead as I've ever been," Alex tried to joke. There was no laughter, nor even the hint of a grin.

After a few moments, Diriglia began nodding his head, as if in agreement with himself. "Twenty-eight hours," Diriglia mumbled to himself. He looked Alex straight in the eyes and smiled, "Then I guess you are well-rested for the afternoon workout." Diriglia nodded affirmatively, sat back down behind his desk, and went back to his paperwork. Alex just stood there, shocked and dumbfounded. Diriglia looked up, both surprised and annoyed to see Alex still standing there. He put his pen down and leaned back in his old leather desk chair. "Is there anything else, Mr. Williams?"

"Uh . . . no! Sorry!" Alex turned around and, eager to take advantage of an unexpected gift, began to walk away. Then Alex stopped, turned around, and uttered, "Coach?"

Diriglia responded softly, yet not without some annoyance, "Yes?"

"I guess I'm a bit surprised."

"About?"

"I thought you would be more upset about me missing morning practice."

Diriglia nodded his head, stood up, returned to the front of his beat up mahogany desk, and leaned on the edge. In silence, the coach looked Alex straight in the eyes for a few moments. Finally, the coach looked at the floor, put his right hand on his chin, and said, "I've been coaching crew for twenty-six years. The first few were at a prep school, then a couple of freshman and varsity assistant positions at smaller schools, and, finally, I was offered this position eighteen years ago. I was on the team the same time as The Cruiser, but I lied to you guys. I never made it to the 1V, never experienced that level of excitement firsthand. I guess for the last quarter century, I thought that, if I willed it enough, it would happen, but it never did. Maybe I should have changed my name to Coach Mediocrity. I've coached some very good teams here, but I never had that one that all coaches dream about, until now. From that first week of practice out on the lake, when I began clocking you guys, I knew this was the best I would ever see. I noticed something different about this team. You all have very different personalities. Although you clearly stand out as the least likely crew athlete, no offense, the other guys are also more different than you might think." Alex puzzled over that last sentence for some time, as Diriglia continued, "Remember that day the team wouldn't row without you? When I wanted you to sit out because you were late? I must tell you that took some balls for you guys to do. If I had any chutzpah, I would have sat the whole team out. After all, this is college; we're supposed to have principles here. But as Johnson stood before me, with what was clearly an immovable pronouncement, I knew that not to let you row would have cost me the dream as much as anyone else. After all, you're all kids with bigger ambitions." Diriglia pointed to the staircase wall, which was adorned with crew teams past, and went on, "At the least, this will be a bright memory for many of you. This is it for me. This is my soul. It's what I live for at this little boathouse by the lake that I call my home." Alex stared at Diriglia during a momentary silence. He was as serious as a hot metal poker up your ass.

Diriglia continued, "So I gave in. It's as much for me as it is for you. We're going to the Eastern Sprints Regatta next week. We do well there, then kick some butt at the National Championships at the end of the month, and we are the undisputed, number one, college crew team in the United States. It's very possible that you'll be considered one of the greatest collegiate crew teams to ever pick up oars, and I wouldn't mind seeing myself listed in the record books as the coach of that goddamn team. I'm not about to rock this applecart. So, if you want to dance naked in front of Nassau Hall with just a top hat and a bottle of whiskey, be my guest. Just be ready to row on Saturday."

Alex wanted to reply, but he had no idea what to say to all that. Instead, he chose to nod as if in agreement. Diriglia offered a single nod in return, sat back in his desk chair, and resumed his work. In that moment, Alex felt sympathy for his coach that he hadn't felt since he joined the varsity squad as a sophomore. It was tough to knock someone who let you know where they were coming from, even if that place was different than one's own.

"Thanks, coach," Alex heard himself say. He backed out of the room as Diriglia waved in response without looking up from his papers. Alex walked outside into the bright day. Walking down Washington Road, Alex felt like the world had become a little better place.

XXIV

May felt like a blur to Alex. He was wrapping up classes and getting swept into the hoopla accompanying graduation, but the reality of Boder's death was really beginning to hit home. Alex was having a tough time keeping his mind off it. Sometimes it was so consuming that he would be in a conversation, walk away, and have no idea what had been said.

Alex was having an especially tough time focusing on rowing. He had done ok in Ithaca, but the timing was close enough to the tragedy that he had little time to think about it. Since then, he felt as though he was just going through the motions. It was all he could do to drag himself to practice. The team and the coaches had been very supportive, and he was trying not to let them down. Alex would do what he needed to see it through. After almost four years, and especially the demanding work of the last few months, he figured he could row hard in his sleep. Nevertheless, he felt troubled that his joy for racing seemed to be gone.

Between the last of his crew practices, Alex spent a few

hours putting together his final paper for his Contemporary Drama class. Although Alex hadn't spent substantial time and effort on it, his proximity to graduation made his putting together a ten-page paper a bit like a toll taker giving change. The title of Alex's paper was "A Comparison of Issues in the Modern American Drama and the Modern American Musical." Alex really wanted to entitle his paper "Why Does the Music in All of Andrew Lloyd Weber's Musicals Sound the Same?" however, he didn't think there would be much interest.

*****

On the second Friday in May, the crew team set off to Lake Quinsigamond, near Worcester, Massachusetts, for the Eastern Sprints Regatta. Although this was classified as a national race, its participants were mostly the best Northeast teams. It was a two-day event for the first varsity heavyweight boat, with heats on Saturday and finals on Sunday.

Lake Quinsigamond was not the most picturesque lake Alex had rowed on. It was long and very narrow. The starting line for the races was in the shadow of the Kenneth Burns Memorial Bridge, part of heavily traveled Route 9 into Boston. The coastline was littered with a mishmash of houses, apartments, and factories. Because the lake was narrow, it was usually calm with little current; therefore, it had become the site of many crew regattas.

It was all Coach Diriglia could do to keep the team from becoming overconfident. In the past year, except for Holy Cross and Northeastern, Alex's boat had beaten every other team at the Regatta. The coach got a little help bringing Princeton back to earth when, in their heat race, Jim Daley tore a muscle in his right shoulder with just a hundred meters to go. Daley tried his best, screaming with each stroke of his oar, but the boat slowed down and Pennsylvania nipped Princeton at the finish. Princeton would qualify for the finals but would have to row out of lane one. The least desirable, lane one was closest to the shoreline, which resulted in waves bouncing back at the boat. In addition, there was limited visibility of the other teams.

In the finals on Sunday, McGill replaced Daley on the first varsity heavyweight boat. It was raining steadily as the team rowed to the starting line. Alex noticed that McGill had been quiet all morning, prompting Alex to remember his first time in the top boat. It seemed like eons ago that McGill nearly drowned in his row-off with Alex. "McGill?"

"Yes?" McGill didn't look back.

"You're as good as any man on this boat. I know you are better than me, and I'm not just trying to blow smoke up your ass. Do what you've been doing all season, and it will be fine." From his coxswain position, staring directly at McGill, Vales nodded in agreement. McGill took a deep breath and gave a thumbs up. Alex looked at the nearby shoreline. Due to the weather, the crowds were much sparser than the day before. Alex spotted a boy of about four, who was wearing a yellow raincoat and green boots, splashing in a puddle. His mother was unsuccessfully attempting to direct his attention to the start of the race. There's something to be said for a time in your life, Alex thought, when a puddle makes you happy. When Vales yelled for everyone to be ready for the gun, Alex quickly came back to his harsher reality. The lineup from right to left was Brown, Northeastern, Cornell, Harvard, Boston University, Yale, and Princeton. As Alex bent forward slightly, looking down at his shoes in preparation for the first pull on his oar, he felt remarkably calm. He focused on the rain; individual drops falling off his hair and onto his legs. The starter's voice seemed distant to Alex, bu,t as the gun sounded, Alex immediately pulled back hard on his oar. It was as if his brain had shut off, and his body went into automatic.

Vales got the boat up to desired speed quickly, then had the crew ease up a bit and get into the desired rhythm. Over McGill's shoulder, Alex could see Vales. The look of concern on his face suggested that he was struggling to see the positions of the other boats through the rain. Vales asked for a strong drive from the crew. They were halfway through the race when Vales provided his first real update. "Even with the Crimson at second. Half-length behind Northeastern. Let's bring it up to forty-one in four!" The information whipped through Alex's mind, Northeastern? Fucking Northeastern? In fear that the rain might loosen his grip, Alex grabbed his oar tighter as he felt the boat pick up speed. Vales asked for two hard drives, virtually back-to-back, and Alex knew they were in a dogfight. "Come on, boys!" Vales yelled. "Keep it up. Just us now in second two seats behind Northeastern. One more hard drive in five strokes, and we'll catch 'em! Let's do it now!" Alex counted out the five strokes in his head. On the fifth one, he gave it all he had, knowing it was now or never. Pulling hard on the oar, Alex's back and shoulders were nearly parallel with the boat. Pulling up quickly to get ready for the next drive stroke, Alex felt the boat jerk left as something hard landed in his lap. It was McGill's head. McGill's hands had slipped off the oar. McGill stared up at Alex, utter panic in his face. There was nothing that could be done. The free oar in the water caused the boat to turn, resulting in crabbings by other rowers. The boat wafted aimlessly in a slow circle. Princeton's perfect season was over. "What the fuck!" Vales screamed.

"It slipped out of my hands!" McGill pleaded. Alex had never seen Vales so upset.

"That's why you hold on tight, like the other fifty-five goddamn rowers in the fucking race!" Alex thought that if McGill could go back in time, he would have wished not to be rescued that day in September when he was stuck under his capsized boat. He looked as if he had just been told that his entire family had been murdered.

"Hey, Vales, take it easy," Alex replied. "It could have happened to anyone; I almost lost my oar as well."

"But you didn't!"

Others on the boat joined the cacophony until Johnson, who had just been staring at the finish line, yelled, "Enough! It happened, and that's it. Let's bring the boat in." From that point, until they reached the dock, the only sound heard was the rain hitting the lake.

Describing the bus ride home as "subdued" would be stating the obvious. Coach Diriglia was surprisingly supportive of McGill, but he must have asked Johnson at least half a dozen times what the hell happened. McGill sat by himself and was largely left alone, which was better than everyone telling him not to worry about it. It was inevitable that he'd worry about it. Is that going to be my personal moment, he would undoubtedly wonder, forever entwined in

Princeton crew history? Will I be known as the guy who messed up Princeton's greatest season?

Around eleven Sunday evening, they arrived at the Princeton boathouse, and Alex walked back to the eating club. It was the start of another weeklong reading period before final exams. The sounds emanating from the eating clubs on Prospect Street felt more like those of a Saturday night. Against The Cruiser's wishes, Amanda had gone home for the week to be near him. Alex was tired and hungry. He thought about how much he could have used Boder to lean on. Boder was always good for a laugh. Alex walked to Hoagie Haven on Nassau Street. After gulping down a turkey sub and an orange soda, he crept back into his room and went to sleep.

XXV

The President of the University was speaking, but Alex wasn't listening. He was staring beyond the President's podium at Nassau Hall, the oldest building on campus. Alex remembered the first time he saw that building. He was on his high school visit and fell in love with the college almost immediately. It was so old and majestic, and it was covered in ivy from top to bottom. The ivy didn't just symbolize the prestige of the university, but it covered the bullet holes dating back to the revolutionary war.

For commencement, the main entranceway of Nassau Hall, immediately behind the podium, was covered with a huge white banner with the Princeton insignia. A little ostentatious, Alex thought, like everyone needs to be reminded where we are or something. The fact was, there wasn't another place like it on earth. It was like LeBron James having the inscription *World's Greatest Basketball Player* on the back of his jersey. Everyone already knew.

*****

The last few weeks leading up to graduation were uneventful. Alex had no finals for which to study, so he had a lot of time on his hands. Most of that was spent preparing for the national championships in Lake Natoma, California. It was a bit difficult for Alex, though, because he just wasn't into it. He wasn't sure if it was because he still was sad from Boder's passing, or if it was all part of the process of letting go of Princeton. He knew that, after graduation, he could go back to visit, but it would never be the same.

In comeback fashion, the team did well, defeating the University of Washington. Alex rowed as hard as he ever had, definitively aiding in the win. In fact, Alex passed out shortly after the finish line, and the team had their immediate victory celebration around the back of a medic van. And yet, it was then that he knew his heart was no longer in it, and he was done. On the plane back to New Jersey, he told Coach Diriglia that he couldn't make the trip to Oxford for the Henley Royal Regatta in early July. He blamed his new job, which he claimed was going to start earlier than he originally thought. That was a lie. Mr. Applegate and he had not yet decided on a start date, but Alex knew he had nothing left to give the team. He was ok with that.

*****

Alex looked up through the elm trees, the extending branches challenged by the onslaught of an ever-hotter sun. Through his sunglasses, the leaves appeared dark and the sky a haze of purple. Dad would have loved this, Alex thought, if only to have the opportunity to convey his opinion about what a bunch of bullshit most of the event was. But he would have been proud, Alex was certain of that. Alex's father was no fool, either. He knew, no matter what one decided to do, that a Princeton diploma would not hurt. Alex recalled what his father once told him, "Alex, I don't believe much in luck but, nevertheless, never look a gift horse in the mouth."

The sound of a Princeton tradition brought Alex out of his thoughts. The ceremony closed with the singing of "Old Nassau." Alex wasn't a member of any of the a cappella groups, the glee club, nor the band, but he had heard that song dozens of times over the previous four years. It was this rendering, though, that Alex would never forget. The graduates stood up, along with the faculty and the administration, as well as any alumni in the crowd.

> In Praise of Old Nassau, we sing,
> Hurrah! Hurrah! Hurrah!
> Our hearts will live, while we shall give,
> Three cheers for Old Nassau.
> Let music rule the fleeting hour,
> Her mantle round us draw;
> And thrill each heart with all her power,
> In praise of Old Nassau.

Alex laughed as he sang. He thought it was cool, and even emotional, but he felt they could have done without the Heil Hitler-like salute that was done in unison during the chorus. Just a little creepy, he thought.

*****

Finally, the trumpets roared and the closing procession began. Alex took one more look at Nassau Hall and tried to lock it in his memory. He knew he would see it again someday, but it would never be as special as at that moment. As Alex walked down the pathway to the entry gates of the school, he looked for his mother once more. She waved to him with enthusiasm, though it was clear to Alex she had been crying. Jennifer clapped gleefully while Madison, on the other hand, had fallen fast asleep and was bent over at the waist like a folding chair.

Alex walked to his mother, Jennifer and a sleepy Madison, and he gave them each a hug. The actual receiving of the diplomas would take place at each student's residential college. After his mother's third delivery of "I am so proud of you," Alex told her he would meet them all at his college in a few minutes. He walked alone past the Chapel and the stained-glass window of the "Divine Comedy" he admired so much. Crossing over Washington Street, Alex stopped at the Fountain of Freedom. Having been freshly painted in preparation for alumni events, it seemed especially beautiful. The water slowly falling onto its pale blue basin was as soothing as ever. A mother stood watching her two small children, as they ran around throwing pennies into the water. The mother encouraged them to make a wish with each throw, but, given the speed at which they followed each toss, it was apparent that they didn't need a wish to make it a special time.

"I miss you," Alex whispered, suddenly realizing that he might not be just thinking of Boder. Alex looked at the little coin-tossers. He thought of the times, when he was their age, spent throwing pieces of bread to the ducks at a pond near his home.

"Hey."

Alex felt a hand on his arm. It was Amanda. She pulled her earplugs out.

"I had a feeling you might be here. You want to go get our diplomas?"

Alex looked at the fountain and grabbed Amanda's hand.

"It can wait."

Amanda nodded in agreement. She gave Alex one of her earplugs, and he put it on. Van Morrison's "Precious Time" was playing. They walked toward the fountain together, kicked off their shoes, and put their feet in the water. The day was too nice to do much else.